"AN EPIC ADVENTURE . . .
Although it's set in the modern world, magic is at its heart."
—*Pitch Weekly* (St. Louis, MO)

"I will be thinking about *Running with the Demon* for weeks, savoring a magnificent story and turning over its mysteries in my mind. It is suspenseful and mesmerizing and, just when you think you have mastered the puzzles inherent in it, you realize you have been led astray. Wonderfully written, full of pure love and bitter hatred, the story line is as intricate as a spider's web. Terry Brooks's best yet, and a treat for us all!"

—ANN RULE

"*Running with the Demon* is by far the best of Terry Brooks's many wonderful novels: darker, starker, classically written, and with a brand-new mythos to fuel its contemporary plot. I couldn't put it down."

—JOHN SAUL

"This fast-paced, contemporary fantasy by the Seattle author of the now-classic *Sword of Shannara* has a lot going for it: believable characters, fallible heroes, and the nostalgic, romanticized taste of small-town life. These qualities blend with a bittersweet feeling of lost innocence and family tragedy, recalling the point where childhood ends and the world will never be the same again."

—*The Seattle Times*

By Terry Brooks
Published by The Random House Publishing Group

RUNNING WITH THE DEMON

Terry Brooks

A Del Rey® Book

THE RANDOM HOUSE PUBLISHING GROUP • NEW YORK

A Del Rey® Book
Published by The Random House Publishing Group
Copyright © 1997 by Terry Brooks
Excerpt from *A Knight of the Word* copyright © 1998 by Terry Brooks

Published in the United States by Del Rey Books, an imprint of The Random House Publishing Group, a division of Random House, Inc., New York, and simultaneously in Canada by Random House of Canada Limited, Toronto.

Del Rey is a registered trademark and the Del Rey colophon is a trademark of Random House, Inc.

www.delreybooks.com

Library of Congress Catalog Card Number: 97-97180

ISBN 0-345-42258-9

Manufactured in the United States of America

First Hardcover Edition: September 1997
First Mass Market Edition: July 1998

OPM   19   18   17   16   15   14   13   12   11   10

TO JUDINE

*FOR SHOWING ME EVERY DAY WHY THE JOURNEY
IS MORE IMPORTANT THAN THE
DESTINATION.*

PROLOGUE

He stands alone in the center of another of America's burned-out towns, but he has been to this one before. Even in their ruined, blackened condition, the buildings that surround him are recognizable. The streets of the intersection in which he finds himself stretch away in windswept concrete ribbons that dwindle and fade into the horizon—south to the bridge that spans the river, north to the parched flats of what were once cornfields, east toward the remains of Reagan's hometown, and west to the Mississippi and the Great Plains. A street sign, bent and weathered, confirms that he stands at the corner of First Avenue and Third Street. The town is eight blocks square, two blocks in any direction from where he stands, petering out afterward in dribs and drabs of homes that have been converted to real-estate offices and repair shops or simply leveled to provide parking. Farther out lie the abandoned ruins of two supermarkets and the mall, and down along the riverbank he can see the broken-down stacks and rusted-out corrugated roofs of what is left of the steel mill.

He looks around slowly, making sure he is in the right place, because it has been a long time. The sky is clouded and dark. Rain threatens and will probably fall before night. Although it is noon, the light is so pale that it seems more like dusk. The air and the earth are washed clean of color. Buildings, streets, abandoned vehicles, trash, and sky are a uniform shade of gray, the paint running from one into the other until nothing remains but shadows and light to differentiate any of it. In the silence, the wind moans softly as it rises off the river and whips down the empty streets. Twigs, leaves, and debris skitter along the concrete. Windows gape dark and hollow where the plate glass has been broken out. Doors hang open and sag. Smears of black ash and soot stain the walls where fires have burned away the wood and plastic veneer of the offices and shops. Cars hunker down on flattened tires and bare axles, stripped of everything useful, abandoned shells turning slowly to rust.

The man looks the town over as he would a corpse, remembering when it was still vital.

A pack of dogs comes out of one of the buildings. There are maybe ten of them, lean and hungry, quick-eyed and suspicious. They study him momentarily before moving on. They want nothing to do with him. He watches them disappear around the corner of a building, and he begins to walk. He moves east toward the park, even though he knows what he will find. He passes the bank, the paint store, the fabric shop, Al's Bar, and a parking lot, and stops at Josie's. The sign still hangs over the entry; the enamel is faded and broken, but the name is recognizable. He walks over and peers inside. The furniture and pastry cases are all smashed, the cooking equipment broken, and the leather banquettes ripped to shreds. Dust coats the countertop, trash litters the ruined floor, and weeds poke out of cracks in the tile.

He turns away in time to catch sight of two children slipping from the alleyway across the street. They carry canvas bags stuffed with items they have scavenged. They wear knives strapped to their waists. The girl is in her teens, the boy younger. Their hair is long and unkempt, their clothes shabby, and their eyes hard and feral. They slow to consider him, taking his measure. He waits on them, turns to face them, lets them see that he is not afraid. They glance at each other, whisper something punctuated by furtive gestures, then move away. Like the dogs, they want nothing to do with him.

He continues up the street, the sound of his boots a hollow echo in the midday silence. Office buildings and shops give way to homes. The homes are empty as well, those that are still intact. Many are burned out and sagging, settling slowly back into the earth. Weeds grow everywhere, even through cracks in *the concrete of the streets. He wonders how long it has been since anyone has lived here. Counting the strays, the dogs and the children and the one or two others that linger because they have no place else to go, how many are left? In some towns, there is no one. Only the cities continue to provide refuge, walled camps in which survivors have banded together in a desperate effort to keep the madness at bay. Chicago is one such city. He has been there and seen what it has to offer. He already knows its fate.*

A woman emerges from the shadows of a doorway in one of the residences, a frail, hollow-eyed creature, dark hair tangled and streaked with purple dye, arms hanging loose and bare, the skin dotted with needle marks. Got anything for me? she asks dully. He shakes his head. She comes down to the foot of the porch steps and stops. She trots out a smile. Where'd you come from? He does not respond. She moves a couple of steps closer, hugging herself with her thin arms. Want to come in and party with me? He stops her with a look. In the shadows of the house from which she has come, he can see movement. Eyes, yellow and flat, study him with cold intent. He knows who they belong to. Get away from me, he tells the woman. Her face crumples. She turns back without a word.

He walks to the edge of the town, a mile farther on, out where the park waits. He knows he shouldn't, but he cannot help himself. Nothing of what he remembers remains, but he wants to see anyway. Old Bob and Gran are gone. Pick is gone. Daniel and Wraith are gone. The park is overgrown with weeds and scrub. The cemetery is a cluster of ruined headstones. The townhomes and apartments and houses are all empty. What lives in the park now can be found only in the caves and is his implacable enemy.

And what of Nest Freemark?

He knows that, too. It is a nightmare that haunts him, unrelenting and pitiless.

He stops at the edge of the cemetery and looks off into the shadows beyond. He is here, he supposes, because he has no better place to go. He is here because he is reduced to retracing

*the steps of his life as a form of penance for his failures. He is
hunted at every turn, and so he is drawn to the places that once
provided refuge. He searches in the vain hope that something of
what was good in his life will resurface, even when he knows
the impossibility of that happening.*

*He takes a long, slow breath. His pursuers will find him
again soon enough, but perhaps not this day. So he will walk
the park once more and try to recapture some small part of
what is lost to him forever.*

*Across the roadway from where he stands, a billboard hangs
in tatters. He can just make out its wording.*

WELCOME TO HOPEWELL, ILLINOIS! WE'RE GROWING YOUR WAY!

John Ross woke with a start, jerking upright so sharply that he
sent his walking staff clattering to the floor of the bus. For a
moment, he didn't know where he was. It was night, and most
of his fellow passengers were asleep. He took a moment to collect himself, to remember which journey he was on, which
world he was in. Then he maneuvered his bad leg stiffly into
the aisle, jockeying himself about on the seat until he was able
to reach down and retrieve the staff.

He had fallen asleep in spite of himself, he realized. In spite
of what that meant.

He placed the walking stick beside him, leaning it carefully
against his knapsack, bracing it in place so that it would not
slide away again. An old woman several seats in front of him
was still awake. She glanced back at him briefly, her look one
of reproof and suspicion. She was the only one who sat close to
him. He was alone at the very back of the bus; the other passengers, all save the old woman, had been careful to take seats
near the front. Perhaps it was the leg. Or the shabby clothes. Or
the mantle of weariness he wore like the ghost of Marley did
his chains. Perhaps it was the eyes, the way they seemed to
look beyond what everyone else could see, at once cool and
discerning, yet distant and lost, an unsettling contradiction.

But, no. He looked down at his hands, studying them. In
the manner of one who has come to terms with being
shunned, he could ignore the pain of his banishment. Sub-

consciously, his fellow passengers had made a perfectly understandable decision.

You leave as many empty seats as possible between yourself and Death.

FRIDAY, JULY 1

CHAPTER 1

"Hssst! Nest!"

His voice cut through the cottony layers of her sleep with the sharpness of a cat's claw. Her head jerked off the pillow and her sleep-fogged eyes snapped open.

"Pick?"

"Wake up, girl!" The sylvan's voice squeaked with urgency. "The feeders are at it again! I need you!"

Nest Freemark pushed the sheet away and forced herself into an upright position, legs dangling off the side of the bed. The night air was hot and sticky in spite of the efforts of the big floor fan that sat just inside her doorway. She rubbed at her eyes to clear them and swallowed against the dryness in her throat. Outside, she could hear the steady buzz of the locusts in the trees.

"Who is it this time?" she asked, yawning.

"The little Scott girl."

"Bennett?" *Oh, God!* She was fully awake now. "What happened?"

Pick was standing on the window ledge just outside the screen, silhouetted in the moonlight. He might be only six inches tall from the tips of his twiggy feet to the peak of his leafy head, but she could read the disgust in his gnarled wooden features as clearly as if he were six feet.

"The mother's out with her worthless boyfriend again, shutting down bars. That boy you fancy, young Jared, was left in charge of the other kids, but he had one of his attacks. Bennett was still up—you know how she is when her mother's not there, though goodness knows why. She became scared and

9

wandered off. By the time the boy recovered, she was gone. Now the feeders have her. Do you need this in writing or are you going to get dressed and come help?"

Nest jumped out of the bed without answering, slipped off her nightshirt, and pulled on her Grunge Lives T-shirt, running shorts, socks, and tennis shoes. Her face peeked out at her from the dresser mirror: roundish with a wide forehead and broad cheekbones, pug nose with a scattering of freckles, green eyes that tended to squint, a mouth that quirked upward at the corners as if to suggest perpetual amusement, and a complexion that was starting to break out. Passably attractive, but no stunner. Pick was pacing back and forth on the sill. He looked like twigs and leaves bound together into a child's tiny stick man. His hands were making nervous gestures, the same ones they always made when he was agitated—pulling at his silky moss beard and slapping at his bark-encrusted thighs. He couldn't help himself. He was like one of those cartoon characters that charges around running into walls. He claimed he was a hundred and fifty, but for being as old as he was, it didn't seem he had learned very much about staying calm.

She arranged a few pillows under the sheet to give the impression that she was still in the bed, sleeping. The ruse would work if no one looked too closely. She glanced at the clock. It was two in the morning, but her grandparents no longer slept soundly and were apt to be up at all hours of the night, poking about. She glanced at the open door and sighed. There was no help for it.

She nudged the screen through the window and climbed out after it. Her bedroom was on the first floor, so slipping away unnoticed was easy. In the summer anyway, she amended, when it was warm and the windows were all open. In the winter, she had to find her coat and go down the hallway and out the back door, which was a bit more chancy. But she had gotten pretty good at it.

"Where is she?" she asked Pick, holding out her hand, palm up, so he could step into it.

"Headed for the cliffs, last I saw." He moved off the sill gingerly. "Daniel's tracking her, but we'd better hurry."

Nest placed Pick on her shoulder where he could get a firm grip on her T-shirt, fitted the screen back in place, and took off at a run. She sped across the back lawn toward the hedgerow that bordered the park, the Midwest night air whipping across her face, fresh and welcoming after the stale closeness of her bedroom. She passed beneath the canopies of solitary oaks and hickories that shaded the yard, their great limbs branching and dividing overhead in intricate patterns, their leaves reflecting dully in the mix of light from moon and stars. The skies were clear and the world still as she ran, the houses about her dark and silent, the people asleep. She found the gap in the hedgerow on the first try, ducked to clear the low opening, and was through.

Ahead, Sinnissippi Park opened before her, softball diamonds and picnic areas bright with moonlight, woods and burial grounds laced with shadows.

She angled right, toward the roadway that led into the park, settling into a smooth, even pace. She was a strong runner, a natural athlete. Her cross-country coach said she was the best he had ever seen, although in the same breath he said she needed to develop better training habits. At five feet eight inches and a hundred twenty pounds, she was lean and rangy and tough as nails. She didn't know why she was that way; certainly she had never worked at it. She had always been agile, though, even when she was twelve and her friends were bumping into coffee tables and tripping over their own feet, all of them trying to figure out what their bodies were going to do next. (Now they were fourteen, and they pretty much knew.) Nest was blessed with a runner's body, and it was clear from her efforts the past spring that her talent was prodigious. She had already broken every cross-country record in the state of Illinois for girls fourteen and under. She had done that when she was thirteen. But five weeks ago she had entered the Rock River Invitational against runners eighteen and under, girls and boys. She had swept the field in the ten-thousand-meter race, posting a time that shattered the state high school record by almost three minutes. Everyone had begun to look at her a little differently after that.

Of course, they had been looking at Nest Freemark differently for one reason or another for most of her life, so she was less impressed by the attention now than she might have been earlier.

Just think, she reflected ruefully, how they would look at me if I told them about Pick. Or about the magic.

She crossed the ball diamond closest to her house, reached the park entrance, and swept past the crossbar that was lowered to block the road after sunset. She felt rested and strong; her breathing was smooth and her heartbeat steady. She followed the pavement for a short distance, then turned onto the grassy picnic area that led to the Sinnissippi burial mounds and the cliffs. She could see the lights of the Sinnissippi Townhomes off to the right, low-income housing with a fancy name. That was where the Scotts lived. Enid Scott was a single mother with five kids, very few life options, and a drinking problem. Nest didn't think much of her; nobody did. But Jared was a sweetheart, her friend since grade school, and Bennett, at five the youngest of the Scott children, was a peanut who deserved a lot better than she had been getting of late.

Nest scanned the darkness ahead for some sign of the little girl, but there was nothing to see. She looked for Wraith as well, but there was no sign of him either. Just thinking of Wraith sent a shiver down her spine. The park stretched away before her, vast, silent, and empty of movement. She picked up her pace, the urgency of Bennett's situation spurring her on. Pick rode easily on her shoulder, attached in the manner of a clamp, arms and legs locked on her sleeve. He was still muttering to himself, that annoyingly incessant chatter in which he indulged ad nauseam in times of stress. But Nest let him be. Pick had a lot of responsibility to exercise, and it was not being made any easier by the increasingly bold behavior of the feeders. It was bad enough that they occupied the caves below the cliffs in ever-expanding numbers, their population grown so large that it was no longer possible to take an accurate count. But where before they had confined their activities to nighttime appearances in the park, now all of a sudden they were starting to surface everywhere in Hopewell, sometimes even in day-light. It was all due to a shifting in the balance of things, Pick advised. And if the balance was not righted, soon the feeders would be everywhere. Then what was he supposed to do?

The trees ahead thickened, trunks tightening in a dark wall, limbs closing out the night sky. Nest angled through the maze, her eyes adjusting to the change in light, seeing everything, picking out all the details. She dodged through a series of park toys, spring-mounted rides for the smallest children, jumped a low chain divider, and raced back across the roadway and into the burial mounds. There was still no sign of Bennett Scott. The air was cooler here, rising off the Rock River where it flowed west below the cliffs in a broad swath toward the Mississippi. In the distance, a freight train wailed as it made its way east through the farmland. The summer night was thick with heat, and the whistle seemed muted and lost. It died away slowly, and in the ensuing silence the sounds of the insects resurfaced, a steady, insistent hum.

Nest caught sight of Daniel then, a dark shadow as he swooped down from the trees just long enough to catch her attention before wheeling away again.

"There, girl!" Pick shouted needlessly in her ear.

She raced in pursuit of the barn owl, following his lead, heading for the cliffs. She ran through the burial mounds, low, grassy hummocks clustered at the edge of the roadway. Ahead, the road ended in a turnaround at the park's highest point. That was where she would find Bennett. Unless . . . She brushed the word aside, refusing to concede that it applied. A rush of bitterness toward Enid Scott tightened her throat. It wasn't fair that she left Jared alone to watch his brothers and sisters. Enid knew about his condition; she just found it convenient now and then to pretend it didn't matter. A mild form of epilepsy, the attacks could last for as long as five minutes. When they came, Jared would just "go away" for a bit, staring off into space, not seeing or hearing, not being aware of anything. Even the medicine he took couldn't always prevent the attacks. His mother knew that. She knew.

The trees opened before her, and Daniel dove out of the shadows, streaking for the cliffs. Nest put on a new burst of speed, nearly unseating Pick. She could see Bennett Scott now, standing at the very edge of the cliffs, just beyond the turn-around, a small, solitary figure against the night sky, all hunched over and crying. Nest could hear her sobs. The feeders were cajoling her, enticing her, trying to cloud her thinking further so that she would take those last few steps. Nest was angry. Bennett made the seventh child in a month. She had saved them all, but how long could her luck hold?

Daniel started down, then arced away soundlessly. It was too dangerous for him to go in; his unexpected presence might startle the little girl and cause her to lose her balance. That was why Pick relied on Nest. A young girl's appearance was apt to prove far less unsettling than his own or Daniel's.

She slowed to a walk, dropping Pick off in the grass. No point in taking chances; Pick preferred to remain invisible anyway. The scent of pine trees wafted on the humid night air, carried out of the cemetery beyond, where the trees grew in thick clumps along the chain-link fence. In the moonlight, the headstones and monuments were just visible, the granite and marble reflecting with a shimmery cast. She took several deep breaths as she came up to Bennett, moving slowly, carefully into the light. The feeders saw her coming and their lantern eyes narrowed. She ignored them, focusing her attention on the little girl.

"Hey, tiny Ben Ben!" She kept her voice casual, relaxed. "It's me, Nest."

Bennett Scott's tear-filled eyes blinked rapidly. "I know."

"What are you doing out here, Ben Ben?"

"Looking for my mommy."

"Well, I don't think she's out here, sweetie." Nest moved a few steps closer, glancing about as if looking for Enid.

"She's lost," Bennett sobbed.

A few of the feeders edged menacingly toward Nest, but she ignored them. They knew better than to mess with her while

Wraith was around—which she fervently hoped he was. A lot of them were gathered here, though. Flat-faced and featureless, squat caricatures of humans, they were as much a mystery to her now as ever, even after all she had learned about them from Pick. She didn't really even know what they were made of. When she had asked Pick about it once, he had told her with a sardonic grin that as a rule you are mostly what you eat, so the feeders could be almost anything.

"I'll bet your mommy is back home by now, Ben Ben," she offered, infusing her voice with enthusiasm. "Why don't we go have a look?"

The little girl sniffled. "I don't want to go home. I don't like it there anymore."

"Sure you do. I'll bet Jared wonders where you are."

"Jared's sick. He had an attack."

"Well, he'll be better by now. The attacks don't last long, sweetie. You know that. Come on, let's go see."

Bennett's head lowered into shadow. She hugged herself, her head shaking. "George doesn't like me. He told me so."

George Paulsen, Enid's latest mistake in the man department. Even though she was only fourteen, Nest knew a loser when she saw one. George Paulsen was a scary loser, though. She came a step closer, looking for a way to make physical contact with Bennett so that she could draw the little girl away from the cliff. The river was a dark, silver shimmer far below the cliffs, flat and still within the confines of the bayou, where the railroad tracks were elevated on the levy, wilder and swifter beyond where the main channel flowed. The darkness made the drop seem even longer than it was, and Bennett was only a step or two away.

"George needs to get an attitude adjustment," Nest offered. "Everybody likes you, Ben Ben. Come on, let's go find your mommy and talk to her about it. I'll go with you. Hey, what about Spook? I'll bet your kitty misses you."

Bennett Scott's moppet head shook quickly, scattering her lank, dark hair in tangles. "George took Spook away. He doesn't like cats."

Nest wanted to spit. That worthless creep! Spook was just

about the only thing Bennett Scott had. She felt her grip on the situation beginning to loosen. The feeders were weaving about Bennett like snakes, and the little girl was cringing and hugging herself in fear. Bennett couldn't see them, of course. She wouldn't see them until it was too late. But she could hear them somewhere in the back of her mind, an invisible presence, insidious voices, taunting and teasing. They were hungry for her, and the balance was beginning to shift in their favor.

"I'll help you find Spook," Nest said quickly. "And I'll make sure that George doesn't take him away again either. What do you say to that?"

Bennett Scott hugged herself some more and looked fixedly at her feet, thinking it over. Her thin body went still. "Do you promise, Nest? Really?"

Nest Freemark gave her a reassuring smile. "I do, sweetie. Now walk over here and take my hand so we can go home."

The feeders moved to intervene, but Nest glared at them and they flinched away. They wouldn't meet her gaze, of course. They knew what would happen if they did. Nevertheless, they were bolder than usual tonight, more ready to challenge her. That was not a good sign.

"Bennett," she said quietly. The little girl's head lifted and her eyes came into the light. "Look at me, Bennett. Don't look anywhere else, okay? Just look right at me. Now walk over here and take my hand."

Bennett Scott started forward, one small step at a time. Nest waited patiently, holding her gaze. The night air had turned hot and still again, the breeze off the river dying away. Insects buzzed and flew in erratic sweeps, and, not wanting to do anything that would startle the little girl, Nest fought down the impulse to brush at them.

"Come on, Ben Ben," she cajoled softly.

As Bennett Scott advanced, the feeders gave way grudgingly, dropping down on all fours in a guarded crouch and skittering next to her like crabs. Nest took a deep breath.

One of the feeders broke away from the others and made a grab for Bennett. Nest hissed at it furiously, caught its eye, and stripped it of its life with a single, chilling glance. That was all it took—one instant in which their eyes met and her magic took control. The feeder collapsed in a heap and melted into the earth in a black stain. The others backed off watchfully.

Nest took a deep, calming breath. "Come on, Bennett," she urged in a tight whisper. "It's all right, sweetie."

The little girl had almost reached her when the headlight of the freight train swept across the bayou as the lead engine lurched out of the night. Bennett Scott hesitated, her eyes suddenly wide and uncertain. Then the train whistle sounded its shrill, piercing wail, and she cried out in fear.

Nest didn't hesitate. She grabbed Bennett Scott's arm, snatched the little girl from her feet, and pressed her close. For a moment she held her ground, facing down the feeders. But she saw at once that there were too many to stand against, so she wheeled from the cliffs and began to run. Behind her, the feeders bounded in pursuit. Already Pick was astride Daniel, and the barn owl swooped down on the foremost pursuers, talons extended. The feeders veered away, giving Nest an extra few yards head start.

"Faster, Nest!" Pick cried, but she was already in full stride, running as hard as she could. She clutched Bennett Scott tightly against her, feeling the child shake. She weighed almost nothing, but it was awkward running with her. Nest cleared the turnaround and streaked past the burial mounds for the picnic ground. She would turn and face the feeders there, where she could maneuver, safely away from the cliffs. Her magic would give her some protection. And Pick would be there. And Daniel. But there were so many of them tonight! Her heart thumped wildly. From the corner of her eye, she saw shadows closing on her, bounding through the park, yellow eyes narrowed. Daniel screeched, and she felt the whoosh of his wings as he sped past her, banking away into the dark.

"I'm sorry, Mommy, I'm sorry, I'm sorry," Bennett Scott sobbed, a prayer of forgiveness for some imagined wrong. Nest gritted her teeth and ran faster.

Then suddenly she went down, arms and legs flying as she

tripped over a road chain she had missed vaulting. She lost her grip on Bennett Scott and the little girl cried out in terror. Then the air was knocked from Bennett's lungs as she struck the ground.

Nest rolled to her feet at once, but the feeders were everywhere, dark, shadowy forms closing on her with wicked intent. She turned to mush the handful that were closest, the ones that were foolish enough to meet her gaze, ripping apart their dark forms with a glance. But the remainder converged in a dark wave.

Then Wraith materialized next to her, a massive presence, fur all stiff and bristling, the hairs raised like tiny spikes off his body. At first glance, he might have been a dog, a demonic German shepherd perhaps, colored an odd brindle. But he was deep-chested like a Rottweiler, and tall at the shoulders like a boxer, and his eyes were a peculiar amber within a mass of black facial markings that suggested tiger stripes. Then you recognized the sloped forehead and the narrow muzzle as a wolf's. And if you looked even closer, which if you were one of the few who could see him you were not apt to do, you realized he was something else altogether.

Scrambling over each other in an effort to escape, the feeders scattered like leaves in a strong wind. Wraith advanced on them in a stiff-legged walk, his head lowered, his teeth bared, but the feeders disappeared as swiftly as shadows at the coming of full sun, bounding back into the night. When the last of them had gone, Wraith wheeled back momentarily to give Nest a dark, purposeful glance, almost as if to take the measure of her resolve in the face of his somewhat belated appearance, and then he faded away.

Nest exhaled sharply, the chill that had settled in the pit of her stomach melting, the tightness in her chest giving way. Her breath came in rapid bursts, and blood throbbed in her ears. She looked quickly to find Bennett. The little girl was curled into a ball, hiding her face in her hands, crying so hard she was hiccuping. Had she seen Wraith? Nest didn't think so. Few people ever saw Wraith. She brushed at the grass embedded in the cuts and scrapes on her knees and elbows, and went to collect her frightened charge. She scooped Bennett up and cradled her gently.

"There, there, Ben Ben," she cooed, kissing the little girl's face. "Don't be frightened now. It's all right. Everything's all right." She shivered in spite of herself. "It was just a little fall. Time to be going home now, sweetie. Look, there's your house, right over there. Can you see the lights?"

Daniel winged past one final time and disappeared into the dark, bearing Pick with him. The feeders were scattered, so the owl and the sylvan were leaving, entrusting the return of Bennett Scott to her. She sighed wearily and began to walk through the park. Her breathing steadied and her heartbeat slowed. She was sweating, and the air felt hot and damp against her face. It was silent in the park, hushed and tender in the blanket of the dark. She hugged Bennett possessively, feeling the little girl's sobs slowly fade.

"Oh, Ben Ben," she said, "we'll have you home in bed before you know it. You want to get right to sleep, little girl, because Monday's the Fourth of July and you don't want to miss the fireworks. All those colors, all those pretty colors! What if you fell asleep and missed them?"

Bennett Scott curled into her shoulder. "Will you come home with me, Nest? Will you stay with me?"

The words were so poignant that Nest felt tears spring to her eyes. She stared off into the night, to the stars and the half-moon in the cloudless sky, to the shadows of the trees where they loomed against the horizon, to the lights of the buildings ahead where the residences and the apartments began and the park came to an end. The world was a scary place for little girls, but the scariest things in it weren't always feeders and they didn't live only in the dark. In the morning she would talk with Gran about Enid Scott. Maybe together they could come up with something. She would look for Spook, too. Pick would help.

"I'll come home with you, Ben Ben," she whispered. "I'll stay for a little while, anyway."

Her arms were tired and aching, but she refused to put the little girl down. By the time she reached the crossbar blocking the entrance to the park and turned left toward the Sinnissippi Townhomes, Bennett Scott was fast asleep.

CHAPTER 2

Robert Roosevelt Freemark—"Old Bob" to everyone but his wife, granddaughter, and minister—came down to breakfast the next morning in something of a funk. He was a big man, three inches over six feet, with broad shoulders, large hands, and a solidity that belied his sixty-five years of age. His face was square, his features prominent, and his snow white hair thick and wavy and combed straight back from his high forehead. He looked like a politician—or at least like a politician ought to look. But Old Bob was a workingman, had been all his life, and now, in retirement after thirty years on the line at Midwest Continental Steel, he still dressed in jeans and blue work shirts and thought of himself as being just like everyone else.

Old Bob had been Old Bob for as long as anyone could remember. Not in his boyhood, of course, but shortly after that, and certainly by the time he came back from the Korean War. He wasn't called Old Bob to his face, of course, but only when he was being referred to in the third person. Like, "Old Bob sure knows his business." He wasn't Good Old Bob either, in the sense that he was a good old boy. And the "old" had never been a reference to age. It was more a designation of status or durability or dependability. Bob Freemark had been a rock-solid citizen of Hopewell and a friend to everyone living there for his entire life, the sort of man you could call upon when you needed help. He'd worked for the Jaycees, the United Way, the Cancer Fund, and the Red Cross at one time or another, spearheading their campaign efforts. He'd been a member of

Kiwanis, the Moose, and the VFW. (He'd kept clear of Rotary because he couldn't abide that phony "Hi, Robert" malarkey.) He'd been a member of the First Congregational Church, been a deacon and a trustee until after Caitlin died. He'd worked at the steel mill as a foreman his last ten years on the job, and there were more than a few in the union who said he was the best they'd ever known.

But this morning as he slouched into the kitchen he was dark-browed and weary-hearted and felt not in the least as if his life had amounted to anything. Evelyn was already up, sitting at the kitchen table with her glass of orange juice laced with vodka, her cigarette, her coffee, and her magazine. Sometimes he thought she simply didn't go to bed anymore, although she'd been sleeping last night when he'd gotten up to look in on Nest. They'd kept separate bedrooms for almost ten years, and more and more it felt like they kept separate lives as well, all since Caitlin . . .

He caught himself, stopped himself from even thinking the words. Caitlin. Everything went back to Caitlin. Everything bad.

"Morning," he greeted perfunctorily.

Evelyn nodded, eyes lifting and lowering like window shades.

He poured himself a bowl of Cheerios, a glass of juice, and a cup of coffee and sat down across from her at the table. He attacked the cereal with single-minded intensity, devouring it in huge gulps, his head lowered to the bowl, stewing in wordless solitude. Evelyn sipped at her vodka and orange juice and took long drags on her cigarette. The length of the silence between them implied accurately the vastness of the gulf that separated their lives.

Finally Evelyn looked up, frowning in reproof. "What's bothering you, Robert?"

Old Bob looked at her. She had always called him Robert, not Old Bob, not even just Bob, as if some semblance of formality were required in their relationship. She was a small, intense woman with sharp eyes, soft features, gray hair, and a no-nonsense attitude. She had been beautiful once, but she was only old now. Time and life's vicissitudes and her own stubborn refusal to look after herself had done her in. She smoked and drank all the time, and when he called her on it, she told him it was her life and she could lead it any way she wanted and besides, she didn't really give a damn.

"I couldn't sleep, so I got up during the night and looked in on Nest," he told her. "She wasn't there. She'd tucked some pillows under the covers to make me think she was, but she wasn't." He paused. "She was out in the park again, wasn't she?"

Evelyn looked back at her magazine. "You leave the girl alone. She's doing what she has to do."

He shook his head stubbornly, even though he knew what was coming. "There's nothing she has to be doing out there at two in the morning."

Evelyn stubbed out her cigarette and promptly lit another one. "There's everything, and you know it."

"You know it, Evelyn. I don't."

"You want me to say it for you, Robert? You seem to be having trouble finding the right words. Nest was out minding the feeders. You can accept it or not—it doesn't change the fact of it."

"Out minding the feeders . . ."

"The ones you can't see, Robert, because your belief in things doesn't extend beyond the tip of your nose. Nest and I aren't like that, thank the good Lord."

He shoved back his cereal bowl and glared at her. "Neither was Caitlin."

Her sharp eyes fixed on him through a haze of cigarette smoke. "Don't start, Robert."

He hesitated, then shook his head hopelessly. "I'm going to have a talk with Nest about this, Evelyn," he declared softly. "I don't want her out there at night. I don't care what the reason is."

His wife stared at him a moment longer, as if measuring the strength of his words. Then her eyes returned to the magazine. "You leave Nest alone."

He looked out the window into the backyard and the park beyond. The day was bright and sunny, the skies clear, the temperature in the eighties, and the heat rising off the grass in a damp shimmer. It was only the first of July, and already they were seeing record temperatures. There'd been good rain in the spring, so the crops were doing all right, especially the early corn and soybeans, but if the heat continued there would be problems. The farmers were complaining already that they would have to irrigate and even that wouldn't be enough without some rain. Old Bob stared into the park and thought about the hardships of farming, remembering his father's struggle when he'd owned the farm up at Yorktown years ago. Old Bob didn't understand farming; he didn't understand why anyone would want to do it. Of course, that was the way farmers felt about fellows who worked in a steel mill.

"Is Nest still in bed?" he asked after a moment.

Evelyn got up to pour herself another drink. Bob watched the measure of vodka she added to the orange juice. Way too much. "Why don't you lighten up on that stuff, Evelyn? It's not even nine o'clock in the morning."

She gave him a hard look, her face pinched and her mouth set. "I notice you weren't in any hurry to get home last night from telling war stories with your pals. And I don't suppose you were drinking tea and playing shuffleboard down there at the hall, were you?" She took a long pull on the drink, walked back to her chair, sat down, and picked up the magazine. "Leave me alone, Robert. And leave Nest alone, too."

Old Bob nodded slowly and looked off again out the window. They had lived in this house for almost the whole of their married life. It was a big, sprawling rambler on two acres of wooded land abutting the park; he'd supervised the building of it himself, back in the late fifties. He'd bought the land for two hundred dollars an acre. It was worth a hundred times that now, even without the house. Caitlin had grown up under this roof, and now Nest. Everything that had meaning in his life had happened while he was living here.

His eyes traveled over the aged wood of the kitchen cabinets to the molding and kickboards and down the hall to the paneled entry. He had even been happy here once.

He stood up, weary, resigned, still in a funk. He felt emasculated by Evelyn, helpless in the face of her fortress mentality, adrift in his life, unable to change things in any way that mattered. It had been bad between them for years and it was getting worse. What was going to become of them? Nest was all that bound them together now. Once she was gone, as she would be in a few years, what would be left for them?

He brushed at his thick white hair with his hand, smoothing it back. "I'm going downtown, see if there's anything new with the strike," he said. "I'll be back in a few hours."

She nodded without looking up. "Lunch will be on the table at noon if you want it."

He studied her a moment longer, then went down the hall and out the front door into the summer heat.

It was another hour before Nest appeared in the kitchen. She stretched and yawned as she entered and helped herself to the orange juice. Her grandmother was still sitting at the kitchen table, smoking and drinking and reading her magazine. She looked up as Nest appeared and gave her a wan smile. "Good morning, Nest."

"Morning, Gran," Nest replied. She took out the bread and stuck a couple of slices in the toaster. Thinking of Bennett Scott, she stood at the counter and rolled her shoulders inside her sleep shirt to relieve the lingering ache in her muscles. "Grandpa around?"

Her grandmother put down the magazine. "He's gone out. But he wants to talk with you. He says you went into the park last night."

Nest hunched her shoulders one final time, then slouched against the counter, her eyes on the toaster. "Yep, he's right. I did."

"What happened?"

"Same as usual. The feeders got Bennett Scott this time." She told her grandmother what had happened. "I walked her to

the front door and handed her over to Jared. You should have
seen his face. He was so scared. He'd looked everywhere for
her. He was about to call the police. His mom still wasn't
home. She's a dead loss, Gran. Can't we do something about
her? It isn't fair the way she saddles Jared with all the responsibility. Did you know he has to make all the meals for those
kids—or almost all? He has to be there for them after school.
He has to do everything!"

Her grandmother took a deep drag on her cigarette. A cloud
of smoke enveloped her. "I'll have a talk with Mildred Walker.
She's involved with the social-services people. Maybe one of
them will drop by for a chat with Enid. That woman checks her
brains at the door every time a man walks in. She's a sorry
excuse for a mother, but those kids are stuck with her."

"Bennett's scared of George Paulsen, too. Next thing, he'll
be living there."

Her grandmother nodded. "Well, George is good at showing
up where there's a free ride." Her eyes shifted to find Nest's,
and her small body bent forward over the table. "Sit with me a
moment. Bring your toast."

Nest gathered up her toast and juice and sat down. She lath-
ered on some raspberry spread and took a bite. "Good."

"What are you going to tell your grandfather when he asks
you what you were doing in the park?"

Nest shrugged, tossing back her dark hair. "Same as always.
I woke up and couldn't get back to sleep, so I decided to go for
a run. I tucked the pillows under the covers so he wouldn't
worry."

Her grandmother nodded. "Good enough, I expect. I told
him to leave you alone. But he worries about you. He can't stop
thinking about your mother. He thinks you'll end up the same
way."

They stared at each other in silence. They had been over
this ground before, many times. Caitlin Freemark, Nest's
mother, had fallen from the cliffs three months after Nest
was born. She had been walking in the park at night. Her
state of mind had been uncertain for some time; she had been

a very fragile and mercurial young woman. Nest's birth and the disappearance of the father had left her deeply troubled. There was speculation that she might have committed suicide. No one had ever been able to determine if she had, but the rumors persisted.

"I'm not my mother," Nest said quietly.

"No, you're not," her grandmother agreed. There was a distant, haunted look in her sharp, old bird's eyes, as if she had suddenly remembered something best left forgotten. Her hands fluttered about her drink.

"Grandpa doesn't understand, does he?"

"He doesn't try."

"Do you still talk to him about the feeders, Gran?"

"He thinks I'm seeing things. He thinks it's the liquor talking. He thinks I'm an old drunk."

"Oh, Gran."

"Its been like that for some time, Nest." Her grandmother shook her head. "It's as much my fault as it is his. I've made it difficult for him, too." She paused, not wanting to go too far down that road. "But I can't get him even to listen to me. Like I said, he doesn't see. Not the feeders, not any of the forest creatures living in the park. He never could see any part of that world, not even when Caitlin was alive. She tried to tell him, your mother. But he thought it was all make-believe, just a young girl's imagination. He played along with her, pretended he understood. But he would talk to me about it when we were alone, tell me how worried he was about her nonsense. I told him that maybe she wasn't making it up. I told him maybe he should listen to her. But he just couldn't ever make himself do that."

She smiled sadly. "He's never understood our connection with the park, Nest. I doubt that he ever will."

Nest ate the last bite of toast, chewing thoughtfully. Six generations of the women of her family had been in service to the land that made up the park. They were the ones who had worked with Pick to keep the magic in balance over the years. They were the ones who had been born to magic themselves.

Gwendolyn Wills, Caroline Glynn, Opal Anders, Gran, her mother, and now her. The Freemark women, Nest called them, though the designation was less than accurate. Their pictures hung in a grouping in the entry, framed against the wooded backdrop of the park. Gran always said that the partnering worked best with the women of the family, because the women stayed while the men too often moved on.

"Grandpa never talks about the park with me," Nest remarked quietly.

"No, I think he's afraid to." Her grandmother swallowed down the vodka and orange juice. Her eyes looked vague and watery. "And I don't ever want you talking about it with him."

Nest looked down at her plate. "I know."

The old woman reached across the table and took hold of her granddaughter's wrist. "Not with him, not with anyone. Not ever. There's good reason for this, Nest. You understand that, don't you?"

Nest nodded. "Yep, I do." She looked up at her grandmother. "But I don't like it much. I don't like being the only one."

Her grandmother squeezed her wrist tightly. "There's me. You can always talk to me." She released her grip and sat back. "Maybe one day your grandfather will be able to talk with you about it, too. But it's hard for him. People don't want to believe in magic. It's all they can do to make themselves believe in God. You can't see something, Nest, if you don't believe in it. Sometimes I think he just can't let himself believe, that believing just doesn't fit in with his view of things."

Nest was silent a moment, thinking. "Mom believed, though, didn't she?"

Her grandmother nodded wordlessly.

"What about my dad? Do you think he believed, too?"

The old woman reached for her cigarettes. "He believed."

Nest studied her grandmother, watched the way her fingers shook as she worked the lighter. "Do you think he will ever come back?"

"Your father? No."

"Maybe he'll want to see how I've turned out. Maybe he'll come back for that."

"Don't hold your breath."

Nest worried her lip. "I wonder sometimes who he is, Gran. I wonder what he looks like." She paused. "Do you ever wonder?"

Her grandmother drew in on the cigarette, her eyes hard and fixed on a point in space somewhere to Nest's left. "No. What would be the point?"

"He's not a forest creature, is he?"

She didn't know what made her ask such a question. She startled herself by even speaking the words. And the way her grandmother looked at her made her wish she had held her tongue.

"Why would you ever think that?" Evelyn Freemark snapped, her voice brittle and sharp, her eyes bright with anger.

Nest swallowed her surprise and shrugged. "I don't know. I just wondered, I guess."

Her grandmother looked at her for a long moment without blinking, then turned away. "Go make your bed. Then go out and play with your friends. Cass Minter has called you twice already. Lunch will be here if you want it. Dinner's at six. Go on."

Nest rose and carried her dishes to the sink. No one had ever told her anything about her father. No one seemed to know anything about him. But that didn't stop her from wondering. She had been told that her mother never revealed his identity, not even to her grandparents. But Nest suspected that Gran knew something about him anyway. It was in the way she avoided the subject—or became angry when he was mentioned. Why did she do that? What did she know that made her so uncomfortable? Maybe that was why Nest persisted in her questions about him, even silly ones like the one she had just asked. Her father couldn't be a forest creature. If he was, Nest would be a forest creature as well, wouldn't she?

"See you later, Gran," she said as she left the room.

She went down the hall to her room to shower and dress. There were all different kinds of forest creatures, Pick had told her once. Even if he hadn't told her exactly what they were. So did that mean there were some made of flesh and blood? Did it mean some were human, like her?

She stood naked in front of the bathroom mirror looking at herself for a long time before she got into the shower.

CHAPTER 3

Old Bob backed his weathered Ford pickup out of the garage, drove up the lane through the wide-boughed hardwoods, and turned onto Sinnissippi Road. In spite of the heat he had the windows rolled down and the air conditioner turned off because he liked to smell the woods. In his opinion, Sinnissippi Park was the most beautiful woods for miles—always had been, always would be. It was green and rolling where the cliffs rose above the Rock River, and the thick stands of shagbark hickory, white oak, red elm, and maple predated the coming of the white man into Indian territory. Nestled down within the spaces permitted by a thinning of the larger trees were walnut, cherry, birch, and a scattering of pine and blue spruce. There were wildflowers that bloomed in the spring and leaves that turned color in the fall that could make your heart ache. In Illinois, spring and fall were the seasons you waited for. Summer was just a bridge between the two, a three-to-four-month yearly preview of where you would end up if you were turned away from Heaven's gates, a ruinous time when Mother Nature cranked up the heat as high as it would go on the local thermostat and a million insects came out to feed. It wasn't like that every summer, and it wasn't like that every day of every summer, but it was like that enough that you didn't notice much of anything else. This summer was worse than usual, and today looked to be typical. The heat was intense already, even here in the woods, though not so bad beneath the canopy of the trees as it would be downtown. So Old Bob breathed in the scents of leaves and grasses and flowers and enjoyed the coolness of the shade as he drove the old truck toward the highway, reminding himself of what was good about his hometown on his way to his regular morning discussion of what wasn't.

The strike at Midwest Continental Steel had been going on for one hundred and seven days, and there was no relief in sight. This was bad news and not just for the company and the union. The mill employed twenty-five percent of the town's working population, and when twenty-five percent of a community's spending capital disappears, everyone suffers. Mid-Con was at one time the largest independently owned steel mill in the country, but after the son of the founder died and the heirs lost interest, it was sold to a consortium. That produced some bad feelings all by itself, even though one of the heirs stayed around as a nominal part of the company team. The bad feelings grew when the bottom fell out of the steel market in the late seventies and early eighties in the wake of the boom in foreign steel. The consortium underwent some management changes, the last member of the founding family was dismissed, the twenty-four-inch mill was shut down, and several hundred workers were laid off. Eventually some of the workers were hired back and the twenty-four-inch was started up again, but the bad feelings between management and union were by then so deep-seated and pervasive that neither side could bring itself ever again to trust the other.

The bad feelings had come to a head six months earlier, when the union had entered into negotiations for a new contract. A yearly cost-of-living increase in the hourly wage, better medical benefits, an expansion of what qualified as piecework, and a paid-holiday program were some of the demands on the union's agenda. A limited increase without escalators in the hourly wage over the next five years, a cutback in medical benefits, a narrowing down of the types of payments offered for piecework, and an elimination of paid holidays were high on the list of counterdemands made by the company. A deadlock was quickly reached. Arbitration was refused by both sides, each choosing to wait out the other. A strike deadline was set by the union. A back-to-work deadline was set by the company. As the deadlines neared and no movement was achieved in the bargaining process, both union and company went public with their grievances. Negotiators for each side kept popping up on television and radio to air out the particulars of the latest outrage perpetrated by the other. Soon both sides were talking to everyone but each other.

Then, one hundred and seven days ago, the union had struck the fourteen-inch and the wire mill. The strike soon escalated to include the twenty-four-inch and the twelve-inch, and then all of MidCon was shut down. At first no one worried much. There had been strikes before, and they had always resolved themselves. Besides, it was springtime, and with the passing of another bitterly cold Midwest winter, everyone was feeling hopeful and renewed. But a month went by and no progress was made. A mediator was called in at the behest of the mayor of Hopewell and the governor of the State of Illinois and with the blessing of both union and management, but he failed to make headway. A few ugly incidents on the picket line hardened feelings on both sides. By then, the effect of the strike was being felt by everyone—smaller companies who did business with the mill or used their products, retailers who relied on the money spent by the mill's employees, and professional people whose clientele was in large part composed of management and union alike. Everyone began to choose sides.

After two months, the company announced that it would no longer recognize the union and that it would accept back those workers who wished to return to their old jobs, but that if those workers failed to return in seven days, new people would be brought in to replace them. On June 1, it would start up the fourteen-inch mill using company supervisors as workers. The company called this action the first step in a valid decertification process; the union called it strikebreaking and union busting. The union warned against trying to use scabs in place of "real" workers, of trying to cross the picket line, of doing anything but continuing to negotiate with the union team. It warned that use of company people on the line was foolhardy and dangerous. Only trained personnel should attempt to operate the machinery. The company replied that it would provide whatever training was deemed necessary and suggested the union start bargaining in good faith.

From there, matters only got worse. The company started up the fourteen-inch several times, and each time shut it down again after only a few days. There were reports by the union of unnecessary injuries and by the company of sabotage. Replacement workers were bused in from surrounding cities, and fights took place on the picket line. The national guard was brought in on two occasions to restore order. Finally MidCon shut down again for good and declared that the workers were all fired and the company was for sale. All negotiations came to a halt. No one even bothered to pretend at making an effort anymore. Another month passed. The pickets continued, no one made any money, and the community of Hopewell and its citizens grew steadily more depressed.

Now, with the summer heat reaching record highs, spring's hopes were as dry as the dust that coated the roadways, and the bad feelings had burned down to white-hot embers.

Old Bob reached Lincoln Highway, turned on the lighted arrow off Sinnissippi Road, and headed for town. He passed the Kroger supermarket and the billboard put up six months ago by the Chamber of Commerce that read WELCOME TO HOPEWELL, ILLINOIS! WE'RE GROWING YOUR WAY! The billboard was faded and dust-covered in the dull shimmer of the late-morning heat, and the words seemed to mock the reality of things. Old Bob rolled up the windows and turned on the air. There weren't any smells from here on in that mattered to him.

He drove the combined four-lane to where it divided into a pair of one-ways, Fourth Street going west into town, Third Street coming east. He passed several fast-food joints, a liquor store, a pair of gas stations, Quik Dry Cleaners, Rock River Valley Printers, and an electrical shop. Traffic was light. The heat rose off the pavement in waves, and the leaves on the trees that lined the sidewalks hung limp in the windless air. The men and women of Hopewell were closeted in their homes and offices with the air conditioners turned on high, going about the business of their lives with weary determination. Unless summer school had claimed them, the kids were all out at the parks or swimming pools, trying to stay cool and keep from being bored. At night the temperature would drop ten to fifteen degrees and there might be a breeze, but still no one would be moving very fast. There was a somnolence to the community that suggested a long siesta in progress, a dullness of pace that whispered of despair.

Old Bob shook his head. Well, the Fourth of July was almost here, and the Fourth, with its fireworks and picnics and the dance in the park, might help take people's minds off their problems.

A few minutes later he pulled into a vacant parking space in front of Josie's and climbed out of the cab. The sun's brightness was so intense and the heat's swelter so thick that for a moment he felt light-headed. He gripped the parking mirror to steady himself, feeling old and foolish, trying desperately to pretend that nothing was wrong as he studied his feet. When he had regained his balance sufficiently to stand on his own, he walked to the parking meter, fed a few coins into the slot, moved to the front door of the coffee shop, and stepped inside.

Cold air washed over him, a welcome relief. Josie's occupied the corner of Second Avenue and Third Street across from the liquor store, the bank parking lot, and Hays Insurance. Windows running the length of both front walls gave a clear view of the intersection and those trudging to and from their air-conditioned offices and cars. Booths lined the windows, red leather fifties-era banquettes reupholstered and restitched. An L-shaped counter wrapped with stools was situated farther in, and a scattering of tables occupied the available floor space between. There were fresh-baked doughnuts, sweet rolls, and breads displayed in a glass case at the far end of the counter, and coffee, espresso, hot chocolate, tea, and soft drinks to wash those down. Josie's boasted black cows, green rivers, sarsaparillas, and the thickest shakes for miles. Breakfast was served anytime, and you could get lunch until three, when the kitchen closed. Takeout was available and frequently used. Josie's had the best daytime food in town, and almost everyone drifted in to sample it at least once or twice a week.

Old Bob and his union pals were there every day. Before the

mill was shut down, only those who had retired came in on a regular basis, but now all of them showed up every morning without fail. Most were already there as Old Bob made his way to the back of the room and the clutch of tables those who had gotten there first had shoved together to accommodate late-comers. Old Bob waved, then detoured toward the service counter. Carol Blier intercepted him, asked how he was doing, and told him to stop by the office sometime for a chat. Old Bob nodded and moved on, feeling Carol's eyes following him, measuring his step. Carol sold life insurance.

"Well, there you are," Josie greeted from behind the counter, giving him her warmest smile. "Your buddies have been wondering if you were coming in."

Old Bob smiled back. "Have they now?"

"Sure. They can't spit and walk at the same time without you to show them how—you know that." Josie cocked one eyebrow playfully. "I swear you get better-looking every time I see you."

Old Bob laughed. Josie Jackson was somewhere in her thirties, a divorcée with a teenage daughter and a worthless ex-husband last seen heading south about half a dozen years ago. She was younger-looking than her years, certainly younger-acting, with big dark eyes and a ready smile, long blondish hair and a head-turning body, and most important of all a willingness to work that would put most people to shame. She had purchased Josie's with money loaned to her by her parents, who owned a carpet-and-tile business. Having worked much of her adult life as a waitress, Josie Jackson knew what she was doing, and in no time her business was the favorite breakfast and lunch spot in Hopewell. Josie ran it with charm and efficiency and a live-and-let-live attitude that made everyone feel welcome.

"How's Evelyn?" she asked him, leaning her elbows on the counter as she fixed him with her dark eyes.

He shrugged. "Same as always. Rock of ages."

"Yeah, she'll outlive us all, won't she?" Josie brushed at her tousled hair. "Well, go on back. You want your usual?"

Old Bob nodded, and Josie moved away. If he'd been

younger and unattached, Old Bob would have given serious consideration to hooking up with Josie Jackson. But then that was the way all the old codgers felt, and most of the young bucks, too. That was Josie's gift.

He eased through the clustered tables, stopping for a brief word here and there, working his way back to where the union crowd was gathered. They glanced up as he approached, one after the other, giving him perfunctory nods or calling out words of greeting. Al Garcia, Mel Riorden, Derry Howe, Richie Stoudt, Penny Williamson, Mike Michaelson, Junior Elway, and one or two more. They made room for him at one end of the table, and he scooted a chair over and took a seat, sinking comfortably into place.

"So this guy, he works in a post office somewhere over in Iowa, right?" Mel Riorden was saying. He was a big, over-weight crane operator with spiky red hair and a tendency to blink rapidly while he was speaking. He was doing so now. Like one of those ads showing how easy it is to open and close a set of blinds. Blink, blink, blink. "He comes to work in a dress. No, this is the God's honest truth. It was right there in the paper. He comes to work in a dress."

"What color of dress?" Richie Stoudt interrupted, looking genuinely puzzled, not an unusual expression for Richie.

Riorden looked at him. "What the hell difference does that make? It's a dress, on a man who works in a post office, Richie! Think about it! Anyway, he comes to work, this guy, and his supervisor sees the dress and tells him he can't work like that, he has to go home and change. So he does. And he comes back wearing a different dress, a fur coat, and a gorilla mask. The supervisor tells him to go home again, but this time he won't leave. So they call the police and haul him away. Charge him with disturbing the peace or something. But this is the best part. Afterward, the supervisor tells a reporter—this is true, now, I swear—tells the reporter, with a straight face, that they are considering psychiatric evaluation for the guy. *Considering!*"

"You know, I read about a guy who took his monkey to the emergency room a few weeks back." Albert Garcia picked up the conversation. He was a small, solid man with thinning dark hair and close-set features, a relative newcomer to the group, having come up from Houston with his family to work at MidCon less than ten years ago. Before the strike, he set the rolls in the fourteen-inch. "The monkey was his pet, and it got sick or something. So he hauls it down to the emergency room. This was in Arkansas, I think. Tells the nurse it's his baby. Can you imagine? His baby!"

"Did it look anything like him?" Mel Riorden laughed.

"This isn't the same guy, is it?" Penny Williamson asked suddenly. He was a bulky, heavy-featured black man with skin that shone almost as blue as oiled steel. He was a foreman in the number-three plant, steady and reliable. He shifted his heavy frame slightly and winked knowingly at Old Bob. "You know, the postal-worker guy again?"

Al Garcia looked perplexed. "I don't think so. Do you think it could be?"

"So what happened?" Riorden asked as he bit into a fresh Danish. His eyes blinked like a camera shutter. He rearranged the sizable mound of sweet rolls he had piled on a plate in front of him, already choosing his next victim.

"Nothing." Al Garcia shrugged. "They fixed up the monkey and sent him home."

"That's it? That's the whole story?" Riorden shook his head.

Al Garcia shrugged again. "I just thought it was bizarre, that's all."

"I think you're bizarre." Riorden looked away dismissively. "Hey, Bob, what news from the east end this fine morning?"

Old Bob accepted with a nod the coffee and sweet roll Josie scooted in front of him. "Nothing you don't already know. It's hot at that end of town, too. Any news from the mill?"

"Same old, same old. The strike goes on. Life goes on. Everybody keeps on keeping on."

"I been getting some yard work out at Joe Preston's," Richie Stoudt offered, but everyone ignored him, because if brains were dynamite he didn't have enough to blow his nose.

"I'll give you some news," Junior Elway said suddenly. "There's some boys planning to cross the picket line if they can get their jobs back. It was just a few at first, but I think there's more of them now."

Old Bob considered him wordlessly for a moment. Junior was not the most reliable of sources. "That so, Junior? I don't think the company will allow it, after all that's happened."

"They'll allow it, all right," Derry Howe cut in. He was a tall, angular man with close-cropped hair and an intense, suspicious stare that made people wonder. He'd been a bit strange as a boy, and two tours in Vietnam hadn't improved things. Since Nam, he'd lost a wife, been arrested any number of times for drinking and driving, and spotted up his mill record until it looked like someone had sneezed into an inkwell. Old Bob couldn't understand why they hadn't fired him. He was erratic and error-prone, and those who knew him best thought he wasn't rowing with all his oars in the water. Junior Elway was the only friend he had, which was a dubious distinction. He was allowed to hang out with this group only because he was Mel Riorden's sister's boy.

"What do you mean?" Al Garcia asked quickly.

"I mean, they'll allow it because they're going to start up the fourteen-inch again over the weekend and have it up and running by Tuesday. Right after the Fourth. I got it from a friend on the inside." Howe's temple pulsed and his lips tightened. "They want to break the union, and this is their best chance. Get the company running again without us."

"Been tried already." Al Garcia sniffed.

"So now it's gonna get tried again. Think about it, Al. What have they got to lose?"

"No one from the union is going back to help them do it," Penrod Williamson declared, glowering at Howe. "That's foolish talk."

"You don't think there's enough men out there with wives and children to feed that this ain't become more important to them than the strike?" Howe snapped. He brushed at his close-cropped hair. "You ain't paying attention then, Penny. The bean counters have taken over, and guys like us, we're history! You think the national's going to bail us out of this? Hell! The

company's going to break the union and we're sitting here letting them do it!"

"Well, it's not like there's a lot else we can do, Derry," Mel
Riorden pointed out, easing his considerable weight back in his
metal frame chair. "We've struck and picketed and that's all the
law allows us. And the national's doing what it can. We just
have to be patient. Sooner or later this thing will get settled."

"How's that gonna happen, Mel?" Howe pressed, flushed
with anger. "Just how the hell's that gonna happen? You see
any negotiating going on? I sure as hell don't! Striking and
picketing is fine, but it ain't getting us anywhere. These people
running the show, they ain't from here. They don't give a rat's
ass what happens to us. If you think they do, well you're a
damn fool!"

"He's got a point," Junior Elway agreed, leaning forward
over his coffee, nodding solemnly, lank blond hair falling into
his face. Old Bob pursed his lips. Junior always thought Derry
Howe had a point.

"Damn right!" Howe was rolling now, his taut features
shoved forward, dominating the table. "You think we're going
to win this thing by sitting around bullshitting each other?
Well, we ain't! And there ain't no one else gonna help us either.
We have to do this ourselves, and we have to do it quick. We
have to make them hurt more than we're hurting. We have to
pick their pocket the way they're picking ours!"

"What're you talking about?" Penny Williamson growled.
He had less use for Derry Howe than any of them; he'd once
had Howe booted off his shift.

Howe glared at him. "You think about it, Mr. Penrod Williamson. You were in the Nam, too. Hurt them worse than they
hurt you, that was how you survived. That's how you get anywhere in a war."

"We ain't in a war here," Penny Williamson observed, his
finger pointed at Howe. "And the Nam's got nothing to do with
this. What're you saying, man? That we ought to go down to
the mill and blow up a few of the enemy? You want to shoot
someone while you're at it?"

Derry Howe's fist crashed down on the table. "If that's what it takes, hell yes!"

There was sudden silence. A few heads turned. Howe was shaking with anger as he leaned back in his chair, refusing to look away. Al Garcia wiped at his spilled coffee with his napkin and shook his head. Mel Riorden checked his watch.

Penny Williamson folded his arms across his broad chest, regarding Derry Howe the way he might have regarded that postal worker in his dress, fur coat, and gorilla mask. "You better watch out who you say that to."

"Derry's just upset," said a man sitting next to him. Old Bob hadn't noticed the fellow before. He had blue eyes that were so pale they seemed washed of color. "His job's on the line, and the company doesn't even know he's alive. You can understand how he feels. No need for us to be angry with each other. We're all friends here."

"Yeah, Derry don't mean nothing," Junior Elway agreed.

"What do you think we ought to do?" Mike Michaelson asked Robert Roosevelt Freemark suddenly, trying to turn the conversation another way.

Old Bob was still looking at the man next to Howe, trying to place him. The bland, smooth features were as familiar to him as his own, but for some reason he couldn't think of his name. It was right on the tip of his tongue, but he couldn't get a handle on it. Nor could he remember exactly what it was the fellow did. He was a mill man, all right. Too young to be retired, so he must be one of the strikers. But where did he know him from? The others seemed to know him, so why couldn't he place him?

His gaze shifted to Michaelson, a tall, gaunt, even-tempered millwright who had retired about the same time Old Bob had. Old Bob had known Mike all his life, and he recognized at once that Mike was trying to give Derry Howe a chance to cool down.

"Well, I think we need a stronger presence from the national office," he said. "Derry's right about that much." He folded his big hands on the table before him and looked down at them. "I think we need some of the government people to do more—

maybe a senator or two to intervene so we can get things back on track with the negotiations."

"More talk!" Derry Howe barely hid a sneer.

"Talk is the best way to go," Old Bob advised, giving him a look.

"Yeah? Well, it ain't like it was in your time, Bob Freemark. We ain't got local owners anymore, people with a stake in the community, people with families that live here like the rest of us. We got a bunch of New York bloodsuckers draining all the money out of Hopewell, and they don't care about us." Derry Howe slouched in his chair, eyes downcast. "We got to do something if we expect to survive this. We can't just sit around hoping for someone to help us. It ain't going to happen."

"There was a fellow out East somewhere, one of the major cities, Philadelphia, I think," said the man sitting next to him, his strange pale eyes quizzical, his mouth quirked slightly, as if his words amused him. "His wife died, leaving him with a five-year-old daughter who was mildly retarded. He kept her in a closet off the living room for almost three years before someone discovered what he was doing and called the police. When they questioned the man, he said he was just trying to protect the girl from a hostile world." The man cocked his head slightly. "When they asked the girl why she hadn't tried to escape, she said she was afraid to run, that all she could do was wait for someone to help her."

"Well, they ain't shutting me up in no closet!" Derry Howe snapped angrily. "I can help myself just fine!"

"Sometimes," the man said, looking at no one in particular, his voice low and compelling, "the locks get turned before you even realize that the door's been closed."

"I think Bob's right," Mike Michaelson said. "I think we have to give the negotiation process a fair chance. These things take time."

"Time that costs us money and gives them a better chance to break us!" Derry Howe shoved back his chair and came to his feet. "I'm outta here. I got better things to do than sit around here all day. I'm sick of talking and doing nothing. Maybe you don't care if the company takes away your job, but I ain't having none of it!"

He stalked away, weaving angrily through the crowded tables, and slammed the door behind him. At the counter, Josie Jackson grimaced. A moment later, Junior Elway left as well. The men still seated at the table shifted uncomfortably in their chairs.

"I swear, if that boy wasn't my sister's son, I wouldn't waste another moment on him," Melvin Riorden muttered.

"He's right about one thing," Old Bob sighed. "Things aren't the way they used to be. The world's changed from when we were his age, and a lot of it's gotten pretty ugly. People don't want to work things out anymore like they used to."

"People just want a pound of flesh," Al Garcia agreed. His blocky head pivoted on his bull neck. "It's all about money and getting your foot on the other guy's neck. That's why the company and the union can't settle anything. Makes you wonder if the government hasn't put something in the water after all."

"You see where that man went into a grocery store out on Long Island somewhere and walked up and down the aisles stabbing people?" asked Penny Williamson. "Had two carving knives with him, one in each hand. He never said a word, just walked in and began stabbing people. He stabbed ten of them before someone stopped him. Killed two. The police say he was angry and depressed. Well, hell, who ain't?"

"The world's full of angry, depressed people," said Mike Michaelson, rearranging his coffee cup and silver, staring down at his sun-browned, wrinkled hands fixedly. "Look what people are doing to each other. Parents beating and torturing their children. Young boys and girls killing each other. Teachers and priests taking advantage of their position to do awful things. Serial killers wandering the countryside. Churches and schools being vandalized and burned. It's a travesty."

"Some of those people you talk about live right here in Hopewell." Penny Williamson grunted. "That Topp kid who killed his common-law wife with a butcher knife and cut her up in pieces a few years back? I grew up with that kid. Old man Peters killed all those horses two weeks back, said they were the spawn of Satan. Tilda Mason, tried to kill herself three times over the past six months—twice in the mental hospital. Tried to kill a couple of the people working there as well. That fellow Riley Crisp, the one they call 'rabbit' lives down on Wallace? He stood out on the First Avenue Bridge and shot at people until the police came, then shot at them, and then jumped off the bridge and drowned himself. When was that? Last month?" He shook his head. "Where's it all going to end, I wonder?"

Old Bob smoothed back his white hair. None of them had the answer to that one. It made him wonder suddenly about Evelyn and her feeders. Might just as easily be feeders out there as something the government had put in the water.

He noticed suddenly that the man who had been sitting with Derry Howe was gone. His brow furrowed and his wide mouth tightened. When had the man left? He tried again to think of his name and failed.

"I got me some more work to do out at Preston's," Richie Stoudt advised solemnly. "You can laugh, but it keeps bread on the table."

The conversation returned to the strike and the intractable position of the company, and the stories started up again, and a moment later Old Bob had forgotten the man completely.

CHAPTER 4

The demon stepped out into the midday heat in front of Josie's and felt right at home. Perhaps it was his madness that made him so comfortable with the sun's brilliant white light and suffocating swelter, for it was true that it burned as implacably hot. Or perhaps it was his deep and abiding satisfaction at knowing that this community and its inhabitants were his to do with as he chose.

He followed Derry Howe and Junior Elway to the latter's Jeep Cherokee and climbed into the cab with them, sitting comfortably in the backseat, neither one of them quite aware that he was there. It was one of the skills he had acquired—to blend in so thoroughly with his surroundings that he seemed to be a part of them, to make himself appear so familiar that even those sitting right beside him felt no need to question his presence. He supposed there was still just enough of them in him that he was able to accomplish this. He had been human once himself, but that was long ago and all but forgotten. What remained of his humanity was just a shadow of a memory of what these creatures were, so that he could appear and act like them to the extent that his duplicity required it. His gradual transformation from human to demon had driven out the rest. He had found, after a time, that he did not miss it.

Junior turned over the Jeep's engine and switched on the air, blowing a thick wash of heat through the vents and into the closed interior. Junior and Derry rolled down their windows to let the heat escape as the Jeep pulled away from the curb, but the demon just breathed in contentedly and smiled. He had been in Hopewell a little more than a week, not wanting to

come any sooner because John Ross still tracked him relentlessly and had displayed a disturbing ability to locate him even
when there was no possible way he should have been able to do
so. But a week had gone by, the Fourth of July approached, and
it seemed possible that this time Ross might prove a step too
slow. It was important that Ross not interfere, for the demon
had sown his destructive seed deep and waited long for it to
grow. Now the seed's harvest was at hand, and the demon did
not want any interference. Everything was in place, everything
that he had worked so long and hard to achieve—a clever subterfuge, an apocalyptic ruin, and an irreversible transformation
that would hasten the coming of the Void and the banishment
of the Word.

His mind spun with the possibilities as the Jeep turned off
Second Avenue onto Fourth Street and headed west out of
town. On his left the long, dark, corrugated-metal roofs of Mid-
Con Steel could be glimpsed through gaps in the rows of the
once-elegant old homes that ran the length of West Third coming in toward town from several blocks above Avenue G. The
air-conditioning had kicked in, and with the windows rolled up
again the demon took comfort instead from his inner heat. His
passion enveloped him, a cocoon into which he could retreat
and from which he could feed, a red haze of intolerance and
hate and greed for power.

"Those old boys don't know nothing," Derry Howe was
saying, slouched back in his bucket seat, his bullet head
shining in the sun. "I don't plan to listen to them no more. All
they do is sit around and talk about sitting around some more.
Old farts."

"Yeah, they ain't seeing it like it is," Junior agreed.

No, not like you, thought the demon contentedly. *Not with
the bright, clear knowledge I have given to you.*

"We got to do something if we want to keep our jobs," Derry
said. "We got to stop the company from breaking the union,
and we got to stop them right now."

"Yeah, but how we gonna do that?" Junior asked, glancing
over uncertainly, then gunning the Jeep through a yellow light
turning red.

"Oh, there's ways. There's ways, buddy."

Yes, there are lots and lots of ways.

Derry Howe looked over at Junior, smiling. "You know what they say? Where there's a will, there's a way. Well, I've got me a will that won't quit. I just need me a way. I'm gonna find it, too, and you can take that to the bank! Old Bob and those others can go shove their patience where the sun don't shine."

They crossed Avenue G past the tire center, gas station, and west-end grocery and rode farther toward the cornfields. The buildings of the mill were still visible down the cross streets and between the old homes, plant three giving way to plant four, plant five still out ahead, back of the old speedway, the whole of MidCon spread out along the north bank of the Rock River. The demon studied the residences and the people they sped past, his for the taking, his to own, dismissing them almost as quickly as they were considered. This was a breeding ground for him and nothing more. On July fourth, all of it and all of them would pass into the hands of the feeders, and he would be on his way to another place. It was his world, too, but he felt no attachment to it. His work was what drove him, what gave him purpose, and his servitude to the dark, chaotic vision of the Void would allow for nothing else. There were in his life only need and compulsion, those to be satisfied through a venting of his madness, and nothing of his physical surroundings or of the creatures that inhabited them had any meaning for him.

The Jeep passed a junkyard of rusting automobile carcasses piled high behind a chain-link fence bordering a trailer park that looked to be the last stop of transients on their way to homelessness or the grave, and from behind the fence a pair of lean, black-faced Dobermans peered out with savage eyes. Bred to attack anything that intruded, the demon thought. Bred to destroy. He liked that.

His mind drifted in the haze of the midday summer heat, the voices of Derry and Junior a comfortable buzz that did not intrude. He had come to Hopewell afoot, walking out of the swelter of the cornfields and the blacktop roadways with the inexorable certainty of nightfall. He had chosen to appear in that manner, wanting to smell and taste the town, wanting it to give something of itself to him, something it could not give if he arrived by car or bus, if he were to be closed away. He had materialized in the manner of a mirage, given shape and form out of delusion and desperation, given life out of false hope. He had walked into a poor neighborhood on the fringe of the town, into a collection of dilapidated homes patched with tar paper and oilcloth, their painted wooden sides peeling, their shingled roofs cracked and blistered, their yards rutted and littered with ruined toys, discarded appliances, and rusting vehicles. Within the close, airless confines of the homes huddled the leavings of despair and endless disappointment. Children played beneath the shade of the trees, dust-covered, desultory, and joyless. Already they knew what the future would bring. Already their childhood was ending. The demon passed them with a smile.

At the corner of Avenue J and Twelfth Street, at a confluence of crumbling sheds, pastureland, and a few scattered residences, a boy had stood at the edge of the roadway with a massive dog. At well over a hundred pounds, all bristling hair and wicked dark markings, the dog was neither one identifiable breed nor another, but some freakish combination. It stood next to the boy, hooked on one end of a chain, the other end of which the boy held. Its eyes were deep-set and baleful, and its stance suggested a barely restrained fury. It disliked the demon instinctively, as all animals did, but it was frightened of him, too. The boy was in his early teens, wearing blue jeans, a T-shirt, and high-top tennis shoes, all of them worn and stained with dirt. The boy's stance, like the dog's, was at once strained and cocky. He was tall and heavyset, and there was no mistaking the bully in him. Most of what he had gotten in life he had acquired through intimidation or theft. When he smiled, as he did now, there was no warmth.

"Hey, you," the boy said.

The demon's bland face showed nothing. Just another stupid, worthless creature, the demon thought as he approached. Just another failed effort in somebody's failed life. He would leave his mark here, with this boy, to signal his coming, to lay claim to what was now his. He would do so in blood.

"You want to go through here, you got to pay me a dollar," the boy called out to the demon.

The demon stopped where he was, right in the middle of the road, the sun beating down on him. "A dollar?"

"Yeah, that's the toll. Else you got to go around the other way."

The demon looked up the street the way he had come, then back at the boy. "This is a public street."

"Not in front of my house it ain't. In front of my house, it's a toll road and it costs a dollar to pass."

"Only if you're traveling on foot, I guess. Not if you're in a car. I don't suppose that even a dog as mean as yours could stop a car." The boy stared at him, uncomprehending. The demon shrugged. "So, does the dog collect the dollar for you?"

"The dog collects a piece of your ass if you don't pay!" the boy snapped irritably. "You want to see what that feels like?"

The demon studied the boy silently for a moment. "What's the dog's name?"

"It don't matter what his name is! Just pay me the dollar!" The boy's face was flushed and angry.

"Well, if I don't know his name," said the demon softly, "how can I call him off if he attacks someone?"

The dog sensed the boy's anger, and his hackles rose along the back of his neck and he bared his teeth with a low growl. "You just better give me the dollar, buddy," said the boy, a thin smile twisting his lips as he looked down at the dog and jiggled the chain meaningfully.

"Oh, I don't think I could do that," said the demon. "I don't carry any money. I don't have any need for it. People just give me what I want. I don't even need a dog like this one to make them do it." He smiled, his bland features crinkling warmly, his strange eyes fixing the boy. "That's not very good news for you, is it?"

The boy was staring at him. "You better pay me fast, butt-head, or I might just let go of this chain!"

The demon shook his head reprovingly. "I wouldn't do that,

if I were you. I'd keep a tight hold on that chain until I'm well down the road from here." He slipped his hands in his pockets and cocked his head at the boy. "Tell you what. I'm a fair man. You just made a big mistake, but I'm willing to let it pass. I'll forget all about it if you apologize. Just say you're sorry and that will be the end of it."

The boy's mouth dropped. "What? What did you say?"

The demon smiled some more. "You heard me."

For an instant the boy froze, the disbelief on his face apparent. Then he mouthed a string of obscenities, dropped to his knee, and released the chain on the dog's collar. "Oops!" he snarled at the demon, flinging the chain away disdainfully, eyes hot and furious.

But the demon had already invoked his skill, a small, spare movement of one hand that looked something like the blessing of a minister at the close of a service. Outwardly, nothing seemed to change. The demon still stood there in the sweltering heat, head cocked in seeming contemplation, bland face expressionless. The boy lurched to his feet as he released the dog, urging him to the attack with an angry shout. But something profound had changed in the boy. His look and smell and movement had become those of a frightened rabbit, flushed from cover and desperately trying to scurry to safety. The dog reacted on instinct. It wheeled on the boy instantly, lunging for his throat. The boy gave a cry of shock and fear as the dog slammed into him, knocking him from his feet. The boy's hands came up as he tumbled into the dirt of his yard, and he tried desperately to shield his face. The dog tore at the boy, and the boy's cries turned to screams. Drops of blood flew through the air. Scarlet threads laced the dusty earth.

The demon stood watching for several moments more before turning away to continue down the road. He read later that if the boy's body hadn't been found in front of his house, the authorities would have needed dental records to identify him. His family couldn't recognize him from what was left of his face. The dog, which one of the neighbors described as the boy's best friend, was quarantined for the mandatory ten days to determine if it had rabies and then put down.

Junior Elway pulled the Jeep Cherokee against the curb in front of the dilapidated apartment complex situated on Avenue L and West Third where Derry Howe rented a small, one-bedroom unit. They talked for a moment while the demon listened, agreeing to meet at Scrubby's for pizza and beer that evening. Both were divorced, on the downside of forty, and convinced that a lot of women were missing a good bet. Derry Howe climbed out of the Jeep, and the demon climbed out with him. Together they went up the walk as Junior Elway drove off.

Inside the apartment, the window fan was rattling and buzzing as it fought to withstand the heat. It was not adequate to the task, and the air in the apartment was close and warm. Derry Howe walked to the refrigerator, pulled out a can of Bud, walked back to the living room, and flopped down on the sofa. He was supposed to be on picket duty at the number-three plant, but he had begged off the night before by claiming that his back was acting up. His union supervisor had probably known he was lying, but had chosen to let it slide. Derry was encouraged. Already he was wondering if he could pull the same scam for Sunday's shift.

The demon sat in the rocker that had belonged to Derry Howe's grandmother before she died, the one his mother had inherited and in turn passed on to him when he was married and she still had hopes for him. Now no one had any hopes for Derry Howe. Two tours in Vietnam followed by his failed marriage to a girl some thought would change him, a dozen arrests on various charges, some jail time served at the county lockup, and twenty years at MidCon with only one promotion and a jacket full of reprimands had pretty much settled the matter. The road that marked the course of his life had straightened and narrowed, and all that remained to be determined was how far it would run and how many more breakdowns he would suffer along the way.

It had not proved difficult for the demon to find Derry Howe. Really, there were so many like him that it scarcely took any effort at all. The demon had found him on the second day of his arrival in Hopewell, just by visiting the coffee shops and bars, just by listening to what the people of the town had to say. He had moved in with Howe right away, making himself an indispensable presence in the other's life, insinuating himself into the other's thoughts, twisting Derry's mind until he had begun to think and talk in the ways that were necessary. Hardly a challenge, but definitely a requirement if the demon's plans were to succeed. He was Derry Howe's shadow now, his conscience, his sounding board, his devil's advocate. His own, personal demon. And Derry Howe, in turn, was his creature.

The demon watched Howe finish his beer, struggle up in the stale air of the apartment, walk to the kitchen, and fish through the cluttered refrigerator for another. The demon waited patiently. The demon's life was wedded to his cause, and his cause required great patience. He had sacrificed everything to become what he was, but he knew from his transformation at the hands of the Void that sacrifice was required. After he had embraced the Void he had concealed himself until his conscience had rotted and fallen away and left him free. His name had been lost. His history had faded. His humanity had dissipated and turned to dust. All that he had been had disappeared with the change, so that now he was reborn into his present life and made over into his higher form. It had been hard in the beginning, and once, in a moment of great weakness and despair, he had even thought to reject what he had so readily embraced. But in the end reason had prevailed, and he had forsaken all.

Now it was the cause that drove him, that fed him, that gave him his purpose in life. The cause was everything, and the Void defined the cause as need required. For now, for this brief moment in time, the cause was the destruction of this town and its inhabitants. It was the release of the feeders that lurked in the caves beneath Sinnissippi Park. It was the subversion of Derry Howe. It was the infusion of chaos and madness into the sheltered world of Hopewell.

And it was one thing more, the thing that mattered most.

Derry Howe returned to the sofa and seated himself with a grunt, sipping at his beer. He looked at the demon, seeing him clearly for the first time because the demon was ready now to talk.

"We got to do something, bud," Derry Howe intoned solemnly, nodding to emphasize the importance of his pronouncement. "We got to stop those suckers before they break us."

The demon nodded in response. "If union men cross the picket line and return to work, the strike is finished."

"Can't let them do that." Howe worked his big hands around the beer bottle, twisting slowly. "Damn traitors, anyway! What the hell they think they're doing, selling out the rest of us!"

"What to do?" mused the demon.

"Shoot a few, by God! That'll show them we mean business!"

The demon considered the prospect. "But that might not stop the others from going back to work. And you would go to jail. You wouldn't be of any use then, would you?"

Derry Howe frowned. He took a long drink out of the bottle. "So what's the answer, bud? We have to do something."

"Think about it like this," suggested the demon, having already done so long ago. "The company plans to reopen the fourteen-inch using company men to fill the skill jobs and scabs to fill the gaps. If they can open one plant and bring back a few of the union men, they can work at opening the others as well. It will snowball on you, if they can just get one mill up and running."

Howe nodded, his face flushed and intense. "Yeah, so?"

The demon smiled, drawing him in. "So, what happens if the company can't open the number-three plant? What happens if they can't get the fourteen-inch up and running?"

Derry Howe stared at him wordlessly, thinking it through.

The demon gave him a hand. "What happens if it becomes clear to everyone that it's dangerous to cross the picket line and work in the mills? What happens, Derry?"

"Yeah, right." A light came on somewhere behind Derry Howe's flat eyes. "No one crosses the line and the strike continues and the company has to give in. Yeah, I get it. But why wouldn't they start up the fourteen-inch? All they need's the workers. Unless . . ."

The demon spoke the words for him, in his own voice, almost as if in his own mind. "Unless there is an accident."

"An accident," breathed Derry Howe. Excitement lit his rawboned features. "A really bad accident."

"It happens sometimes," said the demon.

"Yeah, it does, doesn't it? An accident. Maybe someone even gets killed. Yeah."

"Think about it," said the demon. "Something will come to you."

Derry Howe was smiling, his mind racing. He drank his beer and mulled over the possibilities the demon's words had suggested to him. It would take little effort from here. A few more nudges. One good push in the right direction. Howe had been a demolitions man in Vietnam. It wouldn't take much for him to figure out how to use that knowledge here. It wouldn't even take courage. It required stupidity and blind conviction, and Derry Howe had plenty of both. That was why the demon had picked him.

The demon leaned back in the rocker and looked away, suddenly bored. What happened with Derry Howe was of such little importance. He was just another match waiting to be struck. Perhaps he would catch fire. You never knew. The demon had learned a long time ago that an explosion resulted most often from an accumulation of sparks. It was a lesson that had served him well. Derry Howe was one of several sparks the demon would strike over the next three days. Some were bound to catch fire; some might even explode. But, in the final analysis, they were all just diversions intended to draw attention away from the demon's real purpose in coming to this tiny, insignificant Midwestern town. If things went the way he intended—and he had every reason to think they would—he would be gone before anyone had any idea at all of his interest in the girl.

And by then, of course, it would be too late to save her.

CHAPTER 5

Nest Freemark went down the back steps two at a time, letting the screen door slam shut behind her. She winced at the sound, belatedly remembering how much it irritated Gran. She always forgot to catch the door. She didn't know why, she just did. She skipped off the gravel walk and onto the lawn, heading across the yard for the park. Mr. Scratch lay stretched out in the shade beneath the closest oak, a white and orange tom, his fluffy sides rising and falling with each labored breath. He was thirteen or fourteen, and he slept most of the time now, dreaming his cat dreams. He didn't even look up at her as she passed, his eyes closed, his ragged ears and scarred face a worn mask of contentment. He had long ago forfeited his mouser duties to the younger and sprier Miss Minx, who, as usual, was nowhere to be seen. Nest smiled at the old cat as she passed. Not for him the trials and tribulations of dealing with the feeders of Sinnissippi Park.

Nest had always known about the feeders. Or at least for as long as she could remember. Even when she hadn't known what they were, she had known they were there. She would catch glimpses of them sometimes, small movements seen out of the corner of one eye, bits and pieces of shadow that didn't quite fit in with their surroundings. She was very small then and not allowed out of the house alone, so she would stand at the windows at twilight, when the feeders were most likely to reveal themselves, and keep watch.

Sometimes her grandmother would take her for walks in the stroller in the cool of the evening, following the dark ribbon of the roadway as it wound through the park, and she would

55

see them then as well. She would point, her eyes shifting to find her grandmother, her child's face solemn and inquisitive, and her grandmother would nod and say, "Yes, I see them. But you don't have to worry, Nest. They won't bother you."

Nor had they, although Nest had never really worried about it much back then. Not knowing what the feeders were, she simply assumed they were like the other creatures that lived in the park—the birds, squirrels, mice, chipmunks, deer, and what have you. Her grandmother never said anything about the feeders, never offered any explanation for them, never even seemed to pay them much attention. When Nest would point, she would always say the same thing and then let the matter drop. Several times Nest mentioned the feeders to her grandfather, but he just stared at her, glanced at her grandmother, and then smiled his most indulgent smile.

"He can't see them," her grandmother told her finally. "There's no point talking about it with him, Nest. He just doesn't see them."

"Why doesn't he?" she had asked, mystified.

"Because most people don't. Most people don't even know they exist. Only a lucky few can see them." She leaned close and touched the tip of Nest's small nose. "You and me, we can. But not Robert. Not your grandfather. He can't see them at all."

She hadn't said why that was. Her explanations were always like that, spare and laconic. She hadn't time for a lot of words, except when she was reading, which she did a lot. On her feet she was all movement and little talk, losing herself in her household tasks or her gardening or her walks in the park. That was then, of course. It wasn't the same anymore, because now Gran was older and drank more and didn't move around much at all. Small, gnarled, and gray, she sat at the kitchen table smoking her cigarettes and drinking her vodka and orange juice until noon and, afterward, her bourbon on the rocks until dusk. She still didn't say much, even when she could have, keeping what she knew to herself, keeping her explanations and her secrets carefully tucked away somewhere deep inside.

She told Nest early on not to talk about the feeders. She was quite emphatic about it. She did so about the same time she told the little girl that only the two of them could see the feeders, so there wasn't any point in discussing them with her grandfather. Or with anybody else, she amended soon after, apparently concerned that the increasingly talkative child might think to do so.

"It will just make people wonder about you," she declared. "It will make them think you are a bit strange. Because you can see the feeders and they can't. Think of the feeders as a secret that only you and I know about. Can you do that, Nest?"

Pretty much, she found she could. But the lack of a more thorough explanation on the matter was troubling and frustrating, and eventually Nest tested her grandmother's theory about other people's attitudes on a couple of her friends. The results were exactly as her grandmother had predicted. Her friends first teased her and then ran to their parents with the tale. Their parents called her grandmother, and her grandmother was forced to allay their concerns with an overly convoluted explanation centered around the effects of fairy tales and make-believe on a child's imagination. Nest was very thoroughly dressed down. She was made to go back to her friends and their parents and to apologize for scaring them. She was five years old when that happened. It was the last time she told anyone about the feeders.

Of course, that was just the first of a number of secrets she learned to conceal about the creatures who lived in the park. Don't talk about the feeders, her grandmother had warned, and in the end she did not. But there were a lot of other things she couldn't talk about either, and for a while it seemed there was something new every time she turned around.

"Do you think the feeders would ever hurt me, Gran?" she asked once, disturbed by something she had seen in one of her picture books that reminded her of the furtiveness of their movements in the shadows of summer twilight and the dismal gloom of midday winter. "If they had the chance, I mean?"

They were alone, sitting at the kitchen table playing dominoes on a cold midwinter Sunday, her grandfather ensconced in his den, listening to a debate over foreign aid.

Her grandmother looked up at her, her bright, darkly lumi-
nescent bird's eyes fixed and staring. "If they had the chance,
yes. But that will never happen."

Nest frowned. "Why not?"

"Because you are my granddaughter."

Nest frowned some more. "What difference does that make?"

"All the difference" was the reply. "You and I have magic,
Nest. Didn't you know?"

"Magic?" Nest had breathed the word in disbelief. "Why?
Why do we have magic, Gran?"

Her grandmother smiled secretively. "We just do, child. But
you can't tell anyone. You have to keep it to yourself."

"Why?"

"You know why. Now, go on, it's your turn, make your play.
Don't talk about it anymore."

That was the end of the matter as far as her grandmother was
concerned, and she didn't mention it again. Nest tried to bring
it up once or twice, but her grandmother always made light of
the matter, as if having magic was nothing, as if it were the
same as being brown-eyed or right-handed. She never explained
what she meant by it, and she never provided any evidence that
it was so. Nest thought she was making it up, the same way she
made up fairy tales now and then to amuse the little girl. She
was doing it to keep Nest from worrying about the feeders.
Magic, indeed, Nest would think, then point her fingers at the
wall and try unsuccessfully to make something happen.

But then she discovered Wraith, and the subject of magic
suddenly took on a whole new meaning. It was when she was
still five, shortly after her attempt at telling her friends about
the feeders and almost a year before she met Pick. She was
playing in her backyard on the swing set, pretending at flying
as she rose and fell at the end of the creaking chains, comfortably settled in the cradle of the broad canvas strap. It was a late-
spring day, the air cool yet with winter's fading breath, the
grass new and dappled with jack-in-the-pulpit and bleeding
heart, the leaves on the oaks and elms beginning to bud. Heavy
clouds scudded across the Midwest skies, bringing rain out of
the western plains, and the sunlight was pale and thin. Her

grandparents were busy inside, and since she was forbidden to leave the yard without them and had never done so before, there was no reason for them to believe she would do so now.

But she did. She got down out of the swing and walked to the end of the yard where the hedgerow was still thin with new growth, slipped through a gap in the intertwined limbs, and stepped onto forbidden ground. She didn't know exactly what it was that prompted her to do so. It had something to do with thinking about the feeders, with picturing them as they appeared and faded in shadowy patches along the fringes of her yard. She wondered about them constantly, and on this day she simply decided to have a look. Did they conceal themselves on the other side of the hedge, just beyond her view? Did they burrow into the ground like moles? What did they do back there where she couldn't see? Why, her inquisitive five-year-old mind demanded, shouldn't she try to find out?

So there she was, standing at the edge of the park, staring out across the broad, flat, grassy expanse of ball diamonds and picnic grounds to where the bluffs rose south and the wooded stretches began east, a pioneer set to explore a wondrous new world. Not that day, perhaps, for she knew she would not be going far on her first try. But soon, she promised herself. Soon.

Her eyes shifted then, and she became aware of the feeders. They were crouched within a copse of heavy brush that screened the Peterson backyard some fifty feet away, watching her. She saw them as you would a gathering of shadows on a gray day, indistinct and nebulous. She caught a glimpse of their flat, yellow eyes shining out of the darkness like a cat's. She stood where she was, looking back, trying to see them more clearly, trying to determine better what they were. She stared intently, losing track of time as she did so, forgetting where she was and what she was about, mesmerized.

Then a drop of rain fell squarely on her nose, cold and wet against her skin. She blinked in surprise, and suddenly the feeders were all around her, and she was so terrified that she could feel her fear writhing inside her like a living thing.

And, just as suddenly, they were gone again. It happened so fast that she wasn't sure if it was real or if she had imagined it.

In the blink of an eye, they had appeared. In another blink, they had gone. How could they move so quickly? What would make them do so?

She saw Wraith then, standing a few feet away, a dark shape in the deepening gray, so still he might have been carved from stone. She didn't know his name then, or what he was, or where he had come from. She stared at him, unable to look away, riveted by the sight of him. She thought he was the biggest creature she had ever seen this close up, bigger even, it seemed to her at that moment, than the horses she had petted once on a visit to the Lehman farm. He appeared to be some sort of dog, immense and fierce-looking and as immovable as the massive shade trees that grew in her backyard. He was brindle in color; his muzzle and head bore tiger-stripe markings and his body hair bristled like a porcupine's quills. Oddly enough, she was not frightened by him. She would always remember that. She was awestruck, but she was not frightened. Not in the way she was of the feeders. He was there, she realized, without quite being sure why, to protect her from them.

Then he disappeared, and she was alone. He simply faded away, as if composed of smoke scattered by a sudden gust of wind. She stared into the space he had occupied, wondering at him. The park stretched away before her, silent and empty in the failing light. Then the rain began to fall in earnest, and she made a dash for the house.

She saw Wraith often after that, possibly because she was looking for him, possibly because he had decided to reveal himself. She still didn't know what he was, and neither did anyone else. Pick told her later that he was some sort of cross-breed, a mix of dog and wolf. But really, since he was created from and held together by magic, his genetic origins didn't make any difference. Whatever he was, he was probably the only one of his kind. Pick confirmed her impression that he was there to protect her. Matter of fact, he advised rather solemnly, Wraith had been shadowing her since the first time she had come into the park, still a baby in her stroller. She wondered at first how she could have missed seeing him, but then discovered that she had missed seeing a lot of other things as well, and it didn't seem so odd.

When she finally told her grandmother about Wraith, her grandmother's response was strange. She didn't question what Nest was telling her. She didn't suggest that Nest might be mistaken or confused. She went all still for a moment, her eyes assumed a distant look, and her thin, old hands tightened about the mittens she was knitting.

"Did you see anything else?" she asked softly.

"No," said Nest, wondering suddenly if there was something she should have seen.

"He just appeared, this dog did? The feeders came close to you, and the dog appeared?" Gran's eyes were sharp and bright.

"Yes. That first time. Now I just see him following me sometimes, watching me. He doesn't come too close. He always stays back. But the feeders are afraid of him. I can tell."

Her grandmother was silent.

"Do you know what he is?" Nest pressed anxiously.

Her grandmother held her gaze. "Perhaps."

"Is he there to protect me?"

"I think we have to find that out."

Nest frowned. "Who sent him, Gran?"

But her grandmother only shook her head and turned away. "I don't know," she answered, but the way she said it made Nest think that maybe she did.

For a long time, Nest was the only one who saw the dog. Sometimes her grandmother would come into the park with her, but the dog did not show himself on those occasions.

Then one day, for no reason that Nest could ever determine, he appeared out of a cluster of spruce at twilight while the old woman and her granddaughter walked through the west-end play area toward the cliffs. Her grandmother froze, holding on to the little girl's hand tightly.

"Gran?" Nest said uncertainly.

"Wait here for me, Nest," her grandmother replied. "Don't move."

The old woman walked up to the big animal and knelt

before him. It was growing dark, and it was hard to see clearly, but it seemed to Nest as if her grandmother was speaking to the beast. It was very quiet, and she could almost hear the old woman's words. She remained standing for a while, but then she grew tired and sat down on the grass to wait. There was no one else around. Stars began to appear in the sky and shadows to swallow the last of the fading light. Her grandmother and the dog were staring at each other, locked in a strange, silent communication that went on for a very long time.

Finally her grandmother rose and came back to her. The strange dog watched for a moment, then slowly melted back into the shadows.

"It's all right, Nest," her grandmother whispered in a thin, weary voice, taking her hand once more. "His name is Wraith. He is here to protect you."

She never spoke of the meeting again.

As Nest wriggled her way through the hedgerow at the back of her yard, she paused for a moment at the edge of the rutted dirt service road that ran parallel to the south boundary of the lot and recalled anew how Sinnissippi Park had appeared to her that first time. So long ago, she thought, and smiled at the memory. The park had seemed much bigger then, a vast, sprawling, mysterious world of secrets waiting to be discovered and adventures begging to be lived. At night, sometimes, when she was abroad with Pick, she still felt as she had when she was five, and the park, with its dark woods and gloomy ravines, with its murky sloughs and massive cliffs, seemed as large and unfathomable as it had then.

But now, in the harsh light of the July midday, the sun blazing down out of another cloudless sky, the heat a faint shimmer rising off the burned-out flats, the park seemed small and constrained. The ball fields lay just beyond the service road, their parched diamonds turned dusty and hardened and dry, their grassy outfields gray-tipped and spiky. There were four altogether, two close and two across the way east. Farther on, a cluster of hardwoods and spruce shaded a play area for small children, replete with swings and monkey bars and

teeter-totters and painted animals on heavy springs set in concrete that you could climb aboard and ride.

The entrance to the park was to Nest's immediate right, and
the blacktop road leading into the park ran under the crossbar
toward the river before splitting off in two directions. If you
went right, you traveled to the turnaround and the cliffs, where
the previous night she had rescued Bennett Scott. Beyond the
turnaround, separated from the park by a high chain-link fence
that any kid over the age of seven who was worth his salt could
climb, was Riverside Cemetery, rolling, tree-shaded, and sub-
limely peaceful. The cemetery was where her mother was
buried. If you turned left off the blacktop, you either looped
down under a bridge to the riverbank at the bottom of the cliffs,
where a few picnic tables were situated, or you continued on
some distance to the east end of the park where a large, sheltered pavilion, a toboggan slide, a playground, and the deep
woods waited. The toboggan slide ran all the way from the
heights beyond the parking lot to the reedy depths of the bayou.
A good run in deep winter would take you out across the ice all
the way to the embankment that supported the railroad tracks
running east to Chicago and west to the plains. Stretching a run
to the embankment was every toboggan rider's goal. Nest had
done it three times. There were large brick-chimney and
smaller iron hibachi-style cooking stations and wooden picnic
tables all over the park, so that any number of church outings
or family reunions could be carried on at one time. Farther east,
back in the deep woods, there were nature trails that ran from
the Woodland Heights subdivision where Robert Heppler lived
down to the banks of the Rock River. There were trees that
were well over two hundred years old. Some of the oaks and
elms and shagbark hickories rose over a hundred feet, and the
park was filled with dark, mysterious places that whispered of
things you couldn't see, but could only imagine and secretly
wish for.

The park was old, Nest knew. It had never been anything but
a park. Before it was officially titled and protected by state law,
it had been an untamed stretch of virgin timber. No one had

lived there since the time of the Indians. Except, of course, the feeders.

She took it all in for a moment, embracing it with her senses, reclaiming it for herself as she did each time she returned, familiar ground that belonged to her. She felt that about the park—that through her peculiar and endemic familiarity with its myriad creatures, its secretive places, its changeless look and feel, and its oddly compelling solitude, it was hers. She felt this way whenever she stepped into the park, as if she were fulfilling a purpose in her life, as if she knew that here, of all places in the world, she belonged.

Of course, Pick had more than a little to do with that, having enlisted her years ago as his human partner in the care and upkeep of the park's magic.

She walked across the service road, kicking idly at the dirt with her running shoes, moving onto the heat-crisped grasses of the ball diamond, intent on taking the shortcut across the park to Cass Minter's house on Spring Drive. The others were probably already there: Robert, Brianna, and Jared. She would be the last to arrive, late as usual. But it was summer, and it really didn't matter if she was late. The days stretched on, and time lost meaning. Today they were going fishing down by the old boat launch below the dam, just off the east end of the park. Bass, bluegill, perch, and sunfish, you could still catch them all, if not so easily as once. You didn't eat them, of course. Rock River wasn't clean enough for that, not the way it had been when her grandfather was a boy. But the fishing was fun, and it was as good a way as any to spend an afternoon.

She was skipping off behind the backstop of the closest ball field when she heard a voice call out.

"Nest! Wait up!"

Turning awkward and flushed the moment she realized who it was, she watched Jared Scott come loping up the service road from the park entry. She glanced down at her Grunge Lives T-shirt and her running shorts, at the stupid way they hung on her, at the flatness of her chest and the leanness of her legs and arms, and she wished for the thousandth time that she looked more like Brianna. She was angry at herself for thinking like that, then for feeling so bizarre over a boy, and then because there he was, right in front of her, smiling and waving and looking at her in that strange way of his.

"Hey, Nest," he greeted.

"Hey, Jared." She looked quickly away.

They fell into step beside each other, moving along the third-base line of the diamond, both of them looking at their feet. Jared wore old jeans, a faded gray T-shirt, and tennis shoes with no socks. Nothing fit quite right, but Nest thought he looked pretty cute anyway.

"You get any sleep last night?" he asked after a minute.

He was just about her height (oh, all right, he was an inch or so shorter, maybe), with dark blond hair cut short, eyes so blue they were startling, a stoic smile that suggested both familiarity and long-suffering indulgence with life's vicissitudes, and a penchant for clearing his throat before speaking that betrayed his nervousness at making conversation. She didn't know why she liked him. She hadn't felt this way about him a year ago. A year ago, she had thought he was weird. She still wasn't sure what had happened to change things.

She shrugged. "I slept a little."

He cleared his throat. "Well, no thanks to me, I guess. You saved my bacon, bringing Bennett home."

"No, I didn't."

"Big time. I didn't know what to do. I spaced, and the next thing I knew, she was outta there. I didn't know where she'd gone."

"Well, she's pretty little, so—"

"I messed up." He was having trouble getting the words out. "I should have locked the door or something, because the attacks can—"

"It wasn't your fault," she interrupted heatedly. Her eyes flicked to his, then away again. "Your mom shouldn't be leaving you alone to baby-sit those kids. She knows what can happen."

He was silent a moment. "She doesn't have any money for a sitter."

Oh, but she does have money to go out drinking at the bars, I suppose, Nest wanted to say, but didn't. "Your mom needs to get a life," she said instead.

"Yeah, I guess. George sure doesn't give her much of one."

"George Paulsen doesn't know how." Nest spit deliberately. "Do you know what he did with Bennett's kitten?"

Jared looked at her. "Spook? What do you mean? Bennett didn't say anything about it to me."

Nest nodded. "Well, she did to me. She said George took Spook away somewhere 'cause he doesn't like cats. You don't know anything about it?"

"No. Spook?"

"She was probably scared to tell you. I wouldn't put it past that creep to threaten her not to say anything." She looked off into the park. "I told her I'd help find Spook. But I don't know where to look."

Jared shoved his hands into his jeans pockets. "Me, either. But I'll look, too." He shook his head. "I can't believe this."

They crossed the park toward the woods that bordered the houses leading to Cass Minter's, lost in their separate thoughts, breathing in the heat and the dryness and watching the dust rise beneath their feet in small clouds.

"Maybe your mom will think twice before she goes out with him again, once she learns about Spook," Nest said after a minute.

"Maybe."

"Does she know about last night?"

He hesitated, then shook his head. "No. I didn't want to tell her. Bennett didn't say anything either."

They walked on in silence to the beginning of the woods and started through the trees toward the houses and the road. From somewhere ahead came the excited shriek of a child, followed by laughter. They could hear the sound of a sprinkler running. *Whisk, whisk, whisk.* It triggered memories of times already lost to them, gone with childhood's brief innocence.

Nest spoke to Jared Scott without looking at him. "I don't blame you. You know, for not telling your mom. I wouldn't have told her either."

Jared nodded. His hands slipped deeper into his pockets.

She gripped his arm impulsively. "Next time she leaves you alone to baby-sit, give me a call. I'll come over and help."

"Okay," he agreed, giving her a sideways smile.

But she knew just from the way he said it that he wouldn't.

CHAPTER 6

Nest and her friends spent the long, slow, lazy hours of the hot July afternoon fishing. They laughed and joked, swapped gossip and told lies, drank six-packs of pop kept cool at the end of a cord in the waters of the Rock River, and gnawed contentedly on twists of red licorice.

Beyond the shelter of the park, away from the breezes that wafted off the river, the temperature rose above one hundred and stayed there. The blue dome of the cloudless sky turned hazy with reflected light, and the heat seemed to press down upon the homes and businesses of Hopewell with the intention of flattening them. Downtown, the digital signboard on the exterior brick wall of the First National Bank read 103°, and the concrete of the streets and sidewalks baked and steamed in the white glare. Within their airconditioned offices, men and women began planning their Friday-afternoon escapes, trying to think of ways they could cool down the blast-furnace interiors of their automobiles long enough to survive the drive home.

On the picket lines at the entrances to MidCon Steel's five shuttered plants, the union workers hunkered down in lawn chairs under makeshift canopies and drank iced tea and beer from large Styrofoam coolers, hot and weary and discouraged, angry at the intransigence of their collective fate, thinking dark thoughts and feeling the threads of their lives slip slowly away.

In the cool, dark confines of Scrubby's Bar, at the west edge of town just off Lincoln Highway, Derry Howe sat alone at one end of the serving counter, nursing a beer and mumbling unintelligibly of his plans for MidCon to a creature that no one else could see.

It was nearing five o'clock, the sun sinking west and the dinner hour approaching, when Nest and her friends gathered up their fishing gear and the last few cans of pop and made their way back through the park. They climbed from the old boat launch (abandoned now since Riverside had bought the land and closed the road leading in), gained the heights of the cemetery, and followed the fence line back along the bluff face to where the cliffs dropped away and the park began. They wormed their way through a gap in the chain-link, Jared and Robert spreading the jagged edges wide for the girls, followed the turnaround past the Indian mounds, and angled through the trees and the playgrounds toward the ball diamonds. The heat lingered even with the sun's slow westward descent, a sullen, brooding presence at the edges of the shade. In the darker stretches of the spruce and pine, where the boughs grew thick and the shadows never faded, amber eyes as flat and hard as stone peered out in cold appraisal. Nest, who alone could see them, was reminded of the increasing boldness of the feeders and was troubled anew by what it meant.

Robert Heppler took a deep drink from his can of Coke, then belched loudly at Brianna Brown and said with supreme insincerity, "Sorry."

Brianna pulled a face. She was small and pretty with delicate features and thick, wavy dark hair. "You're disgusting, Robert!"

"Hey, it's a natural function of the body." Robert tried his best to look put-upon. Short and wiry, with a mischievous face, a shock of unruly white-blond hair, Robert eventually aggravated everyone he came in contact with—particularly Brianna Brown.

"There is nothing natural about anything you do!" Brianna snapped irritably, although there wasn't quite enough force behind the retort to cause any of the others to be concerned. The feud between Robert and Brianna was long-standing. It had become a condition of their lives. No one thought much

about it anymore, except where the occasional flare-up exacer-
bated feelings so thoroughly that no one could get any peace.
That had happened only once of late, early in the summer,
when Robert had managed to hide a red fizzie in the lining of
Brianna's swimsuit just before she went into the pool at
Lawrence Park. Mortified beyond any expression of outrage at
the resulting red stain, Brianna would have killed Robert if she
could have gotten her hands on him. As it was, she hadn't said
a word to him for almost two weeks afterward, not until he
apologized in front of everyone and admitted he had behaved
in a stupid and childish manner—and even that seemed to
please Robert in some bizarre way that probably not even he
could fathom.

"No, listen, I read this in a report." Robert looked around to
be sure they were all listening. "Belching and farting are necessary bodily functions. They release gases that would otherwise poison the body. You know about the exploding cows?"

"Oh, Robert!" Cass Minter rolled her eyes.

"No, cows can explode if enough gas builds up inside them.
It's a medical condition. They produce all this methane gas
when they digest grass. If they don't get rid of it, it can make
them explode. There was this whole article on it. I guess it's
like what happens to milk cows if you don't milk them." He
took another drink of Coke and belched again. With Robert,
you never knew if he was making it up. "Think about what
could happen to us if we stopped belching."

"Maybe you should give up drinking Coke," Cass suggested
dryly. She was a big, heavyset girl with a round, cheerful face
and intelligent green eyes. She always wore jeans and loose-
fitting shirts, an unspoken concession to her weight, and her
lank brown hair looked as if no comb had passed through it any
time in recent memory. Cass was Nest's oldest friend, from all
the way back to when they were in second grade together. She
winked at Nest now. "Maybe you should stick to tomato juice,
Robert."

Robert Heppler hated tomato juice. He'd been forced to
drink it once at camp, compelled to do so by a counselor in
front of a dozen other campers, after which he had promptly

vomited it up again. It was a point of honor with him that he would die before he ever did that again.

"Where did you read all this, anyway?" Jared Scott asked with benign interest.

Robert shrugged. "On the Internet."

"You know, you can't believe everything you read," Brianna declared, repeating something her mother frequently told her.

"Well, duh!" Robert sneered. "Anyway, this was a Dave Barry article."

"Dave Barry?" Cass was in stitches. "Now there's a reliable source. I suppose you get your world news from Liz Smith."

Robert stopped and slowly turned to face her. "Oh, I am cut to the quick!" He looked pointedly at Nest. "Like I can't tell the difference between what's reliable and what isn't, right?"

"Leave me out of this," Nest begged.

"Don't be so difficult, Robert!" Brianna chided, smoothing down her spotless white shorts. Only Brianna would wear white shorts to go fishing and somehow manage to keep them white.

"Difficult? I'm not difficult! Am I?" He threw up his hands. "Jared, am I?"

But Jared Scott was staring blankly at nothing, his face calm, his expression detached, as if he had removed himself entirely from everything that was happening around him and gone somewhere else. He was having another episode, Nest realized—his third that afternoon. The medicine he was taking didn't seem to be helping a whole lot. At least his epilepsy never did much more than it was doing now. It just took him away for a while and then brought him back again, snipping out small spaces in his life, like panels cut from a comic book.

"Well, anyway, I don't think I'm difficult." Robert turned back to Brianna. "I can't help it if I'm interested in learning about stuff. What am I supposed to do—stop reading?"

Brianna sighed impatiently. "You could at least stop being so dramatic!"

"Oh, now I'm too dramatic, am I? Gee, first I'm too difficult

and then I'm too dramatic! How ever will I get on with my
life?"

"We all ponder that dilemma on a daily basis," Cass
observed archly.

"You spend too much time in front of your computer!" Brianna snapped.

"Well, you spend too much time in front of your mirror!"
Robert snapped right back.

It was no secret that Brianna devoted an inordinate amount
of time to looking good, in large part as the result of having a
mother who was a hairdresser and who firmly believed that
makeup and clothes made the difference in a young girl's lot in
life. From the time her daughter was old enough to pay attention, Brianna's mother had instilled in her the need to "look the
part," as she was fond of putting it, training her to style her hair
and do her makeup and providing her with an extensive
wardrobe of matching outfits that Brianna was required to
wear whatever the occasion—even on an outing that centered
around fishing. Lately Brianna had begun to chafe a bit under
the constraints of her mother's rigid expectations, but Mom
still held the parental reins with a firm grip and full-blown
rebellion was a year or so away.

The mirror crack brought an angry flush to Brianna Brown's
face, and she glared hotly at Robert.

Cass Minter was quick to intervene. "You both spend too
much time in front of lighted screens, Robert"—she gave Nest
another wink—"but in Brianna's case the results are more
obviously successful."

Nest laughed softly in spite of herself. She envied Brianna's
smooth curves, her flawless skin, and her soft, feminine look.
She was beautiful in a way that Nest never would be. Her tiny,
grade-school girl's body was developing curves on schedule
while Nest's simply refused to budge. Boys looked at Brianna
and were made hungry and awestruck. When they looked at
Nest, they were left indifferent.

Robert started to say something and belched, and everyone
laughed. Jared Scott cleared his throat, and his eyes refocused

on his friends. "Are we going swimming tomorrow?" he asked, as if nothing had happened.

They walked through the center of the park, keeping to the shade of the big oaks that ran along the bluff up from the ball fields bordering Nest's backyard, then cut down toward Cass Minter's rambling two-story. A game was in progress on the fourth field, the one farthest into the park and closest to the toboggan run. They sauntered toward it, caught up in their conversation, which had turned now to the merits of learning a foreign language, and they were almost to the backstop when Nest realized belatedly that one of the players lounging on the benches, waiting his turn at bat, was Danny Abbott. She tried to veer away from him, pushing at Cass to get her to move back toward the roadway, but it was too late. He had already seen her and was on his feet.

"Hey, Nest!" he called out boldly. "Wait up!"

She slowed reluctantly as he started over, already angry with herself for letting this happen. "Oh, great!" Robert muttered under his breath. A scowl twisted his narrow lips.

"Go on," she told Cass, glancing at her shoes. "I'll be along in a minute."

Cass kept moving as if that had been her plan all along, and the other three dutifully followed. All of them drifted on for about twenty feet and stopped. Nest held her ground as Danny Abbott approached. He was big, strong, and good-looking, and for some reason he had a thing for her. A high-school junior in the fall, he was two years older than she was and convinced he was the coolest thing in jeans. A few months ago, at a Y dance, flattered by his interest, she had made the mistake of letting him kiss her. The kiss was all she wanted, and after she experienced it, she decided she wasn't that interested in Danny Abbott after all. But Danny couldn't let it go. He began to talk about her to his friends, and some of the stories got back to her. Danny was saying he had gotten a lot further with her than he had. Worse, he was saying she was anxious for more. She stopped having anything to do with him, but this just seemed to fuel his interest.

He strolled up to her with a confident smile, the big jock

coming on to the impressionable little groupie. She felt her anger build. "So what's happening?" he asked, his voice slow and languid. "Catch anything?"

She shook her head. "Not much. What do you want?"

"Hey, don't be so prickly." He brushed at his dark hair and looked off into the distance, like he was seeing into the future and taking its measure. "I was just wondering why I hadn't seen you around."

She shifted her weight from one foot to the other, forcing herself to look at him, refusing to be intimidated. "You know why, Danny."

He pursed his lips and nodded, as if thinking it through. "Okay, I made a mistake. I said some stuff I shouldn't have. I'm sorry. Can we drop it now? I like you, Nest. I don't want you pissed off at me. Hey, why don't you stick around while I finish this game, and then we'll go out for a burger."

"I'm with my friends," she said.

"So? I'm with mine, too. They can go their way and we can go ours, right?"

He gave her his most dazzling smile, and it made her want to say yes in spite of herself. Stupid, stupid. She shook her head. "No, I've got to get home."

He nodded solemnly. "Okay. Maybe tomorrow night. You know what? There's a dance here at the park Sunday. The Jaycees are putting it on. Want to go with me?"

She shook her head a second time. "I don't think so."

"Why not?" A hint of irritation crept into his voice.

She bit her lip. "I'll probably come with my friends."

He gave a disgusted sigh. "You spend a lot of time with your friends, don't you?"

She didn't say anything.

He glanced past her and shook his head. "Why do you hang out with them, anyway? I don't get it." He was looking right at her now, facing her down. "It seems to me you're wasting your time."

Her lips tightened, but she still didn't say anything.

"I don't mean to be picking on them or anything, but just think about it. They're weird, Nest, in case you hadn't noticed.

Barbie Doll, Big Bertha, Joe Space Cadet, and Bobby the Mouth. Weird, Nest. What are you doing with them?"

"Danny," she said quietly.

"Hey, I'm just trying to make a point. You've got a lot more going for you than they do, that's all I'm saying. You're one of the best runners in the state, and you're not even in high school! You're practically famous! Besides, you're a cool chick. You're nothing like them. I really don't get it."

She nodded slowly. "I know you don't. Maybe that's the point."

He sighed. "Okay, whatever. Anyway, why don't you stick around."

"Hey, Danny, you're up!" someone called.

"Yeah, in a minute!" he shouted back. He put his hands on her shoulders, resting them there casually. "C'mon, Nest. Tell me you'll stay until I finish my at bat."

She stepped back, trying to disengage herself. "I have to go."

"One at bat," he pressed. "Five minutes." He stepped forward, staying with her, keeping his hands in place. "What do you say?"

"Abbott, you're up!"

"Hey, Nest, take your shoulders out from under his hands!" shouted Robert Heppler suddenly. "You're making him nervous!"

Danny Abbott blinked, but kept his dark eyes fixed on Nest. His gaze was so intense, so filled with purpose, that it was all Nest Freemark could do to keep from wilting under its heat. But she was just angry enough by now that she refused to give him the satisfaction.

"I have to go," she repeated, keeping her eyes locked on his.

His hands tightened on her shoulders. "I won't let you," he said. He smiled, but the warmth was missing from his eyes.

"Take your hands away," she told him.

A couple of the boys who had been standing around the backstop started to drift over, curious to see what was happening.

"You're not so hot," he said quietly, so that only she could hear. "Not half as hot as you think."

She tried to twist away, but his grip was too strong.

"Hey, Danny, pick on someone your own size!" shouted Robert, coming forward a few steps.

One thing about Robert, he wasn't afraid of anyone. He'd been in so many fights in grade school that his parents had taken him to a psychiatrist. He'd been suspended more times than Nest could remember. His problem was that he wasn't very careful about choosing his opponents, and today was no exception. Danny Abbott looked over at him with undisguised contempt. Danny was bigger, stronger, quicker, and meaner than Robert, and he was looking for an excuse to slug someone.

"What did you say, Heppler?"

Robert held his ground and shrugged. "Nothing."

"That's what I thought, you little creep."

Robert threw up his hands in exaggerated dismay. "Oh, great! I'm being called a creep by a guy who wrestles with girls!"

Half-a-dozen ballplayers had congregated, and a few snickered at the remark. Danny Abbott dropped his hands from Nest's shoulders. His hands knotted into fists, and he turned toward Robert. Robert gave him a very deliberate smirk, but there was a shadow of doubt in his eyes now.

"Robert," Cass called in a low, warning voice.

"I'm going to wipe up the park with you," Danny Abbott said, and started forward.

Nest Freemark darted in front of him, bringing him to a stop. She stood there shaking, her arms at her sides. "Leave him alone, Danny. I'm the one you're angry at."

Danny shook his head. "Not anymore."

"You're twice his size!"

"Guess he should have thought of that before he opened his big mouth."

"Punch him out, Danny," one of his friends muttered, and a few others quickly echoed the sentiment.

Nest felt the late-afternoon heat scorch her throat as she breathed it in. "Look, forget about this, Danny," she insisted, still blocking his path to Robert. "I'll stay to watch you bat, okay?" She hated herself for saying the words, but she was frightened now. "Leave Robert alone."

He looked at her, and there was undisguised contempt in his eyes. He was enjoying this. "You should have thought about that before. You should have paid a little better attention to your mouth."

He started forward again, and she moved back quickly, still blocking his way. She could feel her control slipping, and her breath came more rapidly. She had promised herself! She had promised Gran! "Danny, don't do this!" she snapped at him.

"Danny, don't do this!" he sneered, mimicking her, and the boys with him laughed.

"Danny, please!"

"Get out of my way," he growled.

He reached for her, their eyes locked, and her magic slammed into him. In an instant he lay sprawled on the ground, his legs and arms tangled, a look of utter shock on his handsome face. The eager shouts of his friends turned to gasps, and Nest stepped quickly away, her face white, her eyes bright and intense with concentration. Danny struggled to his feet, glared at her in rage, not certain what had happened to him, but knowing that somehow she was to blame, and then lunged for her. Her eyes found his. Down he went again, crumpling like a rag doll, as if he could no longer manage to stand upright. He rolled over and over, shrieking unintelligibly, his voice unnaturally high and piercing, his words a jumble of unrecognizable sounds.

Everyone had gone completely still. They stood knotted into two groups, Nest's friends on one side, Danny's on the other, frozen in the swelter of heat and excitement, stunned by what they were witnessing, mesmerized by the spectacle of Danny Abbott's collapse. The park had become a vast arena, carpeted with grass, walled by trees, empty of sound. Magic raced through the air with savage grace and reckless need, but no one except Nest could sense its presence.

Danny came to his hands and knees and stayed there, his head hanging down between his shoulders, his chest heaving. He coughed violently and spit, then drew in several huge gulps

of air. He tried to stand, then gave it up, mouthing a low
obscenity at Nest that faded quickly into a whispered groan.

Nest turned away, feeling cold and empty and sick at heart.
She did not look at Danny Abbott or his friends. She did not
look at Cass or Robert or Brianna or Jared either. "Let's go," she
whispered, barely able to speak the words, and without waiting
to see if anyone would follow, she walked off into the park.

Nest had been eleven before she discovered she could work
magic. She was never sure afterward if she had been able to do
so all along and simply hadn't realized it or if her ability had
matured with growth. Even Gran, when told about it, hadn't
been able to say for sure. By then Nest had lived with the
feeders and Wraith for close to six years and with Pick for
almost that long and knew there was magic out there, so it
wasn't all that weird to discover that a small piece of it was
hers. Besides, Gran had been saying she had magic for so
many years that, even without ever having been presented with
any evidence of it, she had always half believed that it was so.

Her discovery that she really could do magic was due
mainly to Lori Adami. As grade-school classmates, they had
developed a deep and abiding dislike for each other. Each
worked hard at snubbing the other and each made certain she
told her friends what a creep the other was, and that was about
the extent of it. But in the sixth grade the war between them
suddenly escalated. Lori began to go out of her way to make
cutting remarks about Nest, always in front of other kids and
always just within earshot. Nest retaliated by acting as if she
hadn't heard, all the while patiently waiting for Lori to tire of
this latest game.

But Lori Adami was nothing if not persistent, and one day
she said that Nest's mother was crazy and that was why she
killed herself and that Nest was probably crazy, too. It was
winter, and they were standing in the hall by their lockers
before classes, stripping off their coats and boots. Nest heard
the remark, and without even thinking about it, she dropped
her coat and gloves on the floor, turned around, walked right up
to Lori, and hit her in the face. Since Nest had never lifted a

hand against her in all these years, Lori was caught completely by surprise. But Lori had been raised with three older brothers, and she knew how to defend herself. Hissing something awful at Nest, she went after her.

Then a funny thing happened. Nest, who didn't know much about fighting, was unsure what she should do. Anger and fear warred for control. Should she stand her ground or run for it? She stood her ground. Lori grabbed for her, their eyes locked, and Nest, raising her hands to defend herself, thought, *You better not touch me, you better quit right now, you better stop!* And down went Lori in a heap, legs tangled, arms askew, and mouth open in surprise. Lori scrambled up again, furious, but the moment their eyes met she began to stumble about helplessly. She tried to say something, but she couldn't seem to talk, the words all jumbled up and nonsensical. Some of the students thought she was having a fit, and they ran screaming for help. Nest was as shocked as they were, but for a different reason. She knew what had happened. She couldn't explain it, but she understood what it was. She had felt the magic's rush, like a gasp of breath as it left her body. She had felt it entangle Lori, its cords wrapping tightly and implacably about the other girl's ankles. She would never forget the horrified look on Lori Adami's face. She would never forget how it made her feel.

They were suspended from school for fighting. Nest had debated how much she should tell Gran, who was the one she had to answer to for any sort of misbehavior, but in the end, as she almost always did, she told her everything. She found she needed to talk to someone about what had happened, and Gran was the logical choice. After all, wasn't she the one who kept saying Nest had magic? Fine, then—let her explain this!

But Gran hadn't said anything at first on hearing Nest's tale. She merely asked if Nest was certain about what had happened and then let the matter drop. Only later had she taken Nest aside to speak with her, waiting until Old Bob was safely out of the house.

"It isn't as strange as you might think that you should be able to do magic, Nest," she told her. They were sitting at the kitchen table, Nest with a cup of hot chocolate in front of her, Gran with her bourbon and water. "Do you know why that is?"

Nest shook her head, anxious to hear her grandmother's explanation.

"Because you are your mother's daughter and my granddaughter, and the women of this family have always known something about magic. We aren't witches or anything, Nest. But we have always lived around magic, here by the park, by the feeders, and we've known about that magic, and if you live next to something long enough, and you know it's there, some of it will rub off on you."

Nest looked at her doubtfully. *Rub off on you?*

Her grandmother leaned forward. "Now, you listen to me carefully, young lady. Once upon a time, I warned you never to tell anyone about the feeders. You didn't pay attention to me then, did you? You told. And do you remember the sort of trouble it got you into?" Nest nodded. "All right. So you pay attention to me now. Using magic will get you into a whole lot worse trouble than talking about feeders. It will get you into so much trouble I might not be able to get you out. So I am telling you here and now that you are not to use your magic again. Do you hear me?"

Nest chewed her lip. "Yes."

"Good. This is important." Gran's face was scrunched up like a wadded paper sack. "When you are grown, you can decide for yourself when you want to use your magic. You can weigh the risks and the rewards. But you are not to use it while you are a child living in this house. Except," she paused, reminded of something, "if you are threatened, and your life is in danger, and you have no choice." She looked away suddenly, as if fleeing things she would rather not consider. "Then, you can use the magic. But only then."

Nest thought it over for a moment. "How am I supposed to be sure I've really got magic if I don't try it out?"

Her grandmother's gaze fixed on her anew. "You seemed sure enough about it when you were fighting with Lori Adami. Are you telling me that maybe you made it up?"

"No." Nest was immediately defensive. "I just don't know for sure. It all happened so fast."

Her grandmother took a long drink from her glass and lit a cigarette. "You know. Now you do as I say."

So Nest had, although it was very hard. Eventually, she broke her promise, but not for several months, when she used her magic on a boy who was trying to pull down her swimsuit at the pool. Then she used it again on a kid who was throwing rocks at a stray cat. She knew for sure then that the magic was real, and that she could use it on anyone she wished. But the odd thing was, using it didn't make her feel very good. It should have provided her with some measure of satisfaction, but all it did was make her feel sick inside, as if she had done something for which she should feel ashamed.

It was Pick who had straightened her out, telling her that what her grandmother meant was that she wasn't to use her magic against other people. Using it against other people would always make her feel bad, because it was like taking advantage of someone who couldn't fight back. Besides, it would attract a lot of unwanted attention. But the feeders were fair game. Why not use it against them?

Pick's idea had worked. Using her magic against the feeders satisfied her curiosity and gave her an opportunity to experiment. Eventually she told Gran. Gran, saying little in response, had approved. Then Pick had enlisted her aid in dealing with the nighttime activities of the feeders, and summoning the magic had suddenly become serious business. After that, she had been very careful not to use it again on people.

Until now, she thought wearily as she walked home through the park. She had split up with the others as soon as they were in the trees and out of sight of the ball field. See you tomorrow, she had told them, as if nothing had happened, as if everything were all right. See you tomorrow, they'd replied. Hardly a word had been spoken about the incident, but she knew they were all thinking about it, remembering anew some of the stories about her.

Only Robert had ventured a parting comment. "Jeez, it

didn't even look like you touched him!" he'd said in his typically direct, unthinking, Robert way. She was so distressed she didn't even try to respond.

As she reached the edge of the service road, she thought suddenly she might vomit. Her stomach churned and her head ached. The inside of her mouth tasted coppery, and her breathing was quick and uneven. Using the magic on Danny Abbott had been a mistake, even though it had probably saved Robert a beating. She had promised Gran she wouldn't use it again. More important, she had promised herself. But something had happened to her this afternoon. She had been so angry she had forgotten her resolve. She had simply lost control of herself.

She angled through the trees and houses that paralleled the park, closing in now on her home, buoyed by the sight of its familiar white siding and its big stone chimney, her refuge from the world. She knew what troubled her most about what had happened. It was what Danny had said. Your friends are weird. What are you doing with them? But, really, she was the one who was weird, and using the magic as she had just pointed it up. Having magic made her different from everyone—but that was just part of it. How much stranger could you be than to know that you were the only one who could see feeders, the only one with some sort of monster dog for a protector, and the only one with a sylvan for a friend?

She was the one who didn't belong, she knew, tears running down her cheeks, and she wanted desperately not to feel that way.

CHAPTER 7

Nest went for a run before dinner, disdaining to wait for the heat to lessen, needing to escape. She asked Gran if it would be all right, and Gran, with those unerring instincts for evaluating the depth of her granddaughter's needs, told her to go ahead. It was after six, the sun still visible in the western sky, the glare of midday softened to a hazy gold. Colors deepened as the light paled, the green of the leaves and grasses turning damp emerald, the tree trunks taking on an inky cast, and the sky overhead becoming such a clear, depthless blue that it seemed that if gravity's hold could be broken you might swim it like an ocean. As Nest turned out of her drive and ran down Sinnissippi Road, she could feel the branches of the big hardwoods sigh with the faint passing of a momentary breeze, and the sigh seemed collective and all-encompassing. Friday was ending, the work week had come to a close, and now the long Fourth of July weekend could begin in earnest. She ran to the end of Sinnissippi, barely a block from her drive, and turned east onto Woodlawn. Ahead, the road stretched away, a wide, straight racetrack that narrowed between the houses with their lawns, hedgerows, and trees and faded into the horizon. She ran smoothly on its shoulder, feeling her blood hum, her heart pound, her breathing steady, and her thoughts scatter. The movement of her legs and the pounding of her feet absorbed her, enfolded her, and then swallowed her up. She was conscious of the world slipping past like a watercolor running on a canvas backdrop, and she felt herself melt into it. Neighbors worked in their gardens or sat on their porches sipping tea and lemonade and occasionally something stronger. Dogs and cats

lay sleeping. Children played in their yards, and as she passed
a few dashed toward her momentarily before stopping, as if
they, too, were seeking an escape. Now and again someone
waved or called out, making her feel welcome, a part of the
world once more.

She ran the length of Woodlawn, then turned left to Moonlight Bay. She passed boats and trailers on their way to the
launch and campers on their way to White Pines State Park
sixty miles north. She ran the circle drive of the bay past the
shorefront residences, then swung west again and ran back to
her home. Slowly, surely, her trauma eased, left behind with
her footprints in the dust. By the time she turned down her
drive once more, she was feeling better about herself. Her shirt
clung damply to her body and her skin was covered with a
sheen of sweat. She felt drained and loose and renewed. As she
came up to the back door, she permitted herself a quick
glimpse into the park, looking backward in time to the events
of the afternoon, better able now to face what she had done to
Danny Abbott—or perhaps, more accurately, what she had
done to herself. The ache that the memory generated in her
heart was sharp, but momentary. She sighed wearily, telling
herself what she sometimes did when things were bad—that
she was just a kid—and knew as always that it wasn't so.

She showered quickly, dressed in fresh shorts and T-shirt
(this one said Latte Lady), and came down for dinner. She sat
at the kitchen table with her grandparents and ate tuna and
noodle casserole with green beans and peaches off the every-
day china. Gran nursed her bourbon and water and picked at
her food, a voiceless presence. Old Bob asked Nest about her
day, listened attentively as she told him about fishing with her
friends, and didn't say a word about last night in the park.
Through the open screen door came the sounds of the evening,
distant and soft—the shouts of players and spectators as the
night's softball games got under way in the park, the hiss of
tires on hot asphalt from cars passing down Sinnissippi Road,
the muted roar of a lawn mower cutting grass several houses
down, and the faint, silvery laughter of children at play. There
was no air-conditioning in the Freemark house, so the sounds

were clearly audible. Nest's grandparents couldn't stomach the idea of shutting out the world. You can deal better with the heat if you live with it, they liked to say.

"Any news on the strike?" Nest asked her grandfather after they had finished talking about fishing, mostly in an effort to hold up her end of the conversation.

He shook his white head, swallowed the last bite of his dinner, and pushed his plate back. His big shoulders shrugged. "Naw, they can't even agree on what day of the week it is, Nest." He reached for his newspaper and scanned the headlines. "Won't be a resolution any time soon, I don't expect."

Nest glanced at Gran, but her grandmother was staring out the window with a blank expression, a lighted cigarette burning to ash between her fingers.

"Not my problem anymore," Old Bob declared firmly. "At least I got that to be thankful for. Someone else's problem now."

Nest finished her dinner and began thinking about Pick and the park. She glanced outside at the failing light.

"Look at this," Old Bob muttered, shaking out the paper as if it contained fleas. "Just look at this. Two boys dropped a five-year-old out a window in a Chicago apartment. Fifteen stories up, and they just dropped him out. No reason for it, they just decided to do it. The boys were ten and eleven. Ten and eleven! What in the hell is the world coming to?"

"Robert." Gran looked at him reprovingly over the rim of her glass.

"Well, you have to wonder." Old Bob lowered the paper and glanced at Nest. "Excuse my language." He was silent for a moment, reading. Then he opened the inside page. "Oh, my." He sighed and shook his head, eyes bright with anger. "Here's another, this one quite a bit closer to home. One of those Anderson girls used to live out on Route Thirty shot and killed her father last night. She claims he's been molesting all of the girls since they were little. Says she forgot about it until it came to her in a dream." He read on a bit, fuming. "Also says she has a history of mental problems and that the family hasn't had anything to do with her for some time."

He read for a little while longer, then tossed the paper aside. "The news isn't worth the paper it's printed on anymore." He studied the table a moment, then glanced at Gran, waiting for a response. Gran was silent, looking out the window once more. Her hand lowered in a mechanical motion to the ashtray to stub out the cigarette.

Old Bob's eyes turned sad and distant. He looked at Nest. "You going out to play again?" he asked quietly.

Nest nodded, already beginning to push back from the table.

"That's all right," her grandfather said. "But you be back by dark. No excuses."

The way he said it made it plain that, even though he hadn't brought the subject up at dinner, he hadn't forgotten about last night. Nest nodded again, letting him know she understood.

Her grandfather rose and left the table, taking the newspaper with him, retiring to the seclusion of his den. Nest sat for a moment staring after him, then started to get up as well.

"Nest," her grandmother said softly, looking directly at her now. She waited until she had the girl's attention. "What happened this afternoon?"

Nest hesitated, trying to decide what to say. She shrugged. "Nothing, Gran."

Her grandmother gave her a long, hard look. "Carry your dishes to the sink before you go," she said finally. "And remember what your grandfather told you."

Two minutes later, Nest was out the back door and down the porch steps. Mr. Scratch had disappeared and Miss Minx had taken his place. As designated mouser she had assumed a more alert position, crouched down by the toolshed, sniffing at the air and looking about warily. Nest walked over and scratched her white neck, then headed for the hedgerow and the park. Mosquitoes buzzed past her ears, and she swatted at them irritably. Magic didn't seem to do any good when it came to mosquitoes. Pick claimed once that he had a potion that would keep them at bay, but it turned out to be so evil-smelling that it kept everything else at bay as well. Nest grimaced at the memory. Even a hundred-and-fifty-year-old sylvan didn't know everything.

She was nearing the hedgerow, listening to the sounds of the softball games in progress on the other side, when she glanced left into the Peterson backyard and saw the feeders. There were two of them, hiding in the lilac bushes close by the compost heap that Annie Peterson used on her vegetable garden. They were watching Nest, staring out at her with their flat, expressionless eyes, all but invisible in the approaching twilight. Their boldness frightened her. It was as if they were lying in wait for her, hoping to catch her off-guard. They were implacable and relentless, and the certainty of what they would do to her if they had the chance was unnerving. Nest veered toward them, irritated anew by the feelings they aroused in her. It was getting so she couldn't go anywhere without seeing them.

The feeders blinked once as she neared, then simply faded away into the shadows.

Nest stared into the empty gloom and shivered. The feeders were like vultures, waiting to dispose of whatever leavings they could scavenge. Except that feeders were only interested in the living.

She thought back to what Pick had told her years ago when she had asked about the feeders. Her grandmother had avoided the subject for as long as Nest could remember, but Pick was more than willing to address it.

"Your grandmother won't talk about them? Won't say a single word about them? Not a single word? Well, now. Well, indeed!" He'd scrunched up his moss-bearded face and scratched at the side of his head as if to help free up thoughts trapped in his cranium. "All right, then, listen up. First off, you need to understand that feeders are an anomaly. You know what that word means, don't you?"

Since she'd been only eight at the time, she hadn't the slightest idea. "Not really," she'd said.

"Criminy, your education is a mess! Don't you ever read?"

"You don't read," she'd pointed out.

"That's different. I don't have to read. I don't need it in my line of work. But you, why, you should be reading volumes of . . ."

"What does anoma-whatever mean?" she'd pressed, un-willing to wait through the entirety of Pick's by-now-familiar lecture on the plight of today's undereducated youth.

He had stopped in midsentence, harrumphed disapprovingly at her impatience, and cleared his throat. "Anomaly. It means 'peculiar.' It means 'different.' It means feeders are hard to classify. You know that guessing game you used to play? The one where you start by asking, 'Animal, mineral, or vege-table?' Well, that's the kind of game you have to play when you try to figure out what feeders are. Except feeders aren't any of these things, and at the same time they're all of them, because what they are is determined to a large extent by what *you* are."

She'd stared at him blankly.

He'd frowned then, apparently deciding that his explanation was lacking. "Let's start at the beginning," he'd declared, scooting closer to her atop the picnic table in her backyard.

She'd leaned forward so that her chin was resting on her hands and her eyes were level with his. It was late on a spring afternoon, and the leaves of the trees were rustling with the wind's passing, and clouds were drifting across the sun like cottony caterpillars, casting dappled shadows that wriggled and squirmed.

"Feeders," he'd said, deepening his voice meaningfully, "don't come in different sizes and shapes and colors. They don't hardly have any faces at all. They're not like other crea-tures. They don't eat and sleep. They don't have parents or children or go to school or elect governments or read books or talk about the weather. The Word made feeders when he made everything else, and he made them as a part of the balance of things. You remember what I told you about everything being in balance, sort of like a teeter-totter, with some things on one end and some on the other, and both ends weighing the same. Feeders, they're part of that. Frankly, I don't know why. But, then, it's not my place to know. The Word made the decision to create feeders, and that's the end of it. But having said that, having said that it's not my place to know why these feeders were *made*, it is my place to know what they *do*. And that, young lady, is what's interesting. Feeders have only one purpose in this world, only one, single, solitary thing that they do."

He'd moved closer then, and his wizened face had furrowed with delight and his voice had lowered to a conspiratorial whisper. "Feeders, my young friend, devour people!"

Nest's eyes had gone wide, and Pick the sylvan had laughed like a cartoon maniac.

She still remembered him saying it. *Feeders devour people.* There was more to the explanation, of course, for the complexity of feeders could never be defined so simply. There was no mention of the feeders as a force of nature, as sudden, violent, and inexorable as a Midwest twister, or of their strange, symbiotic relationship with the humans they destroyed. Yet it was hard to get much closer to the heart of the matter. Pick's description, provocative and crude, was still the most accurate Nest had ever heard. Even now, six years later, his words resonated with truth.

The pungent smell of spruce filled her nostrils, borne on a momentary breeze, and the memories faded. She turned and jogged quickly to the end of her yard, slipping smoothly into the gap in the hedgerow. She was almost through when Pick appeared on her shoulder as if by magic, springing out of hiding from the leafy branches. At six inches of height and nine ounces of weight, he was as small and light as a bird. He was a wizened bit of wood with vaguely human features stamped above a mossy beard. Leaves grew out of his head in place of hair. His arms and legs were flexible twigs that narrowed to tiny fingers and stubby toes. He looked like a Disney animation that had been roughed up a bit. His fierce eyes were as hard and flat as ink dots on stone.

He settled himself firmly in place, taking hold of her collar. "What have I told you about provoking the feeders?" he snapped.

"Not to," she answered dutifully, swinging west down the service road toward the park entrance.

"Why don't you listen to me, then?"

"I do. But it makes me angry to see them nosing about when it's still light out." She darted a quick look at the ballplayers to make certain that Danny Abbott wasn't among them. "They didn't used to be like that. They never showed themselves when the sun was shining, not even where the shadows were deepest. Now I see them everywhere."

"Times change." Pick sounded disconsolate. "Something's happening, that much is sure, but I don't know what it is yet. Whatever it is, it's caused the balance of things to tip even further. There's been a lot of bad things happening around here lately. That's not good." He paused. "How's the little Scott girl?"

"Fine. But George Paulsen stole her cat, Spook." Nest slowed to a walk again. "I promised Bennett I'd try to find it. Can you help me?"

Even without being able to see him, she knew he was tugging on his mossy beard and shaking his leafy head. "Sure, sure, what else have I got to do but look for someone's lost cat? Criminy!" He was silent a moment as they passed behind the backstop. The spectators grouped at the edge of the ball field were drinking beer and pop and cheering on their favorite players. "Batter, batter, batter—swing!" someone chanted. No one paid any attention to Nest.

"I'll send Daniel out, see if he can find anything," Pick offered grudgingly.

Nest smiled. "Thanks."

"You can thank me by staying away from the feeders!" Pick was not about to be mollified. "You think your magic and that big dog are enough to protect you, but you don't know feeders the way I do. They aren't subject to the same laws as humans. They get to you when you're not expecting it!" She could feel him twisting about angrily on her shoulder. "Creepers! I don't know why I'm telling you this! You already know it, and I shouldn't have to say another word!"

Then please don't, she thought, hiding a grin. Wisely, she swallowed her words without speaking them. "I'll be careful, I promise," she assured him, turning up the blacktop road toward the cliffs.

"See that you do. Now, cut across the grass to the burial

mounds. There's an Indian sitting up there at one of the picnic tables, and I want to know what he's up to."

She glanced sideways at him. "An Indian?"

"That's what I said, didn't I?"

"A real Indian?"

Pick sighed in exasperation. "If you do like I told you, you can decide for yourself!"

Curious now, wondering if there really was an Indian or if the sylvan was just making it up, she stepped off the roadway into the grass and began to jog steadily toward the cliffs.

CHAPTER 8

The Indian was sitting at a picnic table on the far side of the playground just across the roadway from the burial mounds. He was all alone, having chosen a spot well back in the tangle of pines and spruce that warded the park's northern boundary against the heavy winter storms that blew down from Canada. He sat with his back to the roadway and the broad expanse of the park, his gaze directed west toward the setting sun. Shadows dappled his still, solitary form, and if she had not known to look for him, Nest might have missed seeing him altogether.

He did not look up as she neared, and she slowed to a walk. His long, raven hair had been woven into a single braid that fell to the middle of his back, and his burnished skin shone with a copper glint where errant streaks of sunlight brushed against it. He was a big man, even hunched down at the table the way he was, and the fingers of his hands, clasped before him in a twisted knot, were gnarled and thick. He wore what appeared to be an army field jacket with the sleeves torn out, pants that were baggy and frayed, boots so scuffed they lacked any semblance of a shine, and a red bandanna tied loosely about his neck.

Somewhere in the distance a child squealed with delight. The Indian did not react.

Nest moved to a picnic table thirty feet away from the Indian and seated herself. She was off to one side, out of his direct line of sight, where she could study him at her leisure. Pick perched on her shoulder, whispering furiously in her ear. When she failed to respond, he began to jump up and down in irritation.

92

"What's the matter with you?" he hissed. "How can you learn anything from all the way back here? You've got to get closer! Must I tell you how to do everything!"

She reached up, lifted him off her shoulder, and placed him on the table, frowning in reproof. *Patience,* she mouthed.

In truth, she was trying to make up her mind about the man. He looked like he might be an Indian, but how could she be sure? Most of what she knew about Indians she'd learned from movies and a few reports she'd done in school—not what you'd call a definitive education. She couldn't see his face clearly, and he wasn't wearing anything that looked remotely Indian. No jewelry, no feathers, no buckskins, no buffalo robes. He looked more like a combat veteran. She wondered suddenly if he was homeless. A heavy knapsack and a bedroll were settled on the bench beside him, and he had the look of a man who had been out in the weather a lot.

"Who is he, do you think?" she asked softly, almost to herself. Then she glanced down at Pick. "Have you ever seen him before?"

The sylvan was apoplectic. "No, I haven't seen him before! And I don't have the foggiest notion who he is! What do you think we're doing out here? Haven't you heard anything I've said?"

"Shhhhh," she hushed him gently.

They sat there for a time without speaking (although Pick muttered incessantly) and watched the man. He did not seem aware of them. He did not turn their way. He did not move at all. The sun slipped below the treeline, and the shadows deepened. Nest glanced about guardedly, but she did not see the feeders. Behind her, back toward the center of the park, the baseball games were winding down and the first cars were beginning to pull out from the parking spaces behind the backstops and turn toward the highway.

Then suddenly the man rose, picked up his knapsack and bedroll, and came toward Nest. Nest was so surprised she did not even have the presence of mind to think of running away. She sat there, frozen in place as he approached. She could see his face clearly now, his heavy, prominent features—dark brows, flat nose, and wide cheekbones. He moved with the grace and ease of a younger man, but the lines at the corners of his eyes and mouth suggested he was much older.

He sat down across from her without a word, depositing his belongings on the bench beside him. She realized suddenly that Pick had disappeared.

"Why are you looking at me?" he said.

She tried to speak, but nothing came out. He didn't sound or look angry, but his face and voice were hard to read.

"Cat got your tongue?" he pressed.

She cleared her throat and swallowed. "I was wondering if you were an Indian."

He stared at her without expression. "You mean Native American, don't you?"

She bit her lower lip and blushed. "Sorry. Native American."

He smiled, a tight, thin compression of his lips. "I suppose it doesn't matter what you call me. Native American. Indian. Redskin. The words of themselves do not define me. No more so than your histories do my people." The dark eyes squinted at her. "Who are you?"

"Nest Freemark," she told him.

"Huh, little bird's Nest, crafted of twigs and bits of string. Do you live nearby?"

She nodded, then glanced over her shoulder. "At the edge of the park. Why did you call me 'bird's Nest' like that?"

The dark eyes bore into her. "Isn't that what you were called when you were little?"

"By my grandmother, a long time ago. Then by some of the kids in school, when they wanted to tease me." She held his gaze. "How did you know?"

"I do magic," he told her in a whisper. "Don't you?"

She stared at him, not knowing what to say. "Sometimes."

He nodded. "A girl named Nest is bound to be called 'bird's Nest' by someone. Doesn't take much to figure that out. But 'Nest'—that is a name that has power. It has a history in the world, a presence."

Nest nodded. "It is Welsh. The woman who bore it first was the wife and mother of Welsh and English kings." She was surprised at how freely she was talking with the man, almost as if she knew him already.

"You have a good name, Nest. My name is Two Bears. I was given my name by my father, who on seeing me, newly born and quite large, declared, 'He is as big as two bears!' So I was called afterward, although that is not my Indian name. In the language of my people, my name is O'olish Amaneh."

"O'olish Amaneh," Nest repeated carefully. "Where do you come from, Two Bears?"

"First we must shake hands to mark the beginning of our friendship, little bird's Nest," he declared. "Then we can speak freely."

He motioned for Nest to extend her hand, and then he clasped it firmly in his own. His hand was as hard and coarse as rusted iron.

"Good. Because of your age, we will skip the part that involves smoking a peace pipe." He did not smile or change expression. "You ask me where I come from. I come from everywhere. I have lived a lot of places. But this"—he gestured about him—"is my real home."

"You're from Hopewell?" Nest said dubiously.

"No. But my people are of this land, of the Rock River Valley, from before Hopewell. They have all been dead a long time, my people, but sometimes I come back to visit them. They are buried just over there." He pointed toward the Indian mounds. "I was born in Springfield. That was a long time ago, too. How old do you think I am?"

He waited, but she could only shake her head. "I don't know."

"Fifty-two," he said softly. "My life slips rapidly away. I fought in Vietnam. I walked and slept with death; I knew her as I would a lover. I was young before, but afterward I was very old. I died in the Nam so many times, I lost count. But I killed a lot of men, too. I was a LURP. Do you know what that means?"

Nest shook her head once more.

"It doesn't matter," he said, brushing at the air with his big hand. "I was there for six years, and when it was over, I was no longer young. I came home, and I no longer knew myself or my people or my country. I was an Indian, a Native American, and a Redskin all rolled into one, and I was none of these. I was dead, but I was still walking around."

He looked at her without speaking for a moment, his eyes impenetrable. "On the other hand, maybe it was all a dream." His flat features shifted in the failing light, almost as if they were changing shape. "The trouble with dreams is that sometimes they are as real as life, and you cannot tell the two apart. Do you have dreams, little bird's Nest?"

"Sometimes," she replied, fascinated by the way his voice rose and fell as he talked, rough and silky, soft and bold. "Are you really an Indian, Two Bears?"

He glanced down then for a moment, shifting his hard gaze away from her, placing the palms of his big hands flat against the top of the picnic table. "Why should I tell you?"

He kept his eyes lowered, not looking at her. Nest did not know what to say.

"I will tell you because we are friends," he offered. "And because there is no reason not to tell you." His eyes lifted again to find hers. "I am an Indian, little bird's Nest, but I am something more as well. I am something no one should ever be. I am the last of my kind."

He brought the index finger of his right hand to his nose. "I am Sinnissippi, the only one left, the only one in all the world. My grandparents died before I went to Nam. My father died of drink. My mother died of grief. My brother died of a fall from the steel towers he helped to build in New York City. My sister died of drugs and alcohol on the streets in Chicago. We were all that remained, and now there is only me. Of all those who were once Sinnissippi, who filled this valley for miles in all directions, who went out into the world to found other tribes, there is only me. Can you imagine what that is like?"

Nest shook her head, transfixed.

"Do you know anything of the Sinnissippi?" he asked her. "Do you study them in school? Do your parents speak of them? The answer is no, isn't it? Did you even know that we existed?"

"No," she said softly.

His smile was flat and tight. "Think on this a moment, little bird's Nest. We were a people, like you. We had traditions and a culture. We were hunters and fishermen for the most part, but some among us were farmers as well. We had homes; we were the keepers of this park and all the land that surrounds it. All of that is gone, and no record of us remains. Even our burial mounds are believed to belong to another tribe. It is as if we never were. We are a rumor. We are a myth. How is that possible? Nothing remains of us but a name. Sinnissippi. We are a park, a street, an apartment building. Our name is there, preserved after we are gone, and yet our name means nothing, says nothing, tells nothing of us. Even the historians do not know what our name means. I have studied on this, long ago. Some think the name is Sauk, and that it refers to the land. Some think the name is Fox, and that it refers to the river that runs through the land. But no one thinks it is the name of our people. No one believes that."

"Have you ever tried to tell them?" Nest asked when he fell silent.

He shook his head. "Why should I? Maybe they are right. Maybe we didn't exist. Maybe there were no Sinnissippi, and I am a crazy man. What difference does it make? The Sinnissippi, if they ever were, are gone now. There is only me, and I am fading, too."

His words trailed away in the growing silence of the park. The light was almost gone, the sun settled below the horizon so that its brilliant orange glare was only a faint smudge against the darkening skyline west. The buzzing of the locusts had begun, rising and falling in rough cadence to the distant sounds of cars and voices as the last of the ballplayers and spectators emptied out of the park.

"What happened to your people?" Nest asked finally. "Why don't we know anything about them?"

Two Bears' coppery face shifted away again. "They were an old people, and they have been gone a long time. The Sauk and the Fox came after them. Then white Europeans who became the new Americans. The Sinnissippi were swallowed up in time's passage, and no one who lived in my lifetime could tell me why. What they had been told by their ancestors was vague. The Sinnissippi did not adapt. They did not change when change was necessary. It is a familiar story. It is what happens to so many nations. Perhaps the Sinnissippi were particularly ill suited to make the change that was necessary to ensure their survival. Perhaps they were foolish or blind or inflexible or simply unprepared. I have never known." He paused. "But I have come back to find out."

His big hands clasped before his rugged face. "I was a long time deciding that I would do this. It seemed better to me in some ways not to know. But the question haunts me, so I am here. Tomorrow night, I will summon the spirits of the dead from where they lie within the earth. I have shaman powers, little bird's Nest, revealed to me in the madness of the war in Nam. I will use those powers to summon the spirits of the Sinnissippi to dance for me, and in their dance they will reveal the answers to my questions. I am the last of them, so they must speak to me."

Nest tried to picture it. The spirits of the Sinnissippi dancing at night in the park—in the same park where the feeders prowled, unfettered.

"Would you like to watch?" Two Bears asked quietly.

"Me?" She breathed the word as she would a prayer.

"Tomorrow, at midnight. Are you afraid?"

She was, but she refused to admit it.

"I am a stranger, a big man, a combat veteran who speaks of terrifying things. You should be afraid. But we are friends, Nest. Our friendship was sealed with our handshake. I will not hurt you."

The dark eyes reflected pinpricks of light from the rising moon. Darkness cloaked the park, the twilight almost gone. Nest remembered the promise she had made to her grandfather. She had to leave soon.

"If you come," said the big man softly, "you may learn something of your own people's fate. The spirits will speak of more than the Sinnissippi. The dance will reveal things that you should know."

Nest blinked. "What things?"

He shook his head slowly. "What happened to my people can happen to yours as well." He paused. "What if I were to tell you that it is happening now?"

Nest felt a tightening in her throat. She brushed at her short, curly hair with her hand. She could feel the sweat bead on her forehead. "What do you mean?"

Two Bears leaned back, and his face disappeared momentarily into shadow. "All peoples think they are forever," he growled softly. "They do not believe they will ever not be. The Sinnissippi were that way. They did not think they would be eradicated. But that is what happened. Your people, Nest, believe this of themselves. They will survive forever, they think. Nothing can destroy them, can wipe them so completely from the earth and from history that all that will remain is their name and not even that will be known with certainty. They have such faith in their invulnerability.

"Yet already their destruction begins. It comes upon them gradually, in little ways. Bit by bit their belief in themselves erodes. A growing cynicism pervades their lives. Small acts of kindness and charity are abandoned as pointless and somehow indicative of weakness. Little failures of behavior lead to bigger ones. It is not enough to ignore the discourtesies of others; discourtesies must be repaid in kind. Men are intolerant and judgmental. They are without grace. If one man proclaims that God has spoken to him, another quickly proclaims that his God is false. If the homeless cannot find shelter, then surely they are to blame for their condition. If the poor do not have jobs, then surely it is because they will not work. If sickness strikes down those whose lifestyle differs from our own, then surely they have brought it on themselves.

"Look at your people, Nest Freemark. They abandon their old. They shun their sick. They cast off their children. They decry any who are different. They commit acts of unfaithfulness, betrayal, and depravity every day. They foster lies that undermine beliefs. Each small darkness breeds another. Each small incident of anger, bitterness, pettiness, and greed breeds others. A sense of futility consumes them. They feel helpless to effect even the smallest change. Their madness is of their own making, and yet they are powerless against it because they refuse to acknowledge its source. They are at war with themselves, but they do not begin to understand the nature of the battle being fought."

He took a long, slow breath and released it. "Do even a handful among your people believe that life in this country is better now than it was twenty years ago? Do they believe that the dark things that inhabit it are less threatening? Do they feel safer in their homes and cities? Do they find honor and trust and compassion outweigh greed and deceit and disdain? Can you tell me that you do not fear for them?"

There was bleak appraisal in his dark eyes. "We do not always recognize the thing that comes to destroy us. That is the lesson of the Sinnissippi. It can appear in many different forms. Perhaps my people were destroyed by a world which demanded changes they could not make." He shook his head slowly, as if trying to see beyond his words. "But there is reason to think that your people destroy themselves."

He went silent then, staring at the girl, his eyes distant, his look impenetrable. Nest took a deep breath. "It is not that bad," she said, trying to keep the doubt from her voice.

Two Bears smiled. "It is worse. You know that it is. You can see it everywhere, even in this park." He glanced around, as if to find some evidence of it close at hand. Feeders were visible at the edges of the deeper shadows, but the Indian seemed oblivious of them. He looked back at Nest. "Your people risk the fate of the Sinnissippi. Come to the summoning tomorrow at midnight and judge for yourself. Perhaps the spirits of the dead will speak of it. If they do not, then perhaps I am just another Indian with too much firewater in his body."

"You're not that," Nest said quickly, not certain at the same time just exactly what he was.

"Will you come?" he pressed.

She nodded. "Okay."

Two Bears rose, a hulking figure amid the shadows. "The Fourth of July approaches," he said softly. "Independence Day. The birth of your nation, of the United States of America." He nodded. "My nation, too, though I am Sinnissippi. I was born to her. My dreams were nurtured by her. I fought for her in Vietnam. My people are buried in her soil. She is my home, whatever name she bears. So I suppose that I am right to be interested in her fate."

He picked up his knapsack and his bedroll and slung them over his shoulder. "Tomorrow night, little bird's Nest," he repeated.

She nodded in response. "At midnight, O'olish Amaneh."

He gave her a brief, tight-lipped smile. "Tell your little friend he can come out from under the picnic table now."

Then he turned into the darkness and strode silently away.

SATURDAY, JULY 2

CHAPTER 9

The Knight of the Word rode into Hopewell on the nine-fifteen out of Chicago and not one of the passengers who rode with him had any idea who he was. He wore no armor and carried no sword, and the only charger he could afford was this Greyhound bus. He looked to be an ordinary man save for the pronounced limp and the strange, haunted look that reflected in his pale green eyes. He was a bit stooped for thirty-eight years of age, a little weathered for being not yet forty. He was of average height and weight, rather lean, almost gaunt when seen from certain angles. His face was unremarkable. He was the kid who cut your lawn all through high school grown up and approaching middle age. His lank brown hair was combed straight back from his high forehead, cut shoulder-length and tied back with a rolled bandanna. He wore jeans, a blue denim work shirt, and high-top walking shoes that were scuffed and worn, the laces knotted in more than one place.

He had left his duffel bag for storage in the luggage compartment, and when the bus pulled to a stop in front of the Lincoln Hotel he moved to retrieve it. He leaned heavily on a gnarled black walnut staff for support as he made his way to the front of the bus, his knapsack slung loosely across one shoulder. He did not meet anyone's gaze. He appeared to those traveling with him, those whose journey would take them farther west to the Quad Cities and Des Moines, as if he might be drifting, and their assessment was not entirely wrong.

But for as much as he might appear otherwise, he was still a knight, the best that the people of the world were going to get and better perhaps than they deserved. For ten long years he had sought to protect them, a paladin in their cause. There were demons loose in the world, things of such evil that if they were not destroyed they would destroy mankind. Already the feeders were responding to them, coming out of their hiding places, daring to appear even in daylight, feeding on the dark emotions that the demons fostered in humans everywhere. The demons were skillful at their work, and the humans they preyed upon were all too eager to be made victims. The demons could be all things to all people just long enough to blacken their hearts, and by the time the people realized what had happened to them, it was too late. By then the feeders were devouring them.

The Knight of the Word had been sent to put an end to the demons. His quest had taken him from one end of the country to the other countless times over, and still he journeyed on. Sometimes, in his darker moments, he thought his quest would never end. Sometimes he wondered why he had accepted it at all. He had given up everything in its cause, his life irrevocably changed. The dangers it presented were more formidable than any faced by those who had ridden under Arthur's banner. Nor did he have a Round Table and fellow knights awaiting his return—no king to honor him or lady to comfort him. He was all alone, and when his quest was finished, he would still be so.

His name was John Ross.

He retrieved his duffel bag from the driver, thanked him for his trouble, then leaned on his staff and looked about as the bus door closed, the air brakes released, and his silver charger slowly pulled away. He was at the corner of Fourth Street and Avenue A, the hotel before him, a paint store across one street and a library across the other. Kitty-corner was a gas station and tire shop. All of the buildings were run-down and bleached by the sun, washed of every color but beige and sand, their bricks crumbling and dry, their painted wood sidings peeling and splintered with the heat. The concrete of the sidewalks and streets radiated with the sun's glare, and where the street had been patched with asphalt it reflected a damp, shimmering black.

He found himself staring down Fourth Street to its junction

with First Avenue, remembering what he had seen in his dream. His eyes closed against the memory.

He picked up his duffel, limped up the steps to the front door of the hotel, and pushed his way inside. A blast of cool air from the air conditioner welcomed him, then quickly turned him cold. He checked himself in at the desk, taking the cheapest room they had, booking it for a week because the rate was less than for the three days he required. He was frugal with his money, for he lived mostly on the little his parents had left him when they died. Leaving his duffel and his knapsack with the desk clerk, who offered to carry them to his room, he picked up one of the slim pamphlets entitled "Hopewell—We're Growing Your Way" that were stacked next to the register, moved over to the tiny lobby sitting area, and lowered himself into one of the worn wing-back chairs.

The cover of the pamphlet was a collage of pictures—a cornfield, a park, a swimming pool, the downtown, and one of the plants at MidCon Steel. Inside was a rudimentary map. He read briefly that Hopewell had a population of fifteen thousand, was situated in the heart of Reagan country (both the town where Ronald Reagan was born and the one in which he grew up were within twenty miles), boasted more than seventy churches, offered easy freeway access to major cities in all directions, and was the home of Midwest Continental Steel, once the largest independently owned steel company in America. The pamphlet went on to say that while more than twenty percent of the working force of Hopewell was employed at MidCon Steel, the community was a source of employment for others as a result of a diverse and thriving agricultural and business economy.

The desk man returned with his room key. Not another soul had passed through the lobby in the time he had been gone. He seemed grateful when John Ross gave him a dollar for his trouble. Ross finished with the pamphlet and tucked it into the pocket of his jeans with his room key. He sat for a moment in the cool of the lobby, listening to the hum of the air-conditioning, looking down at his hands. He did not have much time to do what was needed. He knew enough from his dreams to make a start, but the dreams were sometimes deceptive and so could not be trusted completely. Nor were the dream memories of his future more than rudimentary. Nor were they stable; they tended to shift with the passing of events and the changing of circumstances. It was like trying to build with water and sand. Sometimes he could not tell which part of his life he was remembering or even at which point of time the events had occurred or would occur. Sometimes he thought it would drive him mad.

He hoisted himself out of the armchair, an abrupt, decisive movement. Leaning on his staff, he went out the front door into the heat and turned up Fourth Street toward the heart of the downtown. He walked slowly and methodically along the gauntlet of burning concrete, the sidewalks baking in the already near one-hundred-degree heat. The buildings had a flattened feel to them, as if weighted by the heat, as if compressed. The people he passed on the streets looked drained of energy, squinting into the glare from behind sunglasses, walking with their heads lowered and their shoulders hunched. He crossed Locust Street, the north-south thoroughfare that became State Route 88 beyond the town limits, continued on to Second Avenue, and turned down Second toward Third Street. Already he could see the red plastic sign on the building ahead that read JOSIE'S.

A church loomed over him, providing a momentary patch of shade. He slowed and looked up at it, studying its rust-colored stone, its stained glass, its arched wooden doors, and its open bell tower. A glass-enclosed sign situated on the patch of lawn at the corner said it was the First Congregational Church. Ralph Emery was the minister. Services were Sunday at 10:30 A.M. with Christian Education classes at 9:15. This Sunday's message was entitled, "Whither Thou Goest." John Ross knew it would be cool and silent inside, a haven from the heat and the world. It had been a long time since he had been in church. He found himself wanting to see how it would feel, wondering if he could still say his prayers in a slow, quiet way and not in a rush of desperation. He wondered if his God still believed in him.

He stood staring at the church for a moment more, then turned away. His relationship with God would have to wait. It was the demon he hunted who demanded his attention now, the one he had come to Hopewell to destroy. He limped on through the midmorning heat, thinking on the nature of his adversary. In a direct confrontation, he was certain he would prevail. But the demon was clever and elusive; it could conceal its identity utterly. It was careful never to permit itself to be fully engaged. Time and again John Ross had thought to trap it, to unmask it and force it to face him, and every time the demon had escaped. Like a sickness that passed itself from person to person, the demon first infected them with its madness, then gave them over to the feeders to devour. Until now Ross had searched in vain for a way to stop it. It had been difficult even to find it, virtually impossible to lay hands on it. But that was about to change. The dreams had finally revealed something useful to him, something beyond the haunting ruin of the future that awaited should he fail, something so crucial to the demon's survival that it might prove its undoing.

John Ross reached the corner of Second Avenue and Third Street and waited for the WALK sign. When it flashed on, he crossed over to Josie's, limped to the front door, and pushed his way inside.

The café was busy, the Saturday-morning crowd filling all but one of the tables and booths, the air pungent with the smell of coffee and doughnuts. Ross glanced about, taking in the faces of the customers, noting in particular the large table of men at the back, then moved to the counter. The stools were mostly vacant. He took one at the far end and lowered himself comfortably in place. The air-conditioning hummed, and the sweat dried on his face and hands. He leaned the black walking stick between the counter and his knee, bracing it there. Talk and laughter drifted about him in the mingling of voices. He did not look around. He did not need to. The man he had come to find was present.

The woman working the counter came over to him. She was pretty, with long, tousled blondish hair tied back in a ponytail, expressive dark eyes, and sun-browned skin. White cotton shorts and a collared blouse hugged the soft curves of her body. But it was her smile that captivated him. It was big and open and dazzling. It had been a long time since anyone had smiled at him like that.

"Good morning," she greeted. "Would you like some coffee?"

He stared at her without answering, feeling something stir inside that had lain dormant for a long time. Then he caught himself and shook his head quickly. "No, thank you, miss."

"Miss?" Her grin widened. "Been quite a while since anyone called me that. Do I know you?"

Ross shook his head a second time. "No. I'm not from around here."

"I didn't think so. I'm pretty good with faces, and I don't remember yours. Would you like some breakfast?"

He thought about it a moment, studying the menu board posted on the wall behind her. "You know, what I'd really like is a Cherry Coke."

She cocked an eyebrow at him. "I think we can fix you up."

She walked away, and he watched her go, wondering at the unexpected attraction he felt for her, trying to remember when he had last felt that way about anyone. He looked down at his hands where they rested on the counter. His hands were shaking. His life, he knew, was a shambles.

A man and a boy came into the coffee shop, approached the counter, glanced at the available seats, and then squeezed themselves in between two men farther down the way. Ross could feel their eyes on him. He did not react. It was always like this, as if somehow people could sense the truth of what he was.

The woman with the smile returned carrying his Cherry Coke. If she could sense the truth, she didn't show it. She set the Coke on a napkin in front of him and folded her arms under her breasts. She was probably somewhere in her thirties, but she looked younger than that.

"Sure you wouldn't like a Danish or maybe some coffee cake? You look hungry."

He smiled in spite of himself, forgetting for a moment his

weariness. "I must be made of glass, the way you see right through me. As a matter of fact, I'm starved. I was just trying to decide what to order."

"Now we're getting somewhere," she declared, smiling back. "Since this is your first visit, let me make a suggestion. Order the hash. It's my own recipe. You won't be sorry."

"All right. Your own recipe, is it?"

"Yep. This is my place." She stuck out her hand. "I'm Josie Jackson."

"John Ross." He took her hand in his own and held it. Her hand was cool. "Nice to meet you."

"Nice to meet you, too. Nice to meet anyone who still calls me 'miss' and means it." She laughed and walked away.

He finished the Cherry Coke, and when the hash arrived he ordered a glass of milk to go with it. He ate the hash and drank the milk without looking up. Out of the corner of his eye, he caught Josie Jackson looking at him as she passed down the counter.

When he was finished, she came back and stood in front of him. There were freckles on her nose underneath the tan. Her arms were smooth and brown. He found himself wanting to touch her skin.

"You were right," he said. "The hash was good."

She beamed, her smile dazzling. "Do you want some more? I think the house can spare seconds."

"No, thank you anyway."

"Can I get you anything else?"

"No, that's fine." He glanced over one shoulder as if checking something, then looked back at her. "Can I ask you a question?"

Her mouth quirked at the corners. "That depends on the question."

He glanced over his shoulder again. "Is that Robert Freemark sitting back there with those men?"

She followed his gaze, then nodded. "You know Old Bob?"

Ross levered himself off the stool with the help of his walking stick. "No, but I was a friend of his daughter." The lie burned in his throat as he said it. "Will you hold my bill for a minute, Josie? I want to go say hello."

He limped from the counter toward the table in back, steel-ing himself against what he must do. The men sitting around it were telling stories and laughing, eating doughnuts and pas-tries, and drinking coffee. It looked like they felt at home here, as if they came often. Bob Freemark had his back turned and didn't see him until some of the others looked up at his approach. Then Old Bob looked around as well, his big, white head lifting, his piercing blue eyes fixing Ross with a thoughtful look.

"Are you Robert Freemark, sir?" John Ross asked him.

The big man nodded. "I am."

"My name is John Ross. We haven't met before, but your daughter and I were friends." The lie went down easier this time. "I just wanted to come over and say hello."

Old Bob stared at him. The table went silent. "Caitlin?" the other man asked softly.

"Yes, sir, a long time ago, when we were both in college. I knew her then." Ross kept his face expressionless.

Old Bob seemed to recover himself. "Sit down, Mr. Ross," he urged, pulling over an empty chair from one of the adjoining tables. Ross seated himself gingerly, extending his leg away from the table so that he was facing Robert Freemark but not the others. The conversations at the table resumed, but Ross could tell that the other men were listening in on them nevertheless.

"You knew Caitlin, you say?" Old Bob repeated.

"In Ohio, sir, when we were both in college. She was at Oberlin, so was I, a year ahead. We met at a social function, a mixer. We dated on and off, but it was nothing serious. We were mostly just friends. She talked about you and Mrs. Freemark often. She told me quite a lot about you. When she left school, I never saw her again. I understand she was killed. I'm sorry."

Old Bob nodded. "Almost fourteen years ago, Mr. Ross. It's all in the past."

He didn't sound as if that were so, Ross thought. "I prom-ised myself that if I was ever out this way, I would try to stop by and say hello to you and Mrs. Freemark. I thought a lot of Caitlin."

The other man nodded, but didn't look as if he quite understood. "How did you find us here in Hopewell, Mr. Ross?"

"Please, sir, call me John." He eased his bad leg to a new position. The men at the table were losing interest in what he had to say. A fourteen-year-old friendship with a dead girl was not important to them. "I knew where Caitlin was from," he explained. "I took a chance that you and Mrs. Freemark were still living here. I asked about you at the hotel where I'm staying. Then I came here. Josie told me who you were."

"Well," Old Bob said softly. "Isn't that something?"

"Yes, sir."

"Where are you from, John?"

"New York City." He lied again.

"Is that so? New York City? What brings you out this way?"

"I'm traveling through by bus to see friends in Seattle. I don't have a schedule to keep to, so I took a small detour here. I suppose I decided it was time to keep my promise."

He paused, as if considering something he had almost forgotten. "I understand that Caitlin has a daughter."

"Yes, that would be Nest," Old Bob acknowledged, smiling. "She lives with us. She's quite a young lady."

John Ross nodded. "Well, that's good to hear." He tried not to think of the dreams. "Does she look at all like her mother?"

"Very much so." Old Bob's smile broadened. "Having Nest helps in some small way to make up for losing Caitlin."

Ross looked at the floor. "I expect it does. I wish I could see her. I think often of Caitlin." He went silent, as if unable to think of anything else to say. "Well, thank you, sir. I appreciate having had the opportunity of meeting you."

He started to rise, levering himself up with the aid of his staff. "Please give my regards to Mrs. Freemark and your granddaughter."

He was already moving away when Old Bob caught up with him. The big man's hand touched his arm. "Wait a minute, Mr. Ross. John. I don't think it's right that you've come all this way and don't get to talk about Caitlin more than this. Why don't you come to dinner tonight? You can meet Evelyn—Mrs.

Freemark—and Nest as well. We'd like to hear more about what you remember. Would you like to come?"

John Ross took a long, deep breath. "Very much, sir."

"Good. That's good. Come about six, then." Old Bob brushed at his thick white hair with one hand. "Can you find a ride or shall I pick you up?"

"I'll manage to get there." Ross smiled.

Robert Freemark extended his hand and Ross took it. The old man's grip was powerful. "It was good of you to come, John. We'll be looking forward to seeing you this evening."

"Thank you, sir," Ross replied, meaning it.

He moved away then, back toward the counter, listening to the conversation of the other men at the table trail after him. *Knew Caitlin, did he? At college? What's his name again? You think he's one of those hippies? He looks a little frayed around the edges. What do you think he did to his leg?* Ross let the words wash off him and did not look around. He felt sad and old. He felt bereft of compassion. None of them mattered. No one mattered, in truth, besides Nest Freemark.

He came back to the counter and Josie Jackson. She handed him his bill and stood waiting while he pried loose several dollars from his jeans pocket.

"You knew Caitlin, did you?" she asked, studying him.

"A long time ago, yes." He held her gaze with his own, wanting to find a way to take something of her with him when he went.

"Is that what brought you to Hopewell? Because the fact of the matter is you don't look like a salesman or a truck driver or a bail bondsman or anything."

He gave her a quick, tight smile. "That's what brought me."

"So where are you off to now?" She took the money he handed her without looking at it. "If you don't mind my asking."

He shook his head. "I don't mind. To tell you the truth, I thought I'd go back to my room for a bit. I'm a little tired. I just came in on the bus, and I didn't sleep much." The word "sleep" sent an involuntary chill through his body.

"Are you staying at the Lincoln Hotel?" she asked.

"For a few days."

"So maybe we'll see some more of you while you're here?"

He smiled anew, liking the way she looked at him. "I don't see how you can avoid it if everything at Josie's is as good as the hash."

She smiled back. "Some things are even better." She kept her gaze level, unembarrassed. "See you later, John."

The Knight of the Word turned and walked out the door into the midday heat, riddled with shards of confusion and hope.

Seated at the table in the back of the café with Old Bob and the others, an invisible presence in their midst, the demon watched him go.

CHAPTER 10

It is night. The sky is clear, and the full moon hangs above the eastern horizon in brilliant opalescence. Stars fill the dark firmament with pinpricks of silver, and the breeze that wafts across his heated skin is cool and soft. He stands looking upward for a moment, thinking that nothing of the madness of the world in which he stands reflects in the heavens he views. He wishes he could find a way to smother the madness with the tranquillity and peace he finds there. He remembers for a moment the way things were.

Then he is moving again, jogging steadily down the concrete highway into the city, hearing already the screams and cries of the captives. The pens are two miles farther in, but the number of prisoners they contain is so vast that the sounds travel all the way to the farmlands. The city is not familiar to him. It lies in what was Kansas or perhaps Nebraska. The country about is flat and empty. Once it grew crops, but now it grows only dust. Nothing lives in the country. All of the fields have dried away. All of the animals have been killed. All of the people have been hunted down and herded into the pens by those who were once like them. In the silence of the night, there is only the buzzing and chirping of insects and the dry, papery whisper of old leaves being blown across stone.

Feeders peer out from the shadows as he passes, but they keep their distance. He is a Knight of the Word, and they have no power over him. They sense this, and they do not offer challenge. They are creatures of instinct and habit, and they react to what they find in humans in the way that predators react to the smell of blood. John Ross knows this about them. He

*understands what they are, a lesson imparted to him long ago
when there was still hope, when there was still reason to
believe he could make a difference. The feeders are a force of
nature, and they respond to instinct rather than to reason. They
do not think, because thinking is not required of them. They do
not exist to think, but to react. The Word made them for reasons
that John Ross does not understand. They are a part of the balance of life, but their particular place in the balance remains a
mystery to him. They are attracted by the darker emotions that
plague human beings. They appear when those emotions can
no longer be contained. They feed on those emotions and in so
doing drive mad the humans who are their victims. Given
enough time and space and encouragement, they would destroy
everything.*

*The Knight of the Word has tried hard to determine why this
must be, but it requires a deeper understanding of human
behavior than he possesses. So he has come to accept the
feeders simply as a force of nature. He can see them, as most
cannot, so he knows they are real. Few others understand this.
Few have any idea at all that the feeders even exist. If they
knew, they would be reminded of Biblical references and cau-
tionary tales from childhood and be quick to describe the
feeders as Satan's creatures or the Devil's imps. But the feeders
belong to the Word. They are neither good nor evil, and their
purpose is far too complex to be explained away in such sim-
plistic terms.*

*He passes through what was once an industrial storage area
of the city, and the amber eyes follow him, flat and expressionless. The feeders feel nothing, reveal nothing. The feeders have
no concern for him one way or the other. That is not their function. The Knight of the Word has to remind himself of this, for
the glimmer of their eyes seems a challenge and a danger to
him. But the feeders, as he has learned, are as impervious to
emotion as fate is to prayers. They are like the wind and the
rain; when conditions warrant, they will appear. Look for them
as you would a change in the weather, for they respond in no
less impersonal and arbitrary a way.*

Nevertheless, it seems to him, as he passes their dark lair, that they know who he is and judge him accordingly. He cannot help himself, for they have been witness to his every failure. It feels as if they judge him now, remembering as he does the many oppor- tunities he has squandered. Tonight provides another test for him. His successes of late might seem to offset his earlier fail- ures, but it is the failures that matter most. If he had not failed in Hopewell with Nest Freemark, he thinks bitterly, there would be no need for successes now. He remembers her, a child of four- teen, how close he was to saving her, how badly he misjudged what was needed. He remembers the demon, prevailing even in the face of his fierce opposition. The memory will not leave. The memory will haunt him to the grave.

But he will not die tonight, he thinks. He carries in his hands the gleaming, rune-carved staff of magic that the Lady gave him all those years ago, wielding it as Arthur would Excalibur, believing there are no numbers great enough to stand against him or weapons strong enough to destroy him or evil dark enough to expunge the light of his magic. It is the legacy of his failure, the talisman bequeathed to him when nothing re- mained but the battle itself. He will fight on because fighting is all that is left. He is strong, pure, and fixed of purpose. He is a knight-errant adrift on a quest of his own making. He is Don Quixote tilting at windmills with no hope of finding peace.

He slows now to a walk, close enough to the pens to be able to see the smoky light of the torches that illuminate the com- pound. He has never been here before, but he knows what he will find. He has seen others of the same sort in other cities. They are all the same—makeshift enclosures into which humans have been herded and shut away. Men, women, and children run to ground and enslaved, there to be separated and pro- cessed, to be designated for a purpose, to be used and debili- tated and ultimately destroyed. It is the way the world is now, the way it has been for more than seven years. All of the cities of America are either armed camps or ruins. Nuclear missiles and poison gas and defoliant were used early, when there were still governments and armies to wield them. Then the missiles and gas and defoliant were discarded in favor of more per- sonal, rudimentary weapons as the governments and armies disintegrated and the level of savagery rose. Washington was obliterated. New York City tore itself apart. Atlanta, Houston, and Denver built walls and stockpiled weapons and began systematically to annihilate anyone who came close. Los Angeles and Chicago became killing grounds for the demons and their followers. Sides were chosen and battles fought at every turn. Reason gave way to bloodlust and was lost.

There are places somewhere, the Knight has heard, where the madness is still held at bay, but he has not found them. Some are in other countries, but he does not know where. Technology is fragmented and does not function in a dependable manner. Airplanes no longer fly, ships no longer sail, and trains no longer run. Knowledge dissipates with the passing of every day and the death of every man. The Void has no interest in technology because technology furthers progress. The demons multiply, and their purpose now is to break down what remains of human reason and to put an end to any resistance. Little stands in their way. The madness that marked the beginning of the end continues to grow.

But the Knight fights on, a solitary champion for the Word, shackled to his fate as punishment for his failure to prevent the madness from taking hold when he still had a chance to do so. He goes from city to city, from armed camp to armed camp, freeing those poor creatures imprisoned by the slave pens, hoping that some few will manage to escape to a better place, that one or two will somehow make a difference in the terrible battle being fought. He has no specific expectations. Hope of any sort is a luxury he cannot afford. He must carry on because he has pledged to do so. There is nothing else left for him. There is nothing else that matters.

John Ross slows to a steady walk, holding the staff crosswise before him with both hands. He remembers what it was like when the staff was his walking stick and gave support against his limp. But his dreams have ended and his future has become his present. Tomorrow's madness has become today's. The limp has disappeared, and he is transformed. The staff is now his sword and shield; he is infused with its power and made strong. The magic he had feared to use before is now used freely. It is a measure of his service that there are no longer any constraints placed on him, but it is also a mark of his failure.

Ahead, the torchlight grows brighter. The tools of living have become rudimentary once more. There is no electricity to power streetlamps, no fuel for turbines or generators, almost no coal or oil left to burn. There is no running water. There is no sewage or garbage disposal. There are few automobiles that run and few roads that will support them. The concrete of the streets is cracked and broken. Patches of grass and scrub push through. The earth slowly reclaims its own.

He slides to one side to keep within the shadows. He is not afraid, but there is an advantage in surprise. The feeders peering out at him draw back, wary. They sense that he can see them when most others cannot—even those who have fallen victim to the madness and serve the demons, even those the feeders rely upon to sustain them. Their numbers are huge now, grown so vast that there is not a darkened corner anywhere in which they do not lurk. They have bred in a frenzy as the madness consumed mankind, but of late their breeding has slowed. Some will begin to disappear soon, for the dwindling population of humans cannot continue to support them. With the passage of time the balance will shift back again, and the world will begin anew. But it is too late for civilization. Civilization is finished. Men are diminished, reduced to the level of animals. Rebirth, when it comes, will be a crapshoot.

He wonders momentarily how bad it is elsewhere in the world. He does not know for certain. He has heard it is not good, that what began in America spread more quickly elsewhere, that what took seed slowly here finds more fertile soil abroad. He believes that every country is under assault and that most are overrun. He believes that the destruction is widespread. He has not been visited by the Lady in a long time. He has seen no evidence that she still exists. He has heard nothing from the Word.

He approaches the pens now, a sprawling maze of wire mesh fences and gates behind which the humans are imprisoned. Torches smoke and blaze on tall stanchions, revealing the extent of the misery visited on the captives. Men, women, and *children, all ages, races, and creeds—they have been flushed from their hiding places in the surrounding countryside, rounded up and herded like cattle into the pens, squeezed together with no thought for their comfort or their needs, provided with just enough of what they require to remain alive. They are used for work and breeding until they are no longer strong enough, and then they are exterminated. Their keepers are once-men, humans who have succumbed to the madness that the demons foster everywhere, the madness that was before isolated and is now rampant. Once it was accepted that all men were created equal, but that is no longer so. Humanity has evolved into two separate and distinct life-forms, strong and weak, hunter and hunted. The Void holds sway; the Word lies dormant. The once-men have given way completely to their darker impulses and now think only to survive, even at the cost of the lives of their fellow men, even at the peril of their souls. Given time, some few will evolve to become demons themselves. The feeders dine upon their victims, finding sustenance in the commission of atrocities so terrible that it is difficult even to contemplate them. It must have been like this in the concentration camps of old. But John Ross cannot imagine it.*

He is close enough now that he can see the faces of the captives. They peer out at him from behind the wire, their eyes dull and empty. They are naked mostly, thrust up against the wire by those who push from behind, waiting for the night to end and the day to begin, waiting without hope or reason or purpose. They mewl and they cry and they curl up in fear. They scratch themselves endlessly. He can hardly bear to look on them, but he forces himself to do so, for they are the legacy of his failure. Once-men stand armed and ready in watchtowers all about the compound, holding automatic weapons. Weapons are still plentiful in this post-apocalyptic world, a paradox. Sentries patrol the perimeter of the compound. John Ross has come up on them so quickly that they are just now realizing he is there. Some turn to look, some swing their weapons about menacingly. But he is only one man, alone and unarmed. They are not alarmed. They are no better now at recognizing what will destroy them than they were when the first of the demons came among them all those years ago.

A few call out to him to halt, to stand where he is, but he comes on without slowing. A command rings out and shots are fired, a warning. He comes on. Shots ring out again, a flurry this time, meant to bring him down. But his magic is already in place. He calls it Black Ice—smooth, slippery, invisible. It coats him with its protective shield. The bullets slide off harmlessly. He pushes aside the closest of the once-men and strides to the wire mesh of the pens. Holding the staff firmly in both hands, he sweeps its tip across the diamond-shaped openings. Light flares, and the mesh falls apart like torn confetti. The occupants of the pens fall back in shock and fear, not certain what is happening, not knowing what to do. Ross ignores them, turning to face the once-men that rush to stop him. He scatters them with a single sweep of his staff. The guards in the watchtowers turn their weapons on him and begin to fire, but the bullets cannot harm him. He points his staff at the towers. Light flares, incandescent and blinding, and one after another the towers collapse and burn.

The compound is in chaos now. The once-men are rushing about frantically, trying to regroup. The Knight of the Word is relentless. He tears at the wire mesh of the pens until it hangs in tatters. He yells at the cowering prisoners, urging them to get up, to run, to escape. At first no one moves. Then a few begin to creep out, the bolder ones, testing the waters of their newfound freedom. Then others follow, and soon the entire camp is rushing away into the night. Some few, those who still cling to some shred of their humanity, stop to help the children and the elderly. The once-men give chase, howling in frustration and rage, but they are swept aside by the tide and by the fire of the Knight's bright magic. John Ross strides through the camp unchallenged, flinging aside those who would stop him. The feeders have appeared by now, vast numbers of them, leaping and cavorting about him, seeing in him the prospect of fresh nourishment. He does not like serving as their catalyst, but he knows it cannot be helped. The feeders respond because it is in their nature to do so. The feeders are there because they *are drawn by the misery and the pain of the humans. There is nothing he can do to change that.*

He is making his way through the greater part of the camp, destroying the pens and freeing their occupants, when he sees the demon. It comes toward him almost casually, appearing out of the shadows. It still looks somewhat human, although grotesquely so, for most of its disguise has fallen away from lack of use. Once-men flank it, mirroring in their faces the hatred and fear that flares in the depths of its bright eyes. Although the demon has come to stop him, John Ross is not afraid. Others of its kind have tried to stop him before. All lie dead.

He swings to face the demon. Behind him, the captives of the pens stream through the empty streets of the ruined city for the flatlands beyond. Perhaps some will escape the pursuit that will follow. Perhaps they will find freedom in another place. The Knight has made what difference he can. It is all he can do.

All about him, the feeders cluster, anticipating that they will soon dine upon the leavings that a battle between the Knight and the demon will create. They creep like shadows in the smoky glow of the torches. Their fluid forms extend and recede like waves on a shore.

The Knight brings up his staff and starts for the demon. As he does so a net falls over him. It is heavy and thick, woven of steel threads and weighted on the ends. It bears him to his knees. Instantly the once-men are upon him, rushing from hiding, charging into the light. It is a trap, and the Knight has stumbled into it. The once-men are on him, seeking to tear the staff from his hands, to strip him of his only weapon. All about, the feeders leap and dart wildly, the frenzy drawing them like moths to a flame. In the background, the demon approaches, eyes intent, eager, and bright with hate.

Light flares along the length of the Knight's staff and surges into the midst of his attackers . . .

John Ross awoke with a cry, tearing at the enemies that were no longer there, thrashing beneath the light blanket he had thrown over himself when he succumbed to his need for sleep.

He stifled his cry and ceased his struggle and lurched to a sitting position, the black walking staff clutched tightly in both hands. He sat staring into space, coming back from his dream, regaining his sense of place and time. The portable air conditioner thrummed steadily from its seating in the window, and the cool air washed over his sweating face. His breathing was quick and uneven, and his pulse pounded in his ears. He felt as if his heart would burst.

It was like this, sometimes. He would dream and then wake in the middle of his dream, his future revealed in tantalizing snippets, but with no resolution offered. Would he escape from the net and the once-men or would he be killed? Either was possible. Time was disjointed in his dreams, so he could not know. Sometimes the answers would be revealed in later dreams, but not always. He had learned to live with the uncertainty, but not to accept it.

He looked over at the bedside clock. It was midafternoon. He had only slept three hours. He closed his eyes against his bitterness. Three hours. He must sleep again tonight if he was to maintain his strength. He must go back again into the world of his dreams, into the future of his life, into the promise of what waited should he fail in the here and now, and there was no help for it. It was the price he paid for being what he was.

He lay back slowly on the bed and stared upward at the ceiling. He would not sleep again now, he knew. He could never sleep right after waking from the dreams, his adrenaline pumping through him, his nerve endings jagged and raw. It was just as well. He tried not to sleep at all anymore, or to sleep only in small stretches in an effort to lessen the impact of the dreams. But it was hard to live that way. Sometimes it was almost more than he could bear.

He let his thoughts drift. His memory of the times and places when he had felt at peace and there had been at least some small measure of comfort were distant and faded. His childhood was a blur, his boyhood a jumbled collection of disconnected faces and events. Even the years of his manhood, from before the coming of the Lady, were no longer clear in his mind. His entire life was lost to him. He had given it all away.

Once it had seemed so right and necessary that he should do so. His passion and his beliefs had governed his reason, and the importance of the charge that had been offered him had outweighed any other consideration.

But that was a long time ago. He was no longer certain he had chosen rightly. He was no longer sure even of himself.

He called up a picture of Josie Jackson in an effort to distance himself from his thoughts. She materialized before him, tousled hair and sun-browned skin, freckles and bright smile. Thinking of her comforted him, but there was no reason for it. She had smiled at him, and they had talked. He knew nothing about her. He could not afford to think about knowing her better. In three days, he would be gone. What did it matter how she made him feel?

But if it did not matter, then why shouldn't he indulge himself for just a minute?

He stared at the ceiling, at the cracks in the plaster, at the lines the shadows threw across the paint, at worlds so far removed that they could only be found in dreams.

Or nightmares.

Josie Jackson disappeared. John Ross blinked. Tears formed at the corners of his eyes, and he was quick to wipe them away.

CHAPTER 11

Nest Freemark spent Saturday morning cleaning house with Gran. It didn't matter that it was the Fourth of July weekend or that Nest was particularly anxious to get outside. Nor did it matter how late you stayed up the night before. Saturday mornings were set aside for cleaning and that took precedence over everything. Gran was up at seven, breakfast was on the table at eight, and cleaning was under way by nine. The routine was set in stone. There was no sleeping in. Old Bob was already out of the house by the time Gran and Nest started work. There was a clear division of duties between Nest's grandparents, and the rough measure of it was whether the work took place inside or out. If it was inside, Gran was responsible. Cutting the grass, raking the leaves, plowing the snow, chopping wood, planting and tending the vegetable garden, fetching and hauling, and just about everything else that didn't involve the flower beds were Old Bob's responsibility. As long as he kept up the yard and the exterior of the house, he stayed on Gran's good side and was relieved of any work inside.

Nest, on the other hand, had responsibility for chores both inside and out, beginning with the Saturday-morning house-cleaning. She rose with Gran at seven to shower and dress, then hurried downstairs for her breakfast of scrambled eggs, toast, and juice. The quicker she got started, she knew, the quicker she would get done. Gran was already chain-smoking and drinking vodka and orange juice, her breakfast untouched in front of her, Old Bob frowning at her in disapproval. Nest ate her eggs and toast and drank her juice in silence, trying not to look at either of them, consumed instead by thoughts of last night and of Two Bears.

"How did he know I was there?" Pick had demanded in exasperation as they made their way back across the park, the hot July darkness settled all about them like damp velvet. "I was invisible! He shouldn't have been able to see me! What kind of Indian is he, anyway?"

Nest had been wondering the same thing. The Indian part notwithstanding, Two Bears wasn't like anyone she had ever met. He was strangely reassuring, big, direct, and well reasoned, but he was kind of scary, too. Sort of like Wraith—a paradox she couldn't quite explain.

She pondered him now as she cleaned with Gran, dusting and polishing the furniture, vacuuming the carpet, sweeping and mopping the floors, wiping down the blinds and windowsills, scrubbing out the toilets and sinks, and washing out the tubs and showers. On a light cleaning day, they would stick to dusting and vacuuming, but on the first Saturday of the month they did it all. She helped Gran with the laundry and the dishes as well, and it was nearing noon when they finally finished. When Gran told her she could go, she wolfed down a peanut butter and jelly sandwich, drank a large glass of milk, and went out the back door in a rush, inadvertently letting the screen slam shut behind her once more. She cringed at the sound, but she didn't turn back.

"He said he was a shaman," Nest had remarked to Pick the previous night. "So maybe that means he sees things other people can't. Aren't Indian medicine men supposed to have special powers?"

"How am I supposed to know what medicine men can or can't do?" Pick had snapped irritably. "Do I look like an expert on Indians? I live in this park and I don't take vacations to parts of the country where there might be Indians like some people I could mention! Why don't you know what Indians do? Haven't you studied Indians in school? What kind of education are you getting, anyway? If I were

you, I'd make certain I knew everything that was important
about the history . . ."

And on and on he had gone, barely pausing for breath to say
good night when she reached her house and left him to go in.
Sometimes Pick was insufferable. A lot of times, really. But he
was still her best friend.

Nest had met Pick at the beginning of the summer of her
sixth year. She was sitting on the crossboard at the corner of
her sandbox one evening after supper, staring out at the park,
catching glimpses of it through gaps in the hedgerow, which
was still filling in with new spring growth. She was humming
to herself, picking idly at the sand as she scrutinized the park,
when she saw the feeder. It was slipping through the shadows
of the Petersons' backyard, hunkered down against the failing
light as it made its way smoothly from concealment to concealment. She stared after it intently, wondering where it was
going and what it was about.

"Weird, aren't they?" a voice said.

She looked around hurriedly, but there was no one to
be seen.

"Down here," said the voice.

She looked down, and there, sitting on the crossboard at the
opposite corner of the sandbox, was what looked like a tiny
wooden man made out of twigs and leaves with a little old face
carved into the wood and a beard made of moss. He was so
small and so still that at first she thought he was a doll. Then he
shifted his position slightly, causing her to start, and she knew
he was alive.

"I don't scare you, do I?" he asked her with a smirk, wig-
gling his twiggy fingers at her.

She shook her head wordlessly.

"I didn't think so. I didn't think you would be scared
of much. Not if you weren't scared of the feeders or that
big dog. Nossir. You wouldn't be scared of a sylvan, I told
myself."

She stared at him. "What's a sylvan?"

"Me. That's what I am. A sylvan. Have been all my life." He

chuckled at his own humor, then cleared his throat officiously. "My name is Pick. What's yours?"

"Nest," she told him.

"Actually, I knew that. I've been watching you for quite a while, young lady."

"You have?"

"Watching is what sylvans do much of the time. We're pretty good at it. Better than cats, as a matter of fact. You don't know much about us, I don't expect."

She thought a moment. "Are you an elf?"

"An elf!" he exclaimed in horror. "An elf? I should guess not! An elf, indeed! Utter nonsense!" He drew himself up. "Sylvans are real, young lady. Sylvans are forest creatures—like tatterdemalions and riffs—but hardworking and industrious. Always have been, always will be. We have important responsibilities to exercise."

She nodded, not certain exactly what he was saying. "What do you do?"

"I look after the park," Pick declared triumphantly. "All by myself, I might add. That's a lot of work! I keep the magic in balance. You know about magic, don't you? Well, there's a little magic in everything and a lot in some things, and it all has to be kept in balance. There's lots of things that can upset that balance, so I have to keep a careful watch to prevent that from happening. Even so, I'm not always successful. Then I have to pick up the pieces and start over."

"Can you do magic?" she asked curiously.

"Some. More than most forest creatures, but then I'm older than most. I've been at this a long time."

She pursed her lips thoughtfully. "Are you like Rumpelstiltskin?"

Pick turned crimson. "Am I like Rumpelstiltskin? Criminy! What kind of question is that? What did I just get through telling you? That's the trouble with six-year-olds! They don't have any attention span! No, I am not like Rumpelstiltskin! That's a fairy tale! It isn't real! Sylvans don't go around spinning straw into gold, for goodness' sake! What kind of education are they giving you in school these days?"

Nest didn't say anything, frightened by the little man's outburst. The leaves that stuck out of the top of his head were rustling wildly, and his twiggy feet were stamping so hard she was afraid they would snap right off. She glanced nervously toward her house.

"Now, don't do that! Don't be looking for your grandmother, like you think you might need her to come out and shoo me away. I just got done telling you that I knew you weren't afraid of much. Don't make a liar out of me." Pick spread his arms wide in dismay. "I just get upset sometimes with all this fairy-tale bunk. I didn't mean to upset you. I know you're only six. Look, I'm over a hundred and fifty years old! What do I know about kids?"

Nest looked at him. "You're a hundred and fifty? You are not."

"Am so. I was here before this town was here. I was here when there were no houses anywhere!" Pick's brow furrowed. "Life was much easier then."

"How did you get to be so old?"

"So old? That's not old for a sylvan! No, sir! Two hundred and fifty is old for a sylvan, but not one hundred and fifty." Pick cocked his head. "You believe me, don't you?"

Nest nodded solemnly, not sure yet if she did or not.

"It's important that you do. Because you and I are going to be good friends, Nest Freemark. That's why I'm here. To tell you that." Pick straightened. "Now, what do you think? Can we be friends, even though I shout at you once in a while?"

Nest smiled. "Sure."

"Friends help each other, you know," the sylvan went on. "I might need your help sometime." He gave her a conspiratorial look. "I might need your help keeping the magic in balance. Here, in the park. I could teach you what I know. Some of it, anyway. What do you think? Would you like that?"

"I'm not supposed to go into the park," Nest advised him solemnly, and glanced furtively over her shoulder at the house again. "Gran says I can only go into the park with her."

"Hmmm. Well, yes, I suppose that makes sense." Pick rubbed at his beard and grimaced. "Parental rules. Don't want to transgress." He brightened. "But that's just for another year or so, not forever. Just until you're a little older. Your lessons could begin then. You'd be just about the right age, matter of fact. Meanwhile, I've got an idea. A little magic is all we need. Here, pick me up and put me in your hand. Gently, now. You're not one of those clumsy children who drop things, are you?"

Nest reached down with her hands cupped together, and Pick stepped into them. Seating himself comfortably, he ordered her to lift him up in front of her face.

"There, hold me just like that." His hands wove in feathery patterns before her eyes, and he began to mutter strange words. "Now close your eyes," he told her. "Good, good. Keep them closed. Think about the park. Think about how it looks from your yard. Try to picture it in your mind. Don't move . . ."

A warm, syrupy feeling slipped through Nest's body, beginning from somewhere behind her eyes and flowing downward through her arms and legs. Time slowed.

Then abruptly she was flying, soaring through the twilight high over Sinnissippi Park, the wind rushing past her ears and across her face, the lights of Hopewell distant yellow pinpricks far below. She was seated astride an owl, the bird's great brown-and-white feathered wings spread wide. Pick was seated in front of her, and she had her arms about his waist for support. Amazingly, they were the same size. Nest's heart lodged in her throat as the owl banked and soared with the wind currents. What if she were to fall? But she quickly came to realize that the motion would not dislodge her, that her perch astride the bird was secure, and her fear turned to exhilaration.

"This is Daniel," Pick called back to her over his shoulder. In spite of the rush of the wind, she could hear him clearly. "Daniel is a barn owl. He carries me from place to place in the park. It's much quicker than trying to get about on my own. Owls and sylvans have a good working relationship in most places. Truth is, I'd never get anything done without Daniel."

The owl responded to a nudge of Pick's knees and dropped earthward. "What do you think of this, Nest Freemark?" Pick asked her, indicating with a sweep of his hand the park below.

Nest grinned broadly and clutched the sylvan tightly about the waist. "I think it's wonderful!"

They flew on through the twilight, crossing the playgrounds and the ballparks, the pavilions and the roadways. They soared west over the rows of granite and marble tombstones that dotted the verdant carpet of Riverside Cemetery, east to the tree-shaded houses of Mineral Springs, south to the precipitous cliffs and narrow banks of the sprawling Rock River, and north to the shabby, paint-worn town houses that fronted the entry to the park. They flew the broad expanse of the Sinnissippi to the wooded sections farther in, skimming the tops of the old growth, of the oaks, elms, hickories, and maples that towered out of the growing darkness as if seeking to sweep the starry skies with their leafy branches. They found the long slide of the toboggan run, its lower section removed and stored beneath, waiting for winter and snow and ice. They discovered a doe and her fawn at the edge of the reedy waters of the bayou, back where no one else could see. Deep within the darkest part of the forest they tracked the furtive movement of shadows that, cloaked in twilight's gray mystery, might have been something alive.

They swept past a massive old white oak, one much larger than its fellows, its trunk gnarled by age and weather, its limbs crooked and twisted in a way that suggested immense fury and desperation captured in midstride, as if a giant had been frozen in place and transformed one bare instant before it had fallen upon the world it now shadowed.

Then a flash of lamplight struck Nest full in the eyes as they crossed back toward Woodlawn, and she blinked in surprise, momentarily blinded.

"Nest!"

It was Gran calling. She blinked again.

"Nest! It's time to come inside!"

She was sitting once more on the crossboard of her sandbox,

staring out into the darkening stretch of her yard toward the park. Her hands were cupped before her, but they were empty. Pick was gone.

She didn't tell Gran about him that night, wary by now of telling anyone anything about the park and its magic, even Gran. She waited instead to see if Pick would return. Two days later he did, appearing at midday while she poked along the hedgerow, sitting on a limb above her head, waving a skinny stick limb in greeting, telling her they had to hurry, there were things to do, places to go, and people to see. Then, when she did tell Gran about him, that very night, the old woman simply nodded, as if the sylvan's appearance was the most natural thing in the world, and told her to pay close attention to what Pick had to say.

Pick was her closest friend after that, closer to her than her school friends, even those she had known all her life. She couldn't explain why that was. After all, he was a forest creature, and for most people such creatures didn't exist. On the surface of things, they had nothing in common. Besides being a sylvan, he was a hundred and fifty years old and a big grouch. He was fastidious and temperamental. He had no interest in the playthings she tried to share with him or in the games she favored.

What drew them together, she decided when she was older, what bonded them in a way nothing else could, was the park. The park with its feeders and its magic, its secrets and its history, was their special place, their private world, and even though it was public and open and everyone could come visit, it belonged only to them because no one else could appreciate it the way they could. Pick was its caretaker, and she became his apprentice. He taught her the importance of looking for damage to the woods and injury to the creatures that inhabited them. He explained to her the nature of the world's magic, how it inhabited everything, why there was a balance to it, and what could be done on a small scale to help keep it in place. He instructed her on how to deal with the feeders when they threatened the safety of those who could not protect themselves. He

enlisted her aid against them. He gave her an insight into the
coexisting worlds of humans and forest creatures that changed
her life.

He told her, eventually, that Gran and her mother and three
generations of her mother's side of the family before Gran had
helped him care for the park.

She was thinking of this as she crossed the backyard that
Saturday morning. She paused to give a sleeping Mr. Scratch
a rub behind his grizzled ears and glanced about in vain for
Miss Minx. The day was hot and slow, and the air was damp
and close. Her friends wanted to go swimming, but she hadn't
made up her mind whether to join them. She was still preoccupied with Two Bears and not yet ready to think of anything
else. She squinted up at the sun, full and brilliant in a cloudless
sky, brushed at a fly that flew into her face, and moved to the
hedgerow and the park. The grass beneath her feet was brittle
and dry and crunched softly. Questions pressed in about her.
Would the spirits of the Sinnissippi appear tonight as Two
Bears believed? Would they reveal to her something of the
future? Only to her? What would they say? How would she
respond?

She brushed at her curly hair, ungluing a handful of strands
from her forehead. Sweat was dampening her skin already, and
a fresh mosquito bite had appeared on her forearm. She
scratched at it ruefully. She had asked Pick repeatedly why it
was that she was the only one who could see the feeders, or see
him, or know about the magic in the park. Pick had told her the
first time she asked that she wasn't the only one, her grandmother could see the forest creatures and the feeders and knew
more about the magic than Nest did, and there were others like
her in other places. After that, when she narrowed the scope of
the question so that it excluded Gran and people in other
places, Pick brushed the matter aside by saying that she was
lucky, was all, and she ought to be grateful and let it go at that.
But Nest couldn't let it go, not even now, after all these years
of living with it. It was what set her apart from everyone else.
It was what defined her. She would not be satisfied until she
understood the reasons behind it.

A few weeks ago she had pressed Pick so hard about it that he had finally revealed something new.

"It has to do with who you are, Nest!" he snapped, facing her squarely. His brow furrowed, his eyes steadied, and his rigid stance marked his determination to lay the matter to rest for good. "You think about it. I'm a sylvan, so I was born to the magic. For you to have knowledge of the magic and me, you must have been born to it as well. Or, in the alternative, share a close affinity with it. You know the word, don't you? 'Affinity'? I don't have time to be teaching you everything."

"Are you saying I have forest-creature blood?" she exclaimed softly. "Is that what you're saying? That I'm like you?"

"Oh, for cat's sake, pay attention!" Pick had turned purple. "Why do I bother trying to tell you anything?"

"But you said . . ."

"You're nothing like me! I'm six inches high and a hundred and fifty years old! I'm a sylvan! You're a little girl! Forest creatures and humans are different species!"

"All right, all right, settle down. I'm not like you. Thank goodness, I might add. Crabpuss." When he tried to object, she hurried on. "So there's an affinity we share, a bond of the sort that makes us both so much at home in the park . . ."

But Pick had waved his hands dismissively and cut her off. "Go ask your grandmother. She's the one who said you could do magic. She's the one who should tell you why."

That was the end of the matter as far as Pick was concerned, and he had refused to say another word about it since. Nest had thought about asking Gran, but Gran never wanted to discuss the origins of her magic, only what the consequences would be if she were careless. If she wanted a straight answer from Gran, she would have to approach the matter in the right way at the right time and place. As of now, Nest didn't know how to do that.

Pick jumped down onto her shoulder from a low-hanging branch as she neared the gap in the hedgerow. It used to frighten her when he appeared unexpectedly like that, like having a large bug land on you, but she had gotten used to it. She glanced down at him and saw the impatience and distress mirrored in his eyes.

"That confounded Indian has disappeared!" he snapped, forgoing any greeting.

"Two Bears?" She slowed.

"Keep moving. You can spit and whistle at the same time, can't you?" He straddled her shoulder, kicking at her with his heels as you might a recalcitrant horse. "Disappeared, gone up in a puff of smoke. Not literally, of course, but he might as well have. I've looked for him everywhere. I was sure I'd find him back at that table, looking off into the sunrise with that blank stare of his. But I can't even find his tracks!"

"Did he sleep in the park?" Nest nudged her way through the hedgerow, being careful not to knock Pick from his perch.

"Beats me. I scouted the whole of the park from atop Daniel early this morning. Flew end to end. The Indian's gone. There's no sign of him." Pick pulled and tugged mercilessly at his beard. "It's aggravating, but it's the least of our troubles."

She stepped into the park and crossed the service road toward the ball diamonds. "It is?"

"Trust me." He gave her a worried glance. "Take a walk up into the deep woods and I'll show you."

Never one to walk when she could run, Nest broke into a steady jog that carried her across the open expanse of the central park toward the woods east. She passed the ball fields, the playgrounds, and the toboggan run. She rounded the east pavilion and skirted a group of picnickers gathered at one of the tables. Heads turned to look, then turned away again. She could smell hot dogs, potato salad, and sweet pickles. Sweat beaded on her forehead, and her breath felt hot and dry in her throat. The sunlight sprinkled her with squiggly lines and irregular spots as she ran beneath the broken canopy of the hardwoods, moving downhill off the high ground toward the bayou and the deep woods beyond. She passed a couple hiking one of the trails, smiled briefly in greeting, and hurried on. Pick whispered in her ear, giving her directions interspersed with unneeded advice about running between trees.

She crossed the wooden bridge at the stream that emptied out of the woods into the bayou and turned uphill again. The woods ahead were thick with shadows and scrub. There were no picnic tables or cooking stations back here, only hiking trails. The trees were silent sentinels all around her, aged dark hulks undisturbed since their inception, witnesses to the passing of generations of life. They towered over everything, a massive and implacable presence. Sunlight was an intruder here, barely able to penetrate the forest canopy, appearing in a scattering of hazy streaks amid the gloom. Feeders skulked at the edges of her peripheral vision, small movements gone as quickly as they were glimpsed.

"Straight ahead," Pick directed as they crested the rise, and she knew at once where they were going.

They plunged deep into the old growth, the trails narrowing and coiling like snakes. Thorny branches of scrub poked in from the undergrowth and sometimes threatened to cut off passage entirely. Itchweed grew in large patches, and mounds of thistles bristled from amid the saw grass. It was silent here, so still you could hear the voices of the picnickers from back across the stream almost a quarter of a mile away. Nest navigated her way forward carefully, choosing her path from experience, no longer relying on Pick to tell her where to go. Sweat coated her skin and left her clothing feeling damp and itchy. Mosquitoes and flies buzzed past her ears and flew at her nose and eyes. She brushed at them futilely, wishing suddenly she had something cold to drink.

She emerged finally in the heart of the deep woods in a clearing dominated by a single, monstrous oak. The other trees seemed to shy away from it, their trunks and limbs twisted and bent, grown so in an effort to reach the nourishing light denied them by the big oak's sprawling canopy. The clearing in which the old tree grew was barren of everything but a few small patches of saw grass and weeds. No birds flitted through the oak's ancient branches. No squirrels built their nests within the crook of its limbs. No movement was visible or sound audible from any part of its gloomy heights. All about, the air was heavy and still with heat and shadows.

Nest stared upward into the old tree, tracing the line of its limbs to the thick umbrella of leaves that shut away the sky. She had not come here for a long time. She did not like being here now. The tree made her feel small and vulnerable. She was chilled by the knowledge of the dark purpose it served and the monstrous evil it contained.

For this was the prison of a maentwrog.

Pick had told her the maentwrog's story shortly after their first meeting. She remembered the aged tree from her flight into the park atop Daniel. She had seen it in the hazy gloom of the deepening twilight, and she had marked it well. Even at six, she knew when something was dangerous. Pick confirmed her suspicions. Maentwrogs were, to use the sylvan's own words, "half predator, half raver, and all bad." Thousands of years ago they had preyed upon forest creatures and humans alike, devouring members of both species in sudden, cataclysmic, frenzied bursts triggered by a need that only they understood. They would tear the souls out of their victims while they still lived, leaving them hollow and consumed by madness. They fed in the manner of the feeders, but did not rely on dark emotions for their response. They were thinking creatures. They were hunters. This one had been imprisoned in the tree a thousand years ago, locked away by Indian magic when it became so destructive that it could no longer be tolerated. Now and again, it threatened to escape, but the magic of the park's warders, human and sylvan, had always been strong enough to contain it.

Until now, Nest thought in horror, realizing why Pick had brought her here. The massive trunk of the ancient oak was split wide in three places, the bark fissured so that the wood beneath was exposed in dark, ragged cuts that oozed a foul, greenish sap.

"It's breaking free," the sylvan said quietly.

Nest stared wordlessly at the jagged rifts in the old tree's skin, unable to look away. The ground about the oak was dry and cracked, and there were roots exposed, the wood mottled and diseased.

"Why is this happening?" she asked in a whisper.

Pick shrugged. "Something is attacking the magic. Maybe the shift in the balance of things has weakened it. Maybe the feeders have changed their diet. I don't know. I only know we have to find a way to stop it."

"Can we do that?"

"Maybe. The fissures are recent. But the damage is far more extensive than I have ever seen before." He shook his head, then glanced left and right into the trees about them. "The feeders sense it. Look at them."

Nest followed his gaze. Feeders lurked everywhere in the shadows, hanging back in the gloom so that only their eyes were visible. There was an unmistakable eagerness in their gaze and in their furtive movements, an expectancy that was unsettling.

"What happens if the maentwrog breaks free?" she asked Pick softly, shivering with the feel of those eyes watching.

Pick cocked an eyebrow and frowned. "I don't know. It's been a prisoner of the tree for so long that I don't think anyone knows. I also don't think anyone wants to find out."

Nest was inclined to agree. "So we have to make sure that doesn't happen. What can I do to help?"

Pick jumped down from her shoulder to her arm, then scooted down her leg to the ground. "Bring me some salt. One of those big bags of the stuff they use in the water conditioners. Rock salt, if that's all you can find. I'll need a bag of compost, too. A wheelbarrow full. A bag of fertilizer or manure is okay. Pitch or tar, too. To fill in those splits." He looked at her. "Do the best you can. I'll stay here and work on strengthening the magic."

Nest shook her head in dismay, looking back again at the tree. "Pick, what's going on?"

The sylvan understood what she was asking. He tugged up his shirtsleeves angrily. "Some sort of war, I'd guess. What does it look like to you? Now get going."

She took a deep breath and darted away through the trees. She raced down the narrow trail, heedless of the brambles and the stinging nettles that swiped at her. Even without hearing him speak the words, she could feel Pick urging her to hurry.

CHAPTER 12

Ten minutes later, she was racing up the gravel drive to Robert Heppler's house. Cass Minter was closer, and Nest might have gone to her instead, but Robert was more likely to have what she needed. The Hepplers lived at the end of a private road off Spring Drive on three acres of woodland that bordered the park at its farthest point east, just up from the shores of the Rock River. It was an idyllic setting, a miniature park with great old hardwoods and a lawn that Robert's dad, a chemical engineer by trade but a gardener by avocation, kept immaculate. Robert found his father's devotion to yard work embarrassing. He was fond of saying his father was in long-term therapy to cure his morbid fascination with grass. One day he would wake up and discover he really wasn't Mr. Green Jeans after all.

Nest reached the Heppler property by climbing a split-rail fence on the north boundary and sprinting across the yard to intercept the gravel drive on its way to the house. The house sat large and quiet in front of her, a two-story Cape Cod rambler with weathered shingle-shake sides and white trim. Patterned curtains hung in the windows, and flowers sprouted in an array of colors from wooden window boxes and planters. The bushes were neatly trimmed and the flower beds edged. The wicker porch furniture gleamed. All the gardening and yard tools were put away in the toolshed. Everything was in its place. Robert's house looked just like a Norman Rockwell painting. Robert insisted that one day he would burn it to the ground.

But Nest spared little thought for the Heppler house today, Pick's words and looks weighing heavily on her mind. She had seen Pick worried before, but never like this. She tried not to dwell on how sick the big oak looked, the rugged bark of its trunk split apart and oozing, its roots exposed in the dry, cracked earth, but the image was vivid and gritty in her mind. She raced up the Heppler drive, her shoes churning up the gravel in puffs of dust that hung suspended in the summer heat. Robert's parents would be at work, both of them employed at Allied Industrial, but Robert should be home.

She jumped onto the neatly swept porch, trailing dust and gravel in her wake, rang the doorbell with no perceptible effect, and then banged on the screen impatiently. "Robert!"

She knew he was there; the front door was open to the screen. She heard him finally, a rapid thudding of footsteps on the stairs as he dashed down from his room.

"All right already, I'm coming!" His blond head bobbed into view through the screen. He was wearing a T-shirt that said Microsoft Rules and a pair of jeans. He saw Nest. "What are you doing, banging on the door like that? You think I'm deaf or something?"

"Open the door, Robert!"

He moved to unfasten the lock. "This better be important. I'm right in the middle of downloading a fractal coding system it took me weeks to find on the Net. I just left it sitting there, unprotected. If I lose it, so help me . . ." His fingers fumbled with the catch. "What are you doing here? I thought you were going swimming with Cass and Brianna. Matter of fact, I think they're waiting for you. Didn't Cass call you at your house? What am I, some sort of messenger service? Why does everything always depend on . . . Hey!"

She had the screen door open now, and she dragged him outside by his arm. "I need a bag of compost and a bag of softener salt."

He jerked his arm free irritably. "What?"

"Compost and softener salt!"

"What are you talking about? What do you want with those?"

"Do you have them? Can we go look? This is important!"

Robert shook his head and rolled his eyes. "Everything is

important to you. That's your problem. Chill out. Be cool. It's summer, in case you hadn't noticed, so you don't have to . . ."

Nest reached out and took hold of his ears. Her grip was strong and Robert gasped. "Look, Robert, I don't have time for this! I need a bag of compost and a bag of softener salt! Don't make me say it again!"

"All right, all right!" Robert was twisting wildly from the neck down, trying not to move his head or put further pressure on his pinioned ears. His narrow face scrunched up with pain. "Leggo!"

Nest released him and stepped back. "This is important, Robert," she repeated carefully.

Robert rubbed at his injured ears and gave her a rueful look. "You didn't have to do that."

"I'm sorry. But you have a way of bringing out the worst in me."

"You're weird, Nest, you know that?"

"I need some pitch, too."

Robert gave her a look. "How about a partridge in a pear tree while we're at it?"

"Robert."

Robert stepped back guardedly. "Okay, let me go take a look out in the toolshed. I think there's a couple bags of compost stored there. And there's some salt for the conditioner in the basement. Jeez."

They trotted out to the storage shed and found the compost, then returned to the house and went down into the basement, where they found the softener salt. The bags weighed fifty pounds, and it took both of them to haul each one out to the front porch. They were sweating freely when they finished, and Robert was still griping about his ears.

They dropped the compost on top of the softener salt, and Robert kicked at the bags angrily. "You better not grab me like that again, Nest. If you weren't a girl, I'd have decked you."

"Do you have any pitch, Robert?"

Robert put his hands on his narrow hips and glared at her. "What do you think this is, a general store? My dad counts all this stuff, you know. Maybe not the salt, since that doesn't have anything to do with his precious yard, but the compost for sure. What am I supposed to tell him when he asks me why he's missing a bag?"

"Tell him I borrowed it and I'll replace it." Nest glanced anxiously towards the park. "How about the pitch?"

Robert threw up his hands. "Pitch? What's that for? You mean like for patching roads? Tar? You want tar? Where am I supposed to find that?"

"No, Robert, not tar. Pitch, the kind you use to patch trees."

"Is that what we're doing here? Patching up trees?" Robert looked incredulous. "Are you nuts?"

"Do you have a wagon?" she asked. "You know, an old one from when you were little?"

"No, but I think it might be a good idea to call one for you! You know, the padded kind?" Robert was apoplectic. "Look, I found the compost and the salt, and that's all I . . ."

"Maybe Cass has one," Nest interrupted. "I'll call her. You go back out to the shed and look for the pitch."

Without waiting for his response, she darted into the house and through the hall and living room to the kitchen phone, the screen door banging shut behind her. She felt trapped. It was hard knowing what she did of the park and of its creatures and their magic and never being able to speak of it to her friends. But what if they knew? What would happen if the maentwrog were to break free of its prison? Something that terrible would be too obvious to miss, wouldn't it? Not like the feeders or Pick or even Wraith. What would that do to the barrier of secrecy that separated the human and forest-creature worlds?

She dialed the phone, chewing nervously on her lower lip. This was all taking too much time. Cass picked up on the second ring. Nest told her friend what she needed, and Cass said she would be right down. Good old Cass, Nest thought as she hung up the phone. No questions, no arguments—just do it.

She went back outside and sat on the porch waiting for Robert. He reappeared a few moments later with a bucket of something labeled Tree Seal that he said he thought would do the trick. He'd found an old stirring stick and a worn brush to apply the contents. He dumped them on the ground and sat down beside her on the steps. Neither of them said anything, staring out into the shaded yard and the heat. Somewhere down the way, off toward Woodlawn, they could hear the music of an ice-cream truck.

"You know, I would have been all right yesterday," Robert said finally, his voice stubborn. "I'm not afraid of Danny Abbott. I'm not afraid to fight him." He scuffed at the porch step with his shoe. "But thanks, anyway, for doing whatever it was you did."

"I didn't do anything," she told him.

"Yeah, sure." Robert smirked.

"Well, I didn't."

"I was there, Nest. Remember?"

"He tripped over himself." She smoothed the skin on her knees with the palms of her hands, looking down at her feet. "I didn't touch him. You saw."

Robert didn't say anything. He hunched forward and buried his face in his knees. "All I know is I'd rather have you for a friend than an enemy." He peeked up at her and rubbed his reddened ears gingerly. "So we're off to patch up a tree, are we? Jeez. What a treat. Good thing I like you, Nest."

A few minutes later Cass arrived with Brianna, pulling a small, red metal wagon. They loaded the softener salt, compost, and bucket of Tree Seal into the bed and headed back down the drive, Nest and Robert pulling the wagon, Cass and Brianna helping to balance its load. They followed the road out to Spring, then turned down Spring until they reached Mrs. Eberhardt's blacktop drive, which ran back through her lot to her garage at the edge of the park. They were halfway down the drive when Alice Eberhardt appeared, yelling at them for trespassing on private property. This was nothing new. Mrs. Eberhardt yelled at every kid who cut through her yard, and there were a lot of them. Robert said it was Mrs. Eberhardt's fault for providing them with a shortcut in the first place. He assured her now, giving her his "don't mess with me" look, that this was an emergency, so the law was on their side. Mrs. Eberhardt, who was a retired insurance adjuster and convinced that all kids were looking to get into trouble, but especially the ones in her yard, shouted back that she knew who Robert was and she was going to speak to his parents. Robert said she should call the house before seven, because his father was still doing nights in jail until the end of the month and his mother would probably go off to visit him after dinner.

They reached the end of the driveway, detoured around the garage to the back of the lot, and set off into the park. The woods began immediately, so they moved to the nearest trail and followed it in.

"You are really asking for it, Robert," Brianna observed, but there was a hint of admiration in her voice.

"Hey, this is how I look at it." Robert cocked his head, a savvy bantam rooster. "Each day is a new chance to get into trouble. I don't ever pass up those kinds of chances. You know why? Because even when I don't go out of the house, I get into trouble. Don't ask me why. It's a gift. So what's the difference if I get into trouble at Mrs. Eberhardt's or at home? It's all relative." He gave Brianna a smirk. "Besides, getting into trouble is fun. You should try it sometime."

They worked their way deeper into the woods, the heat and the silence growing. The sounds of the neighborhood faded. Gnats flew at them in clouds.

"Yuck." Brianna grimaced.

"Just a little additional protein for your diet," Robert cracked, licking at the air with his tongue.

"What are we doing out here?" Cass asked Nest, plodding along dutifully, one hand balancing the sacks of salt and compost in the swaying wagon.

Nest spit out a bug. "There's a big oak that's not looking too good. I'm going to see what I can do to help it."

"With salt and compost?" Robert was incredulous. "Tree Seal, I can see. But salt and compost? Anyway, why are you doing this? Don't they have people who work for the parks who are supposed to patch up sick trees?"

The trail narrowed and the ground roughened. The wagon began to bounce and creak. Nest steered around a large hole. "I tried getting hold of someone, but they're all off for the Fourth of July weekend," she improvised.

"But how do you know what to do?" Cass pressed, looking doubtful as well.

"Yeah, have you nursed other sick trees back to health?" Robert asked with his trademark smirk.

"I watched Grandpa once. He showed me." Nest shrugged dismissively and pushed on.

Fortunately, no one asked her for details. They worked their way along the trail through the weeds and scrub, swatting at bugs and brushing aside nettles, hot and miserable in the damp heat. Nest began to feel guilty for forcing her friends to come. She could probably handle this alone, now that she had the wagon and the supplies. Robert could go back to his computer and Cass and Brianna could go swimming. Besides, what would she do about Pick?

"You don't have to come any farther," she said finally, glancing over her shoulder at them, tugging on the wagon handle. "You can head back. I can manage."

"Forget it!" Robert snapped. "I want to see this sick tree."

Cass nodded in agreement. "Me, too. Anyway, this is more fun than doing hair." She gave Brianna a wry glance.

"Is it much farther?" Brianna asked, stepping gingerly around a huge thistle.

Five minutes later, they reached their destination. They pulled the wagon into the clearing and stood looking at the tree in awe. Nest wasn't sure if any of them had ever seen it before. She hadn't brought them herself, so maybe they hadn't. Whatever the case, she was certain from the looks on their faces that they would never forget it.

"Wow," whispered Robert. Uncharacteristically, he was otherwise at a loss for words.

"That is the biggest oak tree I have ever seen," Cass said, gazing up into its darkened branches. "The biggest."

"You know what?" Robert said. "When they made that tree, they threw away the mold."

"Mother Nature, you mean," Cass said.

"God," Brianna said.

"Whoever," Robert said.

Nest was already moving away from them, ostensibly to

take a closer look at the oak, but really to find Pick. There was
no sign of him anywhere.

"Look at the way the bark is split," said Cass. "Nest was
right. This tree is really sick."

"Something bad has gotten inside of it," Brianna declared,
taking a tentative step forward. "See that stuff oozing out of the
sores?"

"Maybe it's only sap," said Robert.

"Maybe pigs fly at night." Cass gave him a look.

Nest rounded the tree on its far side, listening to the silence,
to the murmur of her friends' voices, to the rustle of the feeders
lurking in the shadows back where they couldn't be seen. She
glanced left and right, seeing the feeders, but not Pick. Irritation shifted to concern. What if something had happened to
him? She glanced at the tree, afraid suddenly that the damage
was more extensive than they had believed, that somehow the
creature trapped within was already loose. Heat and fear closed
about her.

"Hey, Nest!" Robert called out. "What are we supposed to
do, now that we're here?"

She was searching for an answer when Pick dropped from
the tree's branches onto her shoulder, causing her to start in
spite of herself. "Pick!" she gasped, exhaling sharply.

"Took you long enough," he huffed, ignoring her. "Now
listen up, and I'll tell you what to do."

He gave Nest a quick explanation, then disappeared again.
Nest walked back around the tree, gathered her friends together,
and told them what was needed. For the next half hour they
worked to carry out her instructions. Robert was given the Tree
Seal to apply to the splits in the trunk, and he used the stirring
stick and brush to slap the pitchlike material into place in thick
gobs. Cass and Brianna spread the compost over the exposed
roots and cracks, dumping it in piles and raking it in with their
hands. Nest took the conditioner salt and poured it on the
ground in a thin line that encircled the tree some twenty-five
feet out from its base. When Robert asked what she was doing,
she told him she was using the salt to protect the tree from a
particularly deadly form of wood bore that was causing the

sickness. The pitch would heal the sores, the compost would feed the roots, and the salt would keep other wood bores from finding their way back to the tree. It wasn't true, of course, but it sounded good.

When they were done, they stood together for a time surveying their handiwork. Robert gave his theory on tree bores, some wild concoction he said he had picked up on the Internet, and Brianna gave her theory on Robert. Then Cass allowed as how standing there looking at the tree was like watching grass grow, Brianna complained about being hot and thirsty, and Robert remembered the program he was downloading on his computer. It was not yet midafternoon, so there was still time to go swimming. But Nest told them she was tired and thought she would go home instead. Robert snorted derisively and called her a wimp and Cass and Brianna suggested they could just hang out. But Nest persisted, needing to be alone with Pick, distracted by thoughts of the maentwrog and tonight's meeting with Two Bears. The lie felt awkward, and she added to her discomfort by saying that Gran had asked her to do some additional chores around the house. She promised to meet them the following day in the park by the Indian mounds after church services and lunch.

"Hey, whatever." Robert shrugged, failing to hide his irritation and resentment.

"Call you tonight," Cass promised.

She picked up the handle of the wagon and trudged off, with Brianna and Robert trailing after. More than once her friends glanced back at her. She could read the questions in their eyes. She stared after them, unable to look away, feeling selfish and deceitful.

When they were out of sight, she called softly for Pick. The sylvan appeared at her feet, and she reached down, picked him up, and set him on her shoulder.

"Will any of this help?" she asked, gesturing vaguely at the tree, struggling to submerge her feelings.

"Might," he answered. "But it's a temporary cure at best. The problem lies with a shifting in the balance. The magic that wards the tree is being shredded. I have to find out why."

They stood without speaking for a time, studying the big oak, as if by doing so they might heal it by strength of will alone. Nest felt hot and itchy from the heat and exertion, but there was a deeper discomfort working inside her. Her eyes traced the outline of the tree against the sky. It was so massive and old, a great, crooked-arm giant frozen in time. How many years had it been alive? she wondered. How much of the land's history had it witnessed? If it could speak, what would it tell her?

"Do you think the Word made this tree?" she asked Pick suddenly.

The sylvan shrugged. "I suppose so."

"Because the Word made everything, right?" She paused. "What does the Word look like?"

Pick looked at her.

"Is the Word the same as God, do you think?"

Pick looked at her some more.

"Well, you don't think there's more than one God, do you?" Nest began to rush her words. "I mean, you don't think that the Word and God and Mother Nature are all different beings? You don't think they're all running around making different things—like God makes humans and the Word makes forest creatures and Mother Nature makes trees? Or that Allah is responsible for one race and one part of the world and Buddha is responsible for some others? You don't think that, do you?"

Pick stared.

"Because all these different countries and all these different races have their own version of God. Their religions teach them who their God is and what He believes. Sometimes the different versions even hold similar beliefs. But no one can agree on whose God is the real God. Everyone insists that everyone else is wrong. But unless there is more than one God, what difference does it make? If there's only one God and He made everything, then what is the point of arguing over whether to call Him God or the Word or whatever? It's like arguing over who owns the park. The park is for everyone."

"Are you having some sort of identity crisis?" Pick asked solemnly.

"No. I just want to know what you believe."

Pick sighed. "I believe creatures like me are thoroughly misunderstood and grossly underappreciated. I also believe it doesn't matter what I believe."

"It matters to me."

Pick shrugged.

Nest stared at her feet. "I think you are being unreasonable."

"What is the point of this conversation?" Pick demanded irritably.

"The point is, I want to know who made me." Nest took a deep breath to steady herself. "I want to know just that one thing. Because I'm sick and tired of being different and not knowing why. The tree and I are alike in a way. The tree is not what it seems. It might have grown from a seedling a long, long time ago, but it's been infused with magic that imprisons the maentwrog. Who made it that way? Who decided? The Word or God or Mother Nature? So then I think, What about me? Who made me? I'm not like anyone else, am I? I'm a human, but I can do magic. I can see the feeders when no one else can. I know about this other world, this world that you come from, that no one else knows about. Don't you get it? I'm just like that tree, a part of two worlds and two lives—but I don't feel like I really belong in either one."

She took him off her shoulder and held him in the palm of her hand, close to her face. "Look at me, Pick. I don't like being confused like this. I don't like feeling like I don't belong. People look at me funny; even if they don't know for sure, they sense I'm not like them. Even my friends. I try not to let it bother me, but it does sometimes. Like right now." She felt the tears start, and she forced them down. "So, you know, it might help if I knew something about myself, even if it was just that I was right about God and the Word being the same. Even if it was only that, so I could know that I'm not parts of different things slapped together, not something totally weird, but that I was made whole and complete to be just the way I am!"

Pick looked uncomfortable. "Criminy, Nest, I don't have any special insight into how people get made. You don't seem weird to me, but I'm a sylvan, so maybe my opinion doesn't count."

She tightened her mouth. "Maybe it counts for more than you think."

He gave an elaborate sigh, tugged momentarily on his mossy beard, and fixed her with his fierce gaze. "I don't like these kinds of conversations, so let's dispense with the niceties. You pay attention to me. You asked if I believe God and the Word are the same. I do. You can call the Word by any name you choose—God, Mohammed, Buddha, Mother Nature, or Daniel the Owl; it doesn't change anything. They're all one, and that one made everything, you included. So I wouldn't give much credence to the possibility that you were slapped together and modified along the way by a handful of dissatisfied deities. I don't know why you turned out the way you did, but I'm pretty sure it was done for a reason and that you were made all of a piece."

His brows knit. "If you want to worry about something, I don't think it should be about whether you owe your existence to God or the Word or whoever. I think you should worry about what's expected of you now that you're here and how you're going to keep from being a major disappointment."

She shook her head in confusion. "What do you mean?"

"Just this. Everything that exists has a counterpart. The Word is only half of the equation, Nest. The Void is the other half. The Word and the Void—one a creator, one a destroyer, one good, one evil. They're engaged in a war and they've been fighting it since the beginning of time. One seeks to maintain life's balance; the other seeks to upset it. We're all a part of that struggle because what's at risk is our own lives. The balance isn't just out there in the world around us; it's inside us as well. And the good that's the Word and the evil that's the Void is inside us, too. Inside us, each working to gain the upper hand over the other, each working to find a way to overcome the other."

He paused, studying her. "You already understand that you aren't like most people. You're special. You have one foot firmly planted in each of two worlds, forest creature and human. There're not many like you. Like I've said, there's a reason for this, just like there's a reason for everything. Don't you think for a minute that the Void doesn't realize this. You have a presence and a power. You have a purpose. The Void would like to see all that turned to his use. You may think you are a good person and that nothing could change that. But you haven't been tested yet. Not really. You haven't been exposed to the things in life that might change you into something you wouldn't even recognize. Sooner or later, that's going to happen. Maybe sooner, given the amount of unrest among the feeders. Something is going on, Nest. You better concentrate your concerns on that. You better be on your guard."

There was a long silence when he finished as she digested the implications of his admonition. He stood rigid in her hand, arms folded across his wooden chest, mouth set in a tight line, eyes bright with challenge. He was trying to tell her something, she realized suddenly. His words had more than one meaning; his warning was about something else. A sense of uneasiness crept through her, a shadow of deep uncertainty. She found herself thinking back on the past few days, on Bennett Scott's rescue from the cliffs, on the maentwrog's emergence from its prison, and on the increased presence and boldness of the feeders. Did it have to do with these?

What was Pick trying to say?

She knew she would not find out today. She had seen that look on his face before, stubborn and irascible. He was done talking.

She felt suddenly drained and worn. She lowered Pick to the ground, waited impatiently for him to step out of her hand, and then stood up again. "I'm going home after all," she told him. "I'll see you tonight."

Without waiting for his reply, she turned and walked off into the trees.

She didn't go home, however. Instead, she walked through the park, angling down off the heights to the bayou's edge and following the riverbank west. She took her time, letting her emotions settle, giving herself a chance to think through the things that were bothering her. She could put a voice to some of them, but not yet to all. What troubled her was a combination of what had already come about and what she sensed was yet to happen. The latter was not a premonition exactly—more an unpleasant whisper of possibility. The day was hot and still, and the sun beat down out of the cloudless sky on its slow passage west. The park was silent and empty-feeling, and even the voices of the picnickers seemed distant and subdued. As if everyone was waiting for what she anticipated. As if everyone knew it was coming.

She passed below the toboggan slide and above a pair of young boys fishing off the bank by the skating shelter. She glanced up the long, straight, wooden sluice to the tower where the sledders began their runs in winter, remembering the feeling of shooting down toward the frozen river, gathering speed for the launch onto the ice. Inside she felt as if it were happening to her now in another way, as if she were racing toward something vast and broad and slick, and that once she reached it she would be out of control.

The afternoon wore on. She looked for feeders, but did not see any. She looked for Daniel and did not see him either. She remembered that she had forgotten to ask Pick if he was making any progress in the search for Bennett Scott's cat, Spook. Leaves threw dappled shadows on the ground she walked across, and she imagined faces and shapes in their patterns. She found herself wondering about her father and her mother, both such mysterious figures in her life, so removed in time, almost mythical. She thought of Gran and her stubborn refusal to speak of them in any concrete way. A cold, hard determination grew inside her. She would make Gran tell her, she promised herself. She would force her to speak.

She walked to the base of the cliffs, staying back from where the caves tunneled into the rock. Pick had told her never to go there. He had made her promise. It wasn't safe for her, he insisted. It didn't matter that other kids explored the caves regularly and no harm came to them. Other kids couldn't see the feeders. Other kids didn't have use of the magic. She was at risk, and she must keep away.

She shook her head as she turned and began to walk up the roadway that led to the bluff. There it was again, she thought. The realization that she was different. Always different.

She reached the heights and turned toward the cemetery. She thought she might visit her mother's grave. She had a sudden need to do so, a need to connect in some small way with her lost past. She crossed the road in front of the Indian mounds and turned in to the trees. The sun burned white-hot in the afternoon sky, its glare blinding her as she walked into it. She squinted and shaded her eyes with her hand.

Ahead, someone moved in the blaze of light.

She slowed in a patch of shade and tried to see who it was. At first she thought it was Two Bears, returned early for tonight's visit. But then she saw it was a man in forest green coveralls, a maintenance employee of the park. He was picking up trash with a metal-tipped stick and depositing it into a canvas bag. She hesitated, then continued on. As she approached, he turned and looked at her.

"Hot one, isn't it?" His bland face was smooth and expressionless, and his blue eyes were so pale they seemed almost devoid of color.

She nodded and smiled uncertainly.

"Off for a visit to the cemetery?" he asked.

"My mother is buried there," she told him, stopping now.

The man placed the sharp tip of the stick against the ground and rested his hands on the butt. "Hard thing to lose a mother. She been gone a long time?"

"Since I was a baby."

"Yeah, that's a long time, all right. You know, I hardly remember mine anymore."

Nest thought momentarily to tell him about the big oak, but then decided there was nothing he could do in any case, that it was better off in Pick's capable hands.

"You still got your father?" the man asked suddenly.

Nest shook her head. "I live with my grandparents."

The man looked sad. "Not the same as having a father, is it? Old folks like that aren't likely to be around for too much longer, so you got to start learning to depend pretty much on yourself. But then you start to wonder if you're up to the job. Think about one of these trees. It's old and rugged. It hasn't really ever had to depend on anyone. But then along comes a logger and cuts it down in minutes. What can it do? You catch my drift?"

She looked at him, confused.

The man glanced at the sky. "The weather's not going to change for a while yet. Are you coming out for the fireworks Monday?"

She nodded.

"Good. Should be something. Fourth of July is always something." His smile was vaguely mocking. "Maybe I'll see you there."

She was suddenly uneasy. Something about the man upset her. She wanted to move away from him. She was thinking that it was getting close to dinnertime anyway and she should be getting home. She would visit her mother's grave that evening instead, when it was cool and quiet.

"I've got to be going," she said perfunctorily.

The man looked at her some more, saying nothing. She forced herself to smile at him and turned away. Already the shadows of the big trees were lengthening. She went quickly, impelled by her discomfort.

She did not look back, and so she did not see the man's strange eyes turn hard and cold and fixed of purpose as he watched her go.

When Nest Freemark was safely out of sight, the demon hoisted the canvas sack and stick over his shoulder and began walking. He crossed the roadway to the Indian mounds and angled down toward the river, whistling softly to himself. Keeping within the shelter of the trees, he worked his way steadily east through the park. The light was pale and gray where the hillside blocked the sun, the shadows deep and pooled. Afternoon ball games were winding down and picnickers were heading home. The demon smiled and continued on.

Richie Stoudt was waiting at the toboggan slide, seated at one of the picnic tables, staring out at the river. The demon was almost on top of him before Richie realized he was there. Richie leaped up then, grinning foolishly, shaking his head.

"Hey, how's it going?" he sputtered. "Didn't hear you come up. Been waiting though, just like you said to do. Got your message all right. Finished up at the Prestons' and came right over."

The demon nodded, smiled, and kept walking. "Let's get started then."

"Sure, sure." Richie was right on his heels. He was small and wiry, and his thin face peeked out from under a mop of unruly dark hair. He was wearing coveralls over a blue denim shirt and high-top work boots, everything looking ragged and worn. "Didn't know you worked for the park, I guess," he said, trying to make conversation. "Pretty steady hours and all, I suppose. You sure this is all right, this late in the day and all? What is it we're doing, anyway?"

The demon didn't answer. Instead, he led Richie east into the big trees beyond the pavilion toward the slope that ran down to the little creek. The air was hot and still beneath the canopy of branches, and the mosquitoes were beginning to come out in swarms. Richie slapped at them irritably.

"Hate these things," he muttered. When the demon failed to respond, he said, "You said this would pay pretty well and I might have a chance to catch on with the city? That right?"

"Right as rain," the demon replied, not bothering to look at him.

"Well, all right, that's great, just great!" Richie sounded enthused. "I mean, I don't know if that damn strike is ever gonna get settled, and I need me something secure."

They descended the slope to the creek, crossed the wooden bridge, and began to climb the opposite embankment toward the deep woods. In the distance, the bayou was as flat and gray as hammered tin. Richie continued to mutter about the mosquitoes and the heat, and the demon continued to ignore him. They crested the rise, following the path that Nest and Pick had taken earlier, and moments later they were standing in front of the big oak. The demon glanced about cautiously, but there was no sign of anyone except the feeders, who had followed them every step of the way and crouched now at the edge of the clearing, their eyes glimmering watchfully.

"Whoa, will you look at that!" Richie exclaimed, staring up at the sickened tree. "That guy looks like a goner!"

"That's what we're here to determine," the demon explained, his bland face expressionless.

Richie nodded eagerly. "All right. Just tell me what to do."

The demon dropped the canvas sack and took a new grip on the metal-tipped stick. He put his free hand on Richie's shoulder. "Just walk over here to the trunk with me for a moment," he said softly.

The shadows were deep and pervasive as they moved forward, the demon keeping his hand on Richie Stoudt's shoulder. When they were right next to the massive trunk, the demon took his hand away.

"Look up into the branches," he said.

Richie did so, peering intently into the shadows. "I can't see anything. Not in this light."

"Step a little closer. Put your face right up against the trunk."

Richie glanced at him uncertainly, then did as he was told, pressing his cheek against the rough bark, staring up into the branches. "I still can't . . ."

The demon drove the pointed end of his stick through Richie's neck with a furious lunge. Richie gasped in shock and pain as his windpipe and larynx shattered. He tried to cry out, but his voice box was gone and the blood pouring down his throat was choking him. His fingers clawed at the tree as if to tear the bark away, and his eyes bulged. He thrashed wildly, trying to break free, but the demon pressed firmly on the wooden shaft, keeping Richie pinned, watching the dark blood spurt from his ruptured throat.

Feeders raced from among the trees and began throwing themselves on Richie, tearing at his convulsed body, beating past his futile efforts to protect himself, anxious to taste his pain and fear.

Then the bark of the tree, wet with Richie's blood, began to split apart in long, ragged fissures, and parts of Richie were drawn into the cracks. His hands and knees went first, pressing into the trunk as if into soft mud as he struggled to escape. His scream of horror came out a strangled cough, and then more of him was sucked slowly, relentlessly from view. When his head was swallowed, all sound ceased. The demon yanked free his pointed stick and stood watching as Richie's back bucked and heaved in a last futile effort to break free.

A moment later, Richie Stoudt was gone completely. The feeders melted back into the night.

The demon waited for a time, watching as the tree began to ooze what it didn't want of Richie, the bark splitting further and deeper as the blood offering did its work. Within its prison, the maentwrog was feasting, gaining the strength it needed to break free, readying itself for the demon's summons.

The demon looked down. One of Richie's work boots lay on the ground. The demon reached down and picked it up. He would carry it to the riverbank where the water turned rough above the dam and leave it where it could be found. Let people draw their own conclusions.

Humming, he collected his canvas sack and disappeared back into the trees.

CHAPTER 13

Nest pushed open the screen door off the porch just in time to hear the big grandfather clock in the den strike the half hour between five and six. As she paused in the silence that followed, Gran materialized out of the shadows of the kitchen, a thin, gray apparition gripping a pot holder.

"Dinner's in an hour, Nest. Go wash up. We've got company coming."

Nest caught the screen door as it started to swing back on its springs and eased it quietly into place. She could feel the sweat, warm and sticky on her skin beneath her clothes. "Who is it?" she asked.

"Someone your grandfather invited. You'll have to ask him." Gran looked less than pleased. She gestured with the pot holder. "Go clean up first, though. You look like something the cat dragged in."

She disappeared back into the kitchen. Nest could smell pot roast cooking, rich and savory, and she realized suddenly how hungry she was. She went down the hallway past Gran and the good smells and glanced into the den in search of her grandfather, but he was not there. She took a moment longer to listen for him; then, hearing nothing, she continued on to her room, closed the door, popped Nirvana into her CD player, stripped off her clothes, and headed for the shower. She tried not to look at herself in the mirror, but ended up doing so anyway. The girl looking back at her was skinny and flat-chested. She had bony arms and legs and looked as if she would disappear altogether if she turned sideways. She might have been half-pretty if her face hadn't been breaking out so badly. As usual, Nest didn't much care for her.

She spent a long time in the shower washing and soaking. Then she dried, dressed, and stared out the window into the park. She thought about Pick and the big oak tree, about her friends and the magic she hid from them, about the maintenance man and Wraith, and about the feeders. She thought about Two Bears and the dance of the spirits of the Indian dead, now less than six hours away. She wondered if Two Bears could see the feeders. He had seen Pick clearly enough, so shouldn't he be able to see the feeders as well? She had never met anyone who could see the feeders besides herself and Gran. Pick said there were others, but not many and they all lived elsewhere. Pick said only a handful of people could see the feeders, and that was because you had to have some connection with magic. Maybe Two Bears could do magic, she thought. Wouldn't he have to be able to do magic in order to summon spirits?

She left the window and went down the hall toward the living room, wrapped in her speculations. Her hair was still damp and loose. The curls tickled her ears. She brushed at them self-consciously, wishing suddenly that they weren't having company for dinner, thinking about how boring it was likely to be, already planning how she would excuse herself as soon as the meal was consumed . . .

"Hello."

She stopped in surprise. A man was standing just inside the front door looking at her. She had been so preoccupied with her musings she had missed seeing him.

"Hello," she replied.

"Sorry if I startled you."

"No, that's all right. I was thinking about something."

The words sounded stupid, and she colored slightly. The man didn't seem to notice. His green eyes stayed fixed on her, his gaze so intense that she blinked in spite of herself.

"You must be Nest." He smiled as if pleased by this. "My name is John Ross."

He extended his hand, and she took it in her own. His grip was strong, and she thought he must be used to hard work. He seemed to her to be constructed all of bones and muscle, but his clothes hung on him as they would have hung on a scarecrow. He looked strange with his shoulder-length hair tied back in that bandanna, but kind of cool, too. She thought it made him look like a little boy. She wondered suddenly what he was doing there. Was he their dinner company or just someone looking to do yard work?

She realized she was still holding his hand and quickly released it. "Sorry."

He smiled and looked around. His eyes settled on the portraits of the Freemark women, grouped to one side of the entry door. "Your family?" he asked.

She nodded. "Six generations of us."

"Handsome women. This house has a good feel to it. Have you lived here all your life?"

She was pondering whether to answer his question or ask one of her own when her grandfather appeared from the den. "Sorry to take so long. I was just looking for her yearbook, senior year, when she was president of the student council. Nest, have you met Mr. Ross?"

Nest nodded, watching her grandfather closely. It was her mother's yearbook he was holding.

"Mr. Ross knew your mother in school, Nest. In college, in Ohio." He seemed fascinated by the idea. "He came down to visit us, to say hello. I ran into him at Josie's this morning and invited him to join us for dinner. Look here, John, this is Caitlin's picture from her senior year."

He opened the yearbook and held it out for John Ross to see. Ross limped gingerly over for a look, and for the first time Nest noticed the polished black staff leaning against the wall next to the umbrella stand. The staff was covered with strange symbols carved into wood black and depthless beneath the staff's worn sheen. Nest stared at the markings for a long moment as John Ross and her grandfather studied her mother's yearbook. There was something familiar about the markings. She had seen them somewhere before. She was certain of it.

She looked at John Ross anew and wondered how that could be.

Moments later, Gran called them in to dinner. She seated them at the big dining-room table, Nest next to John Ross across from Robert and herself. She placed the food on the table, then finished off her bourbon and made herself another before taking her seat. She picked up her fork and began to eat with barely a glance at her company. Very unlike Gran, who was a stickler for good manners. Nest thought something was clearly troubling her.

"Did you know my mother a long time?" Nest asked, curious now to know more about this stranger.

Ross shook his head. He took small, careful bites as he ate. His green eyes were distant as he spoke. "No, I'm afraid I didn't. I didn't meet her until her second year, and she went home at the end of it. We only had a few months together. I wish I had known her better."

"She was pretty, wasn't she?"

John Ross nodded. "She was."

"You were a year ahead of her at Oberlin, you said," Old Bob encouraged. "Did you stay on and graduate?"

"Caitlin could have graduated, too, if she'd wanted," Gran said quietly, giving him a sharp glance.

"I think Caitlin was one of the smartest people I've ever known, Mrs. Freemark," John Ross offered, looking now at Gran. She looked back at him very deliberately. "But she was fragile, too. Very sensitive. She could be hurt more easily than most. I admired that about her."

Gran put down her fork and sipped at her bourbon. "I don't know that I understand what you're saying, Mr. Ross."

Ross nodded. "It's just that most of us are so hardened to life that we've forgotten how to respond to pain. Caitlin wasn't like that. She understood the importance of recognizing the little hurts that other people ignore. She was always concerned with healing. Not physical injuries, you understand. Emotional hurts, the kind that inflict damage on your soul. She could identify and heal them with a few well chosen words. She was better at it than anyone. It was a genuine gift."

"You said you dated? You and Caitlin?" Old Bob helped himself to more of the roast, ignoring the look Gran shot him. Nest watched the interplay with fascination. Something about John Ross being here had Gran very upset. Nest had never seen her so on edge.

"On and off for some of that year." John Ross smiled, but kept his eyes fixed on his plate. "Mostly we were just friends. We went places together. We talked a lot. Caitlin talked about you all the time. And about her home. She loved the park."

"I have to tell you that she never mentioned you, Mr. Ross," Gran observed pointedly, watching his face.

John Ross nodded. "I'm sorry to hear that. But she kept a lot to herself. I don't suppose I was very important to her in the larger scheme of things. But I admired her greatly."

"Well, she may have mentioned you, and we've just forgotten," Old Bob soothed, giving Gran a warning glance. Gran sniffed and sipped some more of her drink.

"She had a lot of friends while she was at Oberlin," Ross added suddenly, glancing around at their faces as if to confirm that what he was saying was true. He looked at Gran. "This roast is delicious, Mrs. Freemark. I haven't tasted anything this good in a long time. I'm very grateful you included me."

"Well," Gran said, her sharp face softening slightly.

"She did have a lot of friends," Old Bob declared. "Caitlin had a lot of friends, all through school. She had a good heart. People saw that in her."

"Did you know my father?" Nest asked suddenly.

The table went silent. Nest knew at once that she had asked something she should not have. Gran was glaring at her. Her grandfather was staring at his plate, absorbed in his food. John Ross took a drink of his water and set the glass carefully back in place on the table.

"No," he said quietly. "I'm sorry, but I never met him."

The dinner conversation resumed after a few moments and continued throughout in fits and starts, with Nest's grandfather asking questions of John Ross, Ross offering brief replies, and Gran sitting angry and still throughout. Nest finished her meal, asked to be excused, and left almost before permission was given. She walked out onto the porch and down the steps to the backyard. Mr. Scratch was sprawled on the lawn sleeping and Miss Minx was watching him with studied suspicion. Nest moved to the rope swing, seated herself in its weathered old tire, and rocked gently in the evening heat. She felt embarrassed and frustrated by her grandparents' reaction to her question and wondered anew why no one ever wanted to say anything about her father. It was more than the fact that he got her mother pregnant and never married her. That was no big deal; that happened all the time. It was more than the fact that he disappeared afterward, too. Lots of kids grew up in one-parent households. Or with their grandparents, like she was doing. No, it was something more, and she wasn't even sure that it was something anyone could actually explain. It was more like something they suspected, but could not put words to. It was like something that was possible, but they were refusing to look too closely at it for fear that it might be so.

A few minutes later John Ross came out the back door leaning on his cane, carefully negotiated the worn steps, and limped over to where she twisted and bobbed in the swing. Nest steadied herself as he came up, grounding her feet so that she could watch him.

"I guess that question about your father touched a sore spot," he said, his smile faint and pained, his eyes squinting as he looked off toward the approaching sunset. The sky to the west was colored bright red and laced with low-hanging clouds that scraped across the trees of the park.

Nest nodded without replying.

"I was wondering if you would walk me to your mother's grave," Ross continued, still looking west. "Your grandfather said it would be all right for you to do so. Your grandmother gave him one of those looks, but then she agreed, too." He turned back to her, his brow furrowed. "Maybe I'm misreading her, but I have the uncomfortable feeling she thinks she's giving me just enough rope to hang myself."

Nest smiled in response, thinking of Wraith.

Ross ran his hand slowly down the length of his staff. "To tell you the truth, I don't think your grandmother trusts me. She's a very careful woman where you are concerned."

Nest supposed that was so. Gran was fierce about her sometimes, so consumed with watching out for her that Nest would find herself wondering if there was a danger to her that she did not realize.

"So, would that be all right with you?" Ross pressed. "Would you be willing to walk me over to the cemetery?"

Nest nodded, climbed out of the swing, and pointed to the gap in the hedgerow. She led the way wordlessly, setting a slow pace so that he could follow, glancing back to make certain he was able to keep up. In point of fact, he seemed stronger and more agile than she had expected. She wondered what had happened to his leg, if there was a way she could ask him without being rude.

They crossed the yard, pushed through the gap in the hedgerow, and entered the park. The evening ball games were already under way, the diamonds all in use, the benches and grassy areas behind the backstops crowded with families and fans. She led Ross down the service road behind the nearest backstop to the crossing gate at the park entrance, then along the roadway toward the burial mounds and the cliffs. Neither of them spoke. The day's heat hung thick and heavy in the evening air, and there was little indication that the temperature would change with night's coming. The insects buzzed and hummed in dull cacophony in the shade of the trees, and the sounds of the ballplayers rose sharp and sudden with the ebb and flow of the games' action.

After a moment, she dropped back a step to walk beside him. "How long are you visiting?" she asked, wanting to know something more about him, about his involvement with her mother.

"Just a few days." His movements were steady and unhurried. "I think I'll stay for the fireworks. I hear they're pretty spectacular."

"You can sit with us, if you'd like," she offered. "That way you'll be with someone you know. You don't know anyone else in Hopewell, do you?"

He shook his head.

"This is your first visit?"

"This is my first visit."

They crossed the road at the divide and turned west toward the turnaround and the entry to Riverside. John Ross was looking off toward the cliffs, out to where the Rock River flowed west on both sides of the levy and the railroad tracks. Nest watched him out of the corner of her eye. He seemed to be seeing something beyond what he was looking at, his gaze distant and distracted, his expression riddled with pain. He looked almost young to her for an instant, as if the years had dropped away. She thought she could see the boy in him, the way he was maybe twenty years ago, the way he had been before his life had taken him down whatever rough road it was he had traveled.

"Were you in love with my mother?" she asked him suddenly.

He looked at her in surprise, his lean face intense, his green eyes startled. He shook his head. "I think I could have been if I had gotten to know her better, but I didn't get the chance." He smiled. "Isn't that tragic?"

They walked up through the spring-mounted children's toys toward the spruce groves. "You look like her," Ross said after a moment.

Nest glanced over at him, watching him limp alongside her, leaning on his staff, his gaze directed ahead to where they were going. "I don't think I do," she said. "I don't think I look like anybody. Which is just as well, because I don't much like the way I look, just at the moment."

Ross nodded. "We're our own worst critics, sometimes." Then he cocked an eyebrow at her. "But I like the way you look, even if you don't. So sue me."

She smiled in spite of herself. They passed through the spruce trees to the turnaround and the cliffs. There were two cars parked at the cliff edge and a family on the swings nearby.

She thought back to Bennett Scott and the feeders, picturing it in her mind, remembering the night and the heat and the fear. She thought about Two Bears and wondered suddenly if he was there in the park again. She glanced about to see if she could spy him, but he was nowhere in sight. She let her thoughts of Two Bears and the spirits of the dead Sinnissippi drift away.

She led Ross to the gap in the fence line and through to the cemetery beyond. They walked along the edge of the blacktop roadway, through the rows of marble and granite tombstones, across the immaculate grass carpet, and under the stately, silent old hardwoods. The mingled scents of pine and new-mown grass filled the air, rich and pungent. Nest found herself strangely at ease. John Ross made her feel that way. The longer she was with him, the more comfortable she felt—as if she had known him a long time rather than for only a few hours. It was in the way he talked to her, neither as a child nor as an adult, but simply as a person; in the way he moved, neither self-conscious nor protective of his damaged body, not favoring it in an obvious, discomforting way, accepting it as it was; and mostly in the way he was at peace with the moment, as if only the here and now mattered, as if taking this walk with her were enough and what had gone before or what would come after had no place in his thoughts.

They walked through the rolling green of the cemetery and down its tree-shaded rows of markers to where her mother lay, out on a bluff overlooking the river and the land beyond. Her mother's headstone was gray with black lettering and bore the words BELOVED DAUGHTER & MOTHER just beneath her name, Caitlin Anne Freemark. Nest stared at the grave without speaking, immutable and remote, borne to other times and places on the wings of her thoughts.

"I don't remember her at all," she said finally, tears springing to her eyes with her admission.

John Ross looked off into the trees. "She was small and gentle, with sandy hair and blue-gray eyes you couldn't look away from. She was pretty, almost elfin. She was very smart, intuitive about things others would miss entirely. When she laughed, she could transport you to a better time and place in your life if you were sad or make you glad you were there with her if you were happy. She was daring and unafraid. She was never satisfied with just being told how something was; she always wanted to experience it for herself."

He stopped, went silent suddenly, as if he'd come up against something he did not care to explore any further. Nest did not try to look at him. She brushed at her eyes and bit her lip to steady herself. It was always like this when she came to visit. No matter how much time had passed, it was always the same.

Afterward, they walked back through the cemetery to the fence line in the waning light, listening to the dying sounds of a distant mower and the occasional honk of a car horn out on the highway. There was no one in the cemetery this night; its tree-sheltered, rolling green expanse was cradled in silence and empty of movement. The Midwest evening was sultry, the air tasted of sweat, and it felt as if time had slowed its inexorable march to a crawl. There was a sense of something slipping away, gone like chances at love or hopes for understanding.

"Thank you for telling me about her," Nest said quietly as they walked down the blacktop roadway toward the park fence. Her eyes were dry again and her mind was clear.

"Well, you remind me of her," John Ross replied after a moment. "That helps me in telling you what she was like."

"I have pictures," said Nest. "But it isn't the same."

"Not if you don't have the memories of the times those pictures capture, no." Ross limped steadily forward, his staff clicking softly against the blacktop with each step.

"I like your staff," Nest ventured. "Have you had it a long time?"

Ross glanced over at her and smiled. "Sometimes it seems like I have had it all my life. Sometimes it seems like I was born with it. I think maybe, in a sense, I was."

He didn't say anything more. They reached the fence and slipped through the gap and into the park once more. They were back at the turnaround, close by the cliffs. The twilight was deepening, the sun gone down behind the horizon, leaving only its crimson wake to light the world. The family on the swings and the two cars that had been parked at the turnaround were gone. In the distance, the baseball games were winding down.

In the shadows of the trees that bracketed the cliff edge, feeders were gathering, their squat, dark bodies shifting soundlessly, their yellow eyes winking like fireflies. As John Ross and Nest passed down the roadway, their numbers grew. And grew still more. Nest glanced left and right nervously, finding eyes everywhere, watching intently, implacably. Why were there so many? The chilling possibility crossed her mind that they intended to attack, all of them, too many to defend against. They had never done anything like that before, but there was nothing to say they wouldn't do so now. Feeders were nothing if not unpredictable. She tensed expectantly, wondering what she should do. Her heart beat fast and her breathing quickened.

"Don't let them bother you," John Ross told her quietly, his voice soft and calm. "They're not here because of you. They're here because of me."

He said it so matter-of-factly that for a moment the words didn't register. Then she looked at him in surprise and whispered, "You can see them?"

He nodded without looking at her, without appearing to look at anything. "As clearly as you can. It's why I'm here. It's why I've come. To help, if I can. I'm in service to the Word."

Nest was stunned. They continued to walk down the darkening roadway through the masses of feeders as if taking a garden stroll, and Nest fought to collect her thoughts.

"You know about the feeders, don't you?" he asked conversationally. "You know what draws them?" She nodded dully. "They are attracted to me because of the staff." She glanced over immediately, eyes fastening on its black, rune-scrolled walnut length. "The staff is a talisman, and its magic is very powerful. It was given to me when I entered into service to the Word. It is the weapon I carry into battle each and every day. It is also the ball and chain that binds me to my fate."

His words were muted and harsh, but strangely poetic as well, and Nest found herself looking at his face, seeing him anew. He did not look back, but continued to keep his gaze directed forward, away from her, away from the feeders.

"Are you a caretaker?" he asked after a moment. "Are you partnered with a sylvan to look after this park?"

The number of her questions doubled instantly, and she was confused all over again. "Yes. His name is Pick."

"I am a Knight of the Word," he said. "Has Pick told you of the Knights?"

She shook her head no. "Pick doesn't say much about anything that goes on outside of the park."

Ross nodded. They were even with the burial mounds now and turning in to the playground, stepping carefully over the low chain dividers. They moved across the twig-strewn grass beneath the hardwoods, solitary ghosts. Ahead, the baseball diamonds were filling with shadows and emptying of people. Nest could see lights beginning to come on in the houses of the subdivisions bordering the park and in the Sinnissippi Townhomes. Stars were beginning to appear in the darkening sky east, and a crescent moon hung suspended north across the river.

"Did you really know my mother?" Nest asked him, a twinge of doubt nudging at her, suspicious now of everything he had said.

He seemed not to have heard her. He said nothing for a moment, then slowed and looked over at her. "Why don't we sit somewhere and talk, and I'll tell you what I'm doing here."

She studied him carefully while he waited for her answer. "All right," she agreed finally.

They moved out of the hardwoods and away from the playground. The feeders that had been shadowing them fell away as they moved into the open again, unwilling to follow. They stayed on the west side of the road leading out of the park, away from the ball games that were ending and the players and fans packing up their blankets and gear, and moved to a picnic table just at the edge of a solitary spruce close by the crossbar.

They sat across from each other in the failing light, the girl and the man, and they might have been either confidants or combatants from the set of their shoulders and the positioning of their hands, and in the vast, empty space of night and sky that closed about them, their words could not be heard.

"This is how I became a Knight of the Word," John Ross said softly, his green eyes steady and calm as they fixed on her.

And he told Nest Freemark his story.

CHAPTER 14

He was still a young man when he began his odyssey, not yet turned thirty. He was drifting again, as he had been drifting for most of his life. He had earned an undergraduate degree in English literature (he had done his senior thesis on William Faulkner), and his graduation had marked the conclusion of any recognizable focus in his life. Afterward, he had migrated to a series of different schools and graduate programs, twice coming close to completing his masters, each time stepping back when he got too close. He was a classic case of an academic unready and unwilling to confront the world beyond the classroom. He was intelligent and intuitive; he was capable of finding his way. The problem with John Ross was always the same. The way never seemed important enough for him to undertake the journey.

He had always been like that. He had excelled in school from an early age, easily gaining honors recognition, effortlessly garnering high praise and enthusiastic recommendations. While he was attending school full-time, while he was *required* to be there, it was never necessary that he consider doing anything more. It was a comfortable, regimented, encapsulated existence, and he was happy. But with his graduation it became apparent that he must point toward something specific. He might have become a teacher, and thus remained within the classroom, kept himself safe within an academic confinement, but teaching did not interest him. It was the discovery that mattered, the uncovering of truths, the deciphering of life's mysteries that drew him into his studies. And so he moved from college to university, from graduate studies in American literature to funded research

173

in Greek history, all the while waiting for the light to shine down the road his life must necessarily take.

It did not happen, though, and as he approached the age of thirty, he began to think that it never would. His parents, always supportive of him, were beginning to despair of his life. An only child, he had always been the sole focus of their expectations and hopes. They did not say so, but he could read their concerns for him in their studied silence. They no longer supported him—he had long since learned the art of securing scholarships and grants—so money was not an issue. But his options for continued study were drawing to a close, and he was still nowhere close to choosing a career. What could he do with his English degree and his raft of almost completed esoteric studies? If he didn't choose to teach, what could he do? Sell insurance or cars or vacuum cleaners? Go into business? Work for the government? When none of it mattered, when nothing seemed important enough, what could he do?

He chose to go to England. He had saved some money, and he thought that perhaps a trip abroad might give him fresh insight. He had never been outside the United States, save for a brief trip into Canada in his teens and a second into Mexico in his early twenties. He had no experience as a tourist, barely any experience in life beyond the classroom, but he was persuaded to take the plunge by his growing desperation. He would be going to an English-speaking country (well, of course), and he would be discovering (he hoped) something about his substantially English heritage. His one extracurricular activity throughout school had been hiking and camping, so he was strong and able to look after himself. He had some contacts at a few of the universities, and he would find help with lodging and shelter. Perhaps he would even find a smidgen of guest-lecturer work, although that was not important to him. What mattered was removing himself from his present existence in an effort to find his future.

So he applied for and was granted a passport, booked his airline reservation, said good-bye to his parents, and began his journey. He had no timetable for his visit, no date in mind on which he would return, no particular expectation for what he would do. He drifted anew and with careless disregard for his plans to discover himself, traveling through England and Scotland, through London and Edinburgh, south to north and back again. He renewed old acquaintances from his American university days, visited briefly at the places he had marked off on his list of must-see items, and moved on. He walked when he could, finding it the best and most thorough way to see the countryside, saving his money in the not quite acknowledged but inescapable recognition that his travels seemed to be bringing him no closer to his goals.

In the late spring of the year following his summer arrival, the first twelve months of his visit coming to a rapid close, he traveled for the first time into Wales. His decision to go there was oddly precipitated. He was reading on the history of the Welsh and English kings, on Edward I and the iron ring of fortresses he had built to contain the Welsh in Snowdonia, and a friend to whom John Ross had mentioned his reading told him of a cottage her parents owned outside of Betws-y-Coed where he could stay for the asking. Having no better plan for the spending of his time and intrigued by the history he had been reading, he accepted his friend's offer.

So he traveled into Gwynedd, Wales, found the cottage, and began to explore the country surrounding Betws-y-Coed. The village sat in the heart of the Gwydir Forest at the juncture of the Conwy, Llugwy and Lledr valleys within the vast, sprawling wilderness of Snowdonia National Park. Snowdonia, which occupied much of Gwynedd, was mountainous and thickly forested, and his hikes into her wilderness proved long and arduous. But what he found was breathtaking and mysterious, a secretive world that had offered shelter and hiding, but little on which to subsist, to the Welsh during the siege of Edward Longshanks in the late 1200s. He took day trips to the castles, to Harlech, Caernarfon, Beaumaris, and Conwy and all the others that Edward had built, rebuilt, and garrisoned in the forging of his ring of iron. He visited the towns and villages scattered about, poking into their folklore as much as into their history, and he was surprised to discover that some whisper of purpose was drawing him on, that in indulging his curiosity about the past he was embracing an unspoken promise that a

form of revelation on the future of his own life might somehow
be possible. It was an irrational, unfounded hope, but one that
was compelling in its hold over him. He passed that spring and
summer in Betws-y-Coed, and he did not think of leaving. He
wondered now and again if he was overstaying his welcome,
but neither his friend nor her parents contacted him and he was
content to leave well enough alone.

Then, on a summer day filled with sunshine and the smell of
grasses and wildflowers, he came out of a hike south beyond
the Conwy Falls to a sign that said FAIRY GLEN. It was just a
weathered board, painted white with black letters, situated
at the entrance to a rutted dirt and gravel lane leading off
the blacktop through trees and fences, over a rise and into
shadow. There was a small parking lot for cars and a box for
donations. There was nothing else. He stared at the sign,
amused, then intrigued. Why would it be called Fairy Glen?
Because it was magical, of course. Because it had a supposed
connection to a fairy world. He smiled and turned down the
lane. What could it hurt to see? He left a pound in the box and
hiked back along the fence line, over the rise, and through a
corridor of big trees to a barely recognizable opening in the
fence that led toward the sound of rushing water. He stepped
through the opening, went down a winding pathway through
trees and rocks to the source of the rushing water, and found
himself in the glen.

For a long time he just stood there looking about, not
moving, not thinking of anything. The glen was deep and shadowed, but streaked with bright sunlight and roofed by a cloudless blue sky. Massive rocks, broken and cracked, littered the
slopes and floor of the glen, as if in ancient, forgotten times a
volcanic upheaval had ruptured and split the earth. The water
spilled from a series of falls to his left, the rush of their passage
a low thunder against the silence. The stream broadened and
narrowed by turns as it worked its way through channels
formed by the positioning of the boulders. In some places it ran
fast and wild and in others it formed pools so calm and still you
could see the riverbed as clearly as if it were covered over with
glass. Colored rocks littered the bottom of the stream, visible

through the crystalline waters, and wildflowers grew in clusters all along the banks and slopes. The Fairy Glen formed a cathedral of jumbled rocks and trees that closed in the sounds of the twisting waters and shut out the intrusions of the world. Within its sanctuary, you were alone with whatever god you embraced and whatever beliefs you held.

John Ross stepped forward to the water's edge after a moment, squatted, and touched the stream. The water was ice cold, as he had expected. He stared down into its rush for a moment, losing himself in time's passage and the memories of his life. He looked at himself in the water's shimmering reflection, sun-browned from his year of hiking through England, strong and fit, his gaze steady and assured. He did not look like himself, he thought suddenly. What had changed? He had spent another year drifting, accomplishing nothing, arriving at no decision on his life. What was different?

He rose and walked along the jagged rock banks of the glen, working his way over the massive boulders, finding footholds amid the eddies and pools that filled the gaps between. He squinted when he passed through patches of bright sunlight, enjoying the warmth on his face, pausing in the shadows to look more closely at what might be hidden, wondering idly where the fairies were. He hadn't seen any so far. Maybe they were all on vacation.

"If it's magic you're looking for," a deep voice said, "you should come here at night."

John Ross nearly jumped out of his skin, teetering momentarily in midstep on the rocks, then righting himself and looking about quickly for the voice's source.

"It's more a fairy glen when the sun's down, the moon's up, and the stars lend their radiance."

He saw the man then, hunkered down just ahead in a heavy patch of shade, wrapped in a greatcoat and shadowed by a broad-brimmed hat pulled low over his face. He held a fishing pole loosely before him, the line dangling in a deep, still pool. His hands were brown and rough, crosshatched by tiny white scars, but steady and calm as they gently shifted the pole and line.

"You would like to see the fairies, wouldn't you?" he asked, tilting the brim of his hat up slightly.

John Ross shrugged uncomfortably. "I suppose so. At night, you say? You've seen them, have you?" He was trying to find something in their conversation that made sense, to frame a reply that fit.

The man's chuckle was low and deep. "Maybe I have. Maybe I've seen them come out of the falls, tumbling down the waters like tiny bright lights, as if they were stars spilling out of the heavens. Maybe I've seen them come out of the shadows where they hide by day, back there atop the falls, within the rocks and the earth—there, where the sun breaks through the trees."

He pointed, and John Ross looked in spite of himself, peering through a glaze of sunlight across the jumble of rocks to where the falls fell in a dazzling silver sweep. Bits of light danced atop the surface of the water, and behind the shimmering curtain shadows seemed to move . . .

Ross turned back suddenly to the man, anxious to know more. But the man was gone. Ross stared for a moment in disbelief, then glanced hurriedly from one bank to the other, from one place to the next. He searched the shadows and the sunny patches with equal care, but the man was nowhere to be found.

Shaken, he left the glen and walked back up the dirt and gravel lane to the blacktop, and from there back to the village. That night he pondered what he had seen, hunched over his dinner in an alehouse close to his lodgings, nursing a pint of Welsh beer and trying to make sense of it all. There was no way the fisherman could have disappeared so swiftly, so utterly. There was no place for him to go. But if he hadn't disappeared, then he wasn't there in the first place, and Ross wasn't prepared to deal with that.

For several days he refused to return to the glen, even though he wanted to. He thought about going at night, as the fisherman had urged, but he was afraid. Something was waiting for him, he believed. What if it was something he was not prepared to face?

Finally, three days later, he went back during the day. It was gray and overcast, the clouds threatening more of the rain that had already fallen intermittently since dawn. Again, the parking lot was deserted as he made his way off the blacktop and down the rutted lane. Cows looked at him from the pasture on his left, placid, disinterested, and remote. He tightened his rain slicker against the damp and chill, passed through the opening in the fence, and started down the trail. He was thinking that it was a mistake to do this. He was thinking that it was something he would come to regret.

He continued on anyway, stubbornly committed. Almost immediately he saw the fisherman. It was the same man; there was no mistaking him. He wore his broad-brimmed hat and greatcoat and was fishing with the same pole and line. He sat somewhat farther away from the falls than he had the previous day, as if thinking to find better fishing farther downstream. Ross walked carefully across the rocks to reach him, keeping close watch as he approached, making sure that what he was seeing was real.

The fisherman looked up. "Here you are again. Good day to you. Have you done as I suggested? Have you come at night?"

Ross stopped a dozen yards away from him. The man was sitting on a flat rock on the opposite bank, and there was no place close at hand to cross over. "No, not yet."

"Well, you should, you know. I can see in your eyes that you want to. The fairies mean something to you, something beyond what they might mean to an average man. Can you feel that about yourself?"

Ross nodded, surprised to find that he could. "I just . . ." He stopped, not knowing where to go. "I find it hard . . ."

"To believe," the other finished softly.

"Yes."

"But you believe in God, don't you?"

Ross felt a drop of rain nick the tip of his nose. "I don't know. I guess so."

The man adjusted the pole and line slightly. "Hard to believe in fairies if you don't believe in God. Do you see?"

Ross didn't, but he shook his head yes. Overhead, the clouds were darkening, closing in, screening out the light. "Who are you?" he asked impulsively.

The man didn't move. "Owain. And you?"

"John Ross. I'm, uh, traveling about, seeing a little of the world. I was in graduate studies for a number of years, English and Ancient Civilizations, but I, uh . . . I needed . . ."

"To come here," the man said quickly. "To come to the Fairy Glen. To see if the fairies were real. That was what you needed. Still need, for that matter. So will you come, then? As I suggested? Come at night and see them for yourself?"

Ross stared at him, groping for an answer. "Yes," he said finally, the word spoken before he could think better of it.

The man nodded. "Come in two nights, when the moon is new. Then's the best time for catching them at play; there's only the starlight to reveal them and they are less wary." His face lifted slightly, just enough so that Ross could catch a glimpse of his rough, square features. "It will be a clear night for viewing. A clear night for seeing truths and making choices."

Rain was spattering on the rocks and earth, on the surface of the stream. Shadows were deepening within the glen, and there was a rumble of thunder. "Better take shelter now," the man said to John Ross.

Then the skies opened and the rain poured down. Instinctively Ross lowered his head and pulled up the hood to his slicker, covering himself. When he looked back again, the fisherman was gone.

The rain continued all the rest of that day and into the next. John Ross was paralyzed with indecision. He told himself that he would not go back to the Fairy Glen, that he would not put himself at such obvious risk, that what was at stake was not simply his life but possibly his soul. It felt that way to him. He stayed within his rooms reading, trying not to think, and when thinking became inescapable, he went to the pubs and drank until he slept. He would have run if there had been any place left to run to, but he had exhausted his possibilities for running long ago. He knew that he had come as far as he could go that way, and that all that was left to him was to stand. But did standing entail going to the glen or staying clear? He drifted in increasingly smaller circles as the hours passed and the time of his summoning drew closer, and he despaired of his life. What had he done to bring himself to this end, to a strange and unfamiliar land, to a ghost who drew him as a flame did a moth, to a fairy glen in which magic might be possible, to the brink of madness?

After a time, he came to believe that whatever waited in the Fairy Glen was inextricably bound to him, a fate that could not be avoided and therefore must be embraced. With acceptance of this came a sort of peace, and he found himself wondering on the day of his appointed summoning if what had drawn him here and made him feel that self-discovery was at hand was linked in some way to what would happen that night in the glen.

When it was dark and he had eaten his dinner, he put on his warm clothing, his hiking boots, and his slicker, pocketed a flashlight, and went out the door of his cottage. He hitched a ride for part of the distance, then walked the rest. It was nearing midnight when he turned up the dirt and gravel lane past the sign that read FAIRY GLEN. The night was still and empty-feeling, but the skies were clear of clouds and filled with stars, just as the fisherman had foreseen. Ross breathed in the night air and tried to stay calm. His eyes adjusted to the darkness as he moved along the road, through the fence, and down the trail into the glen.

It was darker here, the starlight failing to penetrate much beyond the overhanging branches of the trees. The glen was a world apart, a rush of tumbling water and a jumble of broken rocks. Ross made his way over the massive boulders and along the stream banks to where he had twice seen the fisherman. There was no sign of him now. Within the moss and vine-grown walls of the glen, there was no movement. Belatedly, Ross thought of his failure to advise anyone of his plans. If he should disappear, no one would know where to look for him. No one would know where he might be found.

He reached an open space on the near bank between two

huge boulders, a place where the starlit sky was clearly visible overhead. He glanced back at the falls, but he could not see them, could only hear the sound of the water spilling off the rocks. He stood there waiting, not knowing what he should look for, not certain yet if he should stay or run.

The minutes slipped past. He glanced about expectantly, emboldened by the fact that nothing had happened. Perhaps nothing was going to happen. Perhaps the fisherman had played a joke on him, on a gullible American, leading him on about magic and fairies . . .

"John Ross."

The sound of his name was a silvery whisper in the silence, spoken so softly that it might have come from inside him. He stood perfectly still, afraid even to breathe.

"John Ross, I am here."

He turned then, and he saw her standing at the water's edge across from him, not quite in the stream and not quite out of it either. She seemed to be balanced between water and earth, on the brink of falling either way. She was young and beautiful and so ethereal in the bright starlight that she was almost not there. He stared at her, at her long hair, at her gown, at her slender arms raised toward him.

"John Ross, I have need of you," she said.

She moved slightly, and the light shifted about her. He saw then that she was not real, not solid, but made of the starlight and the shadows, made of the night. She was the ghost he had thought the fisherman to be—still thought he might be now. He swallowed hard against the tightness in his throat and could not speak.

"You were summoned to me by Owain Glyndwr, my brave Owain, as he in his time was summoned by another in my service. I am the Lady. I am the Light. I am the voice of the Word. I have need of you. Will you embrace me?"

Her voice whispered in the deep night silence, low and compelling, vast and unalterable, the sum of all that could ever be. He knew her for what she was instantly, knew her for her power and her purpose. He went to his knees before her on the crushed rock bed of the glen's damp floor, his eyes fixed on her, his arms clutching his body in despair. Behind her, where the waterfall tumbled away in the darkness, lights began to twinkle and shimmer against the black. One by one they blinked on, then soared outward on the cool air, on gossamer wings that glimmered faintly with color, like fireflies. He knew they were the fairies he had come to find, and tears sprang to his eyes.

"I'm sorry," he whispered finally. "I'm sorry I didn't believe."

"You do not believe yet," the Lady sang, as if the words were cotton and the air a net in which they were to be caught and held up for admiration. "You lack reason to believe, John Ross. But that will change when you enter into my service. All will change. Your life and your soul will be transformed. You will become for me, as Owain Glyndwr once was, as others have been, a Knight of the Word. Stand now."

He rose and tried to gather up his scattered thoughts. *Owain Glyndwr.* The fisherman? Was he *that* Owain Glyndwr, the Welsh patriot and warrior? He had read of him. Owain Glyndwr had fought the English Bolingbroke, Henry IV, in the early 1400s. For a time he had prevailed over Henry, and the Welsh were made free again. No one could stand against him, not even the vaunted Prince of Wales, who in time would be Henry V, and the Welsh armies under Glyndwr's command marched into England itself. Then he simply disappeared—vanished so completely that there was no record of what had become of him. And the English marched back into Wales once more.

"It is so," said the Lady, who, though he had not given voice to his thoughts, seemed to have heard them anyway.

"He was in your service?" John Ross whispered. "Owain Glyndwr?"

"For many years." The Lady shimmered with movement as she passed to another point, closer to where the fairies spilled down off the waterfall in a shower of light. "He chose service to me over service to his country, a new life and commitment in exchange for an old. My need for him was greater. He understood that. He understood that only he would do. He sacrificed himself. He was valiant and strong in the face of terrible danger. He was one of the brave. And more. Look closely on his face, John Ross."

One arm gestured, and the fisherman reappeared, standing close beside her. His cloak and broad-brimmed hat were gone, replaced by chain mail and armor plate. His fishing pole was gone as well, and he held instead a broadsword. He looked on John Ross, his face fully revealed by the starlight, and in that face Ross saw himself.

"You carry his blood in your veins." The Lady's voice floated on a whisper of night breeze. "That is why you are summoned to me. What was best in him six hundred years ago reflects anew in you, born of the time and the need, by my will and my command."

The Fairy Glen echoed with her words, the sounds reverberating off the rush of the water, off the shimmer of the light from stars and fairies. John Ross was frozen with fear and disbelief, so petrified he could not move. A part of him thought to run, a part to stand, and a part to scream, to give voice to what roiled within. This was all wrong; it was madness. Why him? Why, even if he was Owain Glyndwr's kin? He was no warrior, no fighter, no leader, no man of courage or strength. He was a failed scholar and a drifter with no purpose or conviction. He might have thought to find himself by coming here, but not in this way, and surely not in whatever cause it was the Lady championed.

"I cannot be like him," he blurted out in despair. "Look at me!"

"Watch," she whispered in reply, and brushed at the air before him with a feathery touch.

What he witnessed next was unspeakable. A black hole opened, and suddenly he stood in a world of such bleak landscape and dark despair that he knew instinctively it lacked even the faintest semblance of hope. What moved through it was unrecognizable—things that looked vaguely human, but walked on all fours, creatures dark and scaled, shadows with blunted, scarred features and eyes that reflected with a flat, harsh light. They moved through the debris of a ruined civilization, through remnants of buildings and roads, the consequences of a catastrophe of monumental proportions. The creatures seemed part of that landscape, wedded to it in the way that ash is to fire, and were one with the shadows that cloaked everything.

The setting shifted. John Ross stood within the camps in which the survivors of the holocaust were penned, imprisoned to live out their lives in servitude to those who had been like them, but had embraced the madness that had destroyed their world. Both showed themselves, victors and victims, born of the same flesh and blood; both had been transformed into something barely recognizable and impossibly sad.

There was more, scene after scene of the destruction, of its aftermath, of the madness that had consumed everything. Ross felt something shift inside him, a lurching recognition, and even before she spoke the words that came next, he knew what they would be.

"It is the future," she said softly, her words as delicate as flower petals. "It approaches."

The vision disappeared. The black hole closed. Ross stood again before her, surrounded by the fairies and the night. Once more, he found his voice. "No," he said. "No, it will never be like that. We would never allow ourselves to become like that. Never."

She floated on the surface of the stream now, balanced on the night air. "Would you change the future, John Ross? Would you be one of those who would forbid it? Then do as Owain Glyndwr once did, as all the others did who entered into my service. Embrace me."

She approached him slowly, a wraith in the starlight, advancing without apparent motion. "This is what is required of you. You must become one of my champions, my paladins, my knights-errant. You must go forth into the world and do battle with those who champion the Void. The war between us is as old as time and as endless. You know of it, for it is revealed by every tongue and written in every language. It is the confrontation between good and evil, between creation and destruction, between life and death. There are warriors that serve each of us, but only a handful like you. You have long sought after yourself, John Ross, searching for the way that you were meant to travel in your life. You have come to me for that reason. Your way lies through me. I am the road that you must take."

Ross shook his head anew. "I can't do this. I haven't the . . . I'm not strong enough, not . . ."

"Give me your hand."

She held forth her own, shimmering like quicksilver in the starlight. Ross flinched away, unwilling to do as she asked. His eyes lowered, and he tried to hide. The Lady waited, her hand held forth, her body still. She had approached to within a yard of him now, so close that he could feel the heat of her, an invisible fire that burned somewhere deep within. Although he tried not to, he could not help himself. He looked at her.

"Oh, my God, my God," he whispered in awe and fear.

"Give me your hand," she repeated.

He did so then, compelled by the force of her voice and the recognition that he could not escape what was about to happen. He placed his hand of flesh and blood within her own of heat and light, and the shock of the contact dropped him instantly to his knees. He threw back his head and tried to scream what he was feeling, but no sound would come from his mouth. He closed his eyes and waited to die, but found instead that it was not death that had come to claim him, but life. Strength filled him, drawn from the well of his heart. Visions flooded his mind, and he saw himself as he could be, as he must be, a man become new again, a man reborn. He saw his future in the Lady's service, saw the roads he would travel down and the journeys he would make, saw the people whose lives he would change and those he might save. In the mix of passion and heat that twisted and built within the core of his being, he found the belief the Lady had foreseen.

She released him then, and he sagged forward, gasping for air, feeling the cool dampness of the earth against his knees and palms, feeling the power of her touch rush through him.

"Rise," she whispered, and he did, surprised to find that he could do so, that there was within him, sparking like flint on stone, the promise that he could do anything.

"Embrace me," she whispered, and he did that as well, without hesitation or deliberation, casting off his doubt and fear and taking on the mantle of his newfound certainty and belief, reaching for her, committing himself irrevocably and forever to her service.

CHAPTER 15

With twilight deepening to night and the park emptying of its last visitors, John Ross walked Nest Freemark home again. He had finished his tale, or as much of it as he wished to confide in her, and they were speaking now of what had brought him to Hopewell. Pick had joined them, come out of nowhere to sit all fidgety and wide-eyed on the girl's shoulder, trying his best not to appear awestruck in the presence of a vaunted Knight of the Word, but failing miserably. Pick knew of the Word's champions—knew as well what having one come to Hopewell meant. It was vindication, of a sort, for his frequently expressed suspicions.

"I told you so!" he declared triumphantly, over and over again, tugging at his mossy beard as if to rid himself of fleas. "I knew it all along! A shift in the balance this extreme could only be the work of something purposefully evil and deliberately ill-intentioned! A demon in the park! Criminy!"

He was the guardian of Sinnissippi Park, and therefore entitled to a certain amount of respect, even from a Knight of the Word, so John Ross indulged his incessant chatter while struggling to complete his explanation to Nest. He had been tracking this particular demon for months, he continued, momentarily silencing Pick. He had sought to bring him to bay on countless occasions, had thought he had done so more than once, but each time had failed. Now he had tracked him here, to Hopewell, where the demon meant to precipitate an event of such far-reaching consequence that it would affect the entire country for years to come. The event itself would not necessarily be dramatic or spectacular enough to draw national attention; that

188

was not how things worked. The event would be the culmination of many other events, all leading to the proverbial last straw that would tip the scales in the demon's favor. Of small events are great catastrophes constructed, and it would be so here.

"The demon will attempt something this weekend that will shift the balance in a way that will make it difficult, if not impossible, to right." John Ross kept his voice calm and detached, taking care not to reveal the rest of what he knew. "What we must do is discover what he intends and put a stop to it."

"How are we supposed to do that?" Pick interrupted for the twentieth time. "Demons can disguise themselves so thoroughly that even a forest creature can't recognize them! If we don't know who he is, how are we supposed to disrupt his plans?"

John Ross was silent for a moment. They were passing down the service road now, the lights of the Freemark house shining ahead through the trees. He had not told them of his dreams. He had not told them of the future he had seen, the future that had revealed to him the truth about what the demon intended to accomplish by coming to Hopewell. He could not tell them that, of course. He could never tell them that.

"The demon is not perfect," he said, choosing his words carefully. "He makes mistakes, just like humans. He was human once; he cannot free himself of his mortal coil completely. If we keep close watch, we will find him out. He will do something to reveal himself. One of us will learn something that will help."

"How much time do we have?" Nest asked quickly.

Ross took a deep breath. "Until Monday. July fourth."

"July fourth?" She looked over at him curiously. "How do you know that?"

Ross slowed and stopped, leaning heavily on his staff, suddenly weary. He had slipped up. "Sometimes the Lady tells me things," he said quietly. "She confides in me."

The lie burned in his mouth, but there was no help for it. He had told her as much as he could, as much as he dared. He would tell her more tomorrow, after she had been given time to consider what she had already learned. He must be careful about this. He must not give away too much too soon.

He said good night to her in her backyard, out by the tire swing, where she said she would remain to talk a bit with Pick. He told her he would see her again tomorrow and they would talk some more. He asked her to keep her eyes open and be careful. Pick was quick to declare that he would keep his eyes open for both of them and if the demon was out there he would find him quickly enough. It was bold talk, but it felt reassuring to hear.

John Ross went inside the house then to thank Nest's grandparents once more for the dinner, moving slowly through the shadows, the staff providing him support and guidance where the light was dimmest. He was conscious of the girl's eyes following after him, aware that already her doubts about him were starting to surface. She was too smart to be fooled easily. He could not expect to do much more than delay giving out the truths she would all too soon demand to know.

He felt the weight of his task settle over him like lead. He wished he had known sooner and been given more time. But his dreams did not work like that. Time was not a luxury permitted him, but a quixotic variable that seemed to thwart him at every turn. He thought again of all the things he had not told her. Of the secret of the staff he bore. Of the reason for his limp. Of the price he paid for the magic he had been given.

Of what would become of Nest Freemark if the future were not changed by his coming.

Nest sat in the tire swing with Pick on her shoulder and told him all of what she had learned about John Ross. As she repeated the tale, she found herself beset by questions she had not thought to ask earlier. She was surprised at how many things Ross had failed to address, and she wished now that she could call him back again. He had come to Hopewell to see her grandparents, to visit her mother's grave, to keep a promise to himself, and to revive old memories. But he had come to stand against the demon as well. It seemed a rather large coincidence that he was there to do both. Were the two connected in some way? What was the demon doing here in the first place, in this tiny town, in the middle of Reagan country? Wasn't there some other, larger place where his efforts might have a more far-reaching result? What was so special about Hopewell?

There was something even more disturbing to her, something that had not been addressed at all. Apparently John Ross had known nothing of her before coming to Hopewell, for he had not seen or spoken with her mother since college. If that was so, then why did she feel that he knew so much about her? He hadn't said anything specific, but the feeling was inescapable. He had recognized her ability to see the feeders. He had known about her relationship with Pick without ever having met the sylvan. He had opened up to her about himself as if this was necessary, as if she was already his ally. Yet what exactly did he expect from her? Was it only that he needed another pair of eyes to help look for the demon? Was it just that if Pick were to know of his coming, so necessarily must she? Or was there something more?

"What do you think?" she asked Pick impulsively.

The sylvan scowled. "What do I think about what?"

"About him. About John Ross."

"I think we are fortunate he is here! What else would I think?" The sylvan looked indignant. "He's a Knight of the Word, Nest—one of the Word's anointed champions! He's come because there's a demon on the loose and that means we're in a lot of trouble! You don't know about demons; I do. A demon is the worst sort of creature. If this one accomplishes whatever it is he's set out to do, the result will be something that none of us wants even to consider! Criminy!"

Nest found herself thinking about Two Bears and his warning of the previous night. *There is reason to think that your people will destroy themselves.* Perhaps, she surmised, they would do so a little more quickly with the help of a demon.

"How do you know he is a Knight of the Word?" she pressed.

"John Ross? Because he is!" Pick snapped irritably. "Why are you being so difficult, Nest?"

She shrugged. "I'm just asking, that's all."

The sylvan sighed laboriously. "I know because of the staff. A staff like that is given only to a Knight of the Word. Been so for centuries. No one else can carry them; no one else is allowed. Every sylvan knows what they look like, how they're marked. The runes—did you notice them? Do they seem familiar to you?"

They did, of course, and now she realized why. Pick had drawn those same runes in the park's earth on several occasions when working his healing magic. That was where she had seen them before.

"He seems very tired," she observed, still musing on what he had revealed about himself, still working it through in her mind.

"You would be tired, too," he sniffed, "if you spent all your time tracking demons. Maybe if you and I do what he's asked of us and spot the demon, then he can get some rest!"

Unperturbed by the rebuke, she looked off into the trees. The shadows had melted into a black wall, and only the faint, silvery streamers of light from moon and stars and the harsher yellow glare of house lamps penetrated the darkness. Mosquitoes buzzed at her, but she ignored them, swinging idly, lazily in the tire, still thinking about John Ross. Something wasn't right. Something about him was different from what he wanted her to believe. What was it?

"Drat!" exclaimed Pick suddenly, springing to his feet on her shoulder. "I forgot to tell him about the maentwrog! Criminy sakes! I'll bet the demon has something to do with weakening the magic that imprisons it! Maybe that's what the demon has come here to do—to set the maentwrog free!"

"He said he was here to see about the feeders," Nest replied thoughtfully.

"Well, of course! But the feeders respond to human behavior, and certainly setting free the maentwrog would stir up a few emotions in the good citizens of Hopewell, don't you think?"

Maybe, maybe not, Nest thought, but she kept her opinion to herself. Why, she wondered once again, were there suddenly so many feeders in Sinnissippi Park? If they were attracted by human emotion, if they responded to what was dark and scary and terrible, why were so many gathered here? What had drawn them to this time and place? Was it whatever John Ross had come to prevent? If so, if it was that, then what were they doing here already, clustered thick as fall leaves even before whatever it was that was going to happen had happened?

She leaned back in the swing, letting her head and shoulders hang down and her legs tilt up. Dislodged from his perch, Pick gave a sharp exclamation, jumped down, and was gone. Nest let him go, weary of talking. She swung slowly in the humid night air, looking up at the stars, wishing suddenly that she could go fishing or hiking or maybe run far out on the roadways that led through the surrounding farmland, wishing that she could be someplace else or maybe even be some other person. She felt a sudden need to escape her present and flee back into her past. She could feel her childhood slipping away, and she despaired suddenly of losing it. She did not want to grow up, even after having struggled so hard to do so. She wanted to go back, just for a little while, just long enough to remember what it was like to have the world be no bigger than your backyard. Then she would be all right. If she could just have one more chance to see things the way they were, she would be all right.

Behind her, Miss Minx strolled out of the shadows, eyes gleaming, paused for a long look, and disappeared back into the dark. Nest watched her go, hanging upside down in the swing, and wondered where she went at night and what she did.

Then her ruminations drifted once more to John Ross, to the mystery that surrounded his coming, and she had a strange, unsettling thought.

Was it possible that he . . . ?

That he was . . . ?

She could not finish the thought, could not put it into words. She held it before her, suspended, a fragile piece of glass. She felt her heart stop and her stomach go cold. No, it was silly. It was foolish and impossible. No.

She closed her eyes and breathed the night air. Then she opened them again and let the thought complete itself.

Could John Ross be her father?

Robert Heppler was sitting alone in his room at his computer, pecking idly at the keys while he talked on the phone with Brianna Brown. "So, what do you think?"

"I think you're making something out of nothing as usual, Robert."

"Well, what does Cass think?"

"Ask her yourself."

He heard the phone being handed off to Cass Minter. He had called Cass first, thinking her the better choice for this conversation, but Mrs. Minter had said she was staying overnight at Brianna's. Now he was stuck with talking to both of them.

"Ask me what?" Cass growled into his ear.

"About Nest. Don't you think she's acting weird? I mean, weirder than usual?"

"Weirder than you, you mean?"

"Sure. Weirder than me. If it makes you happy."

Cass thought it over. "I don't like the word 'weird.' She's got something on her mind, that's all."

Robert sighed heavily. "Look. She comes to my house and practically drags me through the door, collects a bunch of dirt and salt, commandeers you and Brianna and your sister's red wagon, then hauls the bunch of us out to the park to do some voodoo magic stuff on a sick tree. Then, when we're done, she tells us to go on home, she's too tired to go swimming. Just like that. Miss Aqua-Lung, who's never turned down a chance to go swimming in her life. You don't think that's weird?"

"Look, Robert. People do things that other people find strange. That's the way it is. Look at Cher. Look at Madonna. Look at you. Don't be so judgmental!"

"I'm not being judgmental!" Robert was growing exasperated. "I'm worried, that's all. There's a difference, you know. I just wonder if there's something wrong that she's not telling us about. I just wonder if there's something we ought to be doing! We're supposed to be her friends, aren't we?"

Cass paused again. In the background, Robert could hear Brianna arguing with her mother. It had something to do with spending too much time on the phone. Robert rolled his eyes. "Someone ought to tell that woman to get a life," he muttered.

"What?" Cass asked, confused.

"Nothing. So what do you think? Should one of us call her up and ask her if she's all right?"

"One of us?"

"Okay, you. You're her best friend. She'd talk with you. She probably wouldn't tell me if her socks were on fire."

"She might, though, if yours were."

"Big yuck."

He heard the phone being passed again. "Hello? Who is this, please?"

It was Brianna's mother talking. Robert recognized the nasal whine laced with suspicion. "Hello, Mrs. Brown," he answered, trying to sound cheerful. "It's Robert Heppler."

"Robert, don't you have something better to do than call up girls?"

Matter of fact, yes, Robert thought. But he would never admit it to her. "Hmmm, well, I had a question and I was hoping Brianna or Cass could help me with it."

"What sort of question?" Mrs. Brown snapped. "Something a mother shouldn't hear?"

"Mother!" Robert heard Brianna gasp in the background, which gave him a certain sense of satisfaction.

A huge fight broke out, with shouting and screaming, and even the muffling of the receiver by someone's hand couldn't hide what was happening. Robert took the phone away from his ear and looked at it with helpless resignation.

Then Cass came back on the line. "Time to say good night, Robert. We'll see you at the park tomorrow."

Robert sighed. "Okay. Tell Brianna I'm sorry."

"I will."

"Parents are a load sometimes."

"Keep that in mind for when you're one. I'll have a talk with Nest, okay?"

"Okay." Robert hesitated. "Tell her I went back out this evening to see how her tree was coming along. Tell her it looks worse than before. Maybe she should call someone."

There was renewed shrieking. "Good-bye, Robert."

The phone went dead.

Jared Scott came down from his room for a snack to find his mother and George Paulsen drinking beer in front of the television. The other kids were asleep, all of them crammed into a tiny pair of hot, airless bedrooms. Jared had been reading about Stanley and Livingstone, using a tiny night-light that his mother had given him for Christmas. He liked reading stories about exploring faraway places. He thought that this was something he would like to do one day, visit strange lands, see who lived there. He saw the light from the television as he made the bend in the stairs and knew his mother and George were still up, so he crept the rest of the way on cat's paws and was turning in to the kitchen when George called to him.

"Hey, kid, what are you doing?"

He turned back reluctantly, trying not to look at either of them. His mother had been dozing, a Bud Light gripped in her hand. She looked around in a daze at the sound of George's voice. At thirty-two, she was slender still, but beginning to thicken about the waist. Her long dark hair was lank and uncombed, her skin pale, and her eyes dull and lifeless. She had been pretty once, but she looked old and worn-out now, even to Jared. She had five children, all of them by different men. Most of the fathers had long since moved on; Enid was only sure of two of them.

"Jared, why aren't you asleep?" she asked, blinking doubtfully.

"I asked you a question," George pressed him. He was a short, thickset man with dark features and a balding head. He worked part-time at a garage as a mechanic and there was always grease on his hands and clothing.

"I was getting something to eat," Jared answered, keeping his tone of voice neutral. George had hit him several times just for sounding smart-mouthed. George liked hitting him.

"You get what you need, sweetie," his mother said. "Let him be, George."

George belched loudly. "That's your trouble, Enid—you baby him." Jared hurried into the kitchen, George's voice trailing after him. "He needs a firm hand, don't you see? My father would have beat me black and blue if I'd come down from my room after hours. Not to mention thinking about getting something else to eat. You ate your dinner at the table and that was it until breakfast."

His voice was rough-edged and belligerent; it was the same voice he always used around Enid Scott and her children. Jared rummaged through the refrigerator for an apple, then headed back toward the stairs.

"Hey!" George's voice stopped him cold. "Just hold on a minute. What do you have there?"

"An apple." Jared held it up for him to see.

"That all?"

Jared nodded.

"I don't want to catch you drinking any beer around here, kid. You want to do that with your friends, away from home, fine. But not here. You got that?"

Jared felt a flush creep into his cheeks. "I don't drink beer."

George Paulsen's chin jerked up. "Don't get smart with me!"

"George, he can't!" His mother glanced hurriedly at Jared. "He can't drink alcohol of any kind. You know that. His medication doesn't mix with alcohol."

"Hell, you think for one minute that would stop him, Enid? You think it would stop any kid?" George drank from his own can, draining the last of its contents. "Medication, hell! Just another word for drugs. Kids do drugs and drink beer everywhere. Always have, always will. And you think your kid won't? Where'd you check your brain at, anyway? Christ almighty! You better let me do the thinking around here, okay? You just stick to cooking the meals and doing the laundry." He gave her a long look and shook his head. "Change the channel; I want to watch Leno. You can do that, can't you?"

Enid Scott looked down at her hands and didn't say anything. After a moment she picked up the remote and began to flick through the channels. Jared stared at her, stone-faced. He wanted her to tell George to get out of their house and stay out, but he knew she would never do that, that she couldn't make herself. He stood there feeling foolish, watching his mother be humiliated.

"Get on upstairs and stay there," George told him finally, waving him off with one hand. "Take your goddamn apple and get out of here. And don't be coming down here and bothering us again!"

Jared turned away, biting at his lip. Why did his mother stay with him? Sure, he gave her money and bought her stuff, and sometimes he was even halfway nice. But mostly he was bad-tempered and mean-spirited. Mostly he just hung out and mooched off them and found ways to make their lives miserable.

"You remember one thing, buster!" George called after him. "You don't ever get smart with me. You hear? Not ever!"

He kept going, not looking back, until he reached the top of the stairs, then stood breathing heavily in the hallway outside his room, rage and frustration boiling through him. He listened to the guttural sound of George Paulsen's voice, then to the silence that followed. His fists clenched. After a moment, tears flooded his eyes, and he stood crying silently in the dark.

Saturday night at Scrubby's was wild and raucous, the crowd standing three-deep at the bar, all the booths and tables filled, the dance floor packed, and the jukebox blaring. Boots were stomping, hands clapping, and voices lifting in song with Garth Brooks, Shania Twain, Travis Tritt, Wynonna Judd, and several dozen more of country-and-western's favorite sons and daughters. The mingled smells of sweat and cologne and beer permeated the air and smoke hung over everything in a hazy shroud, but at least the air-conditioning was keeping the heat at bay and no one seemed to mind. The workweek was done, the long awaited Fourth of July weekend was under way, and all was right with the world.

Seated in the small, two-person booth crammed into a niche between the storeroom door and the back wall, Derry Howe sat talking to Junior Elway, oblivious of all of it. He was telling Junior what he was going to do, how he had worked it all out the night before. He was explaining to Junior why it would take two of them, that Junior had to be a part of it. He was burning with the heat of his conviction; he was on fire with the certainty that when it was all said and done, the union could dictate its own terms to high-and-mighty MidCon. But his patience with Junior, who had the attention span of a gnat, was wearing thin. He hunched forward over the narrow table, trying to keep his voice down in case anyone should think to listen in, trying as well to keep Junior's mind on the business at hand instead of on Wanda Applegate, seated up at the bar, whom he'd been looking to hit on for the past two hours. Over and over he kept drawing Junior's eyes away from Wanda and back to him. Each time the eyes stayed focused for, oh, maybe thirty seconds before they wandered off again like cats in heat.

Finally he seized the front of Junior's shirt and dragged him halfway across the table, spilling beer and sending ashtrays and napkins flying. "You listen to me, goddamn it!" he screamed. "You listen to me when I talk to you!"

A few people turned to see what was happening, but when they saw the look on Derry Howe's face, they quickly went back to their own conversations. The music boomed out, the dancers yelled and clapped, and the confrontation in the tiny corner booth went mostly unnoticed.

"Okay, okay, I'm listening!" Junior snapped, jerking free. He was twenty pounds heavier and two inches taller, but there was fear in his eyes as he spoke the words. Damn well ought to be, Derry Howe thought with satisfaction.

"You heard anything I said so far, porkypine?" he sneered. "Anything at all?"

Junior ran his hand over his head, feeling the soft bristles of hair that were the product of this afternoon's visit to the Clip Joint, where he'd impulsively decided on a brush cut. He'd thought it would make him look tougher, he'd told Derry afterward. He'd thought it would make him look like a lean, mean cat. What it did was make him look like a jerk. Derry had begun ragging on him right away, calling him names. Porkypine. Cactus head. Nazi brain. Like that.

"I heard every damn thing you said!" Junior snapped furiously, sick and tired of Derry's attitude. "You want me to repeat it, smartass? Want to hear me stand up and shout it out loud maybe?"

If Derry Howe had been angry before, he was positively livid now. His expression changed, his eyes went flat and cold, and all the color drained out of his face. He looked at Junior as if a line had been crossed and Junior were no longer among the living.

Junior's mouth worked against the sudden dryness in his throat. "Look, I just meant . . ."

"Shut up," Derry Howe said softly. Even in the din, Junior heard the words plainly. "You just shut your mouth and listen. I ever hear you say something like that again, and you're history, bub. You believe me? Do you?"

Junior nodded, sitting there as still as stone, staring into the eyes of the man across from him, the man who had been his best friend until just a moment ago and who now was someone else entirely.

"This is too important for me to let you screw it up, you understand?" Derry Howe's voice was a soft hiss. "There's too much at stake for you to be making stupid statements or wiseass remarks. You with me on this or not? Answer me, damn it!"

Junior nodded. He'd never seen Derry like this. "Yeah, sure, course I am."

Derry Howe gave him a long, hard look. "All right, then. Here's the rest of it. Don't say nothing till I'm finished. Just listen. This is for keeps, Junior. We can't go pussyfooting about and hope the company will just come to their senses all on their own. My uncle and those other old farts might think that'll work, but they're whistling down a rat hole. They're old and they're worn-out and the company knows it. The company ain't about to negotiate. Never was. There's just you and me, bub. It's up to us. We have to bring them to the table, kicking and screaming if that's what it takes, but with them understanding they got to reopen the mill. Right? Okay. So we've got to have some leverage."

He leaned so close to Junior that his friend could smell the beer on his breath. "When this thing happens, it's got to be big enough that it will bring the national in. It ain't enough if it looks like an accident. It ain't enough, even if it looks like it's the company's fault. That won't do it. There's got to be casualties. Someone's got to be hurt, maybe even killed."

Junior stared openmouthed, then quickly shook his head. "Man, this is crazy . . ."

"Crazy because it gets the job done?" Derry snapped. "Crazy because it just might work? Hell, because it *will* work? Every war has its sacrifices, Junior. And this is a war, don't kid yourself. It's a war we're going to win. But that won't happen if the company isn't held accountable for something they can't talk their way out of. It won't happen if it don't draw the national's attention."

"But you can't just . . . You can't . . ."

"Go on, say it, Junior," Derry hissed derisively.

"Kill someone, damn it!"

"No? Why not? Why the hell not?"

He could, of course. He'd already decided it, in fact. He would do it because it was necessary. He would do it because it was a war, just like he'd said, and in a war, people got killed. He'd talked it over with himself the day before, after he'd come up with the accident idea. It was almost like having someone sitting there with him, having a conversation with a trusted friend, talking it through, reasoning it out. It all made perfect sense. He was certain of it. He was positive.

Junior kept shaking his head. "Damn it, Derry, you're talking about murder!"

"No, I ain't. Don't use that word. It ain't murder if it's a war. This is just—what do you call it?—a sacrifice for the greater good. For the community, for you and me and all the rest. You can see that, can't you?"

Junior nodded doubtfully, still trying to come to terms with the idea. "All right, okay, it's a war. So that's different. And it's gonna be an accident, right? Just part of something else that happens?" He wiped his mouth with the back of his hand, then looked carefully at Derry once more. "But it's not gonna be deliberate, is it?"

Derry Howe's expression did not change. Junior was such a dork. He forced himself to smile. "Course not. It's gonna be an accident. When there's an accident, people get hurt. It will be a real tragedy when it happens. It will make everyone feel bad, but particularly the company, because it will be the company's fault."

He reached out, fastened his hand around the back of Junior's neck, and pulled his friend's tensed face right up against his own. "Just you remember that, Junior," he whispered. "It won't be our fault. It will be the company's fault. High-and-mighty MidCon's fault." He squeezed Junior's neck roughly. "They'll crawl over broken glass to get back to the bargaining table then. They'll beg to get back. Hide and watch, Junior. Hide and watch."

Junior Elway reached for what was left of his beer.

Nest stayed in the swing another few minutes, lost in her thoughts of John Ross, then climbed out and stood looking off into the blackness of the park. She wondered if the demon he hunted was hiding there. She wondered if it preferred the dark, twisting caves where the feeders concealed themselves to the lighted houses of the humans it preyed upon. Miss Minx crept by, stalking something Nest could not see. She watched the cat move soundlessly through the dark, silken and deadly in its pursuit, and she had a sudden sense of what it would be like to be hunted like that.

She moved toward the house, thinking to go in, knowing she would have only an hour or two of sleep before it was time to meet Two Bears at the Sinnissippi burial mounds. She wondered what Two Bears knew about all this. Did he know of the demon and John Ross and of the war they fought? Did he know of the Word and the Void? Was he aware of the existence of this other world, of its proximity to the human world, and of the ties that bound the two? She felt certain he knew a great deal he wasn't telling her, much like John Ross. She wondered if they shared a common purpose in coming to Hopewell, perhaps a purpose no one else recognized, one tied to both the spirits of the Sinnissippi and the coming of the demon. She sighed and shook her head. It was all speculation, but speculation was all she had.

She moved up to the screen door, then slowed when she heard voices coming from the kitchen. Her grandparents were arguing. She hesitated, then moved down the side of the house to the window that opened above the sink to eavesdrop. It wasn't something she normally did, but she'd heard John Ross's name, and she was curious to know if he was the cause of the argument. She stood silent and unmoving in the shadows, listening.

"He seems like a fine young man to me," her grandfather was saying. He was leaning against the counter at the sink, his back to the window. Nest could see his shadow in a pool of light thrown on the ground. "He was pleasant and straightforward when he came up to speak to me at Josie's. He didn't ask for a thing. It was my idea to invite him to dinner."

"You're too trusting, Robert," her grandmother replied. "You always have been."

"He's given us no reason to be anything else."

"Don't you think it's a bit odd, him showing up like this, unannounced, uninvited, just to see us, to talk about a girl he hasn't seen in over fifteen, sixteen years? A girl who's been dead all that time and never a word from him? Do you remember Caitlin ever saying anything about him, ever even mentioning his name?"

Old Bob sipped from his coffee cup, thinking. "No, but that doesn't mean she didn't know him."

"It doesn't mean he was a friend, either." Nest could picture Gran sitting at the kitchen table, bourbon and water in hand, smoking her cigarette. "I didn't like the way he took to Nest."

"Oh, for God's sake, Evelyn."

"Don't invoke God for my sake, Robert!" Gran shot back. "Use the brain he gave you instead! Suppose, for a minute, John Ross is not who he claims. Suppose he's someone else altogether."

"Someone else? Who?"

"Him, that's who."

There was the sound of ice cubes tinkling in an empty glass and of a fresh cigarette being lit, then silence. Nest watched her grandfather place his coffee cup on the counter, saw his leonine head lower, heard him sigh.

"He's gone, Evelyn. He's not coming back. Ever."

Her grandmother pushed back her chair and rose. Nest could hear her move to the counter and pour herself a drink. "Oh, he's coming, all right, Robert. He's coming. I've known it from the first, from the moment Caitlin died and he disappeared. I've always known it."

"Why would he do that?" Old Bob's voice sounded uneasy. "Evelyn, you can't be serious."

Nest stood transfixed in the heat and the dark, unable to turn away. They were talking about her father.

"He wants Nest," Gran said quietly. She drew on the cigarette and took a long swallow of the drink. Nest heard each sound clearly in the pause between her grandmother's words. "He's always wanted her."

"Nest? Why would he want Nest? Especially after all this time?"

"Because she's his, Robert. Because she belongs to him, and he doesn't give anything up this side of the grave. Don't you know that by now? After Caitlin, don't you know that?"

There was another pause, and then some sounds that Nest could not identify, muttered words perhaps, grumbling. Her grandfather straightened at the window.

"It's been fifteen years, but I remember him well enough." Old Bob spoke softly, but distinctly. "John Ross doesn't look anything like him, Evelyn. They're not the same man."

Gran gave a quick, harsh laugh. "Really, Robert. Sometimes you appall me. Doesn't look like him? You think for a minute that man couldn't change his looks if there was reason enough to do so? You think he couldn't look like anyone he wanted to? Don't you realize what he is?"

"Evelyn, don't start."

"Sometimes you're a fool, Robert," Gran declared sharply. "If you want to go on pretending that I'm a crazy old woman who imagines things that aren't there, that's fine. If you want to pretend there's no feeders in the park, that's fine, too. But there's some things you can't wish away, and he's one of them. You saw what he was. You saw what he did to Caitlin. I wouldn't put anything past him. He's coming here, coming for Nest, and when he does he won't be stupid enough to look the same as he did when he left. You do what you want, Robert, but I plan to be ready for him."

The kitchen was silent again. Nest waited, straining to hear.

"I notice you didn't worry about letting him take her into the park," Old Bob said finally.

Gran didn't say anything. Nest could hear the sound of her glass being raised and lowered.

"So maybe there's not as much to be afraid of as you'd like me to believe. Maybe you're not sure who John Ross is either."

"Maybe," Gran said softly.

"I invited him to come to church tomorrow morning," Old Bob went on deliberately. "I asked him to sit with us. Will you be coming?"

There was a pause. "I don't expect so," Gran replied.

Nest took a long, slow breath. Her grandfather moved away from the window. "I invited him to picnic with us in the park afterward, too. So we could talk some more." Her grandfather cleared his throat. "I like him, Evelyn. I think Nest likes him. I don't think there's any reason to be scared of him."

"You will pardon me if I reserve my opinion on that?" Gran replied after a moment. "That way, we won't all be caught by surprise." She laughed softly. "Spare me that look. And don't ask me if I plan to have another drink either, because I do. You go on to bed, Robert. I'll be just fine by myself. Have been for a long time. Go on."

Nest heard her grandfather move away wordlessly. She stayed where she was for a moment longer, staring up at the empty, lighted kitchen window, listening to the silence. Then she slipped back through the shadows like the ghost of the child she had grown out of being.

CHAPTER 16

Nest did not sleep when she finally reached her bedroom, but lay awake in the dark staring up at the ceiling and listening to the raucous hum of the locusts through the screen window. The air felt thick and damp with the July heat, and even the whirling blades of the big floor fan did little to give relief. She lay atop her covers in her running shorts and T-shirt, waiting for midnight and her rendezvous with Two Bears. The bedroom door stood open; the hallway beyond was silent and dark. Gran might have gone to bed, but Nest could not be certain. She imagined her grandmother sitting alone at the kitchen table in the soft, tree-filtered light of moon and stars, smoking her cigarettes, drinking her bourbon, and reflecting on the secrets she hid.

Nest watched those secrets dance as shadows on her ceiling.

Was John Ross her father? If he was, why had he abandoned her?

The questions repeated themselves over and over in her mind, suspended in time and wrapped in chilly, imperious solitude. They whispered to her, haunting and insidious.

If John Ross was her father, why was Gran so bitter toward him? Why was she so mistrustful of his motives? What was it that her father had done?

She closed her eyes, as if the answers might better be found in darkness. She stilled herself against the beating of her heart, against the pulse of her blood as it raced through her veins, but she could find no peace.

Why was her father such an enigmatic figure, a shadow

barely recognizable as being a part of her life? Why did she know so little about him?

Outside an owl hooted softly, and Nest wondered if Daniel was calling to her. He did that sometimes, reaching out to her from the dark, a gesture she did not fully understand. But she did not rise to look this night, locked in her struggle to understand the doubts and confusion that beset her at every turn. Like a Midwest thunderstorm building out on the plains and working its way east, dark and forbidding and filled with power, a revelation approached. She could feel it, could taste it like rain and smell it like electricity in the air. The increasing boldness of the feeders, the deterioration of the maentwrog's prison, and the coming of John Ross and the demon signaled a shift in the balance of things. In a way Nest did not yet understand, it was all tied to her. She could sense that much from the time she had spent with John Ross. It was in the words he had used and the secrets he had shared. He had taken her into his confidence because she was directly involved. The challenge she faced now, on thinking it through, was in persuading him to tell her why.

When it was nearing midnight, the time reflected by the luminous green numbers on her digital clock, she rose and walked to her open bedroom door and stood listening. The house was dark save for the single lamp that Gran always left burning in the front entry. Nest moved back across the room to turn down the bed and place the extra pillows under the sheet to make it look like she was sleeping. Then she removed the window screen from its fastenings and slipped through, put the screen back in place, and turned toward the park.

In the distance a dog barked, the sound piercing and clear in the deep night silence, and Nest was reminded suddenly of Riley. Riley was the last dog they had owned. A black lab with big feet, sad eyes, and a gentle disposition, he came to her as a puppy, given to her by her grandfather on her third birthday. She had loved Riley from the moment he had bounded into her arms, all rough pads and wet tongue, big ears and squirming body. She had named him Riley because she thought he just looked like a Riley, even though she had never actually known one. Riley had been her dog all through growing up, there for her when she left for school, waiting for her when she came home, with her when she went down the road to visit her friends, at her side when she slipped into the park. He was there when she saw the feeders, Pick, and even Wraith, although he did not seem to see any of them as she did. She was almost twelve when he developed a tumor in his lungs. Inoperable, she was told. She went with her grandfather to have her faithful friend and companion put down. She stood watching, dry-eyed and stoic, as the vet injected Riley and his sleek body stiffened and his soft eyes fixed. She did not cry until later, but then she did not think she would ever stop.

What she remembered most, however, was Gran's reaction. Gran had stayed behind and cried alone; Nest could tell she had cried from her red eyes and the wrinkled Kleenex wads in the waste basket next to the kitchen table where she had begun to take up permanent residence with her bourbon and her cigarettes. Gran said nothing on their return, but at dinner that night she announced in a tone of voice that brooked no argument that they had acquired their last dog. Cats were sufficient. Cats could look after themselves. Dogs were too dependent, required too much, and stole away your heart. Ostensibly, she was speaking of Riley, but Nest had been pretty certain that in an odd way she was speaking of Caitlin as well.

She stood now for a moment in the darkness of the summer night, remembering. She missed Riley more than she could say. She had never told Gran this. She knew it was something Gran did not want to hear, that it would only suggest to her how much she, in turn, missed Caitlin.

Nest glanced at the silent house, thinking Gran might appear, that she might somehow know what Nest was about. But there was no movement and no sound from within. Nest turned away once more and crept through the shadows of the backyard, eyes searching. Miss Minx slunk from beneath a big oak, low to the ground and furtive. Another cat, a strange striped one, followed. Out in the park, beyond the wall of the hedge, moonlight bathed the open ball fields and play areas with silver brightness. It was her secret world, Nest thought, smiling at the idea. Her secret world, belonging only to her. No one knew it as she did, not even Gran, for whom it was now distant and foreign. Nest wondered if it would become that way for her someday, if by growing she would lose her child's world as she would lose her childhood, that this was the price you paid for becoming an adult. There was that gap between adults and children that reserved to each secrets that were hidden from the other. When you were old enough, you became privy to the secrets that belonged only to adults and lost in turn those that belonged only to children. You did not ever gain all of one or lose all of the other; of each, some you kept and some you never gained. That was the way it worked. Gran had told her that almost a year ago, when Nest had felt her child's body first begin its slow change to a woman's. Gran had told her that life never gave you everything or took everything away.

She slipped through the gap in the hedgerow, and Pick dropped onto her shoulder with an irritated grunt.

"It's about time! What took you so long? Midnight's the appointed time, in case you've forgotten! Criminy!"

She kept her eyes directed forward. "Why are you so angry?"

"Angry? I'm not angry! What makes you think I'm angry?"

"You sound angry."

"I sound the way I always do!"

"Well, you always sound angry. Tonight, especially." She felt him squirming on her shoulder, leaves and twigs rustling, settling into place. "Tell me something about my father."

He spit like a cat. "Your father? What are you talking about?"

"I want to know something about my father."

"Well, I don't know anything about your father! I've told you that! Go ask your grandmother!"

She glanced down at him, riding her shoulder in sullen defiance. "Why is it that no one ever wants to talk about my father?

Why is it that no one ever wants to tell me anything about him?"

Pick kicked at her shoulder, exasperated. "It's rather hard to talk about someone you don't know, so that might explain my problem with talking to you about your father! Are you having a problem with your hearing, too?"

She didn't answer. Instead, she broke into a fast trot, jogging swiftly down the service road and past the nearest backstop, then cutting across the ball diamond toward the cliffs and the river. The humid night air whipped past her face as her feet flew across the newly mowed grass. She ran as if she were being chased, arms and legs churning, chest expanding and contracting with deep, regular breaths, blood racing through her in a hot pulse. Pick gave a surprised gasp and hung on to her T-shirt to keep from falling off. Nest could hear him muttering as she ran, his voice swept away by the rush of the air whipping past her ears. She disappeared into herself, into the motion of her arms and legs, into the pounding of her heart. She covered the open ground of the ball fields and the playgrounds, crossed the main roadway, hurdled the chain dividers, and darted into the trees that fronted the burial mounds. She ran with fury and discontent, thinking suddenly that she might not stop, that she might just keep on going, running through the park and beyond, running until there was nowhere left to go.

But she didn't. She reached the picnic benches across the road from the burial mounds and slowed, winded and shot through with the heat of her exertion, but calm again as well, distanced momentarily from her frustration and doubt. Pick was yapping at her like a small, angry dog, but she ignored him, looking about for Two Bears and the spirits of the dead Sinnissippi. She glanced down at her wristwatch. It was almost midnight, and he was nowhere in sight. The burial mounds were dark and silent against the starry backdrop of the southern horizon where moonlight spilled from the heavens. The park was empty-feeling and still. Nothing moved or showed itself. Even the feeders were nowhere to be seen.

A trace of wood smoke wafted on the still air, pungent and invisible.

"Where is he?" she asked softly, turning slowly in the humid dark, eyes flicking left and right, heart pounding.

"Here, little bird's Nest," his familiar voice answered, and she jumped at the sound of it.

He was standing right in front of her, so close she might have reached out to touch him if she had wished to do so. He had materialized out of nowhere, out of the heat and the night, out of the ether. He was stripped to the waist, to his baggy pants and worn army boots, and he had painted his face, arms, and chest in a series of intricate black stripes. His long hair was still braided, but now a series of feathers hung from it. If he had seemed big to her before, he looked huge now, the coppery skin of his massive chest and arms gleaming behind the bars of paint, his blunt features chiseled by shadows and light.

"So you've come," he said softly, looking down at her with curious eyes. "And you've brought your shy little friend."

"This is Pick." She introduced the sylvan, who was sitting up straight on her shoulder, eyeing the big man.

"Charmed," Pick snapped, sounding anything but. "How come you can see me when no one else can?"

The smile flashed briefly on Two Bears' face. "Indian magic." He looked at Nest. "Are you ready?"

She took a deep breath. "I don't know. What's going to happen?"

"What I have told you will happen. I will summon the spirits of the Sinnissippi and they will appear. Maybe they will speak with us. Maybe not."

She nodded. "Is that why you're dressed like that?"

He looked down at himself. "Like this? Oh, I see. You're afraid I might be wearing war paint, that I might be preparing to ride out into the night and collect a few paleface scalps."

She gave him a reproving frown. "I was just asking."

"I dress like this because I will dance with the spirits if they let me. I will become for a few brief moments one with them." He paused. "Would you like to join me?"

She considered the possibility of dancing with the dead Sinnissippi. "I don't know. Can I ask you something, O'olish Amaneh?"

He smiled anew on hearing his Indian name. "You can ask me anything."

"Do you think the spirits would tell me who my father is if I asked them? Do you think they would tell me something like that?"

He shook his head. "You cannot ask them anything, They do not respond to questions or even to voices. They respond to what is in your heart. They might tell you of your father, but it would have to be their choice. Do you understand?"

She nodded, suddenly nervous at the prospect of discovering the answer to this dark secret. "Do I have to do anything?"

He shook his head once more. "Nothing. Just come with me."

They crossed to a small iron hibachi that sat next to a picnic table. A gathering of embers, the source of the wood smoke, glowed red within. Two Bears removed a long, intricately carved pipe from the top of the picnic table, checked to see that the contents within its charred bowl were tightly packed, then dipped the bowl to the embers, put the other end of the pipe in his mouth, and puffed slowly to light it. The contents of the bowl ignited and gleamed, and smoke curled into the air.

"Peace pipe," he declared, removing it from his lips and winking at her. He puffed on it some more, drawing the smoke deep into his lungs. Then he passed the pipe to her. "Now you. Just a few puffs."

She took the pipe reluctantly. "What's in it?" she asked.

"Herbs and grasses. They won't harm you. Smoking the pipe is ritual, nothing more. It eases the passage of the spirits from their resting place into our world. It makes us more accessible."

She sniffed at the contents of the bowl and grimaced. The night around her was deep and still, and it felt as if she were all alone in it with the Indian. "I don't know."

"Just take a few puffs. You don't have to draw it into your lungs." He paused. "Don't be frightened. You have Mr. Pick to watch over you."

She considered the pipe a moment longer, then put it to her lips and drew in the smoke. She took several quick puffs, wrinkled her nose, and passed the pipe back to Two Bears. "Yuck."

Two Bears nodded. "It's an acquired taste." He inhaled the pungent smoke, then carefully placed the pipe across the rim of the hibachi. "There."

Then he moved out onto the open grass and seated himself cross-legged facing the burial mounds. Nest joined him, sitting cross-legged as well, positioning herself next to him in the dark. Pick still rode her shoulder, but he had gone strangely silent. She glanced down at him, but he was staring out into the night, oblivious of her. She let him be. Overhead, the sky was crosshatched by the limbs of the trees, their dappled shadows cast earthward in a tangled net by the bright moonlight. Nest waited patiently, saying nothing, losing herself in the silence.

Two Bears began to chant, the words coming in a soft, steady cadence. The words were foreign to Nest, and she thought they must be Indian, probably Sinnissippi. She did not look at Two Bears, but looked instead where he looked, out over the roadway to the burial mounds, out into the night. Pick sat frozen on her shoulder, become momentarily a part of her, as quiet as she had ever seen him. She felt a twinge of fear, wondering suddenly if what she was doing was somehow more than she believed, if it would lead to a darker result than she anticipated.

Two Bears continued to chant, his deep voice steady and toneless. Nest felt the first stirrings of doubt mingle with her uneasiness. Nothing was happening; maybe nothing would.

Then a wind blew off the river, cool and unexpected, carrying with it the smell of things forgotten since childhood—of her grandmother's kitchen, of her sandbox, of Riley, of her cedar toy chest, of Wisconsin's lakes in summer. Nest started in surprise. The wind brushed past her and was gone. In the stillness that followed, she felt the hair on the back of her neck prickle.

Small glimmerings of light appeared at the edges of the burial mounds, rising up into the night, flickering and fading again, moving with rhythmic grace against the darkness. At first they were nothing, simply bright movements that lacked definition. Slowly they began to take shape. Arms and legs appeared, then bodies and heads. Nest felt her throat tighten and her mouth grow dry. She leaned forward, peering expectantly, trying to make certain of what she was seeing. On her shoulder, she heard Pick utter a faint, surprised exclamation.

Then up from the darkness rose the Sinnissippi, their spirits taking form, coming back into a shadowy semblance of their lost bodies. They lifted free of the earth to hang upon the air, twisting and turning in small arcs. They were dancing, Nest could see, but not in the fashion she had expected, not as Indians did in the television shows and movies she had seen, rising and falling in that familiar choppy motion, but in another way altogether. Their movements were more balletic, more sinuous, and they danced free of one another, as if each had a story to tell, each a different tale. Nest watched, awed by the beauty of it. After a time, she felt the dance begin to draw her in. She thought she could sense something of what the dancers were trying to convey. She felt herself swaying with them, heard the sounds of their breathing, smelled the sweat of their bodies. They were ghosts, she knew, but they were real, too. She wanted to call out to them, to make them turn and look at her, to acknowledge her presence. But she stayed silent.

Suddenly Two Bears was on his feet and striding forward. He reached the dancers and joined in their dance, his big, powerful body swaying and weaving as smoothly as their own. Nest marveled at the ease with which he moved, smiled at his grace. She felt the heat of his body fill her own, as if his pulse had mingled with hers. She watched in shock, then with a glimmer of terror, as his flesh-and-blood body began to fade into the darkness and turn as ghostly as the spirits of the dead Sinnissippi. There were drums now, their booming rising out of the night—or maybe the sounds were only in her mind, the rhythm of her heartbeat. She watched Two Bears become one with the dead, watched him become as they were, translucent and ephemeral, ghostly and unreal. She stared transfixed as he danced on, the sound of the drums heightening, the movements of the dancers quickening. She felt the summer's heat flood through her, causing her to blink against sudden flashes of crimson and gold.

Then she was on her feet as well, dancing with Two Bears, moving through the ghosts of the Sinnissippi. She did not feel herself rise or walk to him, did not know how it came to pass, but suddenly she was there among the Indian spirits. She floated as they did, not touching the earth, suspended on the night air, caught between life and death. She heard herself cry out with joy and hope. She danced with wild abandon and frantic need, whirling and twisting, reaching for something beyond what she could see, reaching past memories, past her own life, past all she knew . . .

Like a fever dream, the vision appears to her then. It comes out of nowhere, filling her mind with bright colors and movement. She is in another part of the park, a part she does not recognize. It is night, black and clouded, empty of moon and stars, a devil's night filled with pitch. Dark figures run through the trees, hunched over, lithe and supple. Feeders, she sees, dozens of them, their yellow eyes gleaming in the black. She feels her stomach knot with the realization that they are certain to see her. Across the grassy stretches and along the pathways they bound, swift and certain. A woman leads them, young and strong, her shadowed face smiling and wild-eyed, her long, dark hair streaming out behind her. Nest blinks against the sight—a human at play with feeders, running with them, unafraid. The woman spins and wheels, and everywhere she goes, the feeders chase after her. She teases and taunts them, and it is clear that they are infatuated by her. Nest stands spellbound within the darkened park, staring in disbelief as the woman rushes toward her, all wicked smiles and laughter. She looks into the woman's eyes, and sees there the lines that have been crossed and the taboos that have been broken. She sees the woman's life laid bare, sees her soul unfettered and her heart unafraid. She will dare anything, this woman, and has. She will not be cowed or chastened; she will not be made ashamed.

She dashes into Nest's arms, draws her close, and holds her tight. Nest recoils, then stares in shock. She knows this woman. She recognizes her face. She has seen her face, just

*as it is now, in a collection of framed photographs that sits
upon the mantel over the fireplace in the living room. It is
Caitlin Anne Freemark. It is her mother.*

*And yet it isn't. Not quite. Something is amiss. It is almost
her mother, but it is someone else, too. Nest gasps in shock, not
quite certain what she is seeing. The woman breaks free, her
face suddenly filled with regret and despair. Behind her, barely
visible in the darkness, a man appears. He materializes suddenly, and the feeders, who are clustered all about the woman,
give way instantly at his approach. Nest tries to see his face,
but cannot. The woman sees him and hisses in anger and frustration. Then she flees into the night, racing away shadow-
quick with the feeders bounding in pursuit, and is gone.*

Nest blinked anew against the darkness and the sudden
bright pain that stabbed her eyes. Images whirled and faded,
and her vision cleared. She was sitting once more on the
grass, cross-legged in the darkness, her hands clasped before
her as if in prayer. Two Bears was seated next to her, his eyes
closed, his chiseled body still. In the distance, the burial
mounds rose silent and empty of life. No lights moved across
the grassy slopes; no warriors danced on the air above. The
ghosts of the Sinnissippi had gone.

Two Bears opened his eyes and stared out into the darkness, calm and distanced. Nest seized his arm.

"Did you see her?" she asked, unable to keep the anguish
from her voice.

The big man shook his head. His painted copper face was
bathed in sweat, and his brow was furrowed. "I did not share
your vision, little bird's Nest. Can you tell me of it?"

She tried to speak, to say the words, and found she could
not. She shook her head slowly, feeling paralyzed, her skin
hot and prickly, her face flushed with shame and confusion.

He nodded. "Sometimes it is better not to speak of what
we see in our dreams." He took her hand in his own and held
it. "Sometimes our dreams belong only to us."

"Did it really happen?" she asked softly. "Did the Sinnissippi come? Did we dance with them?"

He smiled faintly. "Ask your little friend when you find him again."

Pick. Nest had forgotten him. She glanced down at her shoulder, but the sylvan was gone.

"I learned many things tonight, little bird's Nest," Two Bears told her quietly, regaining her attention. "I was told of the fate of the Sinnissippi, my people. I was shown their story." He shook his head. "But it is much more complicated than I thought, and I cannot yet find the words to explain it, even to myself. I have the images safely stored"—he touched his forehead—"but they are jumbled and vague, and they need time to reveal themselves." His brow furrowed. "This much I know. The destruction of a people does not come easily or directly, but from a complex scheme of events and circumstances, and that, in part, is why it can happen. Because we lack the foresight to prevent it. Because we do not guard sufficiently against it. Because we do not truly understand it. Because we are, in some part, at least, the enemy we fear."

She squeezed his hand. "I don't think I learned anything. Nothing of what might destroy us. Nothing of what threatens. Nothing of Hopewell or anywhere else. Just . . ." She shook her head.

Two Bears rose, pulling her up with him, lifting her from the ground as if she were as light as a feather. The black paint gleamed on his face. "Maybe you were shown more than you realize. Maybe you need to give it more time, like me."

She nodded. "Maybe."

They stood facing each other in awkward silence, contemplating what they knew and what they didn't. Finally, Nest said, "Will you come back tomorrow night and summon the spirits of the Sinnissippi again?"

Two Bears shook his head. "No. I am leaving now."

"But maybe the spirits . . ."

"The spirits appeared, and I danced with them. They told me what they wished. There is nothing more for me to do."

Nest took a deep breath. She wanted him to stay for her. She found comfort in his presence, in his voice, in the strength of his convictions. "Maybe you could stay until after the Fourth. Just another few days."

He shook his head. "There is no reason. This is not my home, and I do not belong here."

He walked to the hibachi and retrieved his pipe. He knocked the contents of the bowl into the hibachi, then stuck the pipe in his belt. He took a cloth and carefully wiped the black paint from his face and arms and chest, then slipped into his torn army field jacket. He retrieved his backpack and bedroll from the darkness and strapped them on. Nest stood watching, unable to think of anything to say, watching as he transformed back into the man he had been when she had first encountered him, ragged and worn and shabby, another nomad come off the nation's highways.

"This could be your home," she said finally, her voice taking on an urgency she could not conceal.

He walked over to her and stared into her eyes. "Speak my name," he commanded softly.

"O'olish Amaneh."

"And your own."

"Nest Freemark."

He nodded. "Names of power. But yours is the stronger, little bird's Nest. Yours is the one with true magic. There is nothing more that I can do for you. What remains to be done, you must do for yourself. I came to speak with the dead of my people, and I have done so. I saw that it would help you to be there with me, and so I asked you to attend. What there was that I could offer, I have given. Now you must take what you have gained and put it to good use. You do not need me for that."

She stood staring at him in the humid dark, at his strong, blunt features, at the implacable certainty mirrored in his eyes. "I'm afraid," she said.

"Yes," he agreed. "But fear is a fire to temper courage and resolve. Use it so. Speak my name once more."

She swallowed. "O'olish Amaneh."

"Yes. Say it often when I am gone, so that I will not be forgotten."

She nodded.

"Good-bye, little bird's Nest," he whispered.

Then he turned and walked away.

Nest stood watching after him until he was out of sight. She could see him until he reached the edge of the park, and then he seemed to fade into the darkness. She thought more than once to call him back or to run after him, but she knew he would not want that. She felt drained and worn, emptied of emotion and strength alike, and she found herself wondering if she would ever see Two Bears again.

"O'olish Amaneh," she whispered.

She started back across the park, wondering anew what had become of Pick. One moment he had been sitting on her shoulder, all quiet and absorbed in the spirit dance, and the next he had been gone. What had happened? She trudged through the dark, moving toward home and bed, starting to be sleepy now in spite of all that had happened. She tried to make sense of the vision she had seen of the young woman and the feeders and the shadowy figure who accompanied them, but failed. She tried to draw something useful from what Two Bears had told her and failed there, as well. Everything seemed to confuse her, one question leading to another, none of them leading to the answers she sought.

In the shadows about her, a handful of feeders kept pace, as if predators waiting for their prey to falter. They watched her with their steady, implacable gaze, and she could feel the weight of their hunger. They did not stalk her, she knew; they simply watched. Usually, their presence didn't bother her. Tonight she felt unnerved.

She was out of the park and walking through her backyard toward the house when she realized suddenly what was amiss about the young woman in her vision. She stopped where she was and stared wide-eyed into the darkness, feeling the crawl of her skin turn to dryness in her throat. She knew the woman, of course. She had been right about that. And she had seen the woman's photograph on the fireplace mantel, too. But the photograph wasn't of her mother. It was of another woman, one who had been young a long time ago, before Nest or her mother were even born.

The photograph was of Gran.

SUNDAY, JULY 3

CHAPTER 17

It was approaching seven when Nest awoke the following morning, and the sun had already been up for an hour and a half. She had slept poorly for most of the night, haunted by the vision of Gran, plagued by questions and suspicions and doubts, and she did not sleep soundly until almost sunrise. Bright sunlight and birdsong woke her, and she could tell at once that it was going to be another hot, steamy July day. The air from the fan was warm and stale, and through her open window she could see the leaves of the big oaks hanging limp and unmoving. She lay motionless beneath the sheet for a time, staring up at the ceiling, trying to pretend that last night hadn't happened. She had been so eager to watch the dance of the spirits of the Sinnissippi, so anxious to learn what the spirits would tell her of the future. But she had been shown nothing of the future. Instead, she had been given a strange, almost frightening glimpse of the past. She felt cheated and angry. She felt betrayed. She told herself she would have been better off if she had never met Two Bears.

O'olish Amaneh.

But after a while her anger cooled, and she began to consider the possibility that what she had been shown was more important than she realized. Two Bears had hinted that she would need time to understand the vision, to come to grips with what it meant in her own life. She stared at the ceiling some more, trying to make sense of the shadows cast there by the sun, superimposing her own images, willing them to come to life so that they might speak to her.

Finally she rose and went into the bathroom, stopping at the mirror to look at herself, to see if she had changed in some way. But she saw only the face she always saw when she looked at herself, and nothing of secrets revealed. She sighed disconsolately, stripped off her sleep shirt, and stepped into the shower. She let cold water wash over her hot skin, let it cool her until she was chilled, then stepped out and dried. She dressed for church, knowing her grandfather would be expecting her to go, slipping into a simple print dress and her favorite low heels, and went down to breakfast. She passed through the living room long enough to check the pictures on the mantel. Sure enough, there was Gran, looking just as she had in the vision last night, her face young, her eyes reckless and challenging as they peered out from the scrolled iron frame.

She ate her breakfast without saying much, feeling awkward and uncomfortable in her grandmother's presence. She should speak to Gran of the vision, but she didn't know how. What could she say? Should she tell Gran what the vision had revealed or take a more circumspect approach and ask about her youth, about whether she had ever run with the feeders? And what did that mean, anyway? What did it mean when you ran with the feeders as Gran had done in the vision? Feeders were to be avoided; that was what Nest had been taught from the time she was little. Pick had warned her. Gran had warned her. So what did it mean that she was forbidden from doing something Gran had done?

And what, she wondered suddenly, had her mother done when she was a child? What did any of this have to do with her?

"You should eat something, Evelyn," her grandfather said quietly, breaking the momentary silence.

Gran was drinking her vodka and orange juice and smoking her cigarettes. There was no food in front of her. "I ate some toast earlier," the old woman responded distantly. Her eyes were directed out the window again, toward the park. "Just eat your own; don't worry about me."

Nest watched her grandfather shake his head and finish the last of his coffee. "Ready, Nest?"

She nodded and rose, gathering her dishes to carry to the

sink. "Leave them," Gran called after her. "I'll clean up while you're gone."

"Sure you don't want to come?" Old Bob pressed gently. "It would be good for you."

Gran gave him a sideways look. "It would be good for the church gossips, maybe. You go on. I'll work on the picnic lunch." She paused long enough to take a hard drag on her cigarette. "You might want to give some more thought to inviting that boy, Robert. He's not what you think."

Her meaning was plain. Nest placed her dishes in the sink and waited for someone to speak. When no one did, she left the room and went down the hall to brush her teeth and give her hair a final comb. In the kitchen, she could hear her grandparents' voices, low and deliberate, arguing over John Ross.

She rode downtown in the pickup with her grandfather, neither of them saying anything, the windows rolled down so that Old Bob could smell the trees and flowers. It was just after ten o'clock, so the Illinois heat was not yet unbearable and there was still a hint of night's cool. Traffic on Lincoln Highway was light, and the parking lot at the supermarket as they turned off Sinnissippi Road was mostly empty. Nest breathed the summer air and looked down at her hands. She felt oddly disconnected from everything, as if she had been taken away from the home and the people she had always known and relocated to another part of the country. She felt she should be doing something— she had already been enlisted in the fight against the demon— but she had no idea where she ought to begin.

She looked at her reflection in the windshield and wondered if she really was only fourteen or if she was in fact much older and had missed some crucial part of her life while she slept.

Old Bob parked the pickup on Second Avenue in front of Kelly's Furniture directly opposite the First Congregational Church. They got out and crossed the street, stopping momentarily on the sidewalk to say hello to a handful of others on their way inside. Effusive compliments were extended to Nest on her achievements in running, sprinkled with comments concerning the depth of her competition, the state of her health, and the nature of the town's expectations for her. Nest smiled and nodded dutifully, suffering it all as graciously as she could, all the while looking around without success for John Ross.

Then they were inside the church, passing through wide, double doors into a vestibule that wrapped the sanctuary on two sides. It was cool and dark, the intense heat kept at bay by central air, the burning sunlight filtered by ribbons of stained glass. Greeters stood at each door, waiting to shake hands with those entering, and to pin flowers on the men's coats and the women's dresses. An elderly couple welcomed Nest and her grandfather, and the woman asked after Evelyn. An usher took them to a pew about halfway down on the left side of the sanctuary. The church was filling rapidly, and more than half the pews were occupied already. Nest and her grandfather sat on the aisle, holding their programs and glancing around in the hushed, cool gloom. The cathedral ceiling arched darkly overhead, its wooden beams gleaming. Organ music played softly, and the candles on the altar had already been lit by the acolytes. Nest looked again for John Ross, but he was nowhere to be seen. He wasn't coming, she thought, disappointed. But, after all, why would he?

Robert Heppler was sitting with his parents on the other side of the sanctuary near the back. The Hepplers liked the Congregational Church because it wasn't mired in dogma (this from Robert, purportedly quoting his father) and it embraced a larger span of life choices and secular attitudes. Robert said this was very different from being Catholic. Robert gave Nest a brief wave, and she gave him one back. She saw one of her grandfather's steel-mill friends, Mr. Michaelson, sitting with his wife several rows in front of the Hepplers.

The choir filed in and took their seats in the loft beside the pulpit, and everyone opened their programs and began studying the order of events and their hymnals.

Then John Ross appeared at the far side of the chamber, limping through the doorway with the aid of his black staff. He wore a fresh shirt, slacks, and a tie, and his long hair was carefully combed and tied back. He looked ill at ease and unsure of himself. Nest tried and failed to get his attention. Ross followed the usher down the aisle to a mostly empty row behind the Michaelsons and eased himself gingerly into place.

Now the choir rose, and the organist played a brief introduction. The minister appeared through a side door on the dais and walked to the pulpit. Ralph Emery was round and short and sort of strange-looking, with large ears and heavy jowls, but he was kind and funny and he was well known for giving thought-provoking sermons. He stood now in his black robes looking out over the congregation as if trying to decide whether to proceed. Then he asked the congregation to bow their heads, and he gave a brief invocation. When he was finished, he asked everyone to rise and turn to hymn number 236. The congregation stood, opened their hymnals, and began to sing "Morning Has Broken."

They had just reached the second verse when the feeders began to appear, dozens of them, materializing out of the gloom like ghosts. They crept from behind the empty pews down front where no one liked to sit and from under the offertory and sacrament tables at the chamber's rear. They rose out of the choir loft, from behind the blue velvet drapes that flanked the altar, and from under the cantilevered pulpit. They seemed to be everywhere. Nest was so stunned that she stopped singing. She had never seen feeders in the church. She had never imagined they could enter here. She stared at the closest in disbelief, a pair that slithered beneath the pew in front of her between the legs of the Robinson sisters. She fought down the revulsion she felt at seeing them here, in this place where God was worshipped and from which dark things were banished. She glanced around in horror, finding them hanging from the ceiling rafters, curled around the chandeliers, and propped up within the frescoes and bays. Yellow eyes stared at her from every quarter. Her heart quickened and her pulse began to race. No one could see the feeders but her. But even that didn't help. She could not tolerate having them here. She could not abide their presence. What were they doing in a church? In *her* church! What had drawn them? Despite the cool air of the sanctuary, she began to sweat. She glanced at her grandfather,

but he was oblivious of what was happening, his gaze focused
on his hymnal.

Then she turned in desperation to find John Ross.

John Ross had seen the feeders at the same moment as Nest. But
unlike the girl, Ross knew what was happening. Only the demon's coming could have caused so many feeders to gather—
the demon's coming coupled with his own, he amended, which
now, in hindsight, seemed painfully ill advised. He should not
have done this, come into this holy place, given in to his own
desperate need to ease in some small measure the loneliness
that consumed his life. He should have rejected Robert Freemark's offer and remained in his hotel room. He should not
have been influenced by the attraction he had felt for this church
while on his way to Josie's. He should have done what he knew
was best for everyone and stayed away.

He willed himself to remain calm, not to give away what he
was feeling, not to do anything to startle those around him. His
staff was propped against the seat beside him, and his first
impulse was to seize it and ready himself for battle. But he
could not find his enemy, could not identify him even though
he knew he was there, hiding in plain sight.

An elderly lady several seats away glanced at him and
smiled. He realized he had stopped singing. He forced himself
to smile back, to begin singing anew, first reaching down for
the staff, planting it squarely before him, and leaning on it as if
he were suddenly in need of its support.

It was then that he glanced across the heads of the congregation and saw Nest Freemark looking at him. He met her gaze
squarely, letting her know he understood what she was seeing
and that he was seeing it, too. He saw the fear and horror in her
eyes, saw how deep it tunneled, and he understood far better
than she what it was that motivated it. He fixed her with his
gaze and slowly shook his head. Do nothing, he was warning
her. Stay where you are. Keep your head.

He saw in her eyes that she understood. He saw as well that
she did not know if she could do what he was asking. He
thought to go to her, but there was no way to do that without

drawing attention to himself. The hymn was finished, and the congregation was sitting down again. He cast a quick eye over the assemblage on the off chance he might find the demon. The minister was giving the Scripture lesson. The feeders crawled over the dais at his feet, dark shadows that made the scarlet carpet of the sanctuary appear as if it had been stained by ink. The minister finished the Scripture reading and went on to give the church announcements. John Ross felt his skin turn hot as he sat nailed in place in the pew, unable to act. *I should not be here,* he kept thinking. *I should leave now.*

The choir rose to sing, and John Ross looked back at Nest Freemark. Nest was sitting right on the edge of her seat beside her grandfather, her face pale and drawn, her body rigid. Her eyes were shifting right and left, following the movements of the feeders closest to her. Several were almost on top of her, slithering between the legs of the parishioners like snakes. One drew itself right up in front of her, as if taunting her, as if daring her to do something about it. Ross saw the desperation mirrored in her face. She was on the verge of panic, ready to bolt. He knew he had to do something. The choir finished, and the congregation rose to join the minister in a responsive prayer.

When that happened, something caused Nest Freemark to glance suddenly toward the back of the sanctuary, and Ross saw her expression mirror her shock.

Then he saw it, too.

Wraith stood in the doorway, thick fur bristling, tiger-striped face lowered, ears laid back, green eyes narrowed and glittering. He was so massive that he filled the entire opening, a monstrous apparition stalking out of the gloom. His big head swung left and right with slow deliberation, and his muzzle drew back, revealing all of his considerable teeth. He made no sound as he stood there, surveying the unwary assemblage, but his intent was unmistakable. Nest's fear had drawn him, summoned him to a place he had never been, brought him out of the deep woods and into this unfamiliar setting. His deliberate stare was filled with hunger.

Nest felt her stomach lurch. *No, Wraith, no, go away, go*

away! Feeders scattered everywhere, crawling under pews, skittering down the aisles, and climbing the wood-paneled walls, their dark forms bleeding into the shadows. Their scrambling was so frantic that it stirred the air in the chamber, and among the congregation several heads lifted in surprise.

Wraith took a moment to consider his options, then started forward in that familiar, stiff-legged walk.

Nest was out of her seat and striding up the aisle to intercept him instantly. She did not stop to think about what she was doing. She did not stop to consider that she had never even thought to approach him before, that she had no idea whether she could control him. She did not say anything to her grandfather as she wheeled out of the pew; she did not even look at him. All she could think about was what would happen if Wraith managed to get hold of one of the feeders—here, in her church, among her family and friends and neighbors. She did not know what it would do to the fabric that separated the human and nonhuman worlds, and she did not want to find out.

The responsive reading concluded, and the congregation reseated itself. Heads turned to look at her as she closed on Wraith—on the ghost wolf they could not see—but she ignored them. Wraith seemed to grow even larger as she approached him, and his predatory gaze fixed on her. She felt small and vulnerable in his presence, a fragile bit of life that he could snuff out with barely a thought. But still she came on, fixed of purpose, steeled by her determination to turn him back.

And as she reached him, as it seemed she must come right up against him, right onto the tips of those gleaming teeth and that bristling fur, he simply faded away and was gone.

She continued without slowing through the space he had occupied, eyes closing against the rush of cold that washed over her, until she passed through the doorway and into the hall beyond. She stood there shaking, taking deep breaths to steady herself, leaning against the Christian-literature table, out of sight of those gathered within.

She jumped as a hand touched her shoulder. "Nest?"

John Ross was standing next to her, leaning on his black,

rune-scrolled staff, his pale green eyes intense. He must have followed her out, she realized, and done so quickly.

"Are you all right?" he asked.

She nodded. "Did you see?"

He glanced about the deserted hall as if someone might be listening. Within the sanctuary, Reverend Emery was beginning his sermon, "Whither Thou Goest."

"I saw," he answered. He bent close. "What was that creature? How does it know you?"

She swallowed against the dryness in her throat. "That was Wraith." She shook her head, refusing to offer any further explanation. "Where did all these feeders come from? What's happening?"

Ross shifted uneasily. "I think the demon is here. I think that's what's drawing them."

"Here? Why?"

Ross shook his head. "Because of me." He looked suddenly tired. "I don't know. I'm only guessing."

She felt a deep cold settle in the pit of her stomach. "What should we do?"

"Go back inside. Stay with your grandfather. I'll wait out here until after the service. Maybe the demon will show himself. Maybe I'll catch sight of him." His green eyes fixed on her.

She nodded uncertainly. "I have to go to the bathroom first. I'll be right back."

She hurried off down the hall to the Christian Education wing, Reverend Emery's deep, compelling voice trailing after her, floating over the hush of the congregation. She did not feel very good; her stomach was rolling and her head pounding. She glanced through the open doors into the cavernous gloom of the sanctuary; the feeders had disappeared. She frowned in surprise, then shook her head and went on. It didn't matter why they were gone, she told herself, only that they were. Her footsteps echoed softly on the wooden floor as she crossed the lower foyer. She pushed through the doors leading into the reception room, feeling worn and harried. Mrs. Browning, who had been her fifth-grade teacher, was arranging cups and napkins on several long tables in preparation for the fellowship to be held after the service. The bathrooms lay beyond. Nest slipped past Mrs. Browning without being noticed, went into the kitchen, and disappeared into the women's bathroom.

When she came out, a man was standing there, surveying rows of cookies and cakes arranged on serving trays. He looked up expectantly as she entered.

"Ah, there you are," he greeted, smiling. "Good morning."

"Good morning," she replied automatically, and then stopped in surprise. It was the maintenance man who had spoken with her the previous day when she had wandered through the park after working on the injured tree. She recognized his strange, pale eyes. He was wearing a suit now, rather than his working clothes, but she was certain it was the same man.

"Not feeling so good?" he asked.

She shook her head.

He nodded. "Well, that's too bad. You don't want to miss out on all these treats. Missing out on the sermon is one thing, but missing out on these cookies and brownies and cakes? No, sir!"

She started past him.

"Say, you know," he said suddenly, stepping in front of her, blocking her way, "there's a little something I want to share with you. A private fellowship, you might say. It's this. I remember when sermons meant something. It's been a while, but the old-time evangelists had a way of communicating that made you sit up and take notice. Now there's the televangelists with their high-profile ministries, their colleges and their retreats, but they don't talk about what matters. None of them do. Because they're afraid. You know why? Because what matters is how the world will end."

Nest stared at him, openmouthed.

"Sure, that's what really matters. Because we might all be here to see it happen, you know. There's every reason to think so. Just take a look around you. What do you see? The seeds of destruction, that's what." A comfortable smile creased his bland features. "But you know something? The destruction of the world isn't going to happen in the way people think. Nope. It isn't going to happen in a flood or a fire. It isn't going to happen all at once, brought about by some unexpected catastrophe. It won't be any one thing you can point to. That's not how it works. The Bible had it wrong. It will happen because of a lot of little things, an accumulation of seemingly insignificant events. Like dominoes tipped over, one against the other—that's how it will happen. One thing here, another there, next thing you know it all comes tumbling down." He paused. "Of course, someone has to topple that first domino. It all has to start with someone, doesn't it? Tell me. Does any of this sound familiar to you?"

Nest stood speechless before him, her mind screaming at her to run, her body paralyzed.

"Sure it does," he continued, inclining his head conspiratorially. His strange eyes narrowed, burning with a fire she could not bear to look upon. "Tell you something else. The destruction of the world depends on the willingness of the people in it to harm each other in any way necessary to achieve their own ends and to further their own causes. And we got that part down pat, don't we? We know how to hurt each other and how to think up whatever excuses we need to justify it. We're victims and executioners both. We're just like those dominoes I mentioned, arranged in a line, ready to tip. All of us. Even you."

"No," she whispered.

His smile had turned chilly. "You think you know yourself pretty well, don't you? But you don't. Not yet."

She took a step backward, trying to gauge whether or not she could reach the door before he grabbed her. As she did so, the door swung inward, and Mrs. Browning pushed through.

"Oh, hello, Nest," she greeted. "How are you, dear?" She seemed surprised to see the man standing there, but she smiled at him cheerfully and moved to pick up another tray of brownies.

As she did so, the man said to Nest, "No, I'm afraid you don't know yourself at all."

He gestured swiftly toward Mrs. Browning, who gasped as if she had been struck by a fist. She dropped the tray of brownies and clutched at her chest, sinking toward the floor.

Her eyes went wide in horror, and her mouth gaped open. Nest cried out and started toward her, but the man with the strange eyes intervened, moving swiftly to block her way. Nest cringed from him, riddled with fear. He held her gaze, making sure she understood how helpless she was.

Mrs. Browning was on her knees, her head lowered, her face white, her throat working rapidly as she tried to swallow. Blood spurted from her nose and mouth. Nest's scream froze in her throat, locked away by the man's hard eyes.

Then Mrs. Browning slid forward onto her face and lay still, her eyes open and staring.

The man turned to Nest and cocked one eyebrow quizzically. "You see what I mean? There wasn't a thing you could do, was there?" Then he laughed. "Maybe I won't stay for the fellowship after all. Like I said, church isn't what it used to be. Ministers are all just voices in the wind, and congregations are just marking time." He walked to the back door, stopped with his hand on the knob, and glanced over his shoulder at her. "Be good."

He opened the door and closed it softly behind him. Nest stood alone in the kitchen, looking down at Mrs. Browning, waiting for the shaking to stop.

CHAPTER 18

When she could make herself do so, Nest left the kitchen and walked back through the reception room. She was still shaking, the image of Mrs. Browning's final moments burned into her mind. She found one of the ushers and told him to call for an ambulance right away. Then she continued on. She found John Ross standing in the deserted narthex outside the sanctuary. She drew him down the long corridor to where they could not be seen or heard and related what had happened. Was it the demon? He nodded solemnly, asked if she was all right, and did not look or sound nearly as surprised as she thought he should. After all, if the demon had come looking for him, and that was what had drawn all those feeders into the church, what was it doing talking to her, threatening her, and making an object lesson of poor Mrs. Browning? Why was it talking to her about people destroying themselves, parroting in part, at least, much of what she had heard from Two Bears? What in the world was going on?

"What did the demon want with me?" she blurted out.

"I don't know," John Ross answered, giving her a steady, reassuring look, and she knew at once that he was lying.

But Reverend Emery had finished his sermon and the congregation had risen to sing the closing hymn, so her chance to ask anything further came and went. Ross sent her back inside to be with her grandfather, telling her they would talk later. She did as she was told, dissatisfied with his evasiveness, suspicious of his motives, but thinking at the same time she must tread carefully if she was to learn the truth of things. She slipped back down the aisle and into the pew beside her grand-father, giving him a rueful smile as the voices of the congregation rose all around her. She was starting the third verse of the hymn when it struck her that the demon might be trying to get to John Ross through her, and that was why he had cornered her in the church kitchen. That, in turn, would explain why Ross claimed he didn't know what was going on. It made sense if he was her father, she thought. It made perfect sense.

Mrs. Browning had been taken away by the time the fellowship began, but all the talk was of her sudden, unexpected demise. Nest thought she would be able to speak further with John Ross, but she could not manage to get him alone. First there was her grandfather, greeting Ross in a solemn, subdued voice, telling him how sorry he was that he had been introduced to the church under such tragic circumstances, pleased nevertheless that Ross had come to the worship service, reminding him of the afternoon's picnic and eliciting his promise that he would be there. Then there was Reverend Emery, greeting Ross with a sad face, a firm handshake, and a cautious inquiry into his needs while visiting in Hopewell. Then there was Robert Heppler, who latched on to Nest with such persistence that she finally told him they were breathing the same air and to back off. Robert seemed convinced she was suffering from some hidden malady, and while he was not entirely mistaken, he was annoying enough in his determination to uncover the source of her discontent that she wouldn't have told him the truth if her life had depended on it.

When she finally managed to get free of Robert and all the parishioners who stopped to remark on how awful it was about Mrs. Browning and to inquire after Gran's health, John Ross was gone.

She rode home with her grandfather in a dark mood, staring out the window at nothing, mulling over the events of the past few days and particularly the past few hours, struggling to untangle the web of confusion and contradiction that surrounded her. When her grandfather asked why she had run out of the sanctuary, she told him that she had felt sick and gone to the bathroom. When he asked if she was all right now, she said she was still upset about Mrs. Browning and didn't want to talk about it. It was close enough to the truth that he left her alone. She was getting good at making people believe things that weren't true, but she had an unpleasant feeling that she was nowhere near as good as John Ross.

He knew something about her that he was keeping to himself, she thought darkly. He knew something important, and it had much to do with his coming to Hopewell. It was tied to the demon and tied to her mother. It was at the heart of everything that was happening, and she was determined to find out what it was.

She believed, though she refused as yet to let herself accept it fully and unconditionally, that it had to do with the fact that he was her father.

By the time her grandfather pulled the old pickup down the drive and next to the house, she had made up her mind to confront Gran. She stepped out into the heat, the midday temperature already approaching one hundred, the air thick with dampness and the pungent smell of scorched grasses and weeds, the wide-spread limbs of the big shade trees languid and motionless beneath the sun's relentless assault. Nest walked to the porch, stooped to give Mr. Scratch an ear rub, then went inside. Gran was sitting at the kitchen table in a flowered housedress and slippers, sipping a bourbon and water and smoking a cigarette. She looked up as Nest passed by on her way to her bedroom, but didn't say anything. Nest went into her room, slipped off the dress, slip, shoes, and stockings, and put on her running shorts, a T-shirt that said Never Grow Up, and tennis shoes and socks. She could hear her grandparents talking down the hall. Gran was asking about John Ross, and she didn't seem happy with what she was hearing. Old Bob was telling her to keep her voice down. Nest took a moment to brush her hair while they finished the hottest portion of their conversation, then went back down the hall to the kitchen.

They stopped talking as she entered, but she pretended she didn't notice. She walked to the refrigerator and looked inside. The smell of fried chicken still lingered in the air, so she wasn't

surprised to find a container of it sitting on the top shelf. There
was also a container of potato salad, one of raw vegetables
soaking in water, and a bowl of Jell-O. When had Gran done all
this? Had she done it while they were in church?

She glanced over her shoulder at the old woman. "I'm
amazed," she said, smiling. "It looks great."

Gran nodded. "I had help from the wood fairies." She shot
Old Bob a pointed look.

Old Bob responded with a strangely sweet, lopsided grin.
"You've never needed any help from wood fairies, Evelyn.
Why, you could teach them a thing or two."

Gran actually blushed. "Old man," she muttered, smiling
back at him. Then the smile fell away, and she reached down
for her drink. "Nest, I'm sorry about Mrs. Browning. She was
a good woman."

Nest nodded. "Thanks, Gran."

"Are you feeling all right now?"

"I'm fine."

"Good. You both had phone calls while you were in church.
Cass Minter called for you, Nest. And Mel Riorden wants you
to call him right away, Robert. He said it was urgent."

Old Bob watched wordlessly as she took a long pull on her
drink. He was still wearing his suit coat, and he took time now
to slip it off. He looked suddenly rumpled and tired. "All right.
I'll take care of it. Excuse me, please."

He turned and disappeared down the hallway. Nest took a
deep breath, walked over to the kitchen table, and sat down
across from her grandmother. Sunlight spilled through the
south window and streaked the tabletop, its brightness diffused
by the limbs of the shade trees and the lace curtains so that
intricate patterns formed on the laminated surface. It fell across
Gran's hands as they lay resting beside her ashtray and drink
and made them look mottled and scaly. The tabletop felt warm,
and Nest pressed her palms against it, edging her fingers into
one of the more decorative markings of shadows and light, dis-
rupting its symmetry.

"Gran," she said, then waited for the old woman to look at
her. "I was in the park last night."

Gran nodded. "I know. I was up and looked in on you. You weren't there, so I knew where you'd gone. What were you doing?"

Nest told her. "I know it sounds a little weird, but it wasn't. It was interesting." She paused. "Actually, it was scary, too. At least, part of it was. I saw something I don't understand. I had this . . . vision, I guess. A sort of daydream—except it was night, of course. It was about you."

She watched her grandmother's eyes turn cloudy and unfocused. Gran reached for her cigarette and drew the smoke deep into her lungs. "About me?"

Nest held her gaze. "You were much younger, and you were in the park at night, just like me. But you weren't alone. You were surrounded by feeders. You were running with them. You were part of them."

The silence that followed was palpable.

Old Bob closed the door to his den and stood looking into space. His den was on the north side of the house and shaded by a massive old shagbark hickory, but the July heat penetrated even here. Old Bob didn't notice. He laid his suit coat on his leather easy chair and put his hands on his hips. He loved Evelyn, but he was losing her. It was the drinking and the cigarettes, but it was mostly Caitlin and all the things the two of them had shared and kept from him. There was a secret history between them, one that went all the way back to the time of Caitlin's birth—maybe even further than that. It involved this nonsense about feeders and magic. It involved Nest's father. It went way beyond anything reasonable, and it imprisoned Evelyn behind a wall he could not scale, a wall that had become impenetrable since Caitlin had killed herself.

There. He had said the words. *Since Caitlin had killed herself.*

He closed his eyes to stop the tears from coming. It might have been an accident, of course. She might have gone into the park that night, just as she had done as a child, and slipped and fallen from the cliffs. But he didn't believe it for a minute. Caitlin knew the park like she knew the back of her hand. Like

Nest did. Like Evelyn. It had always been a part of their lives. Even Evelyn had grown up in a house that adjoined the park. They were a part of it in the same way as the trees and the burial mounds and the squirrels and birds and all the rest. No, Caitlin didn't slip and fall. She killed herself.

And he still didn't know why.

He stared out the window at the drive leading up to Sinnissippi Road. It was hard losing Caitlin, but he thought it would be unbearable if he lost Evelyn. Their time together spanned almost fifty years; he couldn't remember what his life had been like before her. There really wasn't anything without her. He hated the drinking and the smoking, hated the way she had retired to the kitchen table and taken up residence, and hated the hard way she had come to view her life. But he would rather have her that way than not have her at all.

But what was he going to do to keep her? She was slipping away from him, one day at a time, as if she were sitting in a raft with the mooring lines slipped, drifting slowly out to sea while he stood helplessly on the shore and watched. He clasped his big hands before him and shrugged his shoulders. He was strong and smart and his life was marked by his accomplishments, but he did not know what to do to save her.

He reached up and loosened his tie. What could he do, after all, that would make a difference? Was there anyone who could tell him? He had spoken with Ralph Emery, but the minister had told him that Evelyn had to want to be helped before anyone could reach her. He had come out to the house to talk with her once or twice, but Evelyn had shown no interest in reaching out. Nest was the only one she cared about, and he thought sometimes that maybe Nest made a small difference in Evelyn just by being there. But Nest was still a child, and there was only so much a child could do.

Besides, he thought uneasily, Nest was too much like her grandmother for comfort.

He pulled off his tie, draped it over the easy chair with his coat, and walked to the phone to call Mel Riorden. He dialed, and the phone rang only once before Mel picked up.

"Riorden."

"Mel? It's Bob Freemark."

"Yeah, thanks for calling back. I appreciate it."

Old Bob smiled to himself. "What were you doing, standing by the phone waiting for me?"

"Something like that. This isn't funny. I've got a problem." Mel Riorden's tone of voice made that abundantly apparent, but Old Bob said nothing, waiting Mel out. "You have to keep this to yourself, Bob, if I tell you. You have to promise me that. I wouldn't involve you if I didn't have to, but I can't let this thing slide and I don't know how to deal with it. I've already tried and been told to go to hell."

Old Bob pulled back the desk chair and seated himself. "Well, this doesn't have to go beyond you and me if you don't want it to, Mel. Why don't you just tell me what it is?"

Mel Riorden gave a worried sigh. "It's Derry. The kid's more trouble than a dozen alligators in the laundry chute and stupid to boot. If he wasn't my sister's kid . . ." He trailed off. "Well, you've heard it all before. Anyway, I'm in church for the early mass with Carol and a couple of the grandkids. Al Garcia's there, too. With Angie and their kids. So afterward, I go in for a coffee and a cookie like everyone else. I say hello to Al and Angie, to a couple of others. Everyone's having a nice visit. I'm standing there, munching my cookie, sipping my coffee, Carol's off with the grandkids, all's right with the world, and up comes my sister. She looks really bad, worried as can be, all bent out of shape. First off, I think she's been drinking. But then I see it's something else. She says to me, 'Mel, you got to talk to him. You got to find out what's going on and put a stop to it.' "

"Put a stop to what?"

"I'm coming to that." Mel Riorden paused, arranging his thoughts in the silence. "See, I keep thinking of those newspaper stories we joke about over coffee at Josie's. The ones about the people who suddenly go berserk. Their minds snap and they go crazy, insane, for no real reason. You wonder how it could happen, how the people who know them could let it. It's like that. Like that schoolteacher walking in and killing all those kindergarten kids in Mississippi because he'd lost his job. You read about that in today's paper?"

Old Bob shook his head at the phone. "I haven't read the paper yet. I just got back from church myself."

"Yeah, well, that's one good reason for being Catholic. You get church out of the way early and have the rest of the day to yourself. Al and I talked it over once, the advantages of being Catholic over being Protestant . . ."

"Mel." Old Bob stopped him midsentence. "What about Derry? Are you saying he's planning to kill someone?"

"No, not exactly." Mel Riorden paused. "Hold on a minute, will you? I want to make sure Carol's not back from the store yet." He put down the phone and was gone for a minute before picking it up again. "I don't want her to hear any of this. I don't want anyone to hear."

"You want to meet me someplace private and talk about this?" Old Bob asked him.

"No, I want to get it out of the way right now. Besides, I don't know how much time we've got if we're going to do anything."

"Do anything? What are we going to do, Mel?"

"Bear with me." Mel Riorden cleared his throat. "My sister tells me, when I get her calmed down a bit and off to the side, that someone called her, some friend, and said they'd heard that Derry was out at Scrubby's last night drinking with Junior Elway and talking about some plan to shut down MidCon. The conversation wasn't all that clear, but there was some mention of an accident, maybe someone getting killed."

Old Bob shook his head slowly. "Maybe they heard it wrong."

"Well, with anyone else, you might shrug it off to talk and booze. But Derry's been short-circuited since Vietnam, and he knows a lot about weapons and explosives. My sister begs me to talk to him. I don't want to do that, because I know Derry thinks I'm an old fart, but I tell her I'll give it a try. So when I get home, I give him a call. He's sleeping, and I wake him. He's not pleased. I decide it's best to get right to the point. I tell him about the conversation with my sister and ask him if there's anything to it. He tells me, hell, yes, there's a lot to it, but it's got nothing to do with me. I tell him he'd better think twice about whatever it is. First off, people already know that if something happens, it's because of him; he made sure of that at the tavern. Second, anything he does outside the union will just get him in trouble with us. He says he doesn't care who knows and that the only way anything will ever get done is outside the union."

"What do you think he's got in mind?" Old Bob pressed.

"I don't know. He wouldn't tell me. But he might tell you. He's still got some respect for you, which is something he doesn't have for me. And I think maybe he's a little afraid of you. Not physically, but . . . you know, of your reputation. If you were to ask him what he's planning, he might open up." There was a long pause. "Bob, I don't know who else to turn to."

Old Bob nodded, thinking it over. Derry Howe was full of himself and his wild ideas, but he was mostly talk. The danger came from his army training and his inability to adjust to any kind of normal life since his return from Vietnam. Mel was right about that; you couldn't just dismiss his talk out of hand.

"Bob, are you still there?"

"I'm here," he answered. He didn't want any part of this. He wasn't sure at all that Derry Howe thought anything about him one way or the other. He wasn't sure at all that Derry would give him the time of day. Mel had more faith in him than he had in himself. Besides, he had problems of his own that needed his attention, and the biggest was sitting just down the hall in the kitchen. This whole business with Derry sounded like trouble he didn't need. "I don't know, Mel," he said.

"You and Evelyn going to the park today? For a picnic and the dance? Didn't you say you were?"

"We're going."

"Well, Derry will be there, too. He's going to enter the horseshoe tournament with Junior and some others. All I'm asking is that you take five minutes of your time and talk with him. Just ask him what's up, that's all. If he won't tell you, fine. But maybe he will. Maybe, if it's you."

Old Bob shook his head. He didn't want to get involved in

this. He closed his eyes and rubbed them with his free hand. "All right, Mel," he said finally. "I'll give it a try."

There was an audible sigh of relief. "Thanks, Bob. I'll see you there. Thanks."

Old Bob placed the receiver gently back on the cradle. After a moment, he stood up and went over to open the door again.

"Nest, I want you to listen to me," Gran said quietly.

They were seated at the kitchen table, facing each other in the hazy sunlight, eyes locked. Gran's hands were shaking, and she put one on top of the other to keep them still. Nest saw disappointment and anger and sadness in her eyes all at the same time, and she was suddenly afraid.

"I won't lie to you," Gran said. "I have tried never to lie to you. There are things I haven't told you. Some you don't need to know. Some I can't tell you. We all have secrets in our lives. We are entitled to that. Not everything about us should be known. I expect you understand that, being who you are. Secrets allow us space in which to grow and change as we must. Secrets give us privacy where privacy is necessary if we are to survive."

She started to reach for her drink and stopped. At her elbow, her cigarette was burned to ash. She glanced at it, then away. She sighed wearily, her eyes flicking back to Nest.

"Was it you, Gran?" Nest asked gently. "In the park, with the feeders?"

Gran nodded. "Yes, Nest, it was." She was silent a moment, a bundle of old sticks inside the housecoat. "I have never told anyone. Not my parents, not your grandfather, not even Caitlin—and God knows, I should at least have told her. But I didn't. I kept that part of my life secret, kept it to myself."

She reached across the table for Nest's hand and took it in her own. Her hands were fragile and warm. "I was young and headstrong and foolish. I was proud. I was different, Nest, and I knew it—different like you are, gifted with use of the magic and able to see the forest creatures. No one else could see what I saw. Not my parents, not my friends, not anyone. It set me apart from everyone, and I liked that. My aunt, Opal Anders, my mother's sister, was the last to have the magic before me, and she had died when I was still quite young. So for a time, there was only me. I lived by the park, and I escaped into it whenever I could. It was my own private world. There was nothing in my other life that was anywhere near as intriguing as what waited for me in the park. I came at night, as you do. I found the feeders waiting for me—curious, responsive, eager. They wanted me there with them, I could tell. They were anxious to see what I would do. So I came whenever I could, mingling with them, trailing after them, always watching, wondering what they were, waiting to see what they would do next. I was never afraid. They never threatened me. There didn't seem to be any reason not to be there."

She shook her head slowly, her lips tightening. "As time passed, I became more comfortable with feeders than with humans. I was as wild as they were; I was as uninhibited. I ran with them because that was what made me feel good. I was self-indulgent and vain. I think I knew there was danger in what I was doing, but it lacked an identity, and in the absence of knowing there was something bad about what I was doing, I just kept doing it. My parents could not control me. They tried keeping me in my room, tried reasoning with me, tried everything. But the park was mine, and I was not about to give it up."

A car backfired somewhere out on Woodlawn, and Gran stopped talking for a moment, staring out the window, squinting into the hot sun. Nest felt the old woman's hand tighten about her own, and she squeezed back to let Gran know it was all right.

"The Indian had no right to tell you," Gran said finally. "No right."

Nest shook her head. "I don't think it was Two Bears, Gran. I don't think he was the one."

Gran didn't seem to hear. "Why would he do such a thing? Whatever possessed him? He doesn't even know me."

Nest sighed, picturing Two Bears dancing with the spirits of the Sinnissippi, seeing anew the vision of Gran, wild-eyed and young, at one with the feeders. "When did you stop, Gran?" she asked softly. "When did you quit going into the park?"

Gran's head jerked up, and there was a flash of fear in her narrowed eyes. "I don't want to talk about it anymore."

"Gran," Nest pressed, refusing to look away. "I have to know. Why did I have this vision of you and the feeders, do you think? I still don't know. You have to help me."

"I don't have to help you do another thing, Nest. I've said everything I have to say."

"Tell me about the other—the shadowy figure whose face I couldn't see. Tell me about him."

"No!"

"Gran, please!"

The door to the library opened and Old Bob shambled down the hall. He stopped in the kitchen doorway, his coat and tie draped over one arm, his big frame stooped and weary-looking. He stared at them, his eyes questioning. Gran took her hand from Nest's and picked up her drink. Nest lowered her gaze to the table and went still.

"Robert, I want you to change into your old clothes and then go out and haul that brush out to the roadway for Monday pickup," Gran said quietly.

Old Bob hesitated. "Tomorrow's a holiday, Evelyn. There's no pickup until Tuesday. We've got plenty of . . ."

"Just do it, Robert!" she snapped, cutting him off. "Nest and I need a little time to ourselves, if you please."

Nest's grandfather flushed, then turned wordlessly and went back down the hallway. Nest and her grandmother listened to his footsteps recede.

"All right, Nest," Gran said, her voice deadly calm. "I'll tell you this one last thing, and then I'm done. Don't ask me anything more." She tossed back the last of her drink and lit a cigarette. Her gray hair was loose and spidery about her face. "I quit going to the park because I met someone else who could see the feeders, who was possessed of the magic. Someone who loved me, who wanted me so badly he would have done anything to get me." She took a long pull on the cigarette and blew out a thick stream of smoke. "Hard to imagine now, someone wanting this old woman. Just look at me."

She gave Nest a sad, ironic smile. "Anyway, that's what

happened. At first, I was attracted to him. We both ran the park with the feeders and used the magic. We dared anything. We dared things I can't even talk about, can't even make myself think about anymore. It was wrong to be like that, to do the things we did. But I couldn't seem to help myself. What I didn't realize at first was that he was evil, and he wanted me to be like him. But I saw what was happening in time, thank God, and I put a stop to it."

"You quit going into the park?"

Gran shook her head. "I couldn't do that. I couldn't give up the park."

Nest hesitated. "Then what did you do?"

For a minute she thought her grandmother was going to say something awful. She had that look. Then Gran picked up her cigarette, ground it out in the ashtray, and gave a brittle laugh.

"I found a way to keep him from ever coming near me again," she said. Her jaw muscles tightened and her lips compressed. Her words were fierce and rushed. "I had to. He wasn't what he seemed."

It was the way she said it. Nest gave her a hard look. "What do you mean, 'He wasn't what he seemed'?"

"Let it be, Nest."

But Nest shook her head stubbornly. "I want to know."

Gran's frail hands knotted. "Oh, Nest! He wasn't human!"

They stared at each other, eyes locked. Gran's face was contorted with anger and frustration. The pulse at her temples throbbed, and her mouth worked, as if she were chewing on the words she could not make herself speak. But Nest would not look away. She would not give it up.

"He wasn't human?" she repeated softly, the words digging and insistent. "If he wasn't human, what was he?"

Gran shook her head as if to rid herself of all responsibility and exhaled sharply. "He was a demon, Nest!"

Nest felt all the strength drain from her body in a strangled rush. She sat frozen and empty in her chair, her grandmother's words a harsh whisper of warning in her ears. *A demon. A demon. A demon.*

Gran bent forward and placed her dry, papery hands over

Nest's. "I'm sorry to have disappointed you, child," she whispered.

Nest shook her head quickly, insistently. "No, Gran, it's all right."

But it wasn't, of course, and she knew in the darkest corners of her heart that it might never be again.

CHAPTER 19

Gran did a strange thing then. She rose without another word, went down the hall to her bedroom, and closed the door behind her. Nest sat at the kitchen table and waited. The minutes ticked by, but Gran did not return. She had left her drink and her cigarettes behind. Nest could not remember the last time Gran had left the kitchen table in the middle of the day like this. She kept thinking the old woman would reappear. She sat alone in the kitchen, bathed in the hot July sunlight. Gran stayed in her bedroom.

Finally Nest stood up and walked to the doorway and looked down the hall. The corridor was silent and empty. Nest nudged the wooden floor with the tip of her tennis shoe. *A demon, a demon, a demon!* Her mind spun with the possibilities. Was the demon Gran had known the same demon that was here now? She remembered John Ross saying he didn't know why the demon was interested in her, and she wondered if it was because of Gran. Perhaps the demon was trying to get to Gran through her, rather than to John Ross. Maybe that was its intention.

She looked down at her feet, down her tanned legs and narrow body, and she wished that someone would just tell her the truth and be done with it. Because she was pretty certain no one was doing that now.

After a few more moments of waiting unsuccessfully for Gran to emerge, she went back into the kitchen and picked up the phone to call Cass. The house felt oppressive and secretive to her, even in the brightness of midday. She listened to its silence over the ringing of the telephone. Cass Minter's mother

251

picked up on the third ring and advised Nest that Cass and Bri-anna had already left and would meet her in the park by the toboggan slide. Nest thanked Mrs. Minter and hung up. She looked around the kitchen as if she might find someone watching, haunted by what Gran had told her. *A demon.* She closed her eyes, but the demon was there waiting for her, bland features smiling, pale eyes steady.

She glanced at the clock and went down the hall and out the back door. The picnic with John Ross was not until three. She had a little less than two hours to spend with Cass and the others before getting back. She stepped out into the heat and squinted up at the brilliant, sunlit sky. The air was thick with the rich smells of dry earth and grasses and leaves. Robins sang in the trees and cars drove down Sinnissippi Road, their tires whining on the hot asphalt. She wet her lips and looked around. Her grandfather came up the drive, returning from carrying up the yard waste. He slowed as he approached, and an uncertain smile creased his weathered face.

"Everything all right?" he asked. His big hands hung limp at his sides, and there was sweat on his brow.

Nest nodded. "Sure. I'm on my way to meet Cass and the others in the park."

Her grandfather glanced toward the house hesitantly, then back at her. "John will be here at three for the picnic."

"Don't worry, I'll be back." She gave him a reassuring smile. How much did he know about Gran and the feeders? "Bye, Grandpa."

She stepped around a sleeping Mr. Scratch and crossed the yard quickly, eyes determinedly forward so she would not look back. She felt as if her grandfather had read everything she was thinking in her eyes, and she did not want that. She felt as if everything was kept secret from her, while she had no secrets of her own. But there was John Ross, of course. She was the only one who knew the truth about him. Well, some of the truth, anyway. Maybe. She sighed helplessly.

She was pushing her way through the gap in the bushes when Pick dropped onto her shoulder.

" 'Bout time," he grumbled, settling himself into place. "Some of us have been up since daybreak, you know."

She gave him an angry look. "Good for you. Some of us have been trying to figure out why others of us aren't a little more truthful about things."

The wooden brow furrowed and the black-pool eyes crinkled. "What's that supposed to mean?"

She stopped abruptly beside the service road and looked off into the park. There were families laying out blankets and picnic baskets on the grassy lawn farther east where the shade trees began. There were baseball games under way, softball pickup contests. Two boys were throwing a Frisbee back and forth and a dog was running hopefully between them, giving chase. It was all familiar to her, but it felt quite alien, too.

"It means you were awfully quick to disappear last night after the spirits of the Sinnissippi appeared." She glared at him. "Why was that?"

The sylvan glared back. "Bunch of mumbo jumbo, that's why. I got bored."

"Don't you lie to me!" she hissed. She snatched him off her shoulder by the nape of his twiggy neck and held him kicking and squirming before her. "You saw the vision, too, didn't you? You saw the same thing I did, and you don't want to admit it! Well, it's too late for that, Pick!"

"Put me down!" he raged.

"Or what? What will you do?" She felt like tossing him out on the grass and leaving him there. "I know who it was! It was Gran! I knew it from a picture on the fireplace mantel! I thought it was Mom at first, but it was Gran! You knew, didn't you? Didn't you?"

"Yes!" He lashed out.

He stopped squirming and stared balefully at her. Nest stared back. After a moment, she placed him in the palm of her hand and squatted down in the grass next to the service road, holding him up to her face. Pick righted himself indignantly, brushing at his arms and legs as if he had been dumped in a pile of dirt.

"Don't you ever do that again!" he warned, so furious he refused even to look at her.

"You stop lying to me and maybe I won't!" she snapped back, just as angry as he was.

His mouth worked inside his mossy beard. "I haven't lied to you. But it isn't my place to tell you things about your family! It isn't right for me to do that!"

"Well, what kind of a friend are you, then?" she demanded. "A real friend doesn't keep secrets!"

Pick snorted. "Everyone keeps secrets. That's part of life. None of us tells the other everything. We can't. Then there wouldn't be any part of us that didn't belong to someone else!" He tugged on his beard in frustration. "All right, so I didn't tell you about your grandmother and the feeders. But she didn't tell you either, did she? So maybe there's a reason for that, and maybe it's up to her to decide if she wants you to know that reason and maybe it's not up to me!"

"Maybe this, maybe that! Maybe it doesn't matter, now! She told me when I asked her, even though she didn't want to! She told me, but it would have been easier if it had come from you!" Nest shook her head, and her voice quieted. "She told me about the demon, too. Is it the same one that's here now?"

Pick threw up his hands. "How am I supposed to answer that when I haven't even seen him?"

Nest studied him doubtfully for a moment. "He probably wouldn't look the same anyway, would he?"

"Hard to say. Demons don't change much once they're demons." He blinked. "Wait a minute. You haven't seen him, have you?"

Nest told him then about the encounter in church, about the appearance of the feeders and Wraith, about poor Mrs. Browning, and about John Ross. When she was done, Pick sat down heavily in her palm and shook his head.

"What's going on here?" he asked softly, not so much of her as of himself.

She looked off into the park again, thinking it over, searching for an answer that refused to be found. Then she stood up, put him back on her shoulder, and began to walk once more along the edge of the service road toward the east end of the park. "Tell me about my grandmother," she asked him after a moment.

Pick looked at her. "Don't start with me. I've said all I have to say about that."

"Just tell me what she was doing with the feeders, running with them, being part of them." Nest felt her voice catch as the ugly vision played itself through again in her mind.

Pick shrugged. "I don't know what she was doing. She was young and wild, your grandmother, and she did a lot of things I didn't much agree with. Running with the feeders was one of them. She did it because she felt like it, I guess. She was different from you."

Nest looked at him. "Different how?"

"She was the first to have the magic in your family when there was no one to guide her in its use," he replied. "She didn't know what to do with it. There wasn't any balance in her life like there is in yours. Not then, at least. She's given you that balance, you know. She's been there to warn you about the magic right from the first. No one was there for her. Opal, the last before her, was dead by the time she was eight. So there was only me, and she didn't want to listen to me. She thought I was out for myself, that what I said didn't mean anything." He pursed his lips. "Like I said, she was headstrong."

"She said she was in love with the demon."

"She was, for a time."

"Until she found out the truth about him."

"Yep, until then."

"What did she do to keep him away from her?"

Pick looked at her. "Didn't she tell you?"

Nest shook her head. "Will you?"

Pick sighed. "Here we go again."

"All right, forget it."

They walked on in silence, passing the east ball diamond and turning up toward the parking lot that fronted the toboggan slide. Ahead, the trees shimmered hotly in the midday sun and the river reflected silver and gold. In the backyards of the houses bordering the park, people were working in their flower beds and mowing the grass. The smell of hamburgers cooking on an open grill wafted heavily on the humid air.

"I shouldn't tell you," Pick insisted quietly.

"Then don't."

"I shouldn't."

"All right."

Pick hunched his shoulders. "Your grandmother," he said wearily, staring straight ahead. For a minute he didn't say anything else. "The demon underestimated her, too bad for him. See, she understood him better than he thought. She'd learned a few things running with him, being part of his life, those nights in the park. She knew it was her magic that attracted him to her. She knew the magic was everything to him. He wanted her because she had it. She was very powerful in those days, Nest. Maybe as powerful as he was. So she told him that if he stayed in the park, if he kept after her, she'd use it against him. She'd use it up, every last bit of it. She'd kill him or herself or both of them. She didn't care which."

He paused. "She would have done it, too. She was very determined, very tough-minded, your grandmother." He scratched his mossy beard. "Anyway, the demon was convinced. He backed down from her. He hated her for that afterward. Hated himself, too. By the time she was finished with him, he didn't want anything to do with her anymore."

Nest tried to imagine Gran confronting the demon, threatening to kill him if he refused to leave her alone. Frail, weary old Gran.

"Now, that's all I'm saying on the subject," Pick interjected heatedly. "If you want to know anything more, ask your grandmother. But I'd think twice about it, if I were you. Just my opinion. Some things are better left alone, and this is one of them. Take my word for it. Let it be."

"The Beatles, 1969?"

"What?"

"Never mind." Nest was sick of the whole subject. Nothing she had heard was making her feel any better. Pick was just irritating her with his refusal to talk about it, but she guessed that he was right, that it should come from Gran. Maybe it was time to ask about her father, too. Maybe it was time to insist on an answer. There were too many secrets in her family, and some of them needed revealing. Didn't she have a right to know?

"I have to be going," Pick announced, rising to his knees on her shoulder. She stopped and looked at his narrow face. His fierce eyes stared back at her. "Just make sure you bring John Ross to the maentwrog's tree so he can have a look for himself at what's happening."

Nest nodded. "I'll bring him up after the picnic."

She lowered Pick to the ground, and he disappeared without a word, vanishing into the grass as if he were an ant. " 'Bye," she murmured at the space he left behind.

She walked on across the grass into the parking lot that fronted the toboggan slide, kicking at rocks and staring at the ground as it passed beneath her feet. Her skin was hot and sticky already. She brushed at her curly damp hair, moving it off her forehead and away from her eyes. She felt awkward and stupid. She hated who she was. She wondered what she could do to change things.

Someone yelled at her from the ball field, and she glanced over. A group of boys was standing by home plate looking at her; she thought it was one of them who had called to her. Worse, she thought it was Danny Abbott. She looked away and kept on walking.

She crossed the parking lot to the toboggan slide and saw Cass and the others grouped at a picnic table under one of the big oaks. Behind them, down the hill, the river flowed with sluggish indifference beyond the levy. A few boats bobbed gently on its surface, their occupants hunched over fishing poles and cans of bait. She strolled over to her friends, trying to appear casual, trying to make herself believe that nothing was different. They were all there—Cass, Brianna, Robert, and Jared. They looked up as she approached, and she had the feeling they had been talking about her.

"Hey," she said.

"Pete and Repeat are out walking," said Robert, straight-faced. "Pete goes home. Who's left?"

"Elvis?" she asked, squeezing in between Cass and Brianna.

"Nice try. Two guys walk into a bar. One's got a Doberman, the other a terrier. Bartender says . . ."

"Robert!" snapped Brianna, cutting him short. "Geez!"

"Enough with the jokes," Cass agreed. "They weren't funny the first time, back when Washington was president."

"Oh, big yuck." Robert looked annoyed. "All right, so what are we going to do, then? And don't tell me we're going to spend the day trying to heal any more sick trees." He gave Nest a pointed look. "Especially since we didn't do so well with the last one."

"What do you mean?" she asked.

"I mean, it looks terrible." He pushed up his glasses on his nose and brushed back his blond hair. "We walked by it on the way over, and it looks like it's a goner. Whatever we did, it didn't help."

"We could go swimming," Brianna suggested brightly, ignoring him.

Nest shook her head. "I can't. I have to be back by two. How bad is it, Robert?"

"The bark's all split open and oozing something green and there's dead leaves everywhere." He saw the look on Nest's face and stopped. "What's going on? What's this sick-tree business all about?"

Nest took a deep breath and bit her lower lip. "Someone is poisoning the trees in the park," she said, giving a slight edge of truth to what was otherwise an outright lie.

They stared at her. "Why would anyone do that?" Cass asked.

"Because . . ." She shrugged. "Because they're nuts, I guess."

Robert frowned. "How do you know this?"

"Grandpa told me. He heard it from the park people. I guess it's happened in some other places, too." She was rolling now, sounding very sure of herself. "It's one guy that's doing it. He was seen in another park, so they got a description. Everyone's been looking for him."

Robert frowned some more. "This is the first I've heard of it. My dad never said anything about anyone poisoning trees in the parks. You sure about this?"

Nest gave him a disgusted look. "Of course I'm sure. Why would I say it if I wasn't?"

"So they know what this guy looks like?" Jared asked quietly. He looked tired, as if he hadn't been sleeping well.

"Yep." She glanced at them conspiratorially. "I'll tell you something else, too. Grandpa thinks he might be in the park this weekend. See, sometimes he dresses like a park maintenance man in order not to be noticed. That's how he gets away with poisoning the trees."

"He might be in the park this weekend?" Brianna parroted, her porcelain features horror-struck.

"Maybe," Nest advised. "So we have to watch for him, keep an eye out. This is what he looks like." She provided a careful description of the demon, from his pale eyes to his bland face. "But if you see him, don't try to go near him. And don't let him know he's been seen. Just come get me."

"Come get you?" Robert repeated suspiciously.

"So I can tell Grandpa, because he knows what to do."

Everyone nodded soberly. Nest held her breath and waited for more questions, but there weren't any. Way to go, she thought, not knowing whether to laugh or cry at her subterfuge. You can lie with the best of them, can't you? You can lie even to your friends.

They walked through the park for a while afterward, killing time. Nest watched her friends surreptitiously checking faces as if they might really find the tree poisoner, and she pondered if she had done the right thing. She needed any help she could get, and this would give her friends something to do besides wonder why she was acting odd, but it made her feel ashamed of herself anyway. She didn't believe any of them would find the demon. She thought only John Ross could do that, and she wasn't sure of him. What persuaded her that she should even try to do something was her memory of the morning's encounter in the church kitchen, of the murder, of the pale eyes studying her, of the calm, even voice talking to her about the way the world would end. She could rationalize what had happened from now until Christmas, but she still felt desperate, almost hopeless.

The park was beginning to fill with families come to picnic and participate in the games the Jaycees were running prior to this evening's community dance. There would be softball, badminton, horseshoes, and footraces of various sorts for adults and children both. Members of the club were already preparing for the events. Food and drink stands were being set up. The smells of hot dogs and hamburgers wafted in the thick July air, and smoke curled lazily from the brick chimneys of the cook centers in the pavilion. Bushy-tailed red squirrels scampered along the limbs of the big oaks, and a few dogs chased after balls. Laughter and shouts rose from all about.

A slight breeze wafted off the river, causing Nest to glance skyward. A thin lacework of clouds drifted across the blue. She had heard her grandfather say there was a chance of rain for the Fourth.

She left the others then, promising to meet up with them later on in the afternoon when family obligations were satisfied. Robert was having a cookout in his backyard with his parents and some cousins. Cass and Brianna were going to a church picnic. Jared had to go home to watch the younger kids while his mother and George Paulsen came over to the park so that George could compete in the horseshoe tournament.

Jared and Nest walked back across the park, neither of them saying anything. Jared seemed preoccupied, but she liked being with him no matter what his mood. She liked the way he was always thinking things over, giving careful consideration to what he was going to say.

"You going to the dance tonight, Nest?" he asked suddenly, not looking at her.

She glanced over in surprise. "Sure. Are you?"

"Mom says I can go for a while. The kids are staying at Mrs. Pinkley's for the night, except Bennett is going to Alice Workman's. You know, the social worker. George and Mom are going out somewhere, then coming back to watch TV."

They walked on, the silence awkward. "You want to go to the dance with me?" he asked after a minute.

Nest felt a warm flush run down her neck. "Sure."

"Cool. I'll meet you about seven." He was so serious. He

cleared his throat and shoved his hands in his jeans pockets. "You don't think this is weird or anything, do you?"

She smiled in spite of herself. "Why would I think that?"

"Because it would be you and me, and not all of us. Robert and Cass and Brianna might think it's weird, us not including them."

She glanced quickly at him. "I don't care what they think."

He thought about it a moment, then nodded solemnly. "Good. Neither do I."

She left him on the service road and slipped through the gap in the bushes at the edge of her backyard, feeling light-headed from more than just the heat.

CHAPTER 20

John Ross rode out to Sinnissippi Park with the desk clerk from the Lincoln Hotel, who was having Sunday dinner with his brother and sister-in-law just to the north. The man dropped him at the corner of Third Street and Sixteenth Avenue, and Ross walked the rest of the way. The man would have driven him to the Freemarks' doorstep—offered to do so, in fact—but it was not yet two o'clock and Ross was not expected until three and did not want to arrive too early. So instead he limped up Third to Riverside Cemetery, leaning heavily on his black staff, moving slowly in the heat, and found his way to Caitlin Freemark's grave. The day was still and humid, but it was cool and shady where he walked beneath the hardwood trees. There were people in the cemetery, but no one paid any attention to him. He was wearing fresh jeans, a pale blue collared shirt, and his old walking shoes. He had washed his long hair and tied it back with a clean bandanna. He looked halfway respectable, which was as good as it got.

He stood in front of Caitlin Freemark's grave and looked down at the marble stone, read the inscription several times, studied the rough, dark shadow of the letters and numbers against the bright glassy surface. CAITLIN ANNE FREEMARK, BELOVED DAUGHTER & MOTHER. He felt something tug at him, a sudden urge to recant his lies and abandon his subterfuge, to lay bare to the Freemarks the truth of who he was and what he was doing. He looked off toward their house, not able to see it through the trees, visualizing it instead in his mind. He pictured their faces looking back at him. He could not tell them the truth, of course. Gran knew most of it anyway, he suspected.

She must. And Robert Freemark? Old Bob? Ross shook his head, not wanting to hazard a guess. In any case, Nest was the only one who really mattered, and he could not tell her. Perhaps she did not ever need to know. If he was quick enough, if he found the demon and destroyed it, if he put an end to its plans before it revealed them fully . . .

He blinked into the heat, and the image of the Freemarks faded from his mind.

Forgive me.

He walked on from there into the park, skirting its edges, following the cemetery fence to Sinnissippi Road, then the road past the townhomes to the park entrance and beyond through the big shade trees to the Freemark residence. Old Bob greeted him at the door, ebullient and welcoming. They stood within the entry making small talk until Gran and Nest joined them, then gathered up the picnic supplies from the kitchen. Ross insisted on helping, on at least being allowed to carry the blanket they would sit on. Nest picked up the white wicker basket that contained the food, Old Bob took the cooler with the drinks and condiments, and with Gran leading the way they went out the back door, down the steps past a sleeping Mr. Scratch, across the backyard to the gap in the bushes, and into the park.

The park was filled with cars and people. Picnickers already occupied most of the tables and cooking stations. Blankets were spread under trees and along the bluff, softball games were under way on all the diamonds, and across from the pavilion the Jaycee-sponsored games were being organized. There was a ring toss and a baseball throw. The horseshoe tournament was about to start. Carts dispensing cotton candy and popcorn had been brought in, and the Jaycees were selling pop, iced tea, and lemonade from school-cafeteria folding tables. Balloons filled with helium floated at the ends of long cords. Red, white, and blue bunting hung from the pavilion's rafters and eaves. A band was playing under a striped tent, facing out onto the pavilion's smooth concrete floor. Parents and children crowded forward, anxious to see what was going on.

"Looks like the whole town is here," Old Bob observed with a satisfied grin.

Ross glanced around. It seemed as if all the good places had been taken, but Gran led them forward determinedly, past the diamonds, the pavilion, the games, the cotton candy and popcorn, the band, and even the toboggan slide, past all of it and down the hill toward the bayou, to a grassy knoll tucked back behind a heavy stand of brush and evergreens that was shaded by an aging oak and commanded a clear view of the river. Remarkably, no one else was there, save for a couple of teenagers snuggling on a blanket. Gran ignored them and directed Ross to place the blanket in the center of the knoll. The teens watched tentatively as the Freemarks arranged their picnic, then rose and disappeared. Gran never looked at them. Ross shook his head. Old Bob caught his eye and winked.

The heat was suffocating on the flats, but here it was eased by the cool air off the water and by the shade of the big oak. It was quieter as well, the sounds of the crowd muffled and distant. Gran emptied the contents of the picnic basket, arranged the dishes, and invited them to sit. They formed a circle about the food, eating fried chicken, potato salad, Jell-O, raw sticks of carrot and celery, deviled eggs, and chocolate cupcakes off paper plates, and washing it all down with cold lemonade poured from a thermos into paper cups. Ross found himself thinking of his childhood, of the picnics he had enjoyed with his own family. It was a long time ago. He visited the memories quietly while he ate, glancing now and again at the Freemarks.

Should I tell them? What should I tell them? How do I do what is needed to help this girl? How do I keep from failing them?

"Did you enjoy the service, John?" Old Bob asked him suddenly, chewing on a chicken leg.

Ross glanced at Nest, but she did not look at him. "Very much, sir. I appreciate being included."

"You say you're on your way to Seattle, but maybe you could postpone leaving and stay on with us for a few more days." Old Bob looked at Gran. "We have plenty of extra room at the house. You would be welcome."

Gran's face was tight and fixed. "Robert, don't be pushy. Mr. Ross has his own life. He doesn't need ours."

Ross forced a quick smile. "I can't stay beyond tomorrow or the day after, thanks anyway, Mr. Freemark, Mrs. Freemark. You've done plenty for me as it is."

"Well, hardly." Old Bob cleared his throat, regarded the leg bone in his hand. "Darn good chicken, Evelyn. Your best yet, I think."

They finished the meal, Old Bob talking of Caitlin as a girl now, recalling stories about how she had been, what she had done. Ross listened and nodded appreciatively. He thought it might have been a while since the old man had spoken of his daughter like this. Gran seemed distracted and distant, and Ross did not think she was paying much attention. But Nest was watching raptly, studying her grandfather's face as he related the stories, listening carefully to his every word. Her concentration was so complete that she did not seem aware of anything else. Ross watched her, wondered what she was thinking, wished suddenly that he knew.

I should tell her. I should take the chance. She's stronger than she looks. She is older than her fourteen years. She can accept it.

But he said nothing. Old Bob finished, sighed, glanced out across the bayou as if seeing into the past, then reached over impulsively to pat his wife's hand. "You're awfully quiet, Dark Eyes."

For just an instant all the hardness went out of Evelyn Freemark's face, all the lines and age spots vanished, and she was young again. A smile flickered at the corners of her mouth, and her eyes lifted to find his.

Ross stood up, leaning on his staff for support. "Nest, how about taking a walk with me. My leg stiffens up if I sit for too long. Maybe you can keep me from getting lost."

Nest put down her plate and looked at her grandmother. "Gran, do you want me to help clean up?"

Her grandmother shook her head, said nothing. Nest waited

a moment, then rose. "Let's go this way," she said to Ross. She glanced at her grandparents. "We'll be back in a little while."

They climbed the hill at an angle that took them away from the crowds, east toward the park's far end, where the deep woods lay. They walked in silence, Nest pacing herself so that Ross could keep up with her, limping along with the aid of his staff. They worked their way slowly through the shady oaks and hickories, passing families seated on blankets and at tables eating their picnic lunches, following the curve of the slope as it wound back around the rise and away from the river. Soon Gran and Old Bob were out of sight.

When they were safely alone, Ross said to her, "I'm sorry about what happened at church. I know it was scary."

"I have to show you something," she said, ignoring his apology. "I promised Pick."

They walked on for a ways in silence, and then she asked sharply, accusingly, "Are you an angel? You know, in the Biblical sense? Is that what you are?"

He stared over at her, but she wasn't looking at him, she was looking at the ground. "No, I don't think so. I'm just a man."

"But if God is real, there must be angels."

"I suppose so. I don't know."

Her voice was clipped, surly. "Which? Which don't you know? If there are angels or if God is real?"

He slowed and then stopped altogether, forcing her to do the same. He waited until she was looking at him. "What I told you was the truth—about the Fairy Glen, and the Lady, and the voice, and the way I became a Knight of the Word. What are you asking me, Nest?"

Her eyes were hot. "If there really is a God, why would He allow all those feeders in His church? Why would He allow the demon in? Why would He allow Mrs. Browning to die? Why didn't He stop it from happening?"

Ross took a long, slow breath. "Maybe that isn't the way it works. Isn't the church supposed to be open to everyone?"

"Not to demons and feeders! Not to things like that! What are they doing here, anyway? Why aren't they somewhere else?" Her voice was hard-edged and shaking now, and her hands were gesturing wildly. "If you really are a Knight of the Word, why don't you do something about them? Don't you have some kind of power? You must! Can't you use it on them? Why is this so hard?"

Ross looked off into the trees. *Tell her.* His hands tightened on the staff. "If I destroy the feeders, I reveal myself." He looked back at her. "I let people know what I am. When that happens, I am compromised. Worse, I weaken myself. I don't have unlimited power. I have . . . only so much. Every time I use it, I leave myself exposed. If the demon finds me like that, he will destroy me. I have to be patient, to wait, to choose my time. Ideally, I will only have to use my power once—when I have the demon before me."

He felt trapped by his words. "Pick must have told you about the feeders. The feeders are only here because of us. They react to us, to us as humans. They feed on our emotions, on our behavior. They grow stronger or weaker depending on how we behave. The Word made them to be a reflection of us. If we behave well, we diminish them. If we behave badly, we strengthen them. Give them too much to feed on and they devour us. But they're not subject to the same laws as we are. They don't have life in the same way we do; they don't have substance. They creep around in the shadows and come out with any release of the dark that's inside us. I can burn them all to ash, but they will just come back again, born out of new emotions, new behavior. Do you understand?"

The girl nodded dubiously. "Are they everywhere, everywhere in the world?"

"Yes."

"But aren't there more in places where things are worse? In places where the people are killing each other, killing their children?"

"Yes."

"Then why aren't you there? What are you doing here, in this little, insignificant Midwestern town? No one is dying here. Nothing is happening here!" Her voice rose. "What is so important about Hopewell?"

Ross did not look away, dared not. "I can't answer that. I go where I'm sent. Right now, I'm tracking the demon. I'm here because of him. I know that something pivotal is going to take place, something that will affect the future, and I have to stop it. I know it seems incredible that anything occurring in a tiny place like Hopewell could have such an impact. But we know how history works. Cataclysms are set in motion by small events in out-of-the-way places. Maybe that's what's happening."

She studied him fixedly. "It has something to do with me, doesn't it?"

Tell her! "It looks that way," he hedged.

She waited a moment, then said, "I had a . . . dream about Gran last night. She was a girl, the way she looks in one of the pictures on the mantel. She was running in the park with the feeders. She was one of them. I asked her about it, and she admitted that she had done that when she was a girl." She paused. "There was a demon with her. She admitted that, too. She said she didn't know at first what it was, and that when she found out, she sent it away. Pick said that was true." She paused. "What I wonder is if this might be the same demon, if it might have come back to hurt Gran through me."

Ross nodded slowly. "It's possible."

She glared at him, needing more, wanting a better answer. "But how would that change anything about the future? What difference would that make to anyone but us?"

Ross started walking again, forcing her to follow. "I don't know. What was it you were going to show me?"

She caught up to him easily, kept her hot gaze turned on him. "If you're hiding something, I'll find out what it is." Her voice was hard-edged and determined, challenging him to respond. When he failed to do so, she moved ahead of him as if to push the matter aside, dismissive and contemptuous. "This way, over there, in those trees."

They descended a gentle slope to a small stream and an old wooden bridge. They crossed the bridge and started up the other side into the deep woods. It was silent here, empty of people, of sound, of movement. The heat was trapped in the undergrowth, and none of the river's coolness penetrated to ease the swelter. Insects buzzed annoyingly in their faces, attracted by their sweat.

"Actually, it wasn't a dream," she said suddenly. "About Gran, I mean. It was a vision. An Indian named Two Bears showed it to me. He took me to see the spirits of the Sinnissippi dance in the park last night after you left. He says he is the last of them." She paused. "What do you think?"

A chill passed over John Ross in spite of the heat. O'olish Amaneh. "Was he a big man, a Vietnam vet?"

She looked over at him quickly. "Do you know him?"

"Maybe. There are stories about an Indian shaman, a seer. He uses different names. I've come across people who've met him once or twice, heard about some others." He could not tell her of this, either. He could barely stand to think on it. O'olish Amaneh. "I think maybe he is in service to the Word."

Nest looked away again. "He didn't say so."

"No, he wouldn't. He never does. He just shows up and talks about the future, how it is linked to the past, how everything is tied together; then he disappears again. It's always the same. But I think, from what I've heard, that maybe he is one of us."

They pushed through a tangle of brush that had overgrown the narrow trail, spitting out gnats that flew into their mouths, lowering their heads against the shards of sunlight that penetrated the shadows.

"Tell me something about Wraith," John Ross asked, trying to change the subject.

The girl shrugged. "You saw. I don't know what he is. He's been there ever since I was very little. He protects me from the feeders, but I don't know why. Even Gran and Pick don't seem to know. I don't see him much. He mostly comes out when the feeders threaten me."

She told him about her night forays into the park to rescue the strayed children, and how Wraith would always appear when the feeders tried to stop her. Ross mulled the matter over in his mind. He had never heard of anything like it, and he couldn't be certain from what Nest told him if Wraith was a creature of the Word or the Void. Certainly Wraith's behavior suggested his purpose was good, but Ross knew that where

Nest Freemark was concerned things were not as simple as they might seem.

"Where are we going?" Ross asked her as they crested the rise and moved into the shadow of the deep woods.

"Just a little farther," she advised, easing ahead on the narrow path to lead the way.

The ground leveled and the trees closed about, leaving them draped in heavy shadow. The air was fetid and damp with humidity, and insects were everywhere. Ross brushed at them futilely. The trail twisted and wound through thick patches of scrub and brambles. Several times it branched, but Nest did not hesitate in choosing the way. Ross marveled at the ease with which she navigated the tangle, thinking on how much at home she was here, on how much she seemed to belong. She had the confidence of youth, of a young girl who knew well the ground she had already covered, even if she did not begin to realize how much still lay ahead.

They passed from the thicket into a clearing, and there, before them, was a giant oak. The oak towered overhead, clearly the biggest tree in the park, one of the biggest that Ross had ever seen. But the tree was sick, its leaves curling and turning black at the tips, its bark split and ragged and oozing discolored fluid that stained the earth at its roots. Ross stared at the tree for a moment, stunned both by its size and the degree of its decay, then looked questioningly at the girl.

"This is what I wanted you to see," she confirmed.

"What's wrong with it?"

"Exactly the question!" declared Pick, who materialized out of nowhere on Nest Freemark's shoulder. "I thought that you might know."

The sylvan was covered with dust and bits of leaves. He straightened himself on the girl's shoulder, looking decidedly out of sorts.

"Spent all morning foraging about for roots and herbs that might be used to make a medicine, but nothing seems to help. I've tried everything, magic included, and I cannot stop the decay. It spreads all through the tree now, infecting every limb and every root. I'm at my wits' end."

"Pick thinks it's the demon's work," Nest advised pointedly.

Ross looked at the tree anew, still perplexed. "Why would the demon do this?"

"Well, because this tree is the prison of a maentwrog!" Pick declared heatedly. Quickly, he told John Ross the tale of the maentwrog's entrapment, of how it had remained imprisoned all these years, safe beyond the walls of magic and nature that combined to shut it away. "But no more," the sylvan concluded with dire gloom. "At the rate the decay is spreading, it will be free before you know it!"

Ross walked forward and stood silently before the great oak. He knew something of the creatures that served the Void and particularly of those called maentwrogs. There were only a handful, but they were terrible things. Ross had never faced one, but he had been told of what they could do, consumed by their need to destroy, unresponsive to anything but their hunger. None had been loose in the world for centuries. He did not like thinking of what it would mean if one were to get loose now.

In his hand, the black staff pulsed faintly in response to the nearness of the beast, a warning of the danger. He stared upward into the branches of the ancient tree, trying to see something that would help him decide what to do.

"I lack any magic that would help," he said quietly. "I'm not skilled in that way."

"It's the demon's work, isn't it?" Pick demanded heatedly.

Ross nodded. "I expect it is."

The sylvan's narrow face screwed into a knot. "I knew it, I just knew it! That's why none of our efforts have been successful! He's counteracting them!"

Ross looked away. It made sense. The maentwrog would be another distraction, another source of confusion. It was the way the demon liked to work, throwing up smoke and mirrors to mask what he was really about.

Nest was telling Pick about the encounter with the demon in church that morning, and the sylvan was jumping up and down on her shoulder and telling her he'd warned her, he'd told her. Nest looked appalled. They began to argue. Ross glanced over at them, then walked forward alone and stood directly before the tree. The staff was throbbing in his hand, alive with the magic, hot with anticipation for what waited. *Not yet.* He reached forward with his free hand and touched the damaged bark gently. The tree felt slick and cold beneath his fingers, as if its sickness had come to the surface, coated its rough skin. A maentwrog, he thought grimly. A raver.

Ross studied the ground about him, and everywhere the earth was damp and pitted, revealing long stretches of the tree's exposed roots. No ants or beetles crawled upon its surface. There was no movement anywhere. The tree and its soil had become anathema to living things.

Ross sighed deeply. His inadequacy appalled him. He should be able to do something. He should have magic to employ. But he was a knight, and the magic he had been given to use could only destroy.

He turned back again. Nest and Pick had stopped arguing and were watching him silently. He could read the question in their eyes. What should they do now? They were waiting on him to provide them with an answer.

There was only one answer he could give. They would have to find the demon.

Which was, of course, like so many things, much easier said than done.

CHAPTER 21

After John Ross and Nest departed, Old Bob helped Evelyn clean up the remains of the picnic lunch. While his wife packed away the dishes and leftovers, he gathered together the used paper plates, cups, and napkins and carried them to a trash bin over by one of the cook stations. When they were done, they sat together on the blanket and looked out through the heat to where the sunlight sparkled off the blue waters of the Rock River in brilliant, diamond bursts.

She liked it when I called her Dark Eyes, he thought as he sat with his hand covering hers, remembering the sudden, warm look she had given him. It took him back to when they were much younger, when Caitlin was still a baby, before the booze and the cigarettes and all the hurt. He remembered how funny she had been, how bright and gay and filled with life. He glanced over at her, seeing the young girl locked deep inside her aging body. His throat tightened. If she would just let me get close again.

On the river, boats were drifting with the current, slow and aimless. Some carried fishermen, poles extended over the water, bodies hunched forward on wooden seats in silent meditation. Some carried sunbathers and swimmers on their way to the smattering of scrub islands that dotted the waters where they widened just west of the park and the bayou. There were a few large cruisers, their motors throbbing faint and distant like aimless bumblebees. Flags and pennants flew from their masts. A single sailboat struggled to catch a breeze with its limp triangular sail. In the sunlight, birds soared from tree to tree, out over the waters and back again, small flickers of light and shadow.

After a time, he said, "I'm going to take a walk up to the horseshoe tournament, talk to a couple of the boys. Would you like to come along?"

She surprised him. "Matter of fact, Robert, I would."

They rose and began the walk up the hill, leaving the blanket, the picnic basket, and the cooler behind. No one would steal them; this was Hopewell. Old Bob was already thinking ahead to what he was about to do. He had promised Mel Riorden he would speak with Derry Howe, and he tried hard to keep the promises he made. He had no idea what he was going to say to the boy. This wasn't his business, after all. He no longer worked at MidCon; he was not an active member of the union. His connection with the mill and those who worked there was rooted mainly in the past, a part of a history that was forever behind him. What happened now would probably not affect him directly, not in the time he had left in this life. It might affect Nest, of course, but he thought she would leave when she was grown, move on to some other life. She was too talented to stay in Hopewell. He might argue that he had a lot of himself invested in the mill, but the truth was he had never been a man in search of a legacy, and he didn't believe much in carrying the past forward.

Still, there were other people to be considered, and it was not in his nature to disregard their needs. If Derry was planning something foolish, something that would affect unfavorably those who had been his friends and neighbors, he owed it to them to try to do something about it.

But what should he say? What, that would make any difference to a boy like Derry, who had little respect for anyone, who had no reason to listen to him, to give him so much as the time of day?

But Mel thought the boy would listen to him, had respect for him. So he would try.

Evelyn's arm linked with his, and he felt her lean into him. There was nothing to her anymore—bird bones held together by old skin and iron determination. He drew her along easily, liking the feel of her against him, the closeness of her. He loved her still, wished he could bring her back to the way she had been, but knew he never could. He smiled down at her, and the sharp, old eyes glanced briefly at him, then away. *Love you forever,* he thought.

They crested the rise and were back among the crowds. Children ran everywhere, trailing balloons and crepe-paper streamers, laughing and shrieking. People stood three and four deep in front of the refreshments, loading up on cans of pop, bags of popcorn, and cones of cotton candy. Old Bob steered a path behind them and veered toward the horseshoe tournament, which was set up out in the flats south of the pavilion. He could see Derry Howe already, standing easily in a crowd of other young men, tall and angular in his jeans, T-shirt, and old tennis shoes, a can of beer in his hand.

Old Bob caught sight of Mike Michaelson and his wife, waved hello, and led Evelyn over to talk to them. Mike wanted to know if Old Bob had heard anything from Richie Stoudt. Richie's landlord had called, said Richie was supposed to do some work for him and hadn't shown up. There was no answer at his apartment either. Old Bob shook his head. Al Garcia wandered over, eager to show his latest pictures of the new grandbaby. After a few minutes, Mel Riorden appeared, touting the lemonade they were selling, giving Old Bob a meaningful glance. His wife Carol joined him, a warm and embracing woman, cooing over the grandbaby and joshing Al Garcia about his camera work. Laughter and warm feelings laced the conversation, but Old Bob felt locked away from it, distanced by the task he had agreed to undertake and the implications it bore. His mind struggled with the problem of how to approach Derry Howe. Was it really necessary? Maybe Mel was mistaken. Wouldn't be the first time. Sure wouldn't be the last.

Penny Williamson strode up, his black skin glistening with sweat, his massive arms streaked with dust. Wasn't anyone going to beat him this year in the horseshoe tournament, he announced. He was on, baby, he was dead on. Four ringers already. He clapped Old Bob on the back and bent to look at the pictures, asking Al Garcia whose grandbaby that was, wasn't Al's for sure, didn't look ugly like Al, must be a ringer. There was more laughter, kidding.

Old Bob took a deep breath, whispered to Evelyn, asking her to wait for him a moment, excused himself, and moved away. He eased through the knots of people, tasting dust and sweat in the air, smelling the popcorn and cotton candy. People said hello, greeted him as he passed. He moved toward Derry Howe, thinking he should probably just let it go. Howe saw him coming, watched him, took a long swig of his beer, shook his head. In his eyes, Old Bob saw suspicion, wariness, and a wealth of impatience.

He walked up to Derry, nodded, said, "Got a moment?"

Howe looked at him, debating whether to give him the moment or not. Then he smiled, the soul of equanimity, sauntered forward to join him, said, "Sure, Robert. What's up?"

Old Bob swung into step with him and they walked slowly past the participants in the horseshoe tournament. He nodded toward the field. "Having any luck?"

Derry Howe shrugged, looked at him, waiting.

"Heard a rumor that you were planning something special for the Fourth."

Derry's expression did not change. "Where'd you hear that?"

"Heard you were planning an accident, maybe." Old Bob ignored him, did not look at him. "Something to persuade the MidCon people they ought to work a little harder at settling this strike."

"Man, the things you hear." Derry tossed the beer can into a metal trash bin and shoved his hands in his jeans pockets. He was smiling, being cool. "You planning on coming out for the fireworks, Robert? Celebrating our independence?"

Old Bob stopped now, faced him, eyes hard. "Listen to me. If I know about it, others know about it, too. You're not being very smart, son."

Derry Howe's smile froze, disappeared. "Maybe certain people ought to mind their own business."

Old Bob nodded. "I'll assume you're not talking about me, because we've both got the same business interests where MidCon is concerned."

There was a long pause as Derry studied him. He had misread the comment. "You saying you want in on this?"

"No."

"Then what are you saying?"

Old Bob sighed. "I'm saying that maybe you ought to think this through a little further before you act on it. I'm saying it doesn't sound like a very good idea. If you do something to the company, something that gets people hurt, it might rebound on you. You might get hurt, too."

Derry Howe sneered. "I ain't afraid of taking a chance. Not like Mel and the rest of you, sitting around talking all day while your lives go right down the toilet. I said it before, I'll say it again. This ain't going to get settled unless we do something to help it along. The company's just going to wait us out. They're starting up the fourteen-inch—hell, already started it up, I expect. They'll have it up and running Tuesday morning, bright and early. They're bringing in scabs and company men to run it. Some of the strikers are talking about going back, giving in because they're scared. You know how it goes. When that happens, we're done, Robert Roosevelt Freemark. And you know it."

"Maybe. But blowing things up isn't the answer either."

Derry pulled a face. "Who said anything about blowing something up? Did I say anything like that? That what you heard?"

"You were a demolitions man in Vietnam. I can put two and two together."

Howe laughed. "Yeah? Well, your addition stinks. That explosives stuff is all ancient history. I barely remember any of that. Time marches on, right?"

Old Bob nodded, patient the way you were with a child. "So it wouldn't be your fault if there was an accident, would it?"

"Not hardly."

"An accident that would make MidCon look like a bunch of clowns, trying to reopen the mill without the union?"

"Sort of like kids playing with matches in a pile of fireworks?"

"Like that."

Derry nodded thoughtfully. "You know, Robert, the thing about fireworks is that they're touchy, unpredictable. Sometimes they don't behave like you think they should. That's how all those accidents happen, people getting their hands blown off and such. They play with explosives they aren't trained to handle. They take foolish chances."

Old Bob shook his head. "We're not talking about fireworks here. We're talking about MidCon and people getting killed!"

Derry Howe's eyes were bright and hard. "You got that right."

Old Bob looked off into the trees, into the cool shade. "I don't like what I'm hearing."

"Then don't listen." Derry smiled disdainfully. "Do yourself a favor, Robert. Sit this one out. It ain't right for you anyway. You or Mel or any of the others. You had your day. Time to step aside. Stay home on the Fourth. Watch a movie or something. Keep away from the fireworks—all of them."

He paused, and a dark, wild look came into his eyes. "It's settled with me, Robert Roosevelt. I know what I'm about. I'm going to put an end to this strike. I'm going to give MidCon a Fourth of July to remember, and when it's over they won't be able to get to the bargaining table quick enough. That's the way it's going to be, and there ain't nothing they can do about it." He ran his fingers through his short-cropped hair, a quick, dismissive movement. "Or you either. You stay out of my way. Be better for you if you did."

He gave Old Bob a wink and walked back to his friends.

Robert Freemark stood watching after him angrily for a moment, then turned away. He moved back through the crowds toward Evelyn, his anger turning to disappointment. He supposed he hadn't really expected to change Derry Howe's mind. He supposed he hadn't really expected to accomplish much of anything. Maybe he was hoping it would turn out Mel Riorden was mistaken, that Derry wasn't really planning something foolish. Whatever the case, his failure to achieve anything left him feeling empty and disgruntled. He should have made a stronger argument, been more persuasive. He should have found a way to get through.

He worked his way back to Evelyn, burdened by both the weight of the July heat and his anger. Somewhere deep inside, where he hid the things he didn't want other people to see, he felt a darkness rise up and begin to take shape. Something bad was going to happen. Maybe Derry intended to damage the machinery at the mill. Maybe he intended to put a serious dent in the company's pocketbook or its image. But for some reason Old Bob felt like it might be even worse than that. He felt it might be catastrophic.

He moved up to Mel and Carol Riorden, Al Garcia, Penny Williamson, and Evelyn, smiling easily, comfortably to hide his concerns. They were still talking about the new grandbaby. Mel gave him a questioning look. He frowned and shook his head slowly. He could see the disappointment in his friend's face.

Evelyn took him by the arm and pulled him away. "Come with me," she directed, steering him through the crowd. "I have a little business of my own to take care of."

He let himself be led back toward the horseshoe tournament, back toward Derry Howe. Old Bob glanced quickly at her, thinking, No, it can't be about Derry, can it? Evelyn did not return the glance, her gaze directed forward, intense and immutable. He had seen that look before, and he knew that whatever she had set herself to do, she would not be dissuaded. He kept his mouth shut.

The crowd observing the horseshoe contest parted before them. Evelyn veered left, taking Old Bob with her, striding down the line of spectators toward the participants at the far end.

"Just stand next to me, Robert," she said quietly. "You don't have to say anything. I'll do the talking."

She released his arm and stepped in front of him, taking the lead. He caught sight of George Paulsen staring at them from among the competitors, but Evelyn seemed oblivious of him. She moved, instead, toward Enid Scott, who was standing with her youngest, Bennett, to one side.

Enid saw Evelyn coming and turned to face her, surprise reflecting in her pale, tired eyes. She was dressed in matching shorts and halter top that had fit better when she was twenty pounds lighter. She brushed back a few loose strands of her lank, tousled hair and dragged out an uncertain smile.

"Hello, Mrs. Freemark," she greeted, her voice breaking slightly as she caught the look in Evelyn's dark eyes.

Evelyn came to a stop directly before her. "Enid, I'll come right to the point," she said softly. They were alone except for Bennett and Old Bob; no one else could hear what was being said. "I know you've had some rough times, and that raising five children all alone is no picnic. I think you've done better than a lot of women would have in your circumstances, and I admire you for it. You've kept your family together the best you could. You've got five children you can be proud of."

"Thank you," Enid stammered, surprised.

"I'm not finished. The flip side of this particular coin is that you've made a whole bunch of decisions in your life that testify to the distinct possibility that you have the common sense of a woodchuck. Sooner or later, some of those decisions are going to come back to haunt you. Your choice in men, for example, is abominable. You've got five fatherless children as proof of that, and I don't see much improvement of late. Your frequent visits to the bars and nightspots of this community suggest that alcohol is becoming a problem for you. And it is no shame to be unemployed and on welfare, but it is a shame not to want to do anything about it!"

Robert blinked in disbelief, hearing the fire in his wife's voice, seeing the stiff set of her back rigid within her flowered dress. Little Bennett was staring at Evelyn, her mouth open.

"Well, I don't think you have the right to tell me . . ." Enid Scott began, flustered and angry now.

"Understand something, Enid. I'm not standing here as an example of how a woman ought to live her life." Evelyn cut her short, brushing aside her attempt at defending herself. "Matter of fact, I've made some of the same mistakes you're making, and I've made them worse. I'm closer to you than you realize. That gives me not only the right to talk to you this way, but the obligation as well. I can see where you're headed, and I can't let you walk off the end of the pier without shouting out a warning of some sort. So this is that warning. You can make a lot of mistakes in this life and get away with it. We both know that. But there's one mistake you can't make—not ever, if you want to live with yourself afterward. And that's not being there for your children when they need you. It's happened several times already. Don't say anything, Enid. Don't say it isn't so, because that would be a terrible lie, and you don't want to add that to your catalogue of sins. Point is, nothing bad has happened yet. But sooner or later, it will. If it does, that will be the end of you."

Evelyn held the other woman's gaze, took a quick breath, and stepped forward. Enid Scott flinched, and Bennett jumped. But all Evelyn did was reach down and take Enid's hand in her own, hold it, and then pat it gently.

"If you ever need anyone, you call me," she said quietly. "Any time, for any reason. You call me. I'll be there. That's a promise."

A few people were looking over now, sensing that something was going on, not sure exactly what it was. George Paulsen detached himself from the horseshoe competitors and sauntered over, mean eyes narrowing. "What's going on here?" he snapped.

Evelyn ignored him. "Are you all right, Enid? I didn't speak too harshly, did I?"

"Well," whispered Enid Scott uncertainly.

"I did, I expect." Evelyn continued to pat her hand, to hold it between her own, her voice soothing and calm. "I speak the way I do because I believe it is best to be direct. But I would like to be your friend, if you would let me. I know you have no family here, and I don't want you to think that you are alone."

"She ain't alone, she's got me!" George Paulsen declared, coming up to them.

Gran fixed him with a withering gaze. "Having you for company is not something I would think she would be anxious to brag on!" she snapped.

Paulsen flushed angrily. "Listen here, old woman . . ."

Old Bob started forward protectively, but Evelyn was too quick for him. She moved right up against George Paulsen, the index fingers of both hands aimed at him like the barrels of guns.

"Don't you mess with me, George," she hissed. "Don't you even think about it. You haven't the iron. Now, you listen to me. You can stay with Enid or not—that's between you and her. But if I hear one more story about you striking that woman or any of her children, if I see one bruise on any of them that I don't like the looks of, if I so much as see you raise a threatening hand against them, you will think that God must have reached down out of heaven and squashed you like a bug. Do you understand me, sir?"

George Paulsen flinched as her fingers slowly extended to touch his chest.

"And don't you believe for one minute that you can hide anything from me, George," she continued softly. "Even if you think I won't find out, I will. I'll come after you, no matter how fast or how far you try to run from me." She lifted her fingers away. "You remember that."

For a moment Old Bob thought George Paulsen would strike Evelyn. But he must have seen something in her face or found something in his own heart that told him it would be a mistake. He tried to speak, failed, shot a venomous look at Enid, and stalked away.

There were a lot of people staring now. Evelyn ignored them, was oblivious of them. She turned back to Enid Scott and Bennett, gave Enid a reassuring nod and Bennett a smile. "You come by for ice cream, little one," she invited. "Nest and I would love to have you any time. Bring your mother with you when you do."

"Mrs. Freemark," Enid Scott tried, but was unable to continue.

Evelyn met her gaze, her own steady and fixed. "My name is Evelyn. That's what all my friends call me. You think on what I've said, Enid. I'll be looking in on you."

She walked back to Old Bob then, took his arm in hers, and turned him back toward the river. "Shame to waste a nice day like this standing about in the heat. Why don't we go sit out by the river and wait for Nest."

He stared at her. "You amaze me, Evelyn," he told her, not bothering to hide the astonishment in his voice. "You really do."

A faint smile played at the corners of her mouth, a hint of mischievousness that appeared and faded all at once. "Now and then, Robert," she replied softly. "Now and then."

CHAPTER 22

Though he had not admitted it to Nest Freemark, John Ross had met O'olish Amaneh before. It was O'olish Amaneh who had given him his limp.

"Your old life is finished, my brave knight-errant," the Lady had whispered that night in the Fairy Glen as she held him to her, accepting the pledge of his faith, taking the measure of his strength. All about them, the fairies darted in the blackness of the water and the cool of the shadows, rippling with the sound of her voice in his ear. "Now, for as long as I deem it necessary, you belong to me. You will care for and be faithful to no other. You will forsake your home. You will forsake your family and your friends. Do you understand?"

"Yes," he had said.

"You will be asked to sacrifice, of your body and your soul, of your heart and your mind, in this world and the world to come. Your sacrifice will be great, but it will be necessary. Do you understand?"

"Yes," he had said once more.

"I brought you to me, John Ross. Now I send you back again. Leave this country and return to your home. It is there that you are needed to do battle in my service. I am the light and the way, the road you must travel and the life you must lead. Go now, and be at peace."

He did as he was told. He went from the Fairy Glen to his cottage in Betws-y-Coed, packed his bags, traveled east into England, and caught a standby flight to the States. He did so in the firm belief that his life had been changed in the way he had always anticipated it one day would and with the hope that here, at last, was the purpose he had sought. He did not know yet what he was supposed to do. He had become a Knight of the Word, but he did not know what was expected of him. He carried inside him the blood of Owain Glyndwr, and he would be the Word's champion and do battle with the Void as his ancestor had before him. He did not know what that meant. He was terrified and exhilarated and filled with passion. The visions of the future that the Lady had shown him were burned into his mind forever, and when he recalled them they brought tears to his eyes. He was just a man, just one man, but he knew that he must do whatever was asked of him—even if it meant giving up his life.

But it was not real to him yet. It was still a dream, and as he traveled farther away from the Fairy Glen and that night, it became steadily more so. He went home to his parents, who were still alive then, to let them know he was well, but would not be staying. He was purposefully vague, and he told them nothing of what had befallen him. He had not been forbidden to do so, but he knew that it would be foolish to speak of it. His parents, whether they believed him or not, would be needlessly worried. Better that they thought him a wanderer still when he left them. Better that they lived without knowing.

So he waited, frozen in time. He tried to envision what his life would be like in service to the Lady. He tried to resolve his doubts and his fears, to settle within himself the feelings of inadequacy that had begun to surface. What could he do, that would make a difference? What would be required of him, that he would be able to respond? Was he strong enough to do what was needed? Was he anything of what the Lady believed?

He waited for her to speak to him, to reveal her purpose for him. She did not. He visited with friends and acquaintances from his past, marking time against an uncertain future. Weeks went by. Still the Lady did not appear. Doubts set in. Had he dreamed it all? Had he imagined her? Or worse, had he mistaken her intent? What if the great purpose he had envisioned, the purpose for which he had searched so long, was a lie?

Doubts turned to mistrust. What if he had been deceived? He was beset by nightmares that woke him shaking and chilled on the hottest nights, sweating and fiery in the coldest of rooms. Something had gone wrong. Perhaps he was not the champion she had been looking for, and she had realized it and abandoned him. Perhaps she had forsaken him entirely.

Strong belief turned slowly to fragile hope, the Lady's whispered promise echoing through the empty corridors of his mind.

Your way lies through me. I am the road that you must take.

Then the Indian came to him. He was sitting on the bed in his room, alone in the house, his parents gone for the afternoon. He was staring at words on a paper before him, words that he had written in an effort to find reason in what had happened to him, when the door opened and the Indian was standing there.

"I am O'olish Amaneh," he said quietly.

He was a big man, his skin copper-colored, his hair braided and black, his eyes intense and probing. He wore old army clothes and moccasins and carried a backpack and bedroll. In one massive hand, he gripped a long black staff.

He came into the room and shut the door behind him. "I have come to give you this," he said, and held out the staff.

Ross stared, saw the sheen of the wood, the rune marks cut into the shiny surface, and the way the light played over both. He sat there on the bed, frozen in place.

"You are John Ross?" O'olish Amaneh asked him.

Ross nodded, unable to speak.

"You are a Knight of the Word?"

Ross blinked rapidly and swallowed against the dryness in his throat. "Do you come from her?" he managed.

The Indian did not answer.

"Are you in service to the Lady?" he pressed.

"The staff belongs to you," O'olish Amaneh insisted quietly, ignoring him. "Take it."

Ross could not do so. He knew with sudden, terrifying certainty that if he did, there would be no turning back. The clarity of his knowledge was appalling. It was the staff, something in the way it gleamed, in its blackness, in the intricacy of its carvings. It was in the implacable way the Indian urged him to take hold of it. If he did so, he was finished. If he did so, it was the end of him. He was not ready for this after all, he saw. He no longer wanted to be a part of what had happened in the Fairy Glen, in Wales, in the realm of the Lady's magic.

The Indian was a rock, standing before him unmoved. "Your faith must be stronger than this," he advised in a whisper. "Your faith must sustain you. You swore to serve. You cannot recant. It is forbidden."

"Forbidden?" Ross repeated in disbelief. He was nearly in tears, filled with contempt for himself, for his weakness, for his failing resolve. "Don't you understand?" he breathed.

The Indian gave no sign as to whether he did or not. "You are a Knight of the Word. You have been chosen. You have need of the staff. Take it."

Ross shook his head slowly. "I can't."

"Stand up," O'olish Amaneh ordered.

There was no change of expression in the big man's face, no sign of disappointment, of anger, of anything. The eyes fixed on John Ross, calm and steady, as dark and deep as night pools, bottomless pits within the shadow of the great brow. Ross could not look away. Slowly he rose to his feet. The Indian came forward and held the staff out to him, before his terrified face, the carved markings, the polished wood, the gnarled length.

"Take the staff," he said quietly.

John Ross tried to step away, struggled to break free of the eyes that held him bound.

"Take the staff," O'olish Amaneh repeated.

Ross brought his hands up obediently, and his fingers closed about the polished wood. Instantly, fire ripped through his body. *Oh, God!* His left foot began to cramp, pain seizing and locking about it, working its way down to the bone. Ross tried to scream, but found he could make no sound. The pain intensified, growing worse than anything he had ever experienced, than anything he had imagined possible. His hands fastened so tightly about the staff that his knuckles turned white. He felt as if his fingers were imprinting the wood. He could not make himself let go. His foot jerked and twisted, and the pain climbed up his leg, cramping his muscles, tearing his ligaments, setting fire to his nerves. It bore into his knee, and now his mouth was open wide and his head thrown back in agony.

Then, just as quickly as it had appeared, the pain was gone. John Ross gasped in shock and relief, his head sagging on his chest. He leaned heavily on the black staff, letting it support him, relying on its strength to hold him erect. *My God, my God!*

Slowly O'olish Amaneh stepped away. "Now it belongs to you," the Indian repeated. "You are bound to it. You are joined as one. You cannot give it up until you are released from your service. Remember that. Do not try to put it from you. Do not try to cast it away. Ever."

Then O'olish Amaneh was gone, out the door and down the hall, as silent as a ghost. Ross waited half a breath, then took a quick step toward the door to close it. He collapsed instantly, his foot turning in, his leg unable to bear the weight of his body. He struggled back to his feet, leaning on the staff for support, and fell again. He sprawled on the floor, staring down at his leg. Once more he climbed to his feet, gritting his teeth, squeezing shut his eyes, so fearful of what had been done to him that he could barely breathe.

He was finally able to stand, but only with the aid of the staff. He was going to have to learn to walk all over again. He leaned against the wall and cried with rage and frustration.

Why has this been done to me?

He would have his answer that night when he dreamed for the first time of the future that was his to prevent.

"Penny for your thoughts, John Ross."

It was evening, the daylight gone hazy and dim with twilight's slow descent, the heat lingering in a thick blanket across the broad stretch of the park. Ross was sitting alone on the grass beneath an old hickory just back from where the band was setting up for the dance in the pavilion. People were milling about, watching the proceedings, eating popcorn, ice cream, and cotton candy and drinking pop, lemonade, and iced tea. Ball games were still under way on the diamonds, but the last of the organized races and the horseshoe tournament had come to a close. Ross had been lost momentarily in the past, in the days before he understood what the Lady required of him and what it meant to be a Knight of the Word.

The familiar voice brought him out of his reverie. He looked up and smiled at Josie Jackson. "A penny? I expect that's more than they're worth. How are you?"

"I'm fine, thank you." She stood looking at him for a moment, openly appraising him. She was wearing a flower-print blouse with a scoop neck and a full, knee-length skirt cinched about her narrow waist. She had tied back her blond hair with a ribbon, and wore sandals and a gold bracelet. She looked fresh and cool, even in the stifling heat. "I missed you at breakfast this morning. You didn't come in."

He smiled ruefully. "My loss. I overslept, then went straight to church. The Freemarks invited me." He drew up his good leg and clasped his hands about his knee. "I don't get to church as much as I should, I'm afraid."

She laughed. "So how was it?"

He hesitated, picturing in his mind the dark shapes of the feeders prowling through the sanctuary, Wraith stalking out of the gloom of the foyer, and the demon hiding somewhere farther back in the shadows. *How was it?* "It wasn't quite what I remember," he replied without a trace of irony.

"Nothing ever is." She came forward a step. "Are you alone this evening?"

The expressive dark eyes held him frozen in place. He looked away to free himself, then quickly back again. Nest had gone off with her friends. Old Bob had taken Evelyn home. He was marking time now, waiting on the demon. "Looks that way," he said.

"Do you want some company?" she asked, her voice smooth and relaxed.

He felt his throat tighten. He was tired of being alone. What harm could it do to spend a little time with her, to give a little of himself to a pretty woman? "Sure," he told her.

"Good." She sat down next to him, a graceful movement that put her right up against him. He could feel the softness of her shoulder and hip. She sat without speaking for a moment, looking at the people gathered about the pavilion, her gaze steady and distant. He studied the freckles on her nose out of the corner of his eye, trying to think of something to say.

"I'm not much of a dancer," he confessed finally, struggling to read her thoughts.

She looked at him as if amazed that he would admit such a thing, then gave him a quirky smile. "Why don't we just talk, then?"

He nodded and said nothing for a moment. He looked off toward the pavilion. "Would you like an ice cream or something to drink?"

She was still looking at him, still smiling. "Yes."

"Which?"

"Surprise me."

He levered himself to his feet using the staff, limped over to the food stand, bought two chocolate ice-cream cones, and limped back again, squinting against the sharp glare of the setting sun. It was just for a little while, he told himself. Just so that he could remember what it was like to feel good about himself. He sat down beside her again and handed her a cone.

"My favorite," she said, sounding like she meant it. She took a small bite. Her freckled nose wrinkled. "Hmmmm, really good." She took another bite and looked at him. "So tell me something about yourself."

He thought a moment, staring off into the crowds, then told her about traveling through Great Britain. She listened intently as he recounted his visits to the castles and cathedrals, to the gardens and the moors, to the hamlets and the cities. He liked talking about England, and he took time to give her a clear picture of what it was like there—of the colors and the smells when it rained, which was often; of the countryside with its farms and postage-stamp fields, walled by stone; of the mist and the wildflowers in the spring, when there was color every-where, diffused and made brilliant in turn by the changes in the light.

She smiled when he was done and said she wanted to go someday. She talked about what it was like to run a coffee shop, her own business, built from scratch. She told him what it was like growing up in Hopewell, sometimes good, some-times bad. She talked about her family, which was large and mostly elsewhere. She did not ask him what he did for a living or about his family, and he did not volunteer. He told her he had been a graduate student for many years, and perhaps she thought he still was one. She joked with him as if she had known him all his life, and he liked that. She made him feel comfortable. He thought she was pretty and funny and smart, and he wanted to know her better. He was attracted to her as he had not been attracted to a woman in a very long time. It was a dangerous way for him to feel.

At one point she said to him, "I suppose you think I'm pretty forward, inviting myself to spend the evening with you."

He shook his head at once. "I don't think that at all."

"Do you think I might be easy?" She paused. "You know."

He stared at her, astonished by the question, unable to reply.

"Good Heavens, you're blushing, John!" She laughed and poked him gently in the ribs. "Relax, I'm teasing. I'm not like that." She grinned. "But I'm curious, and I'm not shy. I don't know you, but I think I'd like to. So I'm taking a chance. I believe in taking chances. I think that if you don't take chances, you miss out."

He thought of his own life, and he nodded slowly. "I guess I agree with that."

The sun had dropped below the horizon, and darkness had fallen over the park. The band had begun playing, easing into a slow, sweet waltz that brought the older couples out onto the dance floor beneath the colored lamps that had been strung about the pavilion. Out in the grass, small children danced with each other, mimicking the adults, taking large, deliberate steps. John Ross and Josie Jackson watched them in silence, smiling, letting their thoughts drift on the music's soft swell.

After a time, he asked her if she would like to take a walk. They climbed to their feet and strolled off into the darkened trees. Josie took his free arm, and moved close to him, matching his halting pace. They walked from the pavilion toward the toboggan slide, then down through the trees toward the river. The music trailed after them, soft and inviting. The night was brilliant with stars, but thick with summer heat, the air compressed and heavy beneath the pinpricked sky. It was dark and silent within the old hardwoods, and the river was a gleaming, silver-tipped ribbon below them.

They stopped on a rise within a stand of elm to stare down at it, still listening to the strains of the distant music, to the jumbled sounds of conversation and laughter, to the buzz of the locusts far back in the woods. On the river, a scattering of boats bobbed at anchor, and from farther out in the dark, over on the far bank of the Rock River, car lights crawled down private drives like the eyes of nocturnal hunters.

"I like being with you, John," Josie told him quietly. She squeezed his arm for emphasis.

He closed his eyes against the ache her words generated within him. "I like being with you, too."

There was a long silence, and then she leaned over and kissed him softly on the cheek. When he turned to look at her, she kissed him on the mouth. He put caution aside and kissed her back.

She broke the embrace, and he saw the bright wonder in her eyes. "Maybe, just this once," she whispered, "I'm going to be a little more forward than I thought."

It took a moment for the import of the words to register, and then another for the familiar chill to run through him as the memories began to scream in the silence of his mind.

When he sleeps the night after O'olish Amaneh has given him the black walnut staff with its strange rune markings and terrible secret, he dreams for the first time of the future the Lady had prophesied. It is not a dream of the sort that he has experienced before. The dream is not fragmented and surreal as dreams usually are. It is not composed of people and places from his life, not formed of events turned upside down by the workings of his subconscious. The dream is filled with the sounds, tastes, smells, sights, and feelings of life, and he knows in a strange and frightening way that what he is experiencing is real.

He is not simply dreaming of the future; he is living in it.

He closes his eyes momentarily against the feelings this revelation generates within him. Then he opens them quickly to look about. The world in which he finds himself is nightmarish. It is dark and misted and filled with destruction. He is on a hillside overlooking the remains of a city. The city was once large and heavily populated; now it lies in ruins, empty of life. It does not smolder or steam or glow with fading embers; it has been dead a long time. It sits lifeless and still, its stones and timbers and steel jutting out of the flattened earth like ravaged bones.

After a time, he begins to see the feeders. There are only a few, prowling the ruins, dark shapes barely visible in the gloom, eyes yellow and gleaming. He knows instinctively what they are. They are far away, down within the rubble, and they do not seem aware of him. He feels a twinge in his right hand, and looks down to find that he holds the black staff. Where he grips it, light pulses softly. The light signals the readiness of the staff's magic to respond to his summons. The magic is his to wield in his service to the Word. It is vast and formidable. It enables him to withstand almost anything. It gives him the power to destroy and to defend. It is the Word's magic, drawn from deep within the earth. It whispers to him in seductive tones and makes him promises it cannot always keep. His immediate response is to want to cast the staff away, but something rooted deep within forbids him from doing so.

He feels exposed on the hillside, and starts to move tentatively toward the shelter of some trees. When he does so, he finds that he no longer limps, that his leg is healed. He is not surprised; he knew it would be so.

When he reaches the trees, the Lady is waiting for him. She is a small, faint whiteness within the dark, as ethereal as gossamer. She looks at him, smiles, and then fades. She is not real after all, he realizes; she is not even there. She is a memory. He has been to this place before, in another, earlier time, before the destruction, and coming here again has triggered the memory.

He begins to understand now. He is living in the future, but only in his sleep. It is the cost of the magic he wields, the title he bears, and the responsibility he shoulders. He will live his life henceforth in two worlds—the present when awake, the future when asleep. The images come in a rush, like the waters of a river overflowing its banks in a flood. He is a Knight of the Word, and he must prevent the future in which he stands. But he needs the knowledge the future can give him in order to do so. He must learn from the future of the mistakes and missed opportunities of the past. If he can discover them, perhaps he can correct them. Each time he sleeps, he has another chance to learn. Each time he sleeps, the future whispers secrets of the past. But the future is never the same because the past advances and alters it. Nor does his sleep lend order, coherence, or chronology to what he witnesses. The future comes to him as it will and reveals itself as it chooses. He cannot control it; he must simply abide it.

And survive. For he is hunted by the demons and their allies, by the once-men who serve them, and by the things that are given over to the Void. Few remain who can resist them. He is one. They hunt him every night of his life. They have caught him more than once. They have killed him, he thinks, but he does not know for sure. The future changes each night. Perhaps it changes his fate as well.

He recalls all of it now. He has his memories of the past to fill in the gaps, so that even though it is his first night, he is a veteran of his dreams already. The truths rise up and confront him. He is crippled so that he will not ever give up the staff. Without the staff, he has no magic. Without the staff, he is helpless. If he cannot walk without the staff to aid him, he is far less likely to be careless with it. After all, it is his only protection. He is crippled so that he will remember.

*So it has been settled on him. His past is linked to his future.
If he fails in his mission of service to the Word, the future he
resides in each night will come to pass. He will be whole again,
but he will inherit the destruction and ruin he surveys. And he
will pay a further price. Magic summoned in the present will be
lost to him in the future. Each time he uses the magic in his
former life, he is deprived of it in the latter for an indeterminate
amount of time. He must use the magic wisely and effectively
when he invokes it, or one day, at a time or place not of his
choosing, in a situation when he needs it most, he may find
himself weaponless.*

*He stands alone within the trees on the hillside above the
ruined city and ponders what it means for him to sleep and why
he must always keep solitary and apart . . .*

"Josie," he said softly, searching for the right words.

There was sudden movement in the shadows, the sound of
rushing footsteps and heavy breathing. Ross turned as the
shadows closed on him, swift and menacing. He stepped away
from Josie, trying to place her behind him. He heard her gasp
in surprise, saw the masked faces of the men who reached for
him. He struggled to comprehend their muttered threats, and
then they were upon him.

They bore him backward toward the crest of the rise,
reaching for his arms and shoulders, trying to tear the staff
from his hands. He cried out to them, *No, wait, what are you
doing?* He fought to free himself, wrenching the staff away,
shielding it. One took a swing at him, trying to hit him in the
face, but he ducked aside. He could not move quickly, could
not run with his bad leg. He was forced to stand. He heard one
of them call him names, ugly and crude, heard another call him
"spy" and "company pig." *I'm not!* he tried to explain. Josie
shouted at them, furious, *What are you doing? Stop it! Get
away from him!* He was in danger of going down. He braced
himself against the rush and swung the high end of the staff
sharply at the nearest attacker. He felt the wood connect with
bone, and the man grunted and staggered back. He used the

lower end to hammer the shins of another man, and that one howled openly in pain.

Then they were all over him, bearing him to the ground. Fists struck at him as he slammed into the earth. Someone was kicking at his ribs. He heard Josie scream, saw her rush forward to try to protect him, arms flailing. A boot slammed into his head, bringing pain and bright light. He tried to throw off the ones who held him down, tried to regain his feet. The staff had been pushed aside so that he could no longer bring it to bear. They were still trying to wrench it from his hands, to take away his only protection. He felt the blows rain down on him, felt blood fill his mouth. It was getting harder to breathe. Josie was still screaming, but her voice was hoarse, and it sounded as if a hand had been clamped over her mouth.

A boot pinned his left wrist to the earth. *Don't do this!* he wanted to scream at them, but could not make himself. He fought in silent, futile desperation to break free. They were wrenching at the staff, tearing at his fingers, leaving him no choice . . .

Stop, please!

The runes carved into the polished black surface began to pulse with light. A fiery heat burned its gnarled length.

No!

The magic exploded from the staff in a rush of white brilliance, detonating with such fury that it seemed to consume the air itself, a whirlwind of power unleashed. It was not summoned, but came alive on its own, reacting to its master's need. With a single incendiary burst, it flung John Ross's attackers into the night. They flew from him as if they were paper cutouts, weightless in a high wind, and he was free once more. He lay gasping for breath in the aftermath, the magic gone as swiftly as it had appeared. In the darkness, his attackers climbed dazedly to their feet and stumbled away, their resolve shattered, their purpose forgotten, their confusion profound.

Too late for me, John Ross thought in despair, knowing the price he would now be forced to pay for having required use of the magic. *Way too late.*

As he closed his eyes against his body's and spirit's pain, he heard Josie call his name, and in the ensuing silence he reached out his hand to find her.

CHAPTER 23

Nest Freemark sat with her friends on the grass at the edge of the pavilion and watched the dancers sway and glide to the strains of the music. All about them, families and couples sat visiting on blankets and lawn chairs, their faces reflecting the colors of the lanterns strung from the pavilion's eaves. The sun's heat lingered, but a faint breeze wafted off the river now and cooled those gathered just enough that they could put the salty aftertaste of the daylight's swelter behind them. The breeze and the music wove together, soothing nerves and easing discomfort. Smiles came out of hiding, and people remembered the importance of using kind words. The night was as soft as velvet, and it cradled them in its arms and eased them toward sleep.

Robert was explaining something about computers to Jared. Brianna and Cass were talking about school clothes and makeup. Nest was wondering how she had let this happen.

It could have been so wonderful, she thought wistfully.

Things weren't working out the way she had planned. Jared had found her easily enough in the twilight hour before sunset when the band was setting up and the floor of the pavilion was being swept clean. For a few brief moments, while they were standing alone beneath one of the old hardwoods, she had thought that now, at last, she would have her chance to talk with him, to really talk with him, just the two of them. She had thought he might confide in her, that he might tell her something he had never told anyone—and that perhaps she would tell him something wonderful or startling in turn. She had come out of the day worn and dejected from her battle to discover the truth behind John Ross and her family, and she had reached a point where she just wanted to let go of everything for a little while. No demon, no maentwrog, no Pick, no magic. Just a boy she liked and wanted to be with. It didn't seem too much to ask. She had looked forward to it all day. She had imagined what it would be like, how good it would make her feel. She would talk with him, dance with him and, if things worked out just right, let him kiss her. She would look at him and feel good about herself for just a few moments.

They were easing in that direction when Robert, Cass, and Brianna joined them. One, two, three, there they were, her friends, all smiles, clueless that she wanted to be alone with Jared, wanted them to get lost, to just disappear. Why she hadn't seen that this might happen, she didn't know. But now that it had, she felt oddly betrayed. It was selfish and small of her to feel that way, but she couldn't help herself. She was feeling trapped at every turn, so hemmed in by the events of her life that she was finding it difficult to breathe. She had thought she might gain a small respite from her troubles at this dance. It didn't look like that was going to happen.

She shifted uncomfortably on the grass, trying to decide what to do. Maybe she should go home. Maybe she should just give it up. She glanced at Jared, her eyes hot and angry, willing him to say something, to do something. Anything. She kept thinking he would, but he just sat there. Maybe she should be the one to say or do something, she fumed, but that didn't seem right either.

So she sat there with her momentarily inconvenient friends, listening to the music, watching the dancers, and wishing for a minor miracle.

She got her miracle when Jared finally stood up and in a breathless rush of words asked her to dance. With a hasty apology to the other three, she scrambled to her feet and followed him out onto the dance floor, a surge of adrenaline sending her pulse racing and her spirits soaring. She took his left hand in her right and moved awkwardly into his embrace.

His arm went about her waist and his hand rested on the small
of her back. She could feel the heat of his skin. They began to
dance, slowly, cautiously, gradually adjusting to each other's
movements. Jared led tentatively, but determinedly, easing her
between the other dancers, moving with the rhythm of the
slow, soft music. Nest was as tall as he was, and she ducked her
chin toward his shoulder to make herself smaller. She liked the
way he held her. She liked how he smelled and how he glanced
at her every so often to see if she was all right. His shy smile
made her want to weep.

She closed her eyes and eased closer to him, feeling his arms
tighten about her. She had her escape. She buried her face in his
shoulder. She did not try to look for Cass or Brianna or Robert.
She did not try to look for anyone. She kept her eyes closed and
moved with Jared Scott, letting him take her wherever he
would, giving herself over to him.

They danced that dance and several more. When the music
quickened, they continued to dance slow. Nest felt her weariness, doubt, and fear slip away, fading into the background of
movement and sound. She felt wonderfully at peace; she felt
loving and hopeful. She held Jared close, pressing herself to
him, her face buried in his neck, in the rough tangle of his hair.
They did not speak, not a word the entire time. There was
nothing to say that needed saying, and any attempt at words
would spoil what was happening.

So good, Nest thought, her breathing soft and slow. So
sweet.

Then she let her eyes slip open for just a moment, and she
saw the demon.

He was walking past the dance floor, weaving through
the families clustered on the grass, a solitary, shadowy figure.
He was still in his human guise as the park maintenance man,
though he did not wear coveralls or work clothes this night, but
plain slacks and a collared shirt. He was not looking at her, or
at anyone, but at some point in the distance beyond what she
could see, his gaze bright and intense. Nest stopped dancing at
once, staring after him as he moved away. Where was John

Ross? She hadn't seen him since her grandparents had gone home after the picnic. She had to find him at once.

But the demon was already disappearing into the darkness, withdrawing from the light. She was going to lose him.

"What's the matter?" Jared asked, his hands releasing her as she backed away. She could tell from the sound of his voice that he was afraid he might have done something wrong. His face was pained and uncertain as he stared at her.

Her eyes locked instantly on his. "That's the man I've been searching for, the one I told you about, the one who's poisoning the trees." Her words came in a rush. "Go get the others, Jared, then go find John Ross. You know John, you saw him earlier with my grandparents. Find him and tell him where I've gone—that way." She pointed in the direction of the demon, who was already almost out of sight. "Hurry, I'll be out there waiting!"

She was moving quickly now, leaving Jared and his futile protests behind, darting through the crowd in an effort to keep up with the demon. She would not approach him, of course. She knew how dangerous that would be. But she would keep him in sight and try to find out where he was going.

She hustled past the people gathered about the pavilion and hurried into the dark. She could still see the demon, just at the edge of her vision as he crossed the grass toward the toboggan slide and turned down along the edge of the roadway leading to the west end of the park. She slowed a bit, not wanting to get too close, relying on the darkness to conceal her. She wished she had Pick or Daniel with her to help track the demon, but she hadn't seen either one in several hours. She would have to make do without them. Her eyes swept the darkness of the trees about her. Was Wraith anywhere close? If the demon should turn on her, would she have any protection at all? She pushed the question aside and went on.

The sounds of the music and the dance faded behind her, giving way to the steady buzz of the locusts and the more distant, intermittent sounds of traffic from the highway. She slipped silently through the park trees, shadowy and invisible in the night. She could move without making any sound; Pick had taught her how to do that. She had good night vision as well. The demon wouldn't lose her easily. Not that it appeared as if he would try. It didn't seem that he was worried about being followed. He walked without looking back, his eyes straight ahead, his pace steady. Nest crept along in his wake.

She followed the demon through the trees above the river from the east end of the park to the west, closing on the bridge that spanned the road where it looped back on itself and descended from the heights to the base of the cliffs. She kept looking over her shoulder, hoping to discover John Ross following, come to her aid, but there was no sign of him. She wondered more than once if she ought to turn back, but each time she told herself she would go on just a little farther. The sky was bright with stars, but the heavy canopy of the trees masked much of their light and left the woods in heavy darkness. There was no one out this far, she knew. Anyone in the park tonight was at the dance. If the demon kept going, he would soon be in the cemetery. Nest wondered suddenly if that was his destination. She thought suddenly of her mother, buried there. She thought next of Two Bears.

Then abruptly the demon stopped beneath a streetlamp just before the bridge span and stood looking off into the distance. Was he expecting someone? Nest crept closer. Careful, she warned herself. This was as close as she needed to be.

She hunched down beside a stand of fir, waiting for something to happen. Then a familiar voice hissed at her from behind. "Hey, Nest, whatcha doing?"

She jumped to her feet and whirled about. Danny Abbott stood six feet away, hands on his hips, grinning broadly. "Who're you spying on?"

"Danny, get out of here!" she hissed furiously.

His grin widened. "That guy over there?" he asked, and pointed behind her.

When she turned to see if the demon was still there, if he had been warned, a rush of shadows closed on her. She cried out and fought to escape, but she was knocked from her feet and slammed to the ground. The air went out of her lungs, and bright lights exploded behind her eyes as her head struck the exposed root of a tree. She could hear Danny Abbott laughing. Someone was sitting astride her, forcing her face into the dirt. A strip of electrician's tape was slapped over her mouth. Her arms were pinned behind her, and more tape was wound about her wrists. Then she was yanked to her feet and a burlap feed sack was pulled over her head and body and more tape was wound about her ankles, securing the open end of the sack below her knees.

When she was thoroughly bagged and trussed, she was slung over a burly shoulder. For a second everything went quiet except for the breathing of her attackers and her own stifled sobs.

"You crying?" Danny Abbott said, his mouth right next to her ear. She heard the pleasure in his voice and went still instantly. "You think you're so tough, don't you? Well, let's just see how tough you really are. Let's put it to the test. We're gonna take you down where the sun don't shine, little girl, and see how you like it. Let you spend a night in the dark. Know what I'm talking about, Nest? Sure, you do. The caves, sweet stuff. That's where you're going. Way down in the deep, dark caves."

They carried her like a sack of grain down the road that wound under the bridge to the base of the cliffs. She was cocooned in hot blackness inside the feed sack and jostled against the bony back and shoulders of the boy carrying her. She screamed against the tape that bound her mouth, but her cries were muffled and futile. She was furious with Danny Abbott and however many of his friends were responsible for this idiotic stunt, but she was mostly afraid. She had been warned over and over again by Pick never to go down into the caves. The caves were where the feeders lived, where they hid themselves from humans. It was not safe for her in the caves. And now she was being taken there.

She was afraid, too, because there was nothing she could do

to help herself. She was bound so tightly by the tape that she could not free her arms and legs. The tape over her mouth kept her from crying out. Because she was inside the feed sack, she could not even see what was happening to her. She could not use the magic because the magic relied on sight contact and she was cloaked in blackness. John Ross would come looking for her, but how would he ever find her? Pick and Daniel were nowhere in sight. Her grandparents had gone home. Her friends were only kids like her.

What about Wraith? Her spirits jumped a notch. Surely he would be able to find her, to do something to help.

She could feel her kidnappers picking their way over uneven ground, their steps growing slow and uncertain. They were leaving the paved road. She heard the click of a flashlight, and Danny Abbott said something about taking it easy. She felt the air grow cooler about her exposed ankles, and then just a bit inside the stifling feed sack. They were entering the caves.

"Set her down over there," Danny Abbott said.

She fought to contain her growing desperation and tried to reason through what had happened. How had Danny and his friends crept up on her like that without her knowing? They couldn't have. They must have been waiting. But for them to have been waiting, they must have known she would be coming. A cold, sinking feeling invaded the pit of her stomach. The demon had arranged it all. He had let her see him at the dance, enticed her to follow, and led her to where the boys were waiting to snatch her up and carry her down into the caves. It had to have happened that way.

But why would the demon do that? She closed her eyes inside the blackness of the sack and swallowed against the dryness in her throat. She wasn't sure she wanted to know the answer to that question.

She was lowered from the shoulder of the boy carrying her onto a cold, flat slab of rock. She lay there without moving, listening to the sounds of shuffling feet and low voices.

She heard the rustle of clothing as someone bent over her. "Guess we'll be going home now," Danny Abbott said, his voice sounding mean and smug. "You have a nice night, Nest. Think about what a bitch you are, okay? If you think about it hard enough, maybe I'll decide to come back in the morning and set you free. Maybe."

They moved away then, laughing and joking about ghosts and spiders, offering up unsavory images of what could happen to someone left alone in the caves. She gritted her teeth and thought with disdain that they didn't know the half of it.

Then it was quiet, the silence profound. All the night sounds had disappeared—from the woods, the river, the park, the homes, the streets, the entire city. It was as if she had been deposited in one of those sensory-deprivation tanks she had read about. Except, of course, that she could feel the chill of the cave rock working its way through the feed sack and into her body. And she could feel herself trying not to scream.

Water was dripping nearby. She mustered her strength, made a tentative effort at moving, and found she could do so. She worked her way onto her side and managed to sit up. She might be able to get to her feet, she thought suddenly. But then what would she do? She stayed where she was, thinking. Someone would come. Her friends, even if they didn't find John Ross. They would not abandon her—even though earlier she had wished they would. Tears came to her eyes as she remembered. She was ashamed and embarrassed about the way she had felt. She wished she could take it back.

She pushed her face against the weave of the feed sack so that she could see out. But it was so black inside the caves that even after giving her eyes time to adjust to whatever light there might be, she still couldn't see a thing. She worked for a long time on freeing her hands, but the tape was strong and pliable, and the adhesive kept it firmly glued to her skin. She was sweating freely within the sack, but even her sweat did not provide sufficient lubrication for her to work her way loose.

She wondered again where Wraith was. Couldn't he find her here? Was it possible that he couldn't come into the caves?

Time passed, and despair began to erode her resolve. Maybe no one could find her. It wasn't as if she had left tracks that

anyone could follow. All anyone knew was that she had left the
dance at the pavilion and gone west into the park. She could be
anywhere. It might take them all night to find her. It might take
them more than that. She could easily be here when Danny
Abbott and his low-life friends returned in the morning. If they
returned at all.

Why had this happened?

She heard voices then. Someone on the road outside! She
tried to call out to them, tried to shout through the tape. She
thrashed inside the feed sack, kicking out at anything she could
reach to signal them. But the voices passed and receded into
silence. No one came. She sat trembling in the dark from her
exertion, the sweat drying on her skin.

When she had calmed herself, she began rethinking the possibility of rescue. Whatever else happened, her grandparents
would not leave her out here all night. When she didn't come
home from the dance, they would begin searching. Lots of
people would help. She would be found. Of course she would
be found. Danny Abbott would be sorry then. Her glee at the
prospect wavered into uncertainty. Didn't he know how this
would turn out? Didn't he know what kind of trouble he would
be in?

Or was there some reason he wasn't worried about it?

Time dragged on. After a while, she became aware that she
wasn't alone. It didn't happen all at once; the feeling crept over
her gradually as she pondered her fate. She couldn't hear or see
anyone, but she could sense that someone was there with her.
She went quiet, a slow sense of dread growing inside. Of
course there was someone else in the caves, she reproached
herself with a mix of fear and anger.

There were the feeders.

They moved almost soundlessly as they surrounded her. She
could feel them looking at her, studying her, maybe wondering
what she was doing there. She fought down her revulsion,
willed herself to stay calm against the sea of despair that threatened to drown her. She felt their hands brush against her, small
pricklings that raised goose bumps on her skin. *Touching her!*

She could not identify the feeling—like old paper sacks, maybe, or clothes stiffened with sweat and oil. They had never touched her before, had never had this opportunity, and the thought that they could do so now made her crazy. She fought against the urge to thrash and scream. She forced herself to breathe normally. She tried to pray. Please, God, come for me. Please, don't let me be hurt.

"It's scary to be down here all alone, isn't it?" a voice whispered.

Nest jumped inside her burlap prison. The demon. She swallowed and exhaled quickly, noisily.

"All alone, down in the dark, in a black pit where your greatest enemies dwell. Helpless to prevent them from doing whatever they choose. You hate being helpless, don't you?"

The demon's voice was soft and silky. It rippled through the silence like bat wings. Nest closed her eyes against its insidious sound and gritted her teeth.

"Will someone come for you, you must be wondering? How long before they do? How much more of this must you endure?" The demon paused as if to consider. "Well, John Ross won't be coming. And your grandparents won't be coming. I've seen to that. So who else is there? Oh, I forgot. The sylvan. No, I don't think so. Have I missed anyone?"

Wraith!

The demon chuckled in a self-satisfied way. "The fact is, you have only yourself to blame for this. You should never have tried to follow me. Of course, I knew you would. You couldn't help yourself, could you? It was all so simple, making the suggestion to young Danny Abbott. He's so angry at you, Nest. He hates you. It was easy to persuade him that he could get even with you if he just did what I told him. He was so eager, he didn't even bother to consider the consequences of his act. None of them did. They are such foolish, malleable boys."

The demon's voice had shifted, moving to another part of the cave. But Nest could not hear the demon himself move, could not pick up a single footfall.

"So, here you are, alone with me. Why, you might have asked yourself? Why am I bothering to do this? Why don't I just . . . drop you into a hole and cover you up?" The demon's voice trailed off in a hiss. "I could, you know."

He waited a moment, as if anticipating her response, then sighed anew. "But I don't want to hurt you. I want to teach you. That's why I brought you here. I want you to understand how helpless you are against me. I want you to realize that I can do whatever I like with you. You can't prevent it. Your friends and family can't prevent it. No one can. You need to accept that. I brought you here so that you could discover firsthand what I was talking about yesterday, about the importance of learning to be alone, of learning to depend only on yourself. Because you can't depend on other people, can you? I mean, who's going to save you from this? Your mother is gone, your grandparents are old, your friends are feckless, and no one else really gives a damn. When it comes right down to it, you have only yourself."

Nest was awash with rage and humiliation. She would have killed the demon gladly if she had been free to do so and been offered a way. She hated the demon as she had never hated anyone in her life.

"I have to be going now," he said, the location of his voice shifting again, moving away. "I have things to do while the night is still young. I have enemies to eliminate. Then I'll be back for you. Danny Abbott won't, of course. By morning, he will have forgotten you are even here. So you have to depend on me. Keep that in mind."

Then the voice dropped into a rough whisper that scraped at her nerve endings like sandpaper. "Maybe it would be wise if you were to use your time among the feeders to consider what's important to you. Because your life is about to change, Nest. It is going to change in a way you would never have dreamed possible. I'm going to see to it. It's what I've come here to do."

The silence returned, slow and thick within the dark. Nest waited for the demon to say something more, to reveal some further insight. But no sound came: She sat wrapped within the hot blackness of the burlap, embittered, frightened, and alone.

Then the feeders returned. When the touching began anew, her resolve gave way completely and she screamed soundlessly into the tape.

CHAPTER 24

Old Bob was finishing up the Sunday edition of the *Chicago Tribune* when the doorbell rang. He'd begun the paper early that morning before church and spent his free time during the course of the day working his way through its various sections. It was part of his Sunday ritual, an unhurried review of the events of the world with time enough to give some measured consideration to what they meant. He was sitting in his easy chair in the den, his feet up on the settee, and he glanced immediately at the wall clock.

Ten-forty. Late, for someone to be visiting.

He climbed to his feet and walked out into the hall, the first stirrings of anxiety roiling his stomach. Evelyn was already standing in the foyer, rooted in place six feet from the front door, as if this was as close as she dared to come. She held her cigarette in one hand, its smooth, white length burning slowly to ash, a silent measure of the promptness of his response. The look his wife gave him was unreadable. They had come home together at dusk, bidding John Ross good night and leaving Nest with her friends. They had unpacked the leftover food and eating utensils from the picnic basket, unloaded the cooler, and put away the blanket. Evelyn had barely spoken as they worked, and Old Bob had not asked what she was thinking.

"Open it, Robert," she said to him now as he came down the hall, as if he might have been considering something else.

He released the latch and swung the door wide. Four youngsters were huddled together in the halo of the porch light, staring back at him through the screen. Nest's friends. He recognized their faces and one or two of their names. Enid Scott's oldest boy. Cass Minter. John and Alice Heppler's son. That pretty little girl who always looked like she was on her way to a photo shoot.

The Heppler boy was the one who spoke. "Mr. Freemark, can you come help us find Nest, please? We've looked everywhere, and it's like she dropped into a hole or something. And we tried to find John Ross, like she asked, but he's disappeared, too. I think Danny Abbott knows what's happened to her, but he just laughs at us."

Robert Heppler, Old Bob remembered suddenly. That was the boy's name. What had he said? "What do you mean, Nest has dropped into a hole?"

"Well, she's been gone for close to two hours," Robert continued, his concern reflected in his narrow face. He pushed his glasses up on his nose and ran a hand through his unruly blond hair. "She went off after this guy, the one who's been poisoning the trees? The one you warned her about? She thought she saw him, so she . . ." He bit off whatever it was he was going to say and looked at the Scott boy. "Jared, you were there; you tell it."

Jared Scott looked pale and anxious as he spoke. His words were slow and measured. "We were dancing, me and Nest, and she saw this guy, like Robert says. She gets this funny look on her face and tells me he's the one who's been poisoning the trees, and I have to find Robert and Cass and Brianna and then we have to find John Ross and tell him to go after her. Then she runs off after this guy. So we all go looking for Mr. Ross, but we can't find him."

Old Bob frowned, thinking, Someone's poisoning trees?

"So, anyway, we can't find Mr. Ross," Robert interrupted Jared impatiently, "so we start looking around for Nest on our own. We try to find where she went, going off in the same direction, and that's when we run into Danny Abbott and his friends coming toward us. They're laughing and joking about something, and when they see us, they go quiet, then really start breaking up. I ask them if they've seen Nest, and they get all cute about it, saying, 'Oh, yeah, Nest Freemark, remember her?' and stuff like that. See, we had this run-in with them just the other day, and they're still pissed off. 'Scuse me. Upset.

Anyway, I tell them this isn't funny, that there's a guy out there poisoning trees, and he might hurt Nest. Danny says something like 'What guy?' and I can tell he knows. Then he and his Neanderthal pals push me and Jared down and go right past us and back to the dance. That's when we decided to come get you."

Old Bob stood there, trying to sort the story through, trying to make some sense of it, still stuck on the part about someone poisoning trees in the park. It was Evelyn who spoke first.

"Robert," she said, coming forward now to stand in front of him, her eyes bright and hard in the porch light. There was no hesitation in her voice. "You get out there right away and find that girl and bring her home."

Old Bob responded with a quick nod, saying, "I will, Evelyn," then turned to Nest's friends and said, "You wait here," and went into the kitchen to find a flashlight. He was back in seconds, carrying a four-cell Eveready, his walk quick and certain. He touched his wife on the shoulder as he brushed past, said, "Don't worry, I'll find her," and went out the door and into the night.

When John Ross was able to stand again, Josie Jackson helped him walk back up the hill, bypass the crowded pavilion, and maneuver his way to her car. She wanted to drive him to the hospital, but he told her it wasn't necessary, that nothing was broken, which he believed, from experience, to be so. She wanted him to file a police report, but he declined that offer as well, pointing out that neither of them had the faintest idea who had attacked him (beyond the fact that they were probably MidCon union men) and that he was a stranger in the community, which usually didn't give you much leverage with the police in a complaint against locals.

"John, damn it, we have to do something about this!" she exclaimed as she eased him into the passenger seat of her Chevy, dabbing at his bloodied face with a handkerchief. She had stopped crying by now and was flushed with anger. "We can't just pretend that nothing happened! Look what they did to you!"

"Well, it was all a mistake," he alibied, forcing a smile through his swollen lips, trying to ease her concern and indignation, knowing it was the demon who was responsible and there was nothing to be done about it now. "Just take me back to the hotel, Josie, and I'll be fine."

But she wouldn't hear of it. It was bad enough that he wouldn't go to the emergency room or file a complaint with the police, but to expect her to take him back to the hotel and leave him was unthinkable. He was going to her house and spending the night so that she could keep an eye on him. He protested that he was fine, that he just needed to wash up and get a good night's sleep (ignoring the pain in his ribs, a clear indication one or more were cracked, and the throbbing in his head from what was, in all likelihood, a concussion), but she was having none of it. She could see the deep gash in his forehead, the cuts and bruises on his face, and the blood seeping through his torn clothing, and she was determined that someone would be there for him if he needed help. Her own face and clothing were streaked with blood and dirt, and her tousled hair was full of twigs and leaves, but she seemed oblivious of that.

"If I ever find out who did this . . ." she swore softly, leaving the threat unfinished.

He put his head back on the seat and closed his eyes as she pulled out of the parking lot and headed toward the highway. He was upset that he had been caught off guard by the attack and forced to use his magic to defend himself, but he was encouraged as well, because it implied that the demon was worried about him. Planting a suggestion in the minds of a bunch of MidCon strikers that he was a company spy was a desperate ploy by any measure. Perhaps his chances at stopping the demon were better than he believed. He wondered if he had missed something in his analysis of the situation, in the content of the dream that had brought him here. Josie told him to open his eyes, not to go to sleep yet, because concussions were nothing to fool with. He did as she advised, turning his head so that he could look at her face. She gave him a quick, sideways smile, warming him inside where thoughts of the demon had left a chill.

She drove him to her home, an aging, two-story wood frame house overlooking the Rock River at the bottom of a dead-end street. She parked in the driveway and came around to help him out. She walked him up the steps, her arm around his waist as he leaned on his staff to support his crippled leg, then guided him through the door and down a hall to the kitchen. She seated him at the wooden breakfast table, gathered up clean cloths, hot water, antiseptic, and bandages, and went to work on his injuries. She was quiet as she repaired his damaged face, her dark eyes intense, her hands gentle and steady. The house was silent about them. Her daughter was staying at a friend's, she explained, then quickly changed the subject.

"You really should have stitches for this," she said, fitting the butterfly bandages in place over the gash in his forehead, closing the wound as best she could. Her eyes left the injury and found his. "What happened out there? That white flash—it looked like something exploded."

He gave her his best sheepish grin. "Fireworks. I had them in my pocket. They spilled out on the ground during the fight, and I guess something caused them to ignite."

Her eyes moved away, back to his damaged face, but not before he caught a glimpse of the doubt mirrored there. "I'm sorry this happened," he said, trying to ease past the moment. "I was enjoying myself."

"Me, too. Hold still."

She finished with his face and moved down to his body. She insisted he remove his shirt, against his protests, and her brow furrowed with worry when she saw the deep bruises flowering over his ribs. "This is not good, John," she said softly.

She cleaned his scrapes and cuts, noting the way he winced when she put pressure on his ribs, then applied a series of cold compresses to the more severely damaged areas. She made him hot tea, then excused herself to go wash up. He heard her climb the stairs, then heard a shower running. He sipped at the tea and looked around the kitchen. It was filled with little touches that marked it as Josie's—a series of painted tea-kettles set along the top of the cupboards; pictures of her daughter, tacked to a bulletin board; drawings taped to the refrigerator that she must have done at different ages, some beginning to fray about the edges; fresh flowers in a vase at the window above the sink; and a small dish with cat food in it sitting by the back door. He studied the bright print curtains and wallpaper, the mix of soft yellows, blues, and pinks that trimmed out the basic white of the plaster and woodwork. He liked it here, he decided. He felt at home.

He was beginning to grow sleepy, so he refilled his teacup and drank deeply, trying to wake himself up with the caffeine. If he went to sleep now, he would dream. If he dreamed, he would be back in the future—only this time, because he had used the staff's magic to save himself in the present, he would be bereft of any protection until he woke. He knew what that would feel like. It had happened before. It would happen again. It was the price he paid for serving as a Knight of the Word. It was the cost of staying alive.

Josie came back downstairs in fuzzy slippers and a white bathrobe, her long, light hair shiny with dampness. She gave him her best smile, radiant and embracing, and asked how he was feeling. He told her he was better, admiring the fresh-scrubbed glow of her skin and the high curve of her cheekbones. She asked him if he was hungry, laughed when he told her no, made him some toast anyway, put out butter and jam, and sat down across from him to watch him eat. She sipped at her tea, telling him about the way her grandmother always made her toast and tea late at night when neither of them could sleep. Ross listened without saying much, finding he was hungry after all. He glanced once at the clock. It was after eleven, later than he had thought.

"Are you tired, John?" she asked when he was finished eating. "You must be. I think it's safe for you to sleep now."

He smiled at the thought. "I should be going, Josie."

She shook her head vehemently. "Not a chance, buster. You're staying here tonight. I've got too much invested in you to let you wander off to that hotel room alone." She paused, realizing the implication of what she had said. She recovered with a shrug. "I thought I made it pretty clear that I would feel better if you slept here tonight. Do you mind?"

He shook his head. "No, I just don't want to be underfoot. I feel bad enough about what's happened."

She stood up, tossing back her hair. "In more ways than one, I bet. You come with me."

She put her arm around his waist to help him to his feet, then kept it there as she guided him down the hall and up the stairs. The house was mostly dark; the light from the kitchen stretched only as far as the first half-dozen steps. After that, they were left in starlit gloom. Beneath their feet, the old wooden stairs creaked softly. Ahead, from farther down the hallway that connected the second-story rooms, lamplight glimmered softly. Ross felt his way up the stairs with his staff and Josie's surefooted guidance, taking his time, leaning on her even when it wasn't necessary, liking the feel of her body against his and the smell of her hair against his face.

"Careful, John," she cautioned as they made their way, her arm tightening about his waist, trying to stay below his injured ribs.

He winced silently. "I'm fine."

At the top of the stairs they paused for a moment, still locked together. "Okay?" she asked, and he nodded. She lifted her face and kissed him on the mouth. His lips were bruised and swollen, and her kiss was gentle. "Does that hurt?" she asked, and he shook his head wordlessly.

She eased him down the hall and into a darkened bedroom, a guest room, he decided, the large bed neatly made, the cushion of the love seat smooth and undisturbed, the dresser top bare. She left him just inside the doorway, moved to the bed, and pulled back the spread and covers. Then she came back for him and walked him over. He could hear the soft throbbing of an air conditioner in the window and feel the cool air on his bare arms and torso. The room was dark and the only light came from down the hallway and from the stars that shone faintly through the curtained window. She eased him onto the bed, bending close to kiss him on the forehead.

"Wait here," she said.

She left the room and disappeared down the hall. A moment

later, the hallway light went out. She reappeared soundlessly, a shadowy figure in the gloom. She crossed to the bed and stood next to him, looking down. He could just make out the sheen of her tousled hair and the curve of her hip.

"Can you take the rest of your clothes off by yourself?" she asked.

He slipped off his walking shoes, socks, and jeans, then eased himself into the cool sheets, letting his head sink into the softness of the pillows. A profound weariness settled over him, and he knew that sleep would claim him soon. There was nothing he could do about it; he would sleep and then he would dream. But perhaps the dream would not be as bad as he feared.

"John?" Josie spoke his name softly in the dark.

He took a deep breath and let it out again slowly. "Yeah, I'm still here. I'll be all right, Josie. You go on to bed. Thanks again for . . ."

He felt her weight settle on the bed, and then she was lying next to him, pressing close, her cool arms enfolding him, her bathrobe gone. "I think I better stay with you," she whispered, kissing his cheek.

He closed his eyes against the smooth, soft feel of her body, against the soap scent of her skin and hair. "Josie . . ."

"John, do me a big favor," she interrupted him, her lips brushing his cheek. The fingers of one hand stroked his arm like threads of silk. "Don't say anything for a little while. I made it this far on raw courage and faith in my instincts. If you say the wrong thing, I'll fall to pieces. I don't want anything from you that you don't want to give me. I just want you to hold me for a while. And to let me hold you. That's all I want. Okay?"

Her touch made the pain in his body ease and his fear of sleep's approach lessen. He knew the risk of what he was doing, but he couldn't help himself. "Okay."

"Put your arms around me, please."

He did as she asked, drawing her close, and all the space between them disappeared.

* * *

Old Bob crossed the grassy expanse of Sinnissippi Park,
heading straight for the pavilion and the crowd, his shoulders
squared, his big face intense. Nest's friends struggled to keep
up with him, whispering among themselves as they marked the
determination in his long strides. Someone was gonna get it
now, he heard the Heppler boy declare gleefully. He ignored
the remark, his brow furrowed, his eyes troubled. Something
wasn't right about all this. That Nest was missing was reason
enough all by itself for concern, but this business about poisoning trees suggested a depth to the matter that he knew he
didn't begin to understand. Nor did he like the fact that a bunch
of older boys were involved. But mostly there was the look in
Evelyn's eyes. Behind the worry and fear for the safety of their
granddaughter, Old Bob had seen something else. Evelyn
knew something about this, something that transcended the
boundaries of his own knowledge. Another secret perhaps, or
maybe just a suspicion. But the look was unmistakable.

He crossed the parking lot fronting the pavilion and slowed
as he approached the crowd. The band was still playing and
couples still danced beneath the colored lanterns and bunting.
The humid night air was filled with the bright, clear sounds of
laughter and conversation. He glanced over his shoulder for
Nest's friends, then waited for them to catch up.

"Which one is Danny Abbott?" he asked.

They glanced about without answering. His heart tightened
in his chest. If the boy had gone home, he was in trouble.

Then Brianna Brown said, "There he is."

She was pointing at a good-looking boy with dark hair and
big shoulders standing in the shadows just beyond the tables
where the soft drinks and lemonade were served. Some other
boys were with him, and all of them were talking and joking
with a pair of young girls dressed in cutoffs and halter tops.

Old Bob took a deep breath. "Stay here," he said, and
started forward.

He was right on top of Danny Abbott before the boy saw
him. He smiled when Danny turned and put a friendly arm
about his shoulder, drawing him close, holding him fast.

"Danny, I'm Robert Freemark, Nest's grandfather." He saw frightened recognition flood the boy's eyes. "Now, I don't want to waste any time on this, so I would appreciate a quick answer. Where is my granddaughter?"

Danny Abbott tried to back away, but Old Bob kept a tight hold on him, taking a quick measure of his friends to see if any of them meant trouble. No one looked anxious to get involved. The girls were already moving away. The boys looked eager to follow. "You gentlemen stick around a minute, please," he ordered, freezing them in their tracks.

"Mr. Freemark, I don't know what . . ." Danny Abbott began.

Old Bob moved his hand to the back of Danny's neck and squeezed hard enough to make the boy wince. "That's a bad beginning, son," he said quietly. "I know your father, Ed. Know your mother, too. They're good people. They wouldn't appreciate finding out that their son is a liar. Not to mention a few other things. So let's get this over with before I lose my temper. Where is Nest?"

"It was just a joke," one of the other boys mumbled, hands digging in his jeans pockets, eyes shifting away.

"Shut up, Pete!" Danny Abbott hissed furiously, the words out of his mouth before he could think better of them. Then he saw the look on Old Bob's face and went pale.

"One more chance, Danny," Old Bob told him softly. "Give me a straight answer and we'll put this behind us. No calls to your parents, nothing more between you and me. Otherwise, the next stop for both of us is the police station. And I will press charges. Are we clear on this?"

Danny Abbott nodded quickly, and his eyes dropped. "She's in the caves, taped up inside a gunnysack." His voice was sullen and afraid. "Pete's right, it was just a joke."

Old Bob studied him a moment, weighing the depth of the truth in the boy's words, then let him go. "If she's come to any harm," he said to all of them, looking deliberately from one face to the next, "you'll answer for it."

He walked back to where Nest's friends waited in a tight knot at the edge of the parking lot, their eyes bright with excitement. He surveyed the crowd, looking to see if there was anyone he could call upon to help. But none of the faces were familiar enough that he felt comfortable involving the few he recognized. He would have to do this alone.

He came up to Nest's friends and gave them a reassuring smile. "You young people go on home now," he told them. "I believe I know what's happened, and it's nothing serious. Nest is all right. You go on. I'll have her call you when she gets home."

He moved away from them without waiting for an answer, not wanting to waste any more time. He followed the edge of the paved road toward the west end of the park and the caves. He went swiftly and deliberately, and he did not look over his shoulder until he was well away from the crowd and deep into the darkness of the trees. No one followed him. He carried the flashlight loosely in his right hand, ready to use it for any purpose it required. He didn't think he would be attacked, but he wasn't discounting the possibility. He glanced around once more, saw nothing, no one, and turned his attention to the darkness ahead.

He followed the roadway to where it looped back on itself under the bridge and turned down. The streetlamps provided sufficient light that he was able to find his way without difficulty, keeping in the open where he could see any movement about him. He was sweating now from his exertion, the armpits and collar of his shirt damp, his forehead beaded. The park was silent about him, the big trees still, their limbs and leaves hanging limp and motionless in the heavy air, their shadows webbing the ground in strange, intricate patterns. A car's headlights flared momentarily behind him, then swung away, following the road leading out of the park. He passed beneath the shadow of the bridge and emerged in muted starlight.

"Hang on, Nest," he whispered quietly.

He moved quickly down the road toward the black mouth of the caves. The river was a silver-tipped satin sheet on his left and the cliffs towered blackly above him on his right. His shoes crunched softly on gravel. In his mind, he saw again the look in Evelyn's eyes, and a cold feeling reached down into his stomach. What did she know that she was hiding from him? He thought suddenly of Caitlin, falling from these same cliffs more than a dozen years earlier to land on the rocks below, broken and lifeless. The image brought a bloodred heat to his eyes and the back of his throat. He could not stand it if he were to lose Nest, too. It would be the end of him—the end of Evelyn as well. It would be the end of everything.

He reached the entrance to the caves and flicked on the flashlight. The four-cell beam cut a bright swath through the darkness, reaching deep into the confines of the rock. He worked his way carefully forward, pausing to listen, hearing something almost immediately—a muffled sound, a movement. He scrambled ahead, plunging inside the caves now, swinging the flashlight's beam left and right with frantic movements, searching the jagged terrain.

Then abruptly the light found her. He knew at once it was Nest, even though she was trussed up inside a gunnysack with only her ankles and feet showing. He scrambled forward, calling out to her, stumbling several times on the loose rock before he reached her.

"Nest, it's me, Grandpa," he said, breathing heavily, thinking, *Thank God, thank God!* He reached into his pants and brought out his pocketknife to cut away the tape and burlap from her ankles. When that was done and the sack was removed, he cut the tape from her hands as well. Then, as gently as he could, he pulled the last strip off her mouth.

Her arms came around him at once. "Grandpa, Grandpa," she sobbed, shaking all over, tears running down her cheeks.

"It's all right, Nest," he whispered softly, stroking her hair the way he had when she was a little girl. "It's all right, kiddo. You're all right."

Then he picked her up, cradling her in his big arms as he would a baby, and carried her back out into the night.

Jared Scott raced across the front lawn of his apartment building, dark hair flying, T-shirt laced with sweat. He caught a glimpse of the television screen through the curtained windows of his living room and knew his mother and George were inside. He picked up his pace, anxious to tell them what had happened, all about Nest and Danny Abbott and Mr. Freemark. He burst through the screen door already yelling.

"Mom, some guys kidnapped Nest and took her down to the caves, and we told Mr. Freemark to come help us . . ."

He drew up short at the living-room entrance, the words freezing in his throat. His mother lay on the couch with George Paulsen next to her. Most of their clothes were on the floor. There were beer cans everywhere.

His mother tried to cover herself with her arms, smiling weakly, ashen-faced as he stared at her.

"Jared, sweetie . . ."

Jared backed away, averting his eyes. "Sorry, Mom, I just . . ."

"What the hell do you think you're doing, you little bastard!" George roared, scrambling up from the couch, lurching toward him in fury.

"George, he didn't mean anything!" His mother was trying to slip back into her blouse, her movements cumbersome and slow.

Jared tried to run, but he caught his foot on the carpet and slipped. George was on top of him instantly, hauling him back to his feet by his shirtfront, yelling at him, screaming at him. Jared tried to say he was sorry, tried to say something in his defense, but George was shaking him so hard he couldn't get the words out. His mother was yelling, too, her face flushed and her eyes bright as she stumbled across the littered floor.

Then George struck him across the face with his hand, and without thinking twice, Jared struck him back. He caught George flush on the nose, and blood spurted out. George released him and stumbled back in surprise, both hands going to his face. In that instant, something raw surged through Jared Scott. He remembered the way Old Bob Freemark had walked up to Danny Abbott and his friends and confronted them. He remembered the set of the old man's shoulders and the determination in his eyes.

"You get out of here!" he shouted at George, bracing himself in a fighter's stance, raising his fists threateningly. "This isn't your home! It's mine and my brothers' and my sisters' and my mom's!"

For a moment George Paulsen just stood there, blood running down his mouth and chin, shock registering on his face. Then a wild look came into his eyes, and he threw himself on Jared, catching him by the throat and bearing him to the floor. Jared twisted and squirmed, trying to get away, but George held him down, screaming obscenities. George rose over him and began to hit him with his fists, striking him in the face with solid, vicious blows that rocked his head and brought bright lights to his eyes. He tried to cover up, but George just knocked his hands aside and kept hitting him. Then dark shapes swarmed out of the shadows, things Jared had never seen before, eyes cat-bright and wild. They fell on George with the raw hunger of predators, their supple, invasive limbs twisting about him, ensnaring him, molding to his body. Their presence seemed to drive George to an even greater frenzy. The blows quickened, and Jared's defenses began to collapse. His mother began screaming, begging George to stop. There was the sound of bones snapping, and a warm rush of blood flooded Jared's mouth and throat.

Then the pain froze him, and all sound and movement ceased, disappearing like a movie's final scene into slow, hazy blackness.

At the beginning of the roadway leading up under the bridge to the cliffs, Nest asked her grandfather to set her on her feet again. She had stopped crying, and her legs were steady enough to support her. Once righted, she stared out across the river for long moments, collecting herself, trying to blot the memory of what had happened from her mind. Her grandfather stood next to her and waited in silence.

"I'm all right," she said finally, repeating his words back to him.

They walked up the road side by side, the old man and the girl, no longer touching, saying nothing, eyes lowered to the pavement. They passed under the bridge and came out of the darkness onto the park's grassy flats. Nest glanced about surreptitiously for the feeders, for their eyes, for some small movement that would signal their presence, but found nothing. She could still feel their hands on her, feel them worming their way beneath her skin, into her blood and her bones, past all her defenses, deep inside where her fear and rage roiled and they might feed.

She felt violated and ashamed, as if she had been stripped naked and left soiled and debased.

"How did you find me?" she asked, keeping her eyes lowered so he could not see what was reflected there.

"Your friends," her grandfather replied, not looking at her. "They came to the house, brought me out to look for you."

She nodded, thinking now of Danny Abbott and the demon, and she was about to say something more when they heard the heavy boom of a shotgun. Her grandfather's white head lifted. Both stopped where they were, staring out into the darkness. The shotgun fired again. And again. Six times, it roared.

"Evelyn," Nest heard her grandfather whisper hoarsely.

And then he was running through the park for the house.

CHAPTER 25

E velyn Freemark walked out onto the big veranda porch and watched Robert and the children disappear around the corner of the house, headed for the park in search of Nest. Even when they were no longer in sight, swallowed up by the night's blackness, she stared after them, standing in the yellow halo of the light cast by the porch lamp, motionless as her thoughts drifted back through the years to Nest and Caitlin and her own childhood. She had lived a long life, and she was always surprised on looking back at how quickly the time had passed and how close together the years had grown.

The screen door started to swing shut behind her, and she reached back automatically to catch it and ease it carefully into place. In the deep night silence, she could hear the creak of its hinges and springs like ghost laughter.

After a moment, she began to look around, searching the shadows where the lawn lengthened in a darkening carpet to the shagbark hickories fronting the walk leading in from Woodlawn Road and to the mix of blue spruce and walnut that bracketed the corners of their two-acre lot. She knew already what she would find, but the porch light was blinding her. She reached inside the doorway and shut it off, leaving her in darkness. Better, she thought. She could see them clearly now, the gleaming yellow eyes, dozens strong, too many to be coincidental, too many to persuade her she had guessed wrong about what was going to happen.

She smiled tightly. If you understood them well enough, the feeders could tell you things even without speaking.

Her eyes were fully adjusted to the darkness now, able to

trace the angular shapes of the trees, the smooth spread of the lawn, the flat, broad stretch of the roadway, and the low, sprawling roofs of the houses farther down the way. She gave the landscape a moment's consideration, then turned her attention to the porch on which she stood—to its eaves and railings, its fitted ceiling boards, and its worn, tongue-and-groove wooden flooring. Finally her eyes settled on the old peg oak rocker that had been with her from the time of her marriage to Robert. She could trace the events of her life by such things. This house had borne mute witness to the whole of her married life—to the joy and wonder she had been privileged to experience, to the tragedy and loss she had been forced to suffer. These walls had given her peace when it was needed. They had lent her strength. They were part of her, rooted deep within her heart and soul. She smiled. She could do worse than end her life here.

She gave the feeders another quick study, then slipped through the screen door and walked to the back of the house. She would have to hurry. If the demon was coming for her, as she was certain now he was, he would not waste any time. With Robert out of the way, he would hasten to put an end to matters quickly. He would be confident that he could do so. She was old and worn, and no longer a match for him. She laughed to herself. He was predictable in ways he did not begin to recognize, and in the end they would prove his undoing.

She went past her own bedroom and into Robert's. She no longer slept there, but she cleaned for him, and she knew where he kept his things. She clicked on the bedside lamp and went into his closet, the light spilling after her in a bright sliver through the cracked door. In the rear of his closet was a smaller door that opened into a storage area. She found the key on the shelf above, where she knew he kept it, fitted the key in place, and released the lock.

Inside was the twelve-gauge pump-action shotgun he had once used for hunting and now kept mostly out of habit. She removed it from its leather slipcase and brought it into the light. The polished wooden stock and smooth metal barrel gleamed softly. She knew he cleaned it regularly, that it would fire if needed. There were boxes of shells in a cardboard box at the back of the storage area. She brought the box into the closet and opened it, bypassing the birdshot for the heavier double-ought shells that could blow a hole through you the size of a fist if the range was close and your aim true. Her hands were steady as she slid six shells through the loading slot into the magazine and dumped another six in a pocket of her housedress.

She stood motionless then, looking down at the shotgun, thinking that it had been almost ten years since she had fired it. She had been a good shot once, had hunted alongside Robert in the crisp fall days when duck season opened and the air smelled musky and the wind had a raw edge. It was a long time ago. She wondered if she could still fire this weapon. It felt familiar and comfortable in her hands, but she was old and not so steady. What if her strength failed her?

She chambered a shell with a quick, practiced movement of her hands, checked to make certain the safety was on, and smiled wryly. That would be the day.

Shotgun in hand, she exited the closet and moved back through the house. She stopped off in Nest's room long enough to scribble a few words on a piece of notebook paper, which she then tucked under her granddaughter's favorite down pillow. Satisfied that she had done what she could, she advanced down the hallway on mouse paws, listening to the silence, feeling the tension within her beginning to mount. It would happen quickly now. She was glad Robert was not there, that she did not have to worry about him. By the time he returned with Nest, it would be over. She wasn't really worried about the girl, despite the urgency of her admonition to Robert to find her. Nest was better protected than any of them; she had seen to that. The monster that had appeared to threaten her didn't know the half of it.

She emerged from the house with the shotgun pressed against her side where it could not be clearly seen, and she stopped just beyond the screen door to survey the darkness beyond, her senses alert. Nothing had changed. He was not there yet. Only the feeders had gathered. She moved down the porch to where her rocker was situated, leaned the gun up against the wall in the deep shadows, and settled herself comfortably in place.

Yea, though I walk through the valley of the shadow of death, I shall fear no evil . . .

The demon would come for her. It would come for her because it hated her for what she had done to it all those years ago and because she was the one human it feared. Odd, that it should still feel this way, now that she was old and frail and virtually powerless. She wondered at the symmetry of life, at the ways the good and the bad of what you did came back to repay you, to reveal you. She had made so many mistakes, but she had made good choices, too. Robert, for openers. He had loved her through everything, even when Caitlin's death had shattered her and her drinking and smoking had left her dissipated and hollowed out and bereft of peace. And Nest, linked to her by blood and magic, the image of herself as a girl, but stronger and more controlled. She closed her eyes momentarily, thinking of her granddaughter. Nest, sweet child, who stood unseeing at the center of the maelstrom that was about to commence.

"Good evening, Evelyn."

Her eyes snapped open, raking the dark. She recognized his voice instantly, the smooth, insinuating lilt rising softly out of the heat. He was standing just off the walk, not quite close enough that she could see him clearly.

She tried to still the shaking inside, rocking slowly to settle her fear. "You took your time," she said.

"Well, time has never been of much concern to me." She could feel as much as see his smile. "It's too bad you can't say the same, Evelyn. You have grown quite old."

She was briefly angry, but she kept her voice calm. "Well, I don't pretend to be something I'm not, either. I'm pretty well content with being who I am. I've learned to live with myself. I doubt that you can say the same."

The demon chuckled, crossing his arms on his chest. "Oh, that's a terrible lie, Evelyn! Shame on you! You hate yourself! You hate your life!" The laugh died away. "That's why you drink and smoke and hide out in your house, isn't it? It wasn't like that before. You should have embraced the magic in the same way I did, years ago, when you were still young and pretty and talented. You had that chance, and you gave it up. You gave me up as well. Look at what it's cost you. So, please. I think I can live with myself better than you can." He paused. "Which is what matters have to come down to, haven't they?"

She nodded. "I suppose they have."

The demon studied her. "You knew I'd come back to finish things, didn't you? You didn't think you could escape me?"

"Not for a moment. But I'm surprised you thought you needed help."

He stared at her, a hint of confusion in his bland face. "I'm afraid you've lost me."

"John Ross."

The demon snorted. "Oh, Evelyn, don't be obtuse. Ross is a creature of the Word. He's been tracking me for some time. Without much success, I might add."

Well, well, it seems I was wrong about Mr. Ross, she thought in surprise.

The demon was watching her closely. "Don't get your hopes up, dear heart. John Ross is not going to change the outcome of things. I've already seen to that."

"I expect you have," she replied quietly.

He made a point of glancing around then, a slow, casual survey of the shadows. His smile was empty and cold. "Look who's come to say good-bye to you."

She had already seen them. Feeders by the dozens, slinking out of the darkness to gather at the edges of the light, crowding forward in anticipation, eyes unblinking and expressionless, dark bodies coiled. Some had already advanced to the far ends of the porch, their heads pressed up against the railing like grotesque children in search of a treat.

She gave him a flat, hard stare. "Perhaps they've come to say good-bye to you, instead." She beckoned casually. "Step closer so I can see you better."

The demon did so, moving just out of the shadows, his arms loose, his pale, washed-out blue eyes looking almost sleepy.

"Oh, you've changed considerably," she told him. "If you think I've aged, you ought to take a close look at yourself. Is that the best you can do? Did you sell your soul for so little? How sad."

There was a long silence between them. Then the demon whispered, "This is the end of the line for you, Evelyn."

She rose to her feet and stood looking at him, feeling small and vulnerable in the presence of his strength. But she was buttressed by her anger and by her certainty that he was not half so clever as he thought. She moved slowly around to the back of her rocker and leaned on it, giving him a broad, sardonic smile.

"Why don't you come up on the porch so we can discuss it?" she said.

He smiled in return. "What are you up to, Evelyn?" He cocked his head to one side as if reflecting on the possibilities.

She waited patiently, saying nothing, and after a moment he started toward her, accepting her challenge. The feeders trailed after him, skittish with anticipation. She had not seen so many in one place in years. Not since she had played with them at night in the park as a young girl. Not since the demon and she were lovers. The memories roiled within her, a bitter stirring of emotions that turned the night's heat and darkness suffocating.

When he was almost to the steps, she reached behind her for the shotgun and brought it up in a single, smooth movement so that the long barrel was leveled directly at his chest. She flipped off the safety and placed her finger over the trigger. He was less than fifteen feet away, a clear target. He stopped instantly, genuine surprise showing on his face.

"You can't hurt me with that," he said.

"I can blow that disguise you're hiding behind to smithereens," she declared calmly. "And it will take you a while to put together another, won't it? A little extra time might be all I need and more than you can afford."

He laughed softly in response, his hands clasping before him as if in childish admiration. "Evelyn, you are astonishing! I missed it completely! How could I have been so stupid? You've lost your use of the magic, haven't you? That's why you have the shotgun! Your magic doesn't work anymore!" He grinned, excited by his discovery. "And to think I was worried that you might prove troublesome. Tell me. What happened? Did you use it all up? No, you wouldn't have done that. You were saving it to use against me. Or against yourself. Remember how you threatened to do that when you found out what I was? That was a long time ago. Oh, I hated you so for that! I've waited patiently to make you pay for what you did to me. But there was always your magic to consider, wasn't there?" He paused. "Ah-ha! That's it! You lost it because you *didn't* use it! You worked so hard at hoarding it, you grew old and tired and lost it completely! That's why you haven't come after me. That's why you've waited for me to come to you. Oh, dear! Poor Evelyn!"

"Poor you," she replied, snapped the gun stock to her shoulder, and blew a hole right through his chest. The whole front of his shirt exploded in a gruesome red shower and the demon was knocked backward onto the shadow-streaked lawn.

Except that a moment later, he wasn't there at all. He simply disappeared, fading away into the ether. Then abruptly he reappeared six feet farther to the right, unharmed, standing there looking at her, laughing softly.

"Your aim was a little off." He smirked.

Feeders raced back and forth, darting toward her with lightning-quick rushes, frantic with hunger. She realized at once what had happened. It wasn't the demon she had fired at. It was an illusion he had created to fool her.

"Good-bye, Evelyn," he whispered.

His hand lifted in a casual gesture, drawing her eyes to his, and she felt a crushing force close about her chest. She wrenched her eyes away, brought up the shotgun, and fired a second time. Again, the demon's chest blew apart and he was flung away. The feeders ran in all directions, clawing their way onto the porch only to leap off again, lantern eyes wild with expectation. Evelyn was already swinging the barrel of the shotgun about, searching for him, firing both left and right of where he had been, the heavy shot ripping the air, lead pellets hammering into the fence posts at the gate and into the trunks

of the old shagbarks and the graceful limbs of the spruce.
Lights started to come on in the houses closest to hers.

"Damn you!" she hissed.

She racked the slide a fifth time, chambering a fresh shell,
swung the barrel to her right, where the feeders were massed
thickest, and fired into their midst, the shotgun booming. Her
arms and shoulders throbbed with weariness and pain, and her
rage burned in her throat and chest like fire. One shell left. She
saw him climbing over the railing at the other end of the porch,
pumped the final shell into the firing chamber, swung the
shotgun left, and fired down the length of the house.

Reload!

She backed against the screen door and fumbled for
the shells in her dress pocket, kicking at the empties underfoot.
He was right in front of her then, reaching out his hand. She felt
his fingers on her chest, pressing. The shotgun fell away as she
sought to claw his face.

Then the feeders swarmed over her, and everything disappeared in a bright red haze.

George Paulsen ran from the Sinnissippi Townhomes and the
screams of Enid Scott, his hands covering his face. He burst
through the screen door of the Scott apartment with such force
that he ripped it from its hinges and tore the skin from his
hands. There was blood on him everywhere, and the stink of it
was in his nostrils. But it was not from the screams or the blood
or even the ragged, broken form he had left crumpled on the
living-room floor that he fled.

It was from Evelyn Freemark.

She was right in front of him, a shimmering image come out
of the ether, dark and spectral. No matter which way he turned,
there she was. She whispered at him, repeating the words she
had spoken earlier that day in the park, her dark warning of
what would happen if he laid a hand on Enid Scott or her children. He screamed against the persistent sound of it, tearing at
the air and at his own face. He ran mindlessly across the barren
dirt yard into the roadway, desperate to escape.

The dark things bounded after him, the creatures that had

appeared as he beat aside Jared Scott's futile defenses. They had encouraged him to hurt the boy; they had wanted the boy to suffer.

But now they were coming after him as well.

He could feel their hunger in the ragged sound of their breathing.

Oh, God! Oh, God! He screamed the words over and over into the silence and the dark.

Staggering blindly up the roadway, he crested the rise that led out to Lincoln Highway, and a car came out of the lights of the buildings ahead. George Paulsen lurched aside as the car raced past, its horn blaring angrily. The dark things caught him then, bore him back against the cemetery fence, and began to rip him apart. His insides were being shredded beneath their claws and teeth; he could hear himself shriek. With the dark things clinging to him, he turned toward the cemetery fence and scrambled up the chain links. He reached the top, lost his footing, and slid back heavily. He grabbed for something to slow his fall, hooked his fingers into the mesh, and caught his neck on the exposed edges of a gap near the fence top.

Jagged steel sliced through soft flesh and exposed arteries, and George Paulsen's blood gushed forth. He sagged weakly, pain flooding through him. The dark things slowed their attack, closing on him more deliberately, taking their time. He wouldn't escape them now, he knew. He closed his eyes against his fear and desperation. They were touching him, their fingers dipping experimentally in his blood. *Oh, God!*

A moment later, the life went out of him.

Chicago is afire. Everywhere the Knight of the Word looks the flames rise up against the darkening skyline, bleeding their red glare into the smoky twilight. It is an exceptionally hot, dry summer, and the parched grasses that fill the empty parks and push through the cracks in the concrete burn readily. The homes closest to the hollowed-out steel-and-glass monoliths of the abandoned downtown wait their turn, helpless victims of the destruction that approaches. Down along the piers and shipyards, old storage tanks and fuel wells blaze brightly, the residue of their contents exploding like cannon shots.

John Ross jogs quickly along the walkway bordering the Chicago River, moving south from the breach in the fortress walls. He carries his staff before him, but he has temporarily lost the use of its **magic**, the consequence of another of those times in the past **when he** was forced to call upon it—before the Armageddon, **before the** fall. Thus he must flee and hide as common men. **Already,** his enemies look for him. They have tracked him here, as they track him everywhere, and they know that somewhere in the conflagration he will be found. A Knight of the Word is a great prize, and those who find him will be well rewarded. But they know, too, that he will not be taken easily, and their caution gives him an edge.

He has come late to the city's fall. The attack has been in progress for months, the once-men and their demon masters laying siege to the makeshift walls and reinforced gates that keep the people within protected. Chicago is one of the strongest bastions remaining, a military camp run with discipline and skill, its people armed and trained. But no bastion is impregnable, and the attackers have finally found a way in. He is told they gain entry through the sewers, that there is no longer any way of keeping them out. Now the end is at hand, and there is nothing anyone can do but flee or die.

Bodies line the streets, flung casually aside by those who leave them lifeless. Men, women, and children—no exceptions are made. Slaves are plentiful and food is scarce. Besides, a lesson is needed. Feeders slink through the shadows, working their way from corpse to corpse, seeking a shred of fading life, of pain, of horror, of helpless rage, of shock and anguish on which to feed. But the battle moves on to other places, and so the feeders follow after. Ross works his way along a brick wall fronting the postage-stamp yards of a line of abandoned brick homes, searching for a way out, listening to the screams and cries of those who have failed to do so. The attack shifts to a point ahead of him, and he recognizes the danger. He must turn back. He must find another way. But his options are running *out, and without the magic to protect him he is less certain of what he should do.*

Finally he begins to retrace his steps, angling west toward the outskirts of the city, away from Lake Michigan and the downtown. It will be nightfall soon, and the hunters will not find him so easily. If he can reach the freeways, he can follow them into the suburbs and be gone before they realize he has escaped. His throat is dry, and his muscles ache, for he has not slept in days. His coming to the city was in response to a dream that foretold of its destruction. But he is mistrusted everywhere, a Cassandra crying out in the wilderness of a crumbling Troy, and his warnings are ignored. Some would imprison him as a spy. Some would throw him from the walls. If they did not fear his magic, he would already be dead. It is a pointless, debilitating life he leads, but it is all he has left.

He comes up against a firefight at an intersection in the streets and spins quickly back into a shadowed niche to hide from the combatants. Automatic weapons riddle wooden doors and pock brick walls and take the lives of everyone caught in their field of fire. The feeders frolic through the carnage, leaping and twisting with unrestrained glee, feeding on the rage and fear of the combatants. Killing is the most powerful form of madness and therefore the feeders' strongest source of food, and they are drawn to it as flies to blood. No sounds come from them, nor is any form of recognition accorded them, for they are a silent, invisible presence. But in their lantern eyes Ross sees the pleasure they derive from the dark emotions the killing releases, and he is reminded of the Furies in the old Greek myths, driving insane those who had committed unconscionable crimes. If there were Furies in real life, he thinks, they would be mothers to these feeders.

When the fighting dies away, he moves on, running swiftly toward the confluence of freeways that lead into the city from the west, anxious to find his way clear. Night slips down about him like window shades drawn against the smoky, fiery light of the city's destruction. The smells that assail his nostrils are acrid and rank—charred flesh and blackened blood. Disease will follow, and many of those who do not die in the fighting will die in the aftermath. Thousands are driven from this city into the wilderness. How many will survive to take refuge somewhere else?

He reaches the arterials winding into the main east/west freeway, but the attackers throng from all quarters before him, lining the four-lane, gathering for an unknown reason. He edges back cautiously and works his way down the back-yards of houses and the shattered glass fronts of businesses to where those who celebrate do not mass so thickly. He finds a rise on which an abandoned housing development is set-tled, and he enters a house that gives him a clear view of the freeway leading in. From an upstairs window, he looks out on a grand procession approaching from the west. He uses his binoculars to get a clearer look, a cold suspicion begin-ning to surface.

There, on the buckled, cracked ribbon of concrete that spreads like a length of worn pewter into the horizon, he sees the first lines of captured humans, shackled and bent as they shuffle forward in long trains, their lives spared so that they may serve as slaves. Cages on wheels contain those who will be accorded a special death. Heads strung on ropes and mounted on poles attest to the number who have found death already.

Then he sees her. She rides on a flatbed wagon pulled by sev-eral dozen of those she has subjugated. She sits amid the demons who are her favorites, tall, regal, and as cold as death, queen of the destruction she surveys. Her history is legend. She was a world-class athlete who medaled twice in the Olympics. She became an activist, first for reform, later for revolution, gifted with charismatic speaking powers. She was revered and trusted by everyone, and she betrayed them all. Along the freeway, the once-men who serve her go quiet and bow their heads in obeisance. John Ross feels his stomach knot. Even from where he hides he can see the emptiness in her eyes. She is devoid of emotion, as dead inside as the creatures she has crushed in her passing. She is a pivotal figure in the Void's implacable war against the Word. She is John Ross's greatest failure.

He knew her when she was different, many years ago, when there was still time to save her.

He knew her as Nest Freemark.

MONDAY, JULY 4

CHAPTER 26

Nest Freemark woke to the sound of voices, hushed and cautious outside her bedroom door. The big floor fan had been turned off and shoved to one side and the door closed, so she could not see who was there. She tried to pick up on what was being said, but the words were indistinct. She lay facing the door, staring at its familiar paneled frame, the bedsheet pulled up to her chin, her fists clenched about the wrinkled border. She did not know when she had finally fallen asleep or how long she had slept. The room's light was gray and muted, and the temperature cool, so she thought it might only be dawn. But when she looked at her bedside clock, she saw it was almost noon.

She took a deep breath and exhaled slowly, then turned over to look out the window. A small section of the sky was visible through the curtains. Clouds drifted slowly across the blue expanse, and the sun cast their shadows on the earth and marked their passing with changes in the light. The breeze that wafted through her open window smelled damp and fetid.

Had it rained during the night? Her thoughts drifted. Gran had always loved the sound of falling rain.

Her eyes teared, and she brushed at them quickly. She would not cry again—not right away. She had cried enough. She felt something scratchy against her bare elbow, and she reached beneath the covers to extract Gran's crumpled note. She had found it beneath her pillow when her grandfather had finally gotten her to bed—after they had taken Gran away, after all the policemen, medics, firemen, and neighbors had gone, after she had refused over and over again to go somewhere else for the night. Alone in the darkness of her room, trapped in the downward spiral of her sadness and rage, she had curled into a ball atop her sheets, the fan blowing cool air over her heated skin, her eyes scrunched tight against her horror and misery, and clutched her pillow to her face. That was when her fingers had come upon the note. She had pulled it out, opened it, and stared at it in disbelief. The note was from Gran. She had read it so many times since that she knew the words by heart.

> When he comes for you,
> use your magic.
> Trust Wraith.
>
> > Love you.
> > Gran

She looked at the writing again now, trying to gain some new insight, to find hidden meaning behind the words. But the note was straightforward and the warning it contained unmistakable. Gran had written the note in the moments before she died. She had written it, in all probability, knowing she was going to die. Nest had thought it all through carefully, looking it over from every conceivable viewpoint, and argued the possibilities with herself until she was certain. The police and the firemen and the medics and the neighbors might agree among themselves that Gran was an old drunk who saw things that weren't there and finally drank so much she took out a shotgun to blow away her phantoms and brought on the heart attack that killed her. They might dismiss her with a shrug, a few words of sympathy, and an unspoken conviction that anyone crazy enough to go around shooting holes in trees and fences was just asking for trouble. They might sleep a whole lot better living with that explanation than with the truth. But the fact remained that the truth was something else entirely. Gran wasn't dead because she drank or she was crazy. She was dead because the demon had killed her.

I have enemies to eliminate.

Nest could still hear his words, spoken to her in the blackness of the caves, disembodied and remote and rife with malice. The demon had gone about the business of eliminating Gran quite deliberately. He had taken great pains to sidetrack everyone who might protect her, and then he had come for her. Nest knew it was so. She had never been so certain of anything in her life.

Now Gran was warning her, in the crumpled note she held in her hands, that the demon was coming for her as well.

Why?

Nest had pondered the question all night and she still didn't have an answer. She had assumed all along that the demon's interest in her was strictly secondary to his interest in Gran or John Ross, that he was using her to get to them. But Gran's note suggested that his intentions were more personal. Gran obviously believed the demon was after Nest as well. *Use your magic. Trust Wraith.* Gran could have written anything in those last few moments, but she had chosen to write this.

Why?

Because Gran had thought it more important than anything else. Because she knew what was going to happen.

Which was more than Nest could say.

What did the demon want with her?

She rolled onto her back and stared at the flat surface of the ceiling. *Use your magic. Trust Wraith.* As if the magic had done Gran any good. And where was Wraith last night when she was fighting to keep her sanity as the feeders crawled all over her? Why should she believe either one would be of any use against the demon? Questions buzzed in her mind like gnats, and she closed her eyes against their persistent whine. The answers that would silence them were nowhere to be found. God, she was going to miss Gran. Her eyes filled with tears immediately. She still couldn't believe her grandmother was gone, that she wasn't sitting there at the kitchen table with her orange juice and vodka and her cigarette and ashtray, that she wouldn't be asking Nest what time she planned to be home from the fireworks that night, that she wouldn't be there to talk about the feeders and the forest creatures and the magic in the park.

Nest sobbed quietly. She could still see the look on Gran's face as she lay lifeless on the porch, the shotgun clutched in her hands. She would always see that look, a cold haunting at the fringes of her warmer memories. She had known the truth about how Gran died the instant she had seen her face. The note only confirmed it.

She turned on her side again, staring at the curtained window and the clouded sky beyond. The back of her throat ached with what she was feeling. She would never get over this, she thought. She would never be the same again.

Footsteps approached along the hallway beyond her room and stopped outside her door. A moment later the door opened, and someone stepped inside. She lay without moving, listening to the silence. She hoped that whoever was there would go away.

"Nest?" her grandfather called softly.

She did not respond, but he crossed to the bed anyway and sat down next to her.

"Did you sleep at all?" he asked.

She closed her eyes against the sound of his voice. "Yes."

"That's good. I know it wasn't easy. But you needed to get some rest." He was quiet for a few moments, and she could feel his eyes on her. She remained motionless beneath the sheet, curled into herself. "Are you hungry?"

"No."

"There's a lot of food out there. People have been stopping by all morning, bringing casseroles and tins filled with everything you can imagine." He chuckled softly. "Looks like some of them emptied out their entire kitchens. We've got enough food to feed an army. I don't know what we're going to do with all of it."

His hand rested on her shoulder. "Why don't you get up and come out and keep me company?"

She was silent a moment, thinking it over. "I heard voices."

"Friends. Neighbors. Everyone's gone now. It's just you and me." He shifted on the bed, and she could hear him sigh. "They say she didn't suffer, Nest. She was gone almost right away. Massive heart attack. I spoke with the doctor a little while ago. He was very kind. I've got to go down to the funeral home and pick out a casket this afternoon. A notice has already been sent to the paper. Reverend Emery helped prepare it. He's agreed to speak at the funeral on Thursday."

He trailed off, as if he didn't quite know where to go next. In the silence, Nest could hear the old clock ticking down the hall.

After a moment, her grandfather said quietly, his voice filled with sadness, "I just don't understand."

She nodded without offering a reply, thinking that she understood better than he did, but didn't know how to explain it to him.

His hand tightened on her shoulder. "You might have heard some comments last night, loose talk about your grandmother. You'll probably hear more. I don't want you to pay any attention to it. Your grandmother was a special person. A lot of people didn't understand that. They thought she was peculiar. I guess she was, but she was good-hearted and caring and she knew how to look after people. You know that. And I don't care what anyone says, she wasn't out there shooting that shotgun at nothing. Your grandmother wasn't like that."

"I know," Nest said quickly, hearing the despair build in his voice.

She twisted about so that she could see his face. It looked careworn and tired, the age lines more deeply etched, the thick white hair mussed and badly combed. When she looked into his eyes she could tell he had been crying.

His voice shook. "She was fine when I left her, Nest. She was worried about you, of course, but she was fine. I just don't know what happened. I don't think she would have brought out the shotgun if she wasn't in danger. She hasn't even looked at it in years."

He paused, his eyes searching her face. He was waiting for

her to speak, to respond to his comments. When she stayed silent, he cleared his throat, and his voice steadied again.

"Your young friends said something strange when they came by the house to ask me to help look for you last night. They said you were chasing after someone who was poisoning trees in the park, someone I'd told you about. But I don't know anything about this." He looked away a moment. "The thing of it is, Nest, I get the feeling I don't know anything about a lot of what's going on. It wasn't so important before." His eyes shifted back to her. "But after what happened last night, I guess now it is."

His eyes stayed locked on hers. Nest felt like a deer caught in the headlights. She didn't know what to say. She didn't even know where to begin.

"Can we talk about this a little later, Grandpa?" she said finally. "I just can't do it right now."

He considered her request a moment, and then nodded. "All right, Nest. That seems fair." He rose, his eyes traveling about the room as if seeking something. "Will you come out and eat?"

She raised herself to a sitting position and forced a smile. "Sure. Just give me a minute, okay?"

He went back through the door and closed it softly behind him. Nest sat in the bed without moving, staring into space. What could she say to him? She got up finally and went into the bathroom and took a shower. She let the water wash over her for a long time, her eyes closed, her thoughts wandering off to other times and places, then returning to focus on what lay ahead. She dried off and began to dress. She had just finished pulling on shorts and a T-shirt and was bending down to tie her tennis shoes when she heard a scrabbling sound at the window.

"Nest!" Pick called urgently.

"Pick!" she exclaimed in relief, and rushed over to push aside the curtains.

The sylvan was standing on the sill looking disheveled and grimy, as if he had been rolled in dirt. His leafy head was soiled and his twiggy feet were caked with mud. "I'm sorry to be late, girl. I've had a dreadful night! If I don't get some help, I don't know what I'm going to do! The balance of things is upset in a way I've never seen! The feeders are all over the place!" He caught his breath, and his face softened. "I heard from Daniel about your grandmother. I'm sorry, Nest. I can't believe it happened."

"Was it the demon?" she asked quickly.

"Of course it was the demon!" He was so matter-of-fact about it, so unshakably certain, so *Pick*, that she smiled in spite of herself. Pick scowled. "The stink of his magic is all over your front yard! He must have come right up to the front door! How did he do that? Where were you and your grandfather?"

Quickly she filled him in on what had happened—how she had been lured away from the dance by the demon, how Danny Abbott and his friends had stuffed her in a burlap bag and hauled her down to the caves, how the demon had come to her there and taunted her, how her grandfather had been summoned by her friends to find her, and how Gran had ended up being left alone.

"Oh, that's a nasty piece of work!" Pick spit indignantly. "Your grandmother would have been a match for him once. More than a match for him, fact of the matter is. I told you as much. Would have split him up the middle if he'd tried something like this!"

Nest knelt at the windowsill, her face even with his. "So why didn't she, Pick?" she asked. "She always said she had magic, that we both did. Why didn't she use it?"

Pick scrunched up his seamed face, his sharp blue eyes narrowing, his mouth disappearing into his beard. "I don't know. She wouldn't have needed a shotgun if she'd had the magic. She was powerful, Nest—strong-minded and able. She'd studied on her magic; she'd learned how to use it. She might not have been as strong as he was, but he would have come out of a fight with her with a whole lot less skin! And there wasn't a sign of her magic amid the leavings of his!" He rubbed his beard. "Truth is, I haven't seen her use it in a

long time—not in a very long time, girl. Not since your
mother . . ."

He trailed off, staring at her as if seeing her in a new light.

"What?" she asked quickly.

"Well, I don't know," he answered vaguely. "I was just
wondering."

She let the matter drop, choosing instead to tell him about
the note. She took it out of her pocket and unfolded it so that he
could see that it was Gran's writing, and then she read it to him.
When he heard the words, his face underwent a strange transformation. "Criminy," he whispered.

"What is it?" she demanded. "Stop making me guess what
you're thinking, Pick!"

"Well, it's just that . . ." He shook his head slowly, his lips
still moving, but no sound coming out.

"Why would the demon be coming after me?" she pressed,
poking at him insistently with her finger.

Then the bedroom door opened, and her grandfather looked
in. Pick disappeared instantly. Nest stood up, smoothing down
the front of her T-shirt, composing her face.

"Your friends are at the back door," her grandfather said. "I
think you ought to see them."

Reluctantly Nest came out of the bedroom and followed him
down the hall. The old grandfather clock marked the cadence
of their steps. As they passed the living room, she glanced in at
the pictures of her mother and Gran resting on the fireplace
mantel. Gran's cross-stitch project rested on the arm of the old
easy chair, unfinished. Her crosswords sat in a pile on the floor
beside the chair. There were small pieces of her everywhere.
Dull slants of gray light wedged their way through the drawn
curtains and window shades, but the room felt musty and
empty of life.

In the kitchen, dozens of containers of food sat unattended
on the table and counters like forgotten guests. Her grandfather
slowed and looked vaguely at the array of dishes. "I better see
to this. You go on outside. It might be more private for you in
the backyard."

She went the rest of the way down the hall to the screen door and opened it. Robert, Cass, and Brianna stood waiting for her. Cass held a bouquet of daisies, mums, and marigolds.

"Hey," she said by way of greeting.

"Hey," they replied in jumbled unison.

Cass passed her the flowers, dark eyes bright with tears. "Sorry about Gran, Nest. We'll all miss her."

"She was the best," Brianna agreed, wiping at her nose.

Robert shoved his hands into his pockets and looked at his shoes in a way that suggested he had never seen them before.

"Thanks for coming by." Nest sniffed at the flowers automatically. "These are really pretty."

"Well, daisies were always her favorite," Cass said.

"You remember when she laid into me for cutting down that stand out back?" Robert asked suddenly. He seemed surprised he had said something and gave Nest a quick, hopeful look. "Man, she was upset. But when you told her I was taking them home to my mom, she said right away that it was all right, and she took us inside and gave us milk and cookies. Remember?"

"I remember when she helped me make that Cinderella costume for Halloween when I was six," Brianna said, smiling. "She did most of the work, but she told my mom we did it together."

"I still can't believe she's gone," Cass said.

They were silent a moment, and then Robert said, "What happened to her anyway, Nest? There's all kinds of stories floating around."

Nest crossed her arms defensively. "She had a heart attack." She tried to think what else she could say. Her gaze shifted away from Robert and back again. "I suppose you heard about the shotgun."

Robert shrugged. "Everybody's talking about that part, and you can guess what some of them are saying. But my dad says people will talk no matter who you are or what you do, so you might as well get used to it."

"People are mean," Brianna said to no one in particular.

No one spoke, eyes shifting uneasily in the silence.

"Thanks for not leaving me last night." Nest tried to change the subject. "You know, for getting Grandpa to come back over and find me."

She told them what had happened to her, only leaving out the part about the demon, then adding at the end that she was all right, no harm had been done, and they should all forget about it.

"What about the man who's poisoning the trees?" Brianna said, her brow knit anxiously.

Nest shook her head. "I don't know. He's still out there."

"Danny Abbott is a butt-face." Robert muttered angrily. "You should have let me punch him out when I had the chance, Nest."

Hearing him say it made her smile. She came through the doorway, and the four of them walked out into the shady back-yard and sat down at the old picnic table. Thick, gray clouds floated overhead, drifting out of the west where the sky was already darkening. Rain was on the way, sure enough. In the park, the first of the softball games had started up. Families were arriving by the carloads to set up their picnic lunches and to settle in for the day's events and the evening's fireworks. Nest watched a line of cars crawl down Sinnissippi Road past the townhomes.

"Where's Jared?" she asked, wondering for the first time why he was missing. No one said anything. Nest saw the discomfort mirrored in their faces. "What's wrong? Where is he?"

"He's in the hospital, Nest," Cass said, her eyes lifting. "That's what we came to tell you. It was on the news this morning, but we thought maybe you hadn't heard."

"George Paulsen beat him up real bad," Brianna said softly.

"He beat him within an inch of his life!" growled Robert, shoving back his shock of blond hair aggressively. "The jerk."

Nest felt her stomach go cold and her throat tighten. She shook her head slowly, awash in disbelief.

"I guess it happened right after your grandpa sent us home," Cass explained. Her round face was filled with pain, and her dark eyes blinked rapidly. "Jared came in the door, and George got mad at him for something and hit him. Jared hit him back, and then George really unloaded."

"Yeah, and then he runs off before the police arrive." Robert's face was flushed with anger. "But it didn't do him much good. He fell trying to climb the cemetery fence and tore his throat open on the exposed ends. Bled to death before anyone could reach him. My dad says it's the best thing that could have happened to him."

Nest felt a vast, empty place open inside. "How's Jared?"

Cass shook her head. "He's in a coma. It's pretty bad."

"Mom says he might die," Brianna said.

Nest swallowed and fought to keep the tears from coming. "He can't die."

"That's what I said," Robert agreed quickly. "Not Jared. He's just gone away, like he does sometimes. He'll be back when he's feeling better." He looked away quickly, as if embarrassed by what he had said.

Nest brushed at her eyes, remembering the shy way Jared always looked at her. She struggled to bring herself under control. "Why would George Paulsen do something like that?"

"You know," Robert snorted. "Old Enid and he were drinking and fooling around." Cass gave him a sharp look. "Well, they were! My dad says they were."

"Your dad doesn't know everything, Robert," Cass said evenly.

"Tell him that."

"Mom says they tried to lie about it at first," Brianna interrupted, "but then Mrs. Scott broke down and told them everything. They didn't arrest her, but they took her kids away and put them in foster care. I guess she's in big trouble."

Everyone in that family is in trouble, Nest thought sadly. But it's Jared who's paying the price. Someone should have done something to help him a long time ago. Maybe it should have been her. She'd helped Bennett when she was lost; why hadn't she found a way to help Jared? Why hadn't she seen he might need her help? She could picture George Paulsen hitting him, could see the feeders rising up out of the shadows to spur

George on. She could see Gran as well, standing on the porch with the shotgun pointed at the demon as hundreds of lantern eyes stared hungrily from the shadows.

"It just isn't fair," said Brianna.

They talked a while longer, sitting out under the oak trees in the seclusion of the backyard while beyond the hedgerow the park continued to fill with picnickers. Finally Nest told them she had to go in and get something to eat. Robert wanted to know if she was coming over to the park later for the fireworks, and Cass gave him a look and told him he was an idiot. But Nest said she might, that she had been thinking about it and there was no reason to just sit around the house. Gran would have wanted her to go. She would ask her grandfather.

She waited until they disappeared through the hedgerow into the park, then rose and walked slowly back toward the house. She had a curious, unpleasant feeling that everything was slipping away from her. She had always felt secure about her life, able to face whatever changes might come. But now she felt her grip loosening, as if she might no longer be able to count on anything. It was not just losing Gran and maybe Jared; it was the dark way the world beyond the park had suddenly intruded on her life. It was John Ross and O'olish Amaneh appearing. It was the coming of the demon. It was the danger the maentwrog posed, threatening to break free of its centuries-old prison. It was the sudden emergence of so many feeders in places they had never been seen before and Pick's warning of a shift in the balance. It was the revival of the mystery surrounding her mother and father. It was Wraith's failure to protect her last night.

But mostly, she thought, it was the fear and uncertainty she felt at the prospect of having to rely on her magic to stay alive—her magic, which she mistrusted and disliked, a genetic gift come out of her own flesh and blood that she had never fully understood. Gran had left her with a single admonition. *When he comes for you, use your magic.* Not "if he comes" or "should he come." There was no room for debate on what was going to happen or what was required of her, and Nest Freemark, at fourteen years of age, isolated by loss and doubt and secrets kept hidden from her, did not feel ready to deal with it.

She was still wrestling with her sense of vulnerability, standing alone not ten feet from her back door, when the demon appeared.

CHAPTER 27

The demon stepped from behind the garage where it opened onto the driveway leading down the lane, emerging from a patch of shadows cast by one of the old shagbark hickories. Nest froze on seeing him, the thoughts that cluttered her mind disappearing with the quickness of fireflies in daylight. She was so surprised by his appearance that she didn't even think to call out. She just stood there, staring at him in shock. His bland face was expressionless, as if coming upon her like this was quite natural. He studied her with his washed-out blue eyes, and his gaze was almost tender. He seemed to be seeing something about her that she herself could not, measuring it, weighing it, giving it full and deliberate consideration. She could hear Gran's words screaming in her ear. *When he comes for you. When he comes for you.* The words faded into a high-pitched ringing that deafened her. She tried to break free of him, to bolt for the safety of the house, but his gaze held her fast. No matter how hard she struggled, she could not escape. She felt tears come to her eyes. Rage and frustration boiled up within her, but even these were not powerful enough to release her.

Then the demon cocked his head, as if his attention had been drawn away. He smiled at her, a quick, empty gesture, a reflection of some private amusement. He lifted his fingers to his lips and blew her a kiss off the tips. A moment later, he was gone, stepping back into the shadows in the lee of the garage and fading away.

Nest stood rooted in place, her hands shaking. She waited

354

for him to reappear, to come for her as Gran had said he would. But nothing happened. The ringing in her ears faded, and she began to hear the sounds of the people in the park again, the robins singing in the trees in her yard, and the cars passing down Woodlawn Road. She took a deep breath and held it, trying to still herself.

"Nest!"

John Ross limped slowly into view through the gap in the hedgerow from off the service road. A surge of relief flooded through her. She ran to him without thinking, racing across the backyard, barely able to contain the cry of gratitude that rose in her throat. Her legs churned and her arms pumped, and she threw off the last links of her immobilizing chains. She ran to outstrip her fear and revulsion, to leave them stymied and powerless in the wake of her quickness.

When she reached John Ross, she threw herself into his arms and clung to him.

"Hey, hey, it's all right," he said quickly, bracing himself with his staff, his free arm coming about her shoulders reassuringly. "What's wrong, Nest? Hey, stop crying."

She shook her head against his chest, fighting the tears, gasping for breath as she tried to speak. Everything washed out of her in a hot flush, all the rage and fear and horror and sadness of last night, evaporating like rainwater on hot concrete in the aftermath of a summer storm.

"I heard about your grandmother, and I came right out," he said quietly. "I'm sorry, Nest. I wish I had known he would do this. I would have tried to prevent it. I know how you must feel. I know how hard it must be."

"I hurt so bad," she said finally, the words coming from her mouth in little gulps.

"It can't be any other way," he replied. "Not when you lose someone you love so much."

She shook her head slowly, rubbing her face against his shirt, still pressing against him. "Why did this happen? Why did he do it? Was he just trying to get back at her for what happened when she was a girl? Is that it?" The pitch of her voice began to rise and the words to come faster. "John, he was just here, standing down by the garage, staring at me. I couldn't move! If you hadn't come . . ."

"Nest, slow down, it's all right." He patted her back in an effort to calm her.

She clutched him more tightly. "Gran left a note, John. Just before she died. She knew what was going to happen. The note says the demon is coming for me, too. For me! Why?"

The words hung sharp-edged and immobile in the silence that followed. John Ross said nothing, but in doing so said everything. Nest felt the precipice she had sought to escape drawing near once more. Ross knew, but would not tell her. Like Gran, he had secrets to hide. Her resolve began to falter. She heard the screen door open and saw her grandfather emerge, looking for her. She felt besieged on all sides, boxed in by her ignorance and confusion. She had to know what was happening. She had to know before it was too late.

A surge of wild determination and reckless courage flooded through her. "John," she said quickly, lifting her face away from his chest to look at him. Her heart pounded. "Are you my father?"

The pain that filled his eyes when she spoke the words was palpable. He stared at her with such intensity that it felt to her as if he was unable to convey with words what he was feeling.

"It's just that Gran seemed so suspicious and resentful of you," Nest hurried on, trying to make the answer easier for him, to let him tell her what she already knew was so. "I heard her talking to Grandpa. She was saying things that made it pretty clear . . . I'm not angry or anything, you know. I just . . . I just . . ."

He brought his hand to her face, resting the palm against her cheek. "Nest," he said softly. "I wish to God I were your father. I would be proud to be your father." He shook his head sadly. "But I'm not."

She stared at him in disbelief, feeling her expectation crumple inside and turn to despair. She had been so sure. She had known he was her father, known it from the way that Gran reacted to him, from the way he spoke of her mother, from his history, from his voice and eyes, from everything he was. How could he not be? How could he not?

Her grandfather came up behind them, and Nest turned toward him. He saw the stricken look in her face, and his jaw tightened. His eyes locked at once on John Ross.

"Morning, John," he said, a decided edge to his voice. He placed a reassuring hand on Nest's shoulder.

"Good morning, sir," Ross answered, taking his own hand away.

"Is something wrong here?"

"No, sir. I just came by to offer my condolences. I'm very sorry about Mrs. Freemark. I believe she was a remarkable woman."

"Thank you for the kind words and for your concern." The old man paused. "Mind telling me what happened to your face?"

Nest, who had been staring at nothing, still stunned from learning that Ross was not her father, glanced up at him quickly and for the first time noticed the cuts and bruises.

"I was attacked by some men from MidCon at the dance last night," Ross said, giving a barely perceptible shrug. "It was a case of mistaken identity. They thought I was a company spy."

"A company spy?" Nest's grandfather looked incredulous. "The company doesn't have any spies. Who would they be spying on? For what reason?"

Ross shrugged again. "It's over now. I'm fine. I just wish I had been here for you and Nest."

Nest's grandfather looked at her. "You've been crying, Nest. Are you all right now?"

Nest nodded, saying nothing, feeling dead inside. She looked at her grandfather, then looked quickly away.

Robert Freemark straightened and turned back to John Ross. "John, I have to tell you something. Evelyn wasn't all that warm toward you, I know. She thought that maybe you were someone other than who you claimed. She was suspicious of your motives. I told her she was being silly, that I thought you were a good man."

He shook his head slowly. "But I have to admit that a lot of strange things have happened since you arrived. Nest hasn't been herself for several days. Maybe she doesn't think I've noticed, but I have. Last night's events have made me think. A lot of things don't add up. I guess I need to ask you to explain some of them."

Ross met his frank gaze with a weary, distant look. He seemed to weigh the matter a moment before answering. "I think you deserve that much, Mr. Freemark."

Nest's grandfather nodded. Nest stepped back so that she could see them both, sensing the start of something that was not going to end pleasantly.

"Well, there's this business of the man who's been poisoning trees in the park." Robert Freemark cleared his throat. "Nest's friends told me about him when they came by to ask for my help in finding her." Quickly, he told John Ross what had happened. "They said she sent them first in search of you, making it pretty clear, I think, that you know about this man, too."

He paused, waiting. John Ross glanced at Nest. "I know about him. I came to Hopewell because I was tracking him."

"Tracking him?"

"It's what I do."

"You track people? Are you with the police? Are you a law-enforcement officer?"

Ross shook his head. "I work on my own."

Nest's grandfather stared. "Are you telling me, John, that you are a private detective? Or a bounty hunter?"

"Something else."

There was a long pause as Nest's grandfather studied the other man, hands resting loosely on his hips. "Did you know my daughter Caitlin at all, John? Was any of that true?"

"I knew of her, but I didn't know her personally. I didn't go to school with her. We weren't classmates. I'm sorry, I made that up. I needed to meet you. More to the point, I needed to meet Nest."

Another pause, longer this time. "Why, John?"

"Because while I didn't know Nest's mother, I do know her father."

Now Nest was staring hard at him, too, a look of horror spreading over her face. She swallowed against the sudden ache in her throat and looked quickly at her grandfather. Old Bob's face was pale. "Maybe you better just spit it out," he said.

John Ross nodded, bringing the black staff around in front of him so that he could lean on it, as if the talk was wearing on him in unseen ways. He looked down at his shoes momentarily, then directly at Nest.

"I'm sorry, Nest, this is going to hurt a lot. I wish I didn't have to tell you, but I do. I hope you'll understand." He looked back at her grandfather. "There's a lot of talk about how your wife died, sir. Some people are saying she was a crazy old woman who died shooting at ghosts. I don't think that's true. I think she was shooting at the man I've been tracking, the man I came here to find. She was trying to defend herself. But he is a very resourceful and dangerous adversary, and she wasn't strong enough to stop him. He's caused a lot of trouble and pain, and he's not finished. He came to Hopewell for a very specific purpose. He doesn't realize it yet, but I know what that purpose is."

Nest took a deep breath as his green eyes shifted back to hers. "He's come for you. Your grandmother knew. That made her a threat to him, so he got rid of her."

His gaze was steady. "He's your father, Nest."

In his dream, the Knight of the Word stands with a ragged band of survivors atop a wooded rise south of the burning city. Men have devoted such enormous time and energy to destroying themselves that they are exhausted from their efforts, and now the demons and the once-men have picked up the slack. At first it was the tented camps and nomads who were prey, but of late the attacks have shifted to the walled cities. The weakest have begun to fall and the nature of the adversary to make itself known. The

Knight has battled the demons all through the destruction of the old world, confronting them at every opportunity, trying to slow the erosion of civilization. But the tide is inexorable and undiminished, and a new dark age has descended.

The Knight looks around to be certain that the women and children are being led to safety while he acts as sentry. Most have already disappeared into the night, and the rest are fading with the swiftness of ghosts. Only a few remain behind to stand with him, a handful of those who have discovered too late that he is not the enemy. Below, the city burns with an angry crackle. Hordes of captives are being led away, those who did not flee when there was time, who did not heed his warning. The Knight closes his eyes against the sadness and despair that wells within him. It does not change. He cannot make them listen. He cannot make them believe.

Look! says a weathered man next to him, his voice a low hiss of fear and rage. It's her!

He sees the woman then, striding forward out of the darkness and into the light, surrounded by men who are careful not to come too near. She is tall and regal, and her features are cold. He has never seen her before, but there is something familiar about her nevertheless. He is immediately intrigued. She radiates power and is an immutable presence. She is clearly the leader of those about her, and they hasten to do her bidding. A captive is brought before her and forced to kneel. He will not look at her, his head lowered stubbornly between his shoulders. She reaches for his hair and jerks savagely on it. When their eyes meet, he undergoes a terrible transformation. He twists and shakes, an animal trapped within a snare, enraged and terrified. He says things, screams them actually, the words indistinct, but the sounds clear. Then she is finished with him and he arches as if skewered on the point of a spear and dies writhing in the dirt.

The woman steps around him without a second glance and continues on, the flames of the city catching in their orange glow the empty look upon her face.

Do you know her? the Knight asks the man who has spoken.

Oh, yes, I know her. The man whispers, as if the night breeze might carry his words to her. His face is scarred and worn. She was a girl once. Before she became what she is. Her name was Nest Freemark. She lived in a little town called Hopewell, Illinois. Her father came for her on the Fourth of July when she was just fourteen and changed her forever. Her father, a demon himself, made her one, too. I heard him say so to a man he knew, just before he killed him. It was in a prison. Her father would have killed me as well, had he known I was listening.

Tell me about her, the Knight says quietly.

He turns the man in to the trees so that they can follow the others to safety, and in the course of their furtive withdrawal from the horror taking place on the plains below, the man does.

When John Ross awoke that morning in Josie Jackson's bed, he was in such pain that he could barely move. All of his muscles and joints had stiffened during the night, and the bruises from his beating had flowered into brilliantly colored splotches on his chest and ribs. He lay next to Josie and tried shifting various parts of himself without waking her. Everything ached, and he knew it would be days before he could function in a normal way again.

Last night's dream hung with veiled menace in the dark seclusion of his mind, a horror he could not dispel, and he was reminded anew of the older dream, the one that had given him his first glimpse of the monster Nest Freemark would become.

Should I tell her? he wondered anew. Now, while there is still time? Will it help her to know?

When they rose, Josie drew a hot bath for him and left him to soak while she made breakfast. He was dressing when she came in with the news of Evelyn Freemark's death. The details were on the radio, and several of Josie's friends had called as well. Ross walked in silence to the kitchen to eat, the momentary joy he had found during the night already beginning to fade. He tried not to show what he was feeling. The demon had outsmarted him. The demon had provoked last night's attack on him not because he was a threat to its plans, but to get him out of the way so he could not help Evelyn Freemark. He had spent so much time worrying about Nest that he had forgotten to consider the people closest to her. The demon was breaking Nest down by stripping away the people and defenses she relied upon. Ross had missed it completely.

He finished his breakfast and told Josie he was going out to see Old Bob, and she offered to come with him. He thanked her, but said he thought he should do this alone. She said that was fine, looking away quickly, the hurt showing in her dark eyes. She walked to the counter and stood there, looking out the kitchen window.

"Is this good-bye, John?" she asked after a minute. "You can tell me."

He studied the soft curve of her shoulders against the robe. "I'm not sure."

She nodded, saying nothing. She ran a hand through her tousled hair and continued to stare out the window.

He groped for something more to say, but it was too late for explanations. He had violated his own rules last night by letting himself get close to her. Involvement with anyone was forbidden for a Knight of the Word. It was one thing to risk his own life; it was something else again to risk the life of another.

"I'll be leaving Hopewell soon, maybe even sometime today. I don't know when I'll be back." His eyes met hers as she turned to look at him. "I wish it could be different."

She studied him a moment. "I'd like to believe that. Can I write you?"

He shook his head slowly. "I don't have an address."

Her smile was wan and fragile. "All right. Will you write me sometimes?"

He told her he would try. He could tell she wanted to say more, to ask him why he was being so difficult, so secretive. But she did not. She just kept looking at him, as if knowing somewhere deep inside that it was useless, that she would never see him again.

She drove him back to the hotel so that he could change his clothes, then drove him out to the Freemarks' and dropped him off at the entrance to the park. She barely spoke the entire time. But when he started to get out of the car, she reached over and put her arms around his neck and kissed him hard on the mouth.

"Don't forget me," she whispered, and gave him a hint of the smile that had drawn him to her that first day.

Then she straightened herself behind the steering wheel while he closed the car door and drove away without looking back.

He had made up his mind in that instant to tell Nest Freemark about her father.

Now, as he stood looking at Nest's shattered face, he wondered if he had made the right decision. The mix of shock and horror that flooded her eyes was staggering. She blinked rapidly, and he could tell that she wanted to look away from him, to hide from his terrible revelation, but she could not. She tried to speak, but no words would come. Old Bob was stunned as well, but his exposure to the truth wasn't as complete. He didn't know what Nest did. He didn't know that her father was a demon.

"My father?" she whispered finally. "Are you sure?"

The words hung between them in the ensuing silence, a poisonous and forbidding accusation.

"Nest," her grandfather began, reaching for her.

"No, don't say anything," she said quickly, silencing him, stepping back. She tore her gaze from Ross and looked out into the park. "I need to . . . I just have to . . ."

She broke off in despair, tears streaming down her face, and bolted from the yard through the hedgerow and into the park. She ran past the ball diamond behind the house, down the service road toward the park entrance, and off toward the cemetery. John Ross and her grandfather stood looking after her helplessly, watching her angular figure diminish and disappear into the trees.

Old Bob looked at Ross then, a flat, expressionless gaze. "Are you certain about this?"

Ross nodded, feeling the grayness of the day descend over him like a pall. "Yes, sir."

"I don't know that you should have told her like that."

"I don't know that I should have waited this long."

"You've tracked him here, her father, to Hopewell?"

"Yes, sir."

"And he's come for Nest?"

Ross sighed. "Yes, sir, he has. He means to take her with him."

Old Bob shook his head in disbelief. "To kidnap her? Can't you arrest him?"

Ross shook his head. "I haven't the authority. Besides, I can't even find him. If I do, I can't prove any of what I've told you. All I can do is try to stop him."

Old Bob slipped his big hands into his pockets. "How did you find all this out?"

"I can't tell you that."

Old Bob looked away, then back again, his face growing flushed and angry. "You come to Hopewell with a story about your college days with Caitlin that's all a lie. You manage to get yourself invited to our home and then you keep from us the truth of what you are really doing here. You do not warn us about Nest's father. You may think you have good reasons for everything you've done, John, but I have to tell you that I've put up with as much of this as I'm going to. You are no longer welcome here. I want you off my property and out of our lives."

John Ross stood firm against the old man's withering stare. "I don't blame you, sir. I would feel the same. I'm sorry for everything." He paused. "But none of what you've said changes the fact that Nest is still in danger and I'm the best one to help her."

"Somehow I doubt that, John. You've done a damn poor job of protecting any of us, it seems to me."

Ross nodded. "I expect I have. But the danger to Nest is something I understand better than you."

Old Bob took his hands out of his pockets. "I don't think

you understand the first thing about that girl. Now you get moving, John. Go find Nest's father, if that's what you want to do. But don't come back here."

John Ross stood where he was a moment longer, looking at the old man, trying in vain to think of something else to say. Then he turned without a word and limped away.

CHAPTER 28

Nest fled into the park in mindless shock, her thoughts scattered, her reason destroyed. Had she known a way to do so, she would have run out of her skin, out of her body, out of her life. The face of the demon would not leave her, the image burned so deeply into her mind that she could not dispel it, his features bland and unremarkable, his blue eyes pale and empty.

Your father . . .

Your father . . .

She flew into a dark stand of pine and spruce, flinging herself into the concealing shadows, desperate to hide from everything, frantic to escape. The leathery branches whipped at her face and arms, bringing tears, but the pain was solid and definable and slowed her flight. She staggered to a halt, grounded anew, lacking a reason to run farther or a better place to go. She moved aimlessly within the tangle of the grove, tears welling in her eyes, fists clenching at her sides. This wasn't happening, she thought. It couldn't be happening. She walked through the conifers to a massive old oak, put her arms about the gnarled trunk, and hugged it to her. She felt the rough bark bite into her arms and legs, into her cheeks and forehead, and still she pressed harder.

Your father . . .

She could not say the words, could not complete the thought. She pressed and pressed, willing her body to melt into the tree. She would become one with it. She would disappear into it and never be seen again. She was crying hard now, tears running down her face, her body shaking. She squeezed her eyes tight. Had her father really killed Gran? Had he killed her mother as well? Would he now try to kill her?

Do something!

She forced herself to go still inside and the tears to stop. Her sobs died away in small gulps as the cold realization settled over her that the crying wasn't doing any good, wasn't helping anything. She pushed away from the tree and stared out into the park through gaps in the conifers, rebuilding her composure from tiny, scattered fragments. She caught glimpses between the needled branches of other lives being led, all of them distant and removed. It was the Fourth of July, America's day of independence. What freedom should she celebrate? She looked down at her arms, at how the oak's bark had left angry red marks that made her skin look mottled and scaly.

A shudder overtook her. Could she ever look at herself again in the same way? How much of her was human and how much something else? She remembered asking Gran only a few days earlier, weary of the years of secrecy, if her father might be a forest creature. She remembered wondering afterward what that would feel like.

Now she could wonder about this.

She shifted her gaze inward, staring at nothing, still unable to believe it was true. Maybe John Ross was mistaken. Why couldn't he be? But she knew there was no mistake. That was why Gran had been so anxious to avoid any discussion of her father all those years. She felt sick inside thinking of it, of the lies and half truths, of the rampant deception. Awash with misery and fear, she felt bereft of anything and anyone she could depend upon, mired in a life history that had compromised and abandoned her.

She moved back to the oak and sat down, leaning against the rugged trunk, suddenly worn out. She was still sitting there, staring at the trees around her, trying to decide what to do next, when Pick dropped out of the tree across the way and hurried over.

"Criminy, I thought I'd never catch up with you!" he gasped, collapsing to his knees in front of her. "If it wasn't for Daniel, I'd never get anywhere in this confounded park!"

She closed her eyes wearily. "What are you doing here?"

"What am I dong here? What do you *think* I'm doing here? Is this some sort of trick question?"

"Go away." Her voice was a flat, hollow whisper.

Pick went silent and stayed that way until she opened her eyes to see what he was doing. He was sitting up straight, his eyes locked on hers. "I'm going to pretend I didn't hear that," he said quietly, "because I know how upset you are about your father."

She started to say something flip, then saw the look in his eyes and caught herself just in time. She felt her throat tighten. "You heard?"

Pick nodded.

"Everything?"

"Everything." Pick folded his wooden arms defensively. "Do me a favor. Don't tell me I should have told you about him before this. Don't make me remind you of something you already know."

She compressed her lips into a tight line to keep the tears in check. "Like what?"

"Like how it's not my place to tell you secrets about your family." Pick shook his head admonishingly. "I'm sorry you had to find out, but not sorry it didn't come from me. In any case, it's no reason for you to leap up and run off. It's not the end of the world."

"Not yours, anyway."

"Not yours, either!" The words snapped at her. "You've had a nasty shock, and you have a right to be upset, but you can't afford to go to pieces over it. I don't know how John Ross found out about it, and I don't know why he decided to tell you. But I do know that it isn't going to help matters if you crawl off into a hole and wait for it all to go away! You have to *do* something about it!"

Nest almost laughed. "Like what, Pick? What should I do? Go back to the house and get the shotgun? A lot of good that did Gran! He's a demon! Didn't you hear? A demon! My father's a demon! Jeez! It sounds like a bad joke!" She brushed away fresh tears. "Anyway, I'm not talking about this with you until you tell me the truth about him. You know the truth, don't you? You've always known. You didn't tell me while Gran was alive because you didn't feel you should. Okay. I understand that. But she's dead now, and somebody better tell me the truth right now or I'm probably going to end up dead, too!"

She was gulping against the sobs that welled up in her throat, angry and afraid and miserable.

"Oh, for goodness' sake!" Pick threw up his hands in disgust and began tugging on his beard. "Exactly what is it you think I should tell you, Nest? What part of the truth haven't you figured out, bright girl that you are? Your grandmother was a wild thing, a young girl who bent a lot of rules and broke a few more. That Indian showed you most of it, with his dancing and his visions. She ran with the feeders in Sinnissippi Park, daring anything, and that led to her involvement with the demon. The demon wanted her, whether for herself or her magic, I don't know. He was furious when she found out what he was and told him she didn't want anything more to do with him. He threatened her, told her the choice wasn't hers to make. But she was tough and hard and not afraid of him, and she wouldn't back down. She told him what she would do if he didn't leave her alone, and he knew she meant business."

The sylvan stamped his foot. "Are you with me so far? Good. Here's the rest of it. He waited for his chance to get even, the way demons do. He was mostly smoke and dark magic, so aging wasn't a problem for him. He could afford to be patient. He waited until your grandmother married and your mother came along. He waited for your mother to grow up. I think your grandmother believed she'd seen the last of him by then, but she was wrong. All that time, he was waiting to get back at her. He did it through your mother. He deceived her with his magic and his lies, and then he seduced her. Not out of love or even infatuation. Out of hate. Out of a desire to hurt your grandmother. Deliberately, maliciously, callously. You were the result. Your grandmother didn't know he was responsible at first, and even if she had, she wouldn't have told your mother. But the demon waited until you were a few months old and then told them both. Together."

Nest stared at him, horrified.

His face knotted. "Told them why, too. Took great delight in it. I was there. Your mother went off the cliffs shortly afterward. I think maybe she did it on purpose, but nobody saw it happen, so I can't be sure."

His frustration with her attitude seemed to dissipate. His voice softened. "The thing that concerns me is that the demon wanted to hurt your grandmother, to get even with her for what she'd done to him, and that was why he destroyed your mother, but I think he's after you for a different reason. I think he believes you belong to him, that you're his child, his flesh and blood, and that's why he's come back—to claim what's his."

Nest hugged her knees to her chest, listening to the soft rustle of spruce and pine boughs as a breeze passed through the shadowed grove. "Why does he think I would go with him? Or stay with him if he took me? I'm nothing like him."

But even as she said it, she wondered if it was so. She looked and talked and acted like a human being, but so did the demon, in his human guise, when it suited him. Underneath was that core of magic that defined them both. She did not know its source in her. But if she had inherited it from her father, then perhaps there was more of him in her than she wished.

Pick pointed a finger at her. "Don't be doubting yourself, Nest. Having him for your father is an accident of birth, nothing more. Having his magic doesn't mean anything. Whatever human part of him went into the making of you is long since dead and gone, swallowed up by the thing he's become. Don't look for something that isn't there."

She tightened her lips stubbornly. "I'm not."

"Then what are you thinking, girl?"

"That I'm not going with him. That I hate him for what he's done."

Pick looked doubtful. "He must know that, don't you expect? And it mustn't matter to him. He must think he can make you come, whether you want to go with him or not. Think it through. You have to be very careful. You have to be smart."

He put his chin in his hands and rested his elbows on his

knees. "This whole business is very confusing, if you ask me. I keep wondering what John Ross is doing in Hopewell, of all places. Why would a Knight of the Word choose to fight this particular battle? To save you? Why, when there's dozens of others being lost everywhere you turn? You're my best friend, Nest, and I'd do anything to help you. But John Ross doesn't have that connection. There's a war being waged out there between the Word and the Void, and what's going on here in Sinnissippi Park seems like an awfully small skirmish, the presence of your father notwithstanding. I think there must be something more to all this, something we don't know about."

"Do you think Gran knew?" she asked hesitantly.

"Maybe. Maybe that's why the demon killed her. But I don't think so. I think he killed your grandmother because he was afraid of her, afraid that she would get in his way and spoil his plans. And because he wanted to get even with her. No, I think John Ross is the one who knows. I think that's what he's doing here. Maybe it was your grandmother's death that prompted him to tell you about your father—because of what he knows that we don't."

Nest shook her head doubtfully. "Why wouldn't he just tell me what it is?"

"I don't know." Pick tugged hard on his beard. "I wish I did."

She gave him a wry, sad grin. "That's not very comforting."

They were silent for a moment, staring at each other through the growing shadows, the sounds of the park distant and muffled. A few stray raindrops fell on Nest's face, and she reached up to brush them away. A dark cloud was passing overhead, but the sky behind it showed patches of brightness. Perhaps there wouldn't be a thunderstorm after all.

"That note your grandmother left you reminds me of something," Pick said suddenly, straightening. "Remember that story you told me about your grandmother seeing Wraith for the very first time? You were in the park, just the two of you, and she went right up to him. Remember that? He was standing just within the shadows, you said, not moving, and they stared at each other for a long time, like they were communicating somehow. Then she came back and told you he was there to protect you." He paused. "Doesn't it make you wonder just exactly where Wraith came from?"

Nest stared at him, her mind racing as she considered where he was going with this. "You think it was Gran?"

"Your grandmother had magic of her own, Nest, and she learned some things from your father before she found out who he was and quit having anything to do with him. Wraith appeared after your mother died, after your father revealed himself, after it was clear that you could be in danger. More to the point, maybe, he appeared about the same time your grandmother quit using her magic, the magic she no longer had to defend herself with when your father came for her last night."

"You think Gran made Wraith?"

"I think it's possible. Hasn't Wraith been there to protect you from the time you were old enough to walk?" Pick's brow furrowed deeply. "He's a creature of magic, not of flesh and blood. Who else could have put him there?"

Disbelief and confusion reflected on Nest's face. "But why wouldn't Gran tell me? Why would she pretend she wasn't sure?"

Pick shrugged. "I don't know the answer to that any more than I know why John Ross won't tell you what he's really doing here. But if I'm right, and Wraith was made to protect you, then that would explain the note, wouldn't it?"

"And if you're wrong?"

Pick didn't answer; he just stared at her, his eyes fierce. He didn't think for a moment he was wrong, she realized. He was absolutely certain he was right. Good old Pick.

"Think about this, while you're at it," he continued, leaning forward. "Say John Ross is right. Say your father has come back for you. Look at how he's going about it. He didn't just snatch you up and cart you off. He's taking his time, playing games with you, wearing you down. He found you in the park and teased you about not being able to rely on anyone. He came to your church and confronted you. He used his magic on that poor woman to demonstrate what could happen to you. He had that Abbott boy kidnap you and take you down into the caves, then teased you some more, telling you how helpless you were. He killed your grandmother, and sidetracked John Ross and your grandfather and me as well. Where do you think I was all night? I was out trying to keep the maentwrog locked up in that tree, and it took everything I had to get the job done. But you see, don't you? Your father's gone to an awful lot of trouble to make you think that he can do anything he wants, hasn't he?"

She nodded, studying his wizened face intently. "And you think you know why?"

"I do. I think he's afraid of you."

He let the words hang in the silence, his sharp eyes fixed on her, waiting for her response. "That doesn't make any sense," she said finally.

"Doesn't it?" Pick cocked one bushy eyebrow. "I know you're scared about what's happened and you think you don't have any way of protecting yourself, but maybe you do. Your grandmother told you what to do. She told you to use your magic and trust Wraith. Maybe you ought to listen to her."

Nest thought it over without saying anything, sitting face-to-face with the sylvan, alone in the shadows of the grove. Beyond her momentary shelter, the world went about its business without concern for her absence. But it would not let her forget where she belonged. Its sounds beckoned to her, reminding her that she must go back. She thought of how much had changed in a single day. Gran was dead. Jared might die. Her father had come back into her life with a vengeance. Her magic had become the sword and shield she must rely upon.

"I guess I have to do something, don't I?" she said quietly. "Something besides running away and hiding." She tightened her jaw. "I guess I don't have much choice."

Pick shrugged. "Well, whatever you decide to do, I'll be right there with you. Daniel and me. Maybe John Ross, too. Whatever his reasons, I think he intends to see this through."

She gave him a skeptical look. "I hope that's good news."

The little man nodded soberly. "Me, too."

* * *

Derry Howe was standing at the window of his tiny apartment in a T-shirt and jeans, looking out at the clouded sky and wondering if the weather would interfere with the night's fireworks, when Junior Elway pulled up in his Jeep Cherokee. Junior drove over the curb trying to parallel park and then straightened the wheels awkwardly as the Jeep bumped back down into the street. Derry took a long pull on his Bud and shook his head in disgust. The guy couldn't drive for spit.

The window fan squeaked and rattled in front of him, blowing a thin wash of lukewarm air on his stomach and chest. The apartment felt hot and close. Derry tried to ignore his discomfort, but his tolerance level was shot. A headache that four Excedrin hadn't eased one bit throbbed steadily behind his temples. His hand ached from where he had cut himself the day before splicing wires with a kitchen knife. Worst of all, there was a persistent buzzing in his ears that had been there on waking and refused to fade. He thought at first that he was losing his hearing, then changed his mind and wrote it off to drinking too much the night before and got out a fresh Bud to take the edge off. Three beers later, the buzzing was undiminished. Like a million bees inside his head. Like dozens of those weed eaters.

He closed his eyes momentarily and worked his jaws from side to side, trying to gain a little relief. Damn, but the noise was aggravating!

Seated comfortably in the rocker that had belonged to Derry's mother, the demon, an invisible presence, cranked up the volume another notch and smiled.

Derry finished off his Bud and walked to the front door. He kept watch through the peephole until Junior was on the steps, then swung open the door and popped out at him like a jack-in-the-box.

Junior jumped a foot. "Damn you, don't do that!" he snapped angrily, pushing his way inside.

Derry laughed, an edgy chuckle. "What, you nervous or something?"

Junior ignored him, looked quickly about to see that they

were alone, decided they were, glanced at Derry's beer, and
went into the kitchen to get one of his own. "I'm here, ain't I?"

Derry rolled his eyes. "Nothing gets by you, does it?" He
lifted his voice a notch. "Bring me a cold one, too, long as
you're helping yourself!"

He waited impatiently for Junior to reappear, took the beer
out of his hands without asking, and motioned him over to the
couch. They sat down together, hands cupped about the chilled
cans, and stared at the remains of a pizza that sat congealing in
an open cardboard box on the battered coffee table.

"You hungry?" Derry asked, not caring one way or the
other, anxious to get on with it.

Junior shook his head and took a long drink of his beer,
refusing to be hurried. "So. Everything set?"

"You tell me. Are you scheduled for tonight's shift?"

Junior nodded. "Like we planned. I went in yesterday, told
them I was sick of the strike, that I wanted back on the line,
asked to be put on the schedule soon as possible. You should
have seen them. They were grinning fools. Said I could start
right away. I did like you told me, said I'd like the four to midnight shift. I go on in . . ." He checked his watch. "Little over
an hour. All dressed and ready. See?"

He pointed down to his steel-toed work boots. Derry gave
him a grudging nod of approval. "We got 'em by the short
hairs, and they don't even know it."

"Yeah, well, let's hope." Junior didn't look convinced.

Derry tried to keep the irritation out of his voice. "Hope ain't
got nothing to do with it. We got us a plan, bub, and the plan is
what's gonna get this particular job done." He gave Junior a
look. "You wait here."

He got up and left the room. The demon watched Junior
fidget on the couch, playing with his beer, taking a cold piece
of sausage off the top of the pizza and popping it in his mouth,
staring at the ancient window fan as if he'd never seen anything like it.

Derry came back carrying a metal lunch box with clips and
a handle. He passed it to Junior, who took it gingerly and held
it at arm's length.

"Relax," Derry sneered, reseating himself, taking another pull on his Bud. "Ain't nothing gonna happen until you set the switch. You can drop it, kick it around, do almost anything, it's safe until you set it. See the metal slide on the back, underneath the hinge? That's the switch. Move it off the green button and over the red and you got five minutes—plenty of time. Take it in with you, leave it in your locker when you start your shift, carry it out on your break like you're having a snack, then slip it under the main gear housing and walk away. When it goes off, it'll look like the roller motors overheated and blew. Got it?"

Junior nodded. "Got it."

"Just remember. Five minutes. It's preprogrammed."

Junior set the lunch box back on the coffee table next to the pizza. "Where's yours?"

Derry shrugged. "Back in the bedroom. Want to see it?"

They got up and went through the bedroom door, finishing off their beers, relaxed now, joking about what it was going to be like come tomorrow. The demon watched them leave the room, then rose from the rocker, walked over to the coffee table, and opened the lid to the lunch box. Sandwiches, a chip bag, a cookie pack, and a thermos hid what was underneath. The demon lifted them away. Derry was exactly right; he had set the clock to trigger the explosives five minutes after the slide was pushed.

The demon shook his head in disapproval and reset it from five minutes to five seconds.

Derry and Junior came back out, sat on the couch, drank another beer, and went over the plan one more time, Derry making sure his buddy had it all down straight. Then Junior picked up the lunch box and left, heading for the steel mill. When he was gone, Derry massaged his temples, then went into the bathroom to get a couple more Excedrin, which he washed down with a fresh beer.

Better go easy on this stuff, he admonished himself, and set the can aside. Want to be sharp for tonight. Want to be cool.

He dumped the pizza in the trash and brought out the second device, this one fashioned a little differently than the other to accomplish its intended purpose, and finished wiring it. When he was done, he placed it inside a plastic picnic cooler, fastened it in place, and closed the lid. He leaned back and studied it with pride. This baby will do the job and then some, he thought.

The demon came over and sat down next to him. Derry couldn't see him, didn't know he was there. "Better take your gun," the demon whispered, a voice inside Derry's head.

Derry looked at the rattling old window fan, matching its tired cadence to the buzzing in his head. "Better take my gun," he repeated absently.

"In case anyone tries to stop you."

"Ain't no one gonna stop me."

The demon laughed softly. "Robert Freemark might."

Derry Howe stared off into space. "Might try, anyway." His jaw was slack. "Be too bad for him if he did."

When he got up to go into his bedroom to collect his forty-five from the back of his closet, the demon opened the picnic cooler and reset that clock, too.

Nest walked back through the park to her home, Pick riding on her shoulder, both of them quiet. It was nearing four o'clock, and the park was filled with people. She skirted the families occupying picnic tables and blankets in the open areas and followed the line of trees that bordered Sinnissippi Road on the north. It wasn't that she was trying to hide now; it was just that she didn't feel like talking to anyone. Even Pick understood that much and was leaving her alone.

Feeders shadowed her, flashes of dark movement at the corners of her eyes, and she struggled unsuccessfully to ignore them.

She passed the park entrance and started down the service road behind her house. Overhead, clouds drifted in thick clusters, and the sun played hide-and-seek through the rifts. Bright, sunny streamers mixed with gray shadows, dappling the earth, and to the west, dark thunderheads massed. Rain was on the way for sure. She glanced skyward and away again without interest, thinking about what she had to do to protect herself. She had assumed right up until last night that the demon and John Ross and the madness they had brought to Hopewell had nothing to do with her personally, that she stood on the periphery of what was happening, more observer than participant. Now she understood that she was not just a participant, but the central player, and she had decided she would be better off not counting on anyone's help but her own. Maybe Pick and Daniel would be able to do something. Maybe John Ross would be there for her. Maybe Wraith would defend her when it mattered. But maybe, too, she would be on her own. There was good reason to think so. The demon had managed to isolate her every time he had appeared, and she had to assume he would manage it again.

Her father.

But she could not think of him that way, she knew. He was a demon, and he was her enemy.

She pondered Gran's note. Should she rely on it? Was Pick right in his assumption that Gran had made Wraith and given up her magic to do so? Was that why she was defenseless against the demon? *Trust Wraith.* She remembered Gran telling her over and over again that the feeders would never hurt her, that she was special, that she was protected. She had never questioned it, never doubted it. But the demon was not a feeder, and perhaps this time Gran was wrong. Why hadn't Gran told her more when she'd had the chance? Why hadn't she given Nest something she could rely upon?

I'm so afraid, she thought.

She pushed through the gap in the hedgerow and entered her backyard. The house loomed dark and gloomy before her, and she was reluctant to enter it. Pick had disappeared from her shoulder, gone back into the trees. She hesitated a moment, then walked up to the back door, half expecting the demon to jump out at her.

But it was her grandfather who appeared, stepping from the shadow of the porch entry. "Are you all right, Nest?" he asked quietly, standing there on the steps, his big hands hanging awkwardly at his sides. He looked gaunt and tired.

She nodded. "I'm okay."

"It was a terrible shock, hearing something like that about

your father," he said, testing her with the words. He shook his head. "I'm still not sure I believe it."

She felt suddenly sad for him, this strong man who had lost so much. She gave him a faint smile and a look that said, *Me either*.

"I sent John away," he said. "I told him I didn't appreciate him coming to my house under false pretenses, whatever his reason for it, and I felt it would be better if he didn't come back. I'm sorry if that upsets you."

Nest stared, uncomprehending. She wanted to ask him if he had lost his mind, but she held her tongue. Her grandfather didn't know what she did about John Ross, so it wasn't fair for her to judge him. It was clear he had acted out of concern for her. Would she have acted any differently in his place?

"I'm going to lie down for a little while, Grandpa," she said, and went past him up the steps and into the house.

She went down the hall to her room and closed the door behind her. Shadows dappled the walls and ceiling, and the air was still and close. She felt suddenly trapped and alone.

Would John Ross abandon her? Would he give up on her in the face of her grandfather's antagonism? Even worse, was it possible there was nothing more he could do?

As she lay down on her bed, she found herself praying fervently, desperately that when the demon appeared next, she would not have to face him alone.

CHAPTER 29

Afternoon passed into evening, a gradual fading away of minutes and hours measured by changes in the light and a lengthening of shadows. The rain did not come, but the clouds continued to build in the west. Old Bob wandered through the house like a restless ghost, looking at things he hadn't looked at in years, remembering old friends from other times, and conjuring up memories of his distant past. Visitors came and went, bringing casseroles and condolences. Fresh-cut flowers and potted plants arrived, small white cards tucked carefully inside their plain white envelopes, words of regret neatly penned. The news of Evelyn Freemark's death had spread by radio and word of mouth; the newspaper article would not appear until tomorrow. Phone calls asked for details, and Old Bob dutifully provided them. Arrangements for the funeral, memorial service, and burial were completed. A fund that would accept monetary donations was established in Evelyn's name by the local Heart Association. Old Bob went through the motions with resigned determination, taking care of the details because it was necessary, trying to come to grips with the fact that she was really gone.

Nest stayed in her room with the door closed and did not reappear until Old Bob called her to dinner. They ate at the kitchen table without speaking. Afterward, as the light began to fail and the dusk to descend, her friends called and asked if she wanted to meet them in the park to watch the fireworks. She asked him if she could, and while he was inclined to say no, to keep her safe in the house and close to him, he realized the foolishness of taking that particular course of action. He might shelter her for a day or even a week, but then what? At some point he would have to let her go off on her own, and there was no reason that he could see to postpone the inevitable. Nest was smart and careful; she would not take chances, especially after last night. In any case, was her father really out there? No one besides John Ross had actually seen him, and he was not sure he trusted Ross anymore. Gran had worried that Nest's father might return, but she had never actually said he was back. Old Bob had thought at first that he should call the police and warn them of his concerns, but on reflection he realized he didn't have anything concrete to offer, only a bunch of vague suspicions, most of them based on John Ross' word.

In the end, he let the matter slide, giving Nest his permission to go, extracting in exchange her firm promise that she would sit with her friends in a crowded place and would not go off alone. The park was safe for her, he believed. She had lived in it all her life, wandered it from end to end, played her childhood games in it, adopted it as her own backyard. He could not see forbidding her to go into it now, especially while she was still dealing with the shock of her grandmother's death.

After she was gone, he began cleaning up the kitchen by putting away the food gifts. The refrigerator and the freezer were soon filled to capacity, and there were still dozens of containers sitting out. He picked up the phone and called Ralph Emery's house, and when the minister answered he asked him if he would mind sending someone around first thing in the morning to take all this food down to the church for distribution to those who could make better use of it. The minister said he would take care of it, thanked him for his generosity, spoke with him about Evelyn for a few minutes, and said good night.

The shadows in the house had melted together in a black mass, and Old Bob walked through the empty rooms and turned on the lights before coming back into the kitchen to finish up. The shotgun was gone, taken by the police for reasons he failed to comprehend, part of their investigation, they told him, and he felt strangely uneasy in its absence. You'd think it would be the other way around, he kept telling himself. He washed some dishes by hand, something he hadn't done in a long time, finding that it helped him relax. He thought always of Evelyn. He glanced over at the kitchen table more than once, picturing her there, her bourbon and water in front of her, her cigarette in hand, her face turned away from the light, her eyes distant. What had she been thinking, all those times she'd sat there? Had she been remembering her childhood in the little cottage several houses down? Had she been thinking of Nest? Of Caitlin? Of him? Had she been wishing that her life had turned out differently, that she had done more with it? Had she been thinking of missed chances and lost dreams? His smile was sad. He regretted now that he had never asked.

He finished the dishes, dried them, and put them away. He glanced around, suddenly lost. The house was alive with memories of his life with Evelyn. He walked into the living room and stood looking at the fireplace, at the pictures on the mantel, at the place in the corner by the bowed window where the Christmas tree always sat. The memories swirled around him, some distant and faded, some as new and sharp as the grief from her loss. He moved to the couch and sat down. Tomorrow his friends would gather at Josie's for coffee and doughnuts, and in his absence they would talk of Evelyn in the same way they had talked of that postal worker in the gorilla suit or the fellow who killed all those children. They would not do so maliciously, but because they had thought her curious and now found her death somehow threatening. After all, she had died here, in Hopewell—not in some other town in some other state. She had died here, where they lived, and she was someone they knew. Yes, she was odd, and it wasn't really any surprise that she had died of a heart attack blasting away at shadows with a shotgun, because Evelyn Freemark had done stranger things. But in the back of their minds was the conviction that she really wasn't so different than they were, and that if it could happen to her, it could happen to them. Truth was, you shared an uneasy sense of kinship with even the most unfortunate, disaffected souls; you felt you had known at least a few of them during your life. You had all been children together, with children's hopes and dreams. The dark future that had claimed those few was never more than an arm's length away from everyone else. You knew that. You knew that a single misfortune could change your life forever, that you were vulnerable, and to protect yourself you wanted to know everything you could about why it had touched another and passed you by.

Old Bob listened to the silence and let the parade of memories march away into the darkness. My God, he was going to miss her.

After a time his thoughts wandered to the call he had received earlier from Mel Riorden. Mel and Carol had been by that morning to offer condolences, promising they would have him over for dinner after the funeral, when he was feeling up to it. Old Bob had taken their hands, an awkward ritual between long-standing friends where something profound had changed their lives and left them insufficient words to convey their understanding of what it meant. Later Mel had called on the phone, keeping his voice down, telling Old Bob that there was something he ought to know. Seemed that Derry had called him up out of the blue and apologized for scaring him with his talk about MidCon. Said he really hadn't meant anything by it. Said he was just blowing off steam, and that whatever the union decided was good enough for him. Said he wanted to know if he could go to the fireworks with Mel and Carol and some of the others and sit with them. Mel paused every so often to make sure Old Bob was still listening, his voice sounding hopeful. Maybe he was mistaken about his nephew, he concluded tentatively. Maybe the boy was showing some common sense after all. He just wanted Old Bob to know.

When Mel hung up, Old Bob stood looking at the phone, wondering if he believed any of it and if it made any difference if he did. Then he dropped the matter, going about the business of his own life, of finishing the funeral preparations and worrying about Nest. But now the matter surfaced anew in his thoughts, and he found himself taking a fresh look at it. Truth was, it just didn't feel right. It didn't sound like Derry Howe. He didn't think that boy would change in a million years, let alone in twenty-four hours. But maybe he was being unfair. People did change—even people you didn't think would ever be any different from what they'd been all their lives. It happened.

He drummed his fingers on the arm of the couch, staring off into space. Going to the fireworks with Mel and Carol, was he? That was a first. Where was his buddy, Junior Elway, that he'd opted for an evening out with the old folks?

He got up from the sofa and went into the kitchen to fish around in the packed-out refrigerator for a can of root beer. When he found it, he popped the top and carried it back into the living room and sat down again.

Fireworks. The word kept digging at him, suggesting something different from the obvious, something he couldn't quite grasp. Hadn't he and Derry talked about fireworks yesterday, when he had approached the boy about what sort of mischief he might be planning? Derry Howe, the Vietnam vet, the demolitions expert, talking about playing with matches in a pile of fireworks, about how fireworks were touchy if you didn't know what you were doing, that they could cause accidents . . .

He sat up straight. What was it Derry had said? *I'm going to give MidCon a Fourth of July to remember.* But more, something else, something personal. A warning. *Stay home on the Fourth. Keep away from the fireworks.*

Old Bob set the can of root beer down on the coffee table, barely aware of what he was doing, his mind racing. What he was thinking was ridiculous. It didn't make any sense. What would Derry Howe gain by sabotaging the Fourth of July fireworks? How would that have any effect on MidCon Steel? He looked the possibilities over without finding anything new. There didn't seem to be any connection.

Then something occurred to him, and he got to his feet quickly and walked out onto the screened porch where he kept the old newspapers. He bent down and began to go through them. Most were old *Chicago Tribunes*, but there were a few *Hopewell Gazettes* among them. Friday's had gone out with the trash, he remembered, used to wrap the garbage. He found the one from Thursday, pulled it out, and went through it quickly, searching. There was nothing on the Fourth of July.

But he seemed to remember seeing something, a big ad of some kind. He wished he had paid better attention, but it had been years since he had concerned himself with what went on in the park over the Fourth. The fireworks were all Evelyn and he had ever cared about, and you knew without having to ask when to be there for them.

He tossed the Thursday paper aside, wondering what had become of the Saturday-morning edition. He went down the hall to his den and looked for it there, but couldn't find it. He stood motionless for a moment, trying to think what he had done with it. Then he walked back to the kitchen. He found the Saturday paper sitting on the counter under several of the casseroles he had set aside for the church. He extracted it gingerly, spread it out on the table, and began to scan its pages.

He found what he was looking for right away. The Jaycees had inserted a flyer for the Sunday-Monday events in Sinnissippi Park, admission free, everyone welcome. Games, food, and fun. The events culminated on Monday, the Fourth, with fireworks at sunset. This year, the flyer proclaimed in bold letters, the fireworks were being sponsored and paid for by MidCon Steel.

For long moments, Old Bob just stared at the flyer, not quite trusting himself. He must be wrong about this, he kept thinking. But it was the way a guy like Derry Howe thought, wasn't it? Sabotage the fireworks sponsored by MidCon, maybe blow up a few people watching, cause a lot of hard feelings. But then what? Everybody blames MidCon? MidCon has to do something to regain favor, so it settles the strike? It was such a stretch that for a few seconds he dismissed his reasoning altogether. It was ludicrous! But Derry Howe wouldn't think so, would he? Old Bob felt a cold spot settling deep in his chest. No, not Derry.

He looked at his watch. After nine o'clock. He glanced out the window. It was growing dark. They would start the fireworks soon now. He thought suddenly of Nest. She would be sitting with everyone else, at risk. He could hear Evelyn saying to him, as she had on the last night of her life, "Robert, you get right out there and find that girl and bring her home."

He grabbed his flashlight off the counter and went out the door in a rush.

By now, the largest part of the Fourth of July crowd had abandoned the playgrounds, ball diamonds, and picnic tables to gather on the grassy slopes that flanked the toboggan slide and ran down to the river's edge. The fireworks would be set off over the bayou from a staging area located on a flat, open stretch of the riverbank below. A line had been strung midway up the slope to cordon off the crowd from the danger zone. Strips of fluorescent tape dangled from the line, and volunteers with flashlights patrolled the perimeter. The spectators were bunched forward on the hillside to the line's edge, settled on blankets and in lawn chairs, laughing and talking as the darkness descended. Children ran everywhere, sparklers leaving bright comet tails in the wake of their passing. Now and again a forbidden firecracker would explode off in the trees to either side, causing old people to jump and parents to frown. Shadows deepened and the outlines of the park and its occupants grew fuzzy. By the blackness of the river, a trio of flashlights wove erratic patterns as the staging crew completed their preparations for the big event.

Nest Freemark sat with her friends on a blanket, eating watermelon slices and drinking pop. They were situated high on the slope to the west of the slide where the darkness was deepest and the park lights didn't penetrate. There were families around them, but Nest couldn't see their faces or recognize their voices. The gloom made everyone anonymous, and Nest felt comfortable in that environment. Aside from her friends, she was anxious to avoid everyone.

She had come into the park late, when dusk had begun to edge toward nightfall and it was already getting hard to see. She had crossed her backyard with a watchful eye, half expecting the demon to leap out at her from the shadows. When Pick had dropped onto her shoulder as she pushed her way through the bushes, she had jumped in spite of herself. He was there to escort her into the park, he had informed her in his best no-nonsense voice. He had been patrolling the park since sunset, riding the windless heat atop Daniel, crisscrossing the woods and ballparks and playgrounds in search of trouble. As soon as Nest was safely settled with her friends, he would resume his vigil. For the moment, everything was peaceful. There was no sign of the demon. There was no sign of John Ross. The maentwrog, still imprisoned in its ravaged tree, was quiet. Even the feeders were staying out of sight. Pick shrugged. Maybe nothing was going to happen after all.

Nest gave him a look.

When Pick left her on nearing the crowded pavilion with its cotton-candy, popcorn, hot-dog, and soft-drink stands, she moved quickly toward the rendezvous point she had settled on with her friends. One or two people glanced her way, but no one called out to her. She was stopped only once, by Gran's friend Mildred Walker, who happened to be standing right in front of her as she passed and couldn't be avoided. Mrs. Walker told her she was sorry about Gran and about her young friend Jared Scott, and that she wasn't to worry, that the Social Services people were going to see to it that nothing further happened to any of those children. She said it with such feeling and such obvious concern that it made Nest want to cry.

Later, Brianna confided to all of them that her mother had told her the Social Services people were already looking for temporary homes for the Scott kids. Her mother also told her that Jared was still in a coma and that wasn't good.

Now Nest sat in the darkness sipping at her can of pop and reflecting on how unfair life could be. Out on the river, in a sea of blackness, the running lights of powerboats shone red and green, motionless on the becalmed waters. There was no wind; the air had gone back to being hot and sticky, and the taste of dust and old leaves had returned. But the sky was thick with clouds, which screened away the moon and stars, and rain was on the way. Nest wished it would hurry up and get here. Maybe it would help cool things down, clean stuff up, and give everyone a fresh attitude. Maybe it would help wash away some of the madness.

A stray firefly blinked momentarily in front of her face and disappeared in the darkness. Somebody in a lawn chair sneezed, and the sneeze sounded like a dog's bark. A ripple of laughter rose. Robert made a comment about the nature of germs in people's mouths, and Brianna told him he was gross and disgusting. Robert stood up and announced he was off to buy some popcorn and would anybody like some? Nobody would, he was informed, and Brianna said he should take his time coming back, maybe even think about going home and checking his mouth in the mirror. Robert walked off whistling.

Nest smiled, at ease with herself. She was thinking how comfortable she felt, sitting here in the darkness, surrounded by all these people. She felt sheltered and safe, as if nothing could touch her here, nothing could threaten. How deceptive that was. She wished she could disappear into the gloom and become one with the night, invisible and substanceless, impervious to harm. She wondered if Pick was having any luck. She tried to picture what the sylvan would do to defend her if the need arose, and couldn't. She wondered if the demon was out there, waiting for her. She wondered if John Ross was waiting, too.

After a time, she began to think of Two Bears, wishing that he was still there and could help her. There was such strength in him, a strength she didn't feel in herself, even though he had told her it was there. They had names of power, he said. But hers was the stronger, the one with true magic. He had given her what he could; the rest must come from her.

But what was it he had given her? That brief vision of her grandmother as a young girl, running wild in the park with the feeders and the demon? An insight into her convoluted and tragic family history? She didn't know. Something more, she believed. Something deeper, more personal. *Think.* It was his desire to commune with the spirits of his people, the Sinnissippi, that had brought him to Hopewell, but it was her ties to the magic that had drawn him to her. Your people risk the fate of mine, he had warned, wanting her to know, to understand. No one knows who my people were. No one knows how they perished. It can happen to your people, too. It is happening now, without their knowledge and with their considerable help. Your people are destroying themselves.

We do not always recognize the thing that comes to destroy us. That is the lesson of the Sinnissippi.

But he might have been speaking of her father as well.

She stared into the darkness, lost in thought. It was all tied together. She could feel it in her bones. The fate of her friends and family and neighbors and of people she didn't even know. Her own fate. The fates of the demon and John Ross. Of O'olish Amaneh, too, perhaps. They were all bound up by a single cord.

I am not strong enough for this.

I am afraid.

She stared at nothing, the words frozen in her mind, immutable. Then she heard Two Bears' clear response, the one he had given her two nights earlier.

Fear is a fire to temper courage and resolve. Use it so.

She sat alone in the darkness, no longer comfortable with pretending at invisibility, and tried to determine if she could do as Two Bears expected.

Twenty feet away, a shadowy figure in the deepening gloom, John Ross kept watch over her.

After Old Bob had dismissed him, he had walked into the park in search of the demon, determined to hunt him down. He went to the caves where the feeders made their lair, followed the riverbank east toward the toboggan slide and the deep woods beyond, and climbed to the prison of the maentwrog, that aging, ravaged oak that held the monster bound, but the demon was nowhere to be found.

He debated returning to Nest Freemark then, but did not. What could he say to her that he hadn't already said—or decided against saying? It was sufficient that he had told her the truth about her father. Telling her more would risk undermining what courage and resolve she could still muster. The best he could do was to watch over her, to wait for the demon to come to her, to be there when it appeared, and to do what he could to save her then.

He left the park and walked out to Lincoln Highway to have dinner at a McDonald's, then walked back again. Sitting in a crowd of spectators on the bleachers at the ball diamond closest to the Freemark house, he watched the sun move west toward the horizon. When dusk approached and the game began to break up, he walked to a stand of pine bordering the service road. Using magic to make certain they could not see him, he stood for a time in the shelter of the trees, watching Pick and Daniel as they wheeled overhead. When Nest went into the park, he followed.

Now he stood waiting, close enough to make certain he could act when the demon appeared, close enough to go to her aid if the need arose. All about him, the Fourth of July spectators were shrouded in gloom, vague and featureless in the night. Shouts and laughter rose from the crowded hillside amid the bang of firecrackers and the whistle of small rockets. The air was humid and still, filled with the erratic buzzing of insects and the raw smell of pine needles and wood smoke. He gripped his staff tightly in his hand, feeling anxious and uncertain. He needed only one chance at the demon, but would he get even that? How strong would Nest Freemark be then? He edged his way east toward the woods behind the pavilion, changing his location yet again, trying to avoid notice from the people gathered, concentrating on Nest. He could just make her out, sitting with his friends near the back of the crowd.

Then he caught sight of a familiar face and turned his head aside quickly as Robert Heppler walked past on his way back from the popcorn stand.

"So, did I miss anything?" Robert asked the girls as he plopped back down comfortably on the blanket, his bag of popcorn firmly in hand. "Want some?" he asked Brianna Brown. "I only breathed on it a little. Or did you pig out on the rest of the watermelon while I was gone?"

Brianna grimaced. "I leave the pigging out in life to you, Robert. You're so good at it."

Nest was staring off into space, barely aware of the conversation. Robert glanced over. "Hey, Nest, guess who I just saw standing . . ."

A child flew out of the darkness and into their midst, a little boy running blindly through the night, sparklers waving in both hands. He saw them too late, veering aside when he was already on top of them, nearly losing his balance and toppling onto Robert. Robert yelled angrily at him, and sparks showered everywhere. Cass and Brianna leaped to their feet, stamping at the embers that had tumbled onto the blanket.

Nest rose with them, stepping back, distracted, and as she did so she heard Pick scream. He was screaming inside her head, throwing his voice so that only she could hear, throwing it from somewhere far away so that it was faint and fragmented. But it was terror-stricken, too.

Nest, Nest . . . quick, run . . . here, the oak collapsing . . . demon . . . knows you are . . . the maentwrog breaking . . .

Then the screaming stopped, abruptly, completely, leaving an echo that rang in her ears as she stood shocked and frozen amid the crowd and her friends.

"Pick?" she whispered into the silence he had left behind. Her hand groped blindly at the air before her. "Pick?"

Her friends were staring at her, eyes filled with uncertainty. "Nest, what's wrong?" Cass asked urgently.

But Nest was already turning from her, beginning to run. "I have to go," she shouted over her shoulder, and raced away into the night.

CHAPTER 30

It was an act of instinct rather than of reason, a response to an overwhelming, terrifying fear that another life precious to her was about to be lost. Nest did not hesitate as she bolted through the crowd. Of course the demon was drawing her out. Of course it was a trap. She didn't have to think twice about it to know it was true. If she stayed where she was, safe within the crowd gathered on the slopes of Sinnissippi Park, he could not reach her so easily. But it was Pick who was at risk, her best friend in the whole world, and she would not abandon him even to save her own life.

She darted through the crowd as if become one of the wild children who waved their sparklers, dodging lawn chairs and coolers, avoiding blankets filled with people, seeking the open blackness of the woods beyond. She knew where to go, where the demon would be waiting, where Pick could be found; the sylvan's frantic words had told her that much. The deep woods. The maentwrog's prison. The aging oak from which, it seemed, the monster was threatening to break free. She thought she heard shouts trailing after her, calling her name, but she ignored them, burying them in her determination not to be slowed. She vaulted the last of the coolers that obstructed her passage and broke for the trees.

In the open, beyond the scattering of flashlights and sparklers, she slowed just enough to let her vision adjust to the change of light. Ahead, the trees rose in dark, vertical lines against the softer black of the night. She angled past picnic tables and cook stations, running toward the rolling hills that fronted the deep woods. The sounds of the crowd faded behind her, receding into the distance, leaving her alone with the huff of her breathing and the beat of her heart. She heard her name called clearly then, but she forced herself to go on, trying to ignore the unwelcome summons, trying to outdistance it. When it continued, and she determined with certainty its source, she slowed reluctantly and turned to face a hard-charging Robert Heppler.

"Wait up, Nest!" he shouted as he rushed up to her from out of the darkness, blond hair swept back from his angular face.

She shook her head in disbelief. "Robert, what are you doing? Go back!"

"Not a chance." He came to a ragged halt before her, breathing hard. "I'm going with you."

"You don't even know what I'm doing!"

"Doesn't matter. You're not doing it alone."

"Robert . . ."

"The last time I let you wander off by yourself," he interrupted heatedly, "you ended up in the caves and I had to get your grandfather to come find you! I'm not going through that again!"

He brushed at his tousled hair, his mouth set, his eyes determined. He looked pugnacious and challenging. "You're going out to that big oak, aren't you? This has something to do with that tree, doesn't it? What's going on?"

"Robert!" she snapped at him, suddenly angry. "Get out of here!"

He stared back at her defiantly. "No way. I'm going with you. You're stuck with me."

"Robert, don't argue with me! This is too dangerous! You don't know what you're . . ." She stopped in exasperation. "Turn around, Robert! Right now!"

But he refused to budge. She came toward him menacingly. "I'm not afraid of you, Nest," he said quickly, clenching his fists. "I'm not Danny Abbott, either. You can't make me do anything I don't want to do. I don't know what's going on, but I . . ."

She locked his eyes with hers and struck out at him with her magic in a swift, hard attack. Robert Heppler went down like a stone, his muscles turned to jelly and his words became mush. He jerked once where he lay in the thinning forest grass, gave a long sigh, and blacked out.

She blocked the feelings of guilt that immediately assailed her and turned away, racing on. It was better this way. She knew Robert; he would not turn back. She would attempt an explanation later. If there was a later. Desperation and anger swept aside her attempts at forming an apology. She had done what she had to do. It didn't matter that she had promised not to use the magic, that she hated to use it, that it left her feeling sullied and drained. Gran was gone, and in moments she would face her killer, and all she had to rely on was the magic she had just used on Robert.

A fierce glee rocked her, a strange sense of chains being cast aside and freedom being gained. The defiance she felt at having done something forbidden lent her a certain satisfaction. The magic was a part of her. Why should it ever be wrong to use it?

She charged down the slope into the ravine that separated the picnic grounds from the deep woods, feeling her feet beginning to slide on the loose earth and long grasses. She caught herself with her hands to keep from falling, straightened up again as she reached the base of the ravine, and ran on. The bridge that spanned the little creek appeared through the gloom, and she thundered onto it, tennis shoes pounding as she crossed to the far side and began to climb the slope into the woods.

When she reached the top of the rise, she slowed again. Ahead, a wicked green light pulsed faintly within the trees, like the heartbeat of something alive. She pushed the thought aside and went on, jogging now, her breathing slowing, her eyes flicking from side to side watchfully, trying to penetrate the wall of shadows. The trail had narrowed, choked with brush and hemmed by the trees, a twisting serpent's spine. It was black there, so dark that only the greenish light gave any illumination against the night. She was being drawn to it; she could not pretend otherwise. She repeated the words of Gran's note over and over in her mind, a litany to lend her courage.

She brushed at the insects that buzzed at her, thick clouds of them that flew at her eyes and mouth. Her fear returned in a sudden wave as she pictured what waited ahead. But she did not turn back. She could not. It was no different now than it had been when she had gone to save Bennett Scott from the feeders. No different at all.

Please, Pick, don't give up. I'm coming.

Moments later, she stepped from the woods into the clearing where the big oak stood. The tree was a vast, crooked monster within the darkness, its bark wet-looking and ravaged, as if skin split from the bones and muscles of a corpse. The wicked green light emanated from here, given off by the trunk of the old tree, pulsing slowly, steadily against the darkness. Nest stared in dismay. The tree was still intact, but it had the look of a dying creature. It reminded her of pictures she had seen of animals caught in steel traps, their limbs snared, their eyes glazed with fear and pain.

The demon stood next to the tree, his calm eyes fixed on her. He seemed to think nothing was out of place, nothing awry. It was all she could do to make herself meet his gaze.

"Where is Pick?" she demanded.

Her voice sounded impossibly childish and small, and she saw herself as the demon must see her, a young girl, weaponless and desperate in the face of power she could not even begin to comprehend.

The demon smiled at her. "He's right over there," he replied, and pointed.

Five feet or so off the ground, a small metal cage hung from the branches of a cherry. Within its shadowed interior, Nest could just make out a crumpled form.

"Safely tucked away," the demon said. "To keep him from meddling where he shouldn't. He was flying about on that owl, trying to see what I was up to, but he wasn't very smart about it." He paused. "A cage wasn't necessary for the owl."

A feathered heap lay at the edge of the trees, wings splayed wide. Daniel. "He came right at me when I knocked the sylvan off his back," the demon mused. "Can you imagine?"

He motioned vaguely at the cage. "You do know about sylvans and cages, don't you? Well, perhaps not. Sylvans can't stand being caged. It drains away their spirit. Happens rather swiftly, as a matter of fact. A few hours, and that's it. That will be the fate of your friend if someone doesn't release him."

Nest! Pick gasped in a frantic attempt to signal her. Then he went silent again, his voice choked off.

"Your little friend would like to say something to you about his condition, I'm sure," the demon breathed softly, "but I think it best he save his strength. Don't you?"

Nest felt alone and vulnerable, felt as if everything was being stripped from her. But that was the plan, wasn't it? "Let him go!" she ordered, staring at the demon as if to melt him with the heat of her anger.

The demon nodded. "After you do what I tell you." He paused. "Child of mine."

Her skin crawled at the sound of his words, and a new wave of rage swept through her. "Don't call me that!"

The demon smiled, satisfaction reflecting in his eyes. "You know then, don't you? Who told you? Evelyn, before she died? The sylvan?" He shrugged. "I guess it doesn't matter. That you know is what matters. That you appreciate the special nature of our relationship. Who you are will determine what you become, and that is what we are here to decide."

He looked past her, suddenly startled. A hint of irritation flashed across his strange empty features. "Ah, it's the bad penny. He's turned up after all."

John Ross emerged from the trees, sweat-streaked and hard-eyed. He seemed taller and broader than she remembered, and the black staff gleamed and shimmered with silver light. "Get behind me," he said at once, his green eyes fixed on the demon.

"Oh, she doesn't want to do that!" the demon sneered, and threw something dark and glittering at the ravaged oak.

Instantly the tree exploded in a shower of bark and wood splinters, and the green light trapped within burst forth.

Old Bob crossed to the fireworks from his home as the crow flies, not bothering with the service road or any of the path-

ways, the beam of his flashlight scanning the darkness before
him as he went. The weariness he had felt earlier fell away in
the face of his fear, and a rush of adrenaline surged through
him, infusing him with new strength. The sounds of laughter
and conversation and the momentary flare of sparklers guided
him through the broad expanse of the grassy flats, and in
moments he had reached the rear edge of the crowd.

He began to ask at once if anyone had seen Mel Riorden. He
knew most of the people gathered, and once he got close
enough to make out their faces, he simply offered a perfunctory greeting and inquired about Mel. He was a big man with a
no-nonsense way about him, a man who had just suffered a terrible loss, and those he spoke with were quick to reply. He
moved swiftly in response, easing forward through the crowd
toward the cordoned perimeter west of the slide. He was
sweating freely, his underarms and back damp, his face flushed
from his efforts. He did not have a definite plan. He was not
even certain that he needed one. He might be mistaken about
Derry Howe. He might be overreacting. If he was, fine. He
would feel foolish, but relieved. He could live with that. He
would find Derry, talk to him, possibly confront him with his
suspicions, and deal with his feelings later.

He wove his way through knots of people sprawled on blankets and seated in lawn chairs, through darting children and
ambling teens. The viewing area was packed. Some looked at
him with recognition, and a few spoke. Some he stopped to
talk with took time to offer condolences on his loss, but most
simply answered his questions about Mel and let him go his
way. His eyes flicked left and right as he proceeded, searching
the darkness. He could no longer see the riverbank clearly, and
the trees had faded into a black wall. The fireworks would
begin any moment.

Finally, he found Mel and Carol seated together on a blanket
at the very edge of the crowd with a handful of family and
friends. Mel's sister was among them, but not her son. Old Bob
said hello to everyone, then drew Mel aside where they could
talk privately.

"Did Derry come to the fireworks with you?" he asked quietly, trying to keep his voice calm, to keep his fear hidden.

"Sure, you just missed him," his friend answered. "Been here with us all evening. Something wrong?"

"No, no, I just wanted to talk with him a moment. Where is he?"

"He took some drinks down to the guys shooting off the fireworks. Guess he knows one of them." Mel glanced over his shoulder. "I told him I didn't know if they'd let him go down there, but he seemed to think they would."

Old Bob nodded patiently. "He took them some drinks?"

"Yeah, beer and pop, like that. He had this cooler he brought with him. Hey, what's this about, Robert?"

Old Bob felt the calm drain away in a sudden rush, and the fears that had been teasing and whispering at him from the shadows suddenly emerged like predators. "Nothing," he said. He looked toward the river and the movement of flashlights. "He's still down there?"

"Yeah, he just left." Mel cocked his head and his eyes blinked rapidly. "What's the matter?"

Old Bob shook his head and began to move away. "I'll tell you when I get back."

He moved more quickly now, following the line that cordoned off the staging area as it looped down toward the river's edge. He passed several of the Jaycees responsible for patrolling it, younger men he did not know well or at all, and he asked each of them in turn if he had seen Derry Howe. The third man he passed told him Derry had just gone inside the line, that he had been permitted inside only after identifying a member of the staging crew who he claimed was a friend. Old Bob nodded, told him that this was a violation of the agreement the Jaycees had signed with the park district in order to be allowed to sponsor this event, but that he would forget about reporting it if he could go down there right now and bring Derry back before anything happened. He gave the impression without saying so that he was with the park service, and the younger man was intimidated sufficiently by his words and the look on his face to stand aside and let him pass.

Seconds later, Old Bob was inside the line and working his way down the slope toward the moving flashlights of the men preparing to set off the fireworks. He had to hurry now. The fireworks were scheduled to begin at ten o'clock sharp, and it was almost nine-fifty. He turned off his own flashlight, letting his eyes adjust to the darkness. As he neared, he could make out the figures of the staging crew moving through the firing platforms to make their last-minute preparations.

He saw Derry Howe then, his tall, lank figure unmistakable, even in the darkness, standing with one of the crew, talking. As Old Bob swerved toward them, the crewman started to move away. Old Bob waited a few heartbeats, then flicked on the flashlight.

"Derry!" he called out boldly. Derry Howe turned into the light, squinting. Old Bob slowed. "Been looking all over for you."

Derry's eyes flicked right and left. He was holding a small cooler in his left hand. His grin was weak and forced. "What are you doing down here, Robert? You're not supposed to be here."

"Neither are you." Old Bob gave him an indulgent smile. He was less than fifteen feet away now and closing. "You done here? Give everyone a drink yet? Got one left for me?"

Derry held up his hand quickly. "Stop right there. Right there, Bob Freemark."

Old Bob stopped, and gave him a calm, steady look. "What's in the cooler, Derry?"

Derry Howe's face flushed and tightened with sudden anger. "Get out of here!" he spat angrily. "Get away from me!"

Old Bob shook his head. "I can't do that. Not unless you come with me."

Derry took a quick step back from him. "I'm not going anywhere with you! Get the hell out of my face!"

"What are you doing down here, Derry?" Old Bob pressed, starting forward again.

He could see the desperation in the younger man's eyes as they fixed on him. He looked trapped, frustrated. Suddenly, he laughed. "You want to know what I'm doing?" He was backing off as he spoke, edging down the line of platforms and scaffolding, away from the flashlight's steady beam. Abruptly he stopped. "All right, I'll show you."

He turned away a moment, his movements concealed by the darkness. When he turned back again, he was holding a gun.

The buzzing inside Derry's head had become a dull roar, a Niagara Falls of pounding white noise. He leveled the gun at Robert Freemark and his finger tightened on the trigger.

"Turn off the flashlight, old man."

Old Bob glanced to his left where the staging crew was gathered around the framework that supported the flag display. But they were too far away to see what was happening. No help was coming from there. Old Bob looked back at Derry and the flashlight went dark.

Derry nodded. "First smart thing you've done yet." He licked at his dry lips. "Walk toward me. Stop, that's far enough. You want to know what I'm up to? Fine, I'll tell you. Tell you everything. You know why? No, don't say anything, damn you, just listen! I'll tell you because you got a right to know. See, I knew you were coming. I knew it. Even though I told you to stay away, I knew you'd be here. Big mistake, old man."

"Derry, listen—" Old Bob began.

"Shut up!" Derry's face contorted with rage. "I told you not to say anything, and I damn well mean it! You listen to me! While you and those other old farts have been sitting around waiting for a miracle to end this damn strike, I've found a way to make the miracle happen!"

He edged back toward a grouping of rocket launchers, the cooler dangling from his hand, his eyes on Old Bob, ten feet away. He held the gun level on the old man, making sure it didn't waver, not wanting Old Bob to do something stupid, force him to fire the gun now, before he was ready, ruin everything. Oh, sure, he was going to shoot Mr. Robert Freemark, no question about that. But not quite yet. Not until he was somewhere no one could hear or see. He glanced over to where the staging crew shone their flashlights on the flag display, making sure they were still busy with their work. He grinned. Everything was working out just right.

He knelt in the shadows and set the cooler behind him, close to the launching platform. "Don't you move," he told Old Bob softly. "Just stand there. You ain't carrying a gun, are you?"

Old Bob shook his head. His big hands hung limply at his sides, and his body slumped. "Don't do this, Derry. There are women and children up there. They could be hurt."

"Ain't nobody going to be hurt, old man. What do you think I am, stupid?"

He kept the gun leveled as he lifted the cooler onto the platform and shoved it back into the shadows between the fireworks cases where it couldn't be seen if you weren't looking. Well, okay, maybe a few people would end up getting hurt, hit by debris or something. After all, that was part of the plan, wasn't it? Someone gets hurt, MidCon looks even worse. Derry gave a mental shrug. Point is, the strike will be over and in the long run everyone'll be happy.

He reached behind the cooler to where he had placed the timer switch and activated it. He had five minutes. He stood up, feeling good. "See, easy as pie. Now you turn around and walk down along the riverbank, Robert Freemark, nice and slow. I'll be right behind . . ."

Then everything flared white hot about him, and it felt as if a giant fist had slammed into his back.

The force of the bomb's blast blew Derry Howe forward into Old Bob and carried both of them fifteen feet through the air before it dumped them in a tangled heap. Old Bob lay crumpled in the grass, one arm twisted awkwardly, Derry sprawled half on top of him. His ears rang and his head throbbed, and after a minute he felt the pain begin. I'm dying, he thought. Fireworks were exploding all around him, rockets going off in their launcher tubes or spinning wildly off into the darkness or streaming fire into the trees and sky and out over the river. The launching platform was in flames, and the frameworks for the flag display and others hung in ragged, half-burned tatters. The spectators were running and screaming in all directions, blankets scattered, lawn chairs dumped, coolers abandoned. Deep booms and ear-piercing whistles marked the detonation of explosive after explosive from within the white-hot inferno below. Old Bob felt blood on his chest and face and could not tell if it was his or Derry's. He could feel blood leaking inside his mouth and down his throat. When he tried to free himself from Derry, he found he could not move.

He closed his eyes against his pain and weariness.

Well, that's it, that's all she wrote.

He had just enough time left to wonder about Nest, and then everything went black.

CHAPTER 31

The creature that emerged from the shattered remnants of the old oak was so loathsome that it defied comparison with anything John Ross had ever seen. It slouched out of the smoke and ruin, materializing as the pulsating green light fragmented, a nightmare come to life. It walked upright on two legs, but it was hunched over and crook-backed, as if its huge shoulders would not permit it to straighten. Tufts of coarse, black hair dotted its scaly surface, and it had a snake's hooded yellow eyes and wicked tongue. Toes and fingers split in tripods from its feet and hands, ending in claws that seemed better suited to a great cat. Its face was long and narrow and featureless except for the slits that served as its eyes and mouth, and its head was a smooth, sinuous extension of its corded neck. It was big, fully ten feet in height, even stooped as it was, and its mass suggested that it weighed well over five hundred pounds. It swung around guardedly as it stepped forward into the clearing, casting its flat, empty gaze left and right, looking over the unfamiliar world into which it had emerged.

After centuries of being locked away, the maentwrog was free once more.

John Ross stared at the monster. It looked too huge to have been contained by the old tree, and he wondered how it could ever have been imprisoned. Not that it mattered now. All that mattered now was whether he was going to do anything about the fact that it was loose. His purpose in coming to Hopewell had nothing to do with the maentwrog. The maentwrog was an unneeded and dangerous distraction. He knew what he should do, what he had been sent to do. He should let the monster go its way, let it do what it would, let someone else deal with it. But there was no one else, of course. There was only him. By the time sufficient force was brought to bear, the maentwrog would have killed half the people of the town. It was a berserker, a killing machine that lacked any other purpose in life. It did not kill out of hunger or in self-defense, but out of primal need. It was not his responsibility, but he knew he could not let it pass.

And that was what the demon was counting on—the reason he had set the maentwrog free. John Ross was being given a choice, and the fact that he was human and not a forest creature made the outcome of his choosing a foregone conclusion.

He turned to Nest Freemark, who stood transfixed behind him, her eyes wide and staring, her curly hair wild and damp against her heated face. "Move back from me," he told her softly.

"John, no, it's too big," she whispered, her eyes filled with fear and terror.

"Move back, Nest."

She did so reluctantly, slowly withdrawing toward the wall of the trees. The clearing was lit by the remnants of the oak, a scattering of shards which were still infused with the green light and clung to the limbs and tall grasses. Overhead, the sky was dark and choked with clouds, the moon and stars hidden. In the distance, he heard the slow rumble of thunder. A sad, wistful resignation filled him. There was no way out of this. In his hands, the black walnut staff pulsed with light.

Ignoring the demon, who backed to the tree line, bland features lit with expectation, Ross stepped forward. He kept his eyes on the maentwrog, who was watching him now, seeing him for the first time, realizing that a confrontation was at hand. The creature dropped down on all fours, muscles bunching, tongue flicking out experimentally. Its mouth parted to reveal multiple rows of sharpened teeth, and it gave a deep, slow hiss of warning.

Ross summoned the magic from his staff, and it flowed over him like liquid light, encasing him in its armor, giving him protection for the battle ahead. The maentwrog cringed in revulsion as Ross slowly transformed, becoming less himself, less the human he had been, turning bright and hard within the magic's armor. His features melted, smoothing out within the light, and when he advanced in a slow, almost sensual glide, his limp had disappeared completely.

Within the shadows of the clearing, time seemed to slow and sound to cease.

Then the maentwrog threw itself at its adversary in a stunningly swift attack, claws ripping. But the Knight of the Word sidestepped with ease, and the gleaming black staff hammered into the monster as it hurtled past. Fire flared like molten steel, and the creature howled, a high-pitched, ragged snarl, its neck arching, its body writhing. It spun about as it was struck, one arm whipping at the Knight, who was not quite quick enough to avoid it. The blow sent him sprawling backward across the clearing, and he felt the impact even through the shield of his magic.

He scrambled to his feet as the creature launched itself at him a second time. Again he avoided the attack, using the staff to block the deadly claws. The staff's magic flared and burned, stripping off ragged lengths of reptilian skin, and the maentwrog spun away.

The Knight of the Word righted himself and moved to the center of the clearing, close to the remains of the maentwrog's shattered prison. From the corner of his eye, he saw Nest crouched down at the fringe of the trees, ready to bolt. But she would not run. She would not leave Pick. Or him, he believed. Whatever happened, she would stand her ground. She might be only a young girl, but she had the heart and soul of a warrior. He knew that much about her. He wished anew that he had been able to tell her more, to give her something else with which to defend herself. But it was a pointless exercise; whether he lived or died, he had done everything for her that he could.

He edged left toward the demon. There was his real enemy. If the maentwrog gave him even a moment's respite, he could . . . But no, it was too late for that, too late for anything but letting events unfold as they would. He felt a great despair at his limitations, at the narrowness of the charge he had been given, at the hard truths that belonged to him alone.

The maentwrog crept toward him once more, body lowered to the earth, eyes bright and gleaming. It would not stop until one of them was dead. The Knight understood the nature of his adversary, and he knew there would be no quarter. The beast had killed stronger creatures in its time, and it was not afraid. Fueled by savagery and rage, it knew only one way.

It attacked, feinting several times in an effort to distract the Knight, then launched itself across the clearing, an unstoppable juggernaut of muscle, claws, and teeth. The Knight of the Word stood his ground and delivered a powerful blow, lashing out with such force that the magic's fire engulfed the maentwrog. But the monster's rush carried it past his defenses and right into him. The Knight was slammed against the earth, the armored light that protected him crushed downward like plastic. He rolled aside as the maentwrog thrashed within the cloak of fire, trying to reach him but tearing only the earth. He struck it repeatedly, slamming his staff against the massive body, fire bursting from its polished length. The maentwrog screamed and struggled to pin him to the ground, twisting and arching in fury. Twice the Knight was felled, the breath knocked from his lungs, pain filling his body, his strength momentarily leaving him. Both times he rallied, refusing to back away. He could no longer see either the demon or Nest. He could barely make out where he was, the clearing filled with smoke and soot, the shards of light from the devastated tree obscured. He moved in a world of sound and sudden movement, of responses born of instinct and swift reaction, where an instant's hesitation would mean his death.

He broke from the maentwrog momentarily, sliding away through the murky gloom like a ghost, knowing he must wait for an opening. His strength was beginning to fail, and his magic was tiring. If he did not bring this battle to a swift conclusion, he would lose it. He was so battered already that he could no longer move without pain, his legs cramped, his arms leaden and weak. He had not been much of a fighter in the time before he had become a Knight of the Word, and so fighting did not come instinctively to him. He had learned what little he knew from his dreams of the future and his confrontations in the present, and he was a novice compared with the thing he battled. His magic had made the difference so far, but his magic was not without limits and it was tailored to a different end.

Then the maentwrog swiped at him from out of the smoke and dust, knocking him from his feet. In an instant, the creature was on top of him, bearing down with its forelegs, pinning him fast. Its jaws snapped at his head, scraping against the magic's armored light, ripping at the fabric. The Knight drove his feet into the monster's chest, fire exploding at the contact, but could not break free.

In that instant, Nest Freemark rushed out of the smoke and darkness, screaming in fury, no longer able simply to stand by and watch. Wielding a six-foot piece of deadwood, she swung it at the maentwrog in an effort to distract it, desperate to do something to help. The Knight cried out at her to go back, but she ignored him. Surprised, the maentwrog swiped at her with one massive foreleg, and sent her cartwheeling back into the night.

One arm suddenly free, the Knight thrust the black staff deep into the monster's maw and sent the magic forth. Fire lanced into the monster's throat, burning and consuming, and the maentwrog reared backward in pain, trying to break free. But the Knight clung to it stubbornly as the maentwrog beat at him with its arms and tore at him with its claws, shrieking. The Knight felt as if everything was breaking apart inside his body, but the staff remained buried in the beast's throat, the fire exploding out of it.

The maentwrog stumbled and fell, then lay writhing on the earth, frantically trying to rise, to rid itself of the fire within. The Knight yanked the staff from its throat and drove it into one baleful eye, feeling the maentwrog's head shudder beneath the blow. He struck a second time, then a third, as fire flared in brilliant spurts and smoke billowed into the night.

When he could no longer lift his staff to strike, he tried to disengage himself from the shapeless mass at his feet, but his legs refused to respond.

Don't leave Nest alone! he screamed in silent desperation, and then his strength gave out completely and he collapsed.

In the smoky aftermath, the clearing went still.

Raindrops fell on Nest Freemark's face, soft, cool splashes against her heated skin. They fell out of the blackness in a ragged scattering, and then began to quicken. Nest brushed at them absently as she lay sprawled on the earth at the edge of the clearing, her eyes locked on the mix of smoke and gloom that roiled before her. She could not see what was happening. In the last desperate moments of the struggle between John Ross and the monster, everything had disappeared. Fire belched and inhuman shrieks rent the air, and then suddenly there was only silence.

"John," she said softly, his name a whisper that only she was meant to hear.

A sudden breeze rose off the waters of the Rock River, gusted through the deep woods, and began to sweep away the haze. As the night air cleared, she could see both combatants, sprawled on the ground, motionless. She climbed slowly to her feet. Steam was rising off the maentwrog, and as she watched, it began to disintegrate, collapsing on itself as if a shell in which air had been trapped and released. The massive body broke apart and fell earthward in a cloud of dust and ash, and in seconds only an outline remained, a dark shadow against the torn and bloodied earth.

John Ross remained where he was, motionless and crumpled. The black staff no longer gleamed. Nest moved to where he lay and stared down at him in horror.

A sudden, violent explosion shattered the silence, and the force of the explosion was so powerful that the shock wave rocked her as it passed. The explosion had come from some distance off. She turned to look for its source, and she saw fire-works exploding everywhere. But they were not going off in any pattern, and the flashes of color that identified their location were not only overhead, but at ground level as well.

She swung back to find the demon standing only a dozen feet away, come forward out of the gloom to confront her. Shock and surprise jolted her.

"It's only you and me now," he said quietly, a serene look on his face, his hands folded comfortably before him. "I suspected that Mr. Ross might try to intervene in this, so I arranged a minor distraction. It looks to me as if it did the job. Care to check for yourself?"

She straightened, forcing herself to stand fast, closing away her emotions so that he would not see them. "What do you want from me?" she asked, keeping her tone of voice flat and expressionless.

"I want you, child. My daughter. I want you with me, where you belong."

She choked back the urge to scream in rage. "I told you not to call me that. I am not your daughter. I am nothing like you. I have no intention of going with you anywhere. Not now, not ever. If you make me go, I will run away from you the first chance I get."

He shook his head admonishingly. "You are in deep denial, Nest. Do you know what that means? You can pretend all you want, but when all is said and done, I am still your father. You can't change that. Nothing can. I made you. I gave you life. You can't just dismiss the fact of my existence."

Nest laughed. A surge of adrenaline rushed through her. "You gave me life out of hate for my mother and my grandmother. You gave me life for all the wrong reasons. My mother is dead because of you. I don't know if you killed her or if she killed herself, but you are responsible in either case."

"She killed herself," the demon interjected with a shrug. "She was weak and foolish."

Nest felt her face turn hot. "But my grandmother didn't kill herself, did she?"

"She was dangerous. If I had let her live, she might have killed me."

"And so now I belong with you?" Nest was openly incredulous. "Why would you think I would even consider such a thing?"

The demon's bland features tightened. "There is no one else to look after you."

"What are you talking about? What about Grandpa?" She pointed at him threateningly, aggressively. "Get out of here! Leave me alone!"

"You have no one. Your grandfather is dead. Or if not, he will be soon."

"You're lying!"

The demon shrugged again. "Am I? In any case, none of them matter. Only me."

Nest was shaking with fury. "Why you would think, after all you've done, that I would do *anything* you wanted, is beyond me. I hate you. I hate what you are. I hate it that I am any part of you. You don't matter to me. You matter less than nothing!"

"Nest." He spoke her name calmly and evenly. "You can say or do anything you like, but it won't change what's going to happen."

She took a deep breath to steady herself. "Nothing's going to happen."

"You are my flesh and blood, Nest. We are the same."

"We are not the same. We will never be the same."

"No?" The demon smiled. "You want to believe that, I expect. But you're not certain, are you? How can you be? Don't you wonder how much of me is inside you?" He paused. "Don't you owe it to yourself to find out?"

He started forward. "Don't touch me!" Nest snapped, clenching her fists at her sides.

The demon stopped, laughing. "But I must. I must touch you if I am to help you see who you can become, who you really are. I must, if I am to help you free the part of me you keep buried."

She shook her head rapidly from side to side. "Keep away from me."

He looked skyward, as if discovering the rain for the first time. It was falling more rapidly now, a slow, steady patter against the leaves of the trees, its dampness spreading darkly across the bare ground. Nest glanced down at John Ross, but he still wasn't moving. She looked over at Pick, slumped on the floor of his iron cage.

You have to help them.

Then, for the first time that night, she saw the feeders. They had ringed the clearing, hundreds—perhaps thousands—of them, bodies scrunched together within the shadows cast by the trees, eyes bright with expectation as they gleamed catlike in the darkness. She had never seen so many gathered in one place, never in numbers like this. It seemed, on looking about, as if all the feeders in the world had come together in these woods.

"You belong to me," the demon repeated, watching her closely. "Child of mine."

She closed her eyes momentarily, blinking rapidly against the tears that were threatening to form. She was all alone, she knew. He had seen to that. He had done that to her. She stared balefully at him, daring him to come closer, hating him as she had never hated anyone. Her father. *A demon. A demon. A demon.*

"Step away from Mr. Ross, please," he ordered softly.

She stood her ground in challenge. "No."

The demon smiled coldly. "No?"

He gestured at her almost casually, and she was assailed with such fear that her legs buckled and her breath caught in her throat. She staggered under the weight of the attack, and as she did so the feeders came at her from every side. She whirled to meet their assault, her eyes locking quickly on those of her attackers, her magic turning them to mush. One by one they crumpled before her, falling to the sodden earth and melting away. But for each one she destroyed, two more took its place. She hissed at them like a cat, enraged and terrified by their closeness and numbers. They were touching her now, grappling for her, too many to fend off completely, and she was back once more in the darkness of the caves beneath the park, wrapped in electrician's tape and unable to help herself. She fought on, striking out wildly, destroying any feeder who would look at her, forcing some to cringe away as she wheeled on them, thrashing against those who tried to crawl over her.

But there were so many. *Too many! Too many!*

She clasped her head between her arms and closed her eyes, screaming defiantly.

Then suddenly the feeders were gone back into the night, and she was alone again. She lifted her head and found the demon watching her, amusement reflected in his pale eyes.

He started toward her again, a slow advance through the empty gloom and soft rain.

"Wraith!" she cried out desperately.

Abruptly, the big ghost wolf appeared. He emerged from the trees behind the demon and stalked into the ravaged clearing with his massive head lowered and his hackles raised. Nest felt her heart leap as her giant protector advanced on the demon.

The demon stopped and looked casually over his shoulder. Wraith stopped as well.

The demon turned back to Nest, smiling. "I have a confession to make," he said. "I have been keeping something from you. Would you like to know what it is? It's rather important." Nest said nothing, suddenly terrified. He was enjoying the moment. "It's about this creature. Your protector. It's an elemental, a thing created of magic and the elements, a sort of familiar. You probably think your grandmother made it; maybe she even told you she did. But she didn't. I did."

His words spun through the silence like chips of jagged metal, cutting apart what remained of Nest's courage and resolve. She stared at him in disbelief. "You're lying."

He shook his head. "Think about it. I left you behind after you were born. Why would I do that if I thought any harm would come to you? You were my child; quite possibly you would have magic at your command. The feeders would be drawn to you. At times, you would be in danger." He shrugged. "So I created a protector to watch over you, to keep you from harm."

She shook her head slowly. "I don't believe you."

"No?" He laughed softly. "Watch."

He turned back to Wraith and made a quick gesture. Wraith sat back on his haunches obediently. The demon smiled at

Nest. He made another gesture, and Wraith lay down and put his head between his paws, docile and responsive.

The demon faced Nest once more. "See?" He gave her a wink.

Nest felt the last of her hope fade, watched her last chance for survival drift off into the night. *Use your magic. Trust Wraith.* But Wraith was his creature. *His.* The truth burned in her throat and left her dizzy and sick inside.

Oh, my God, my God! What am I supposed to do now?

The demon spread his arms in a gesture intended to convey his sympathy. "You're all alone, Nest. There isn't anyone left for you to turn to except me. But maybe that isn't as bad as you think. Let me take your hands in mine. Just for a few moments. Let me touch you. I can make you see things in different ways. I can give you an understanding of who you really are. What harm can come from that? If you don't like what you see, I'll leave."

But he wouldn't, she knew. He would never leave. And if she let him touch her as he wanted, she would be destroyed forever. She would be subverted in ways she could not begin to imagine. Her father was anathema to her. To any human. He was a demon, and there was nothing good that could come from embracing any part of what he offered.

"Stay away from me," she told him for the second time that night.

But he came toward her anyway, certain of himself now, confident that he held her fate in his hands, that there was nothing she could do to stop him. Nest was shaking with fear and helpless anger, but she stood her ground. There was nowhere to run and no reason to try. Sooner or later, he would find her. The feeders began to edge out from the shadows again, their eyes brightening. She felt the rain fall steadily on her face, and she realized her clothing was soaked. Behind, through the trees of the deep woods, the fireworks were still exploding in a series of ragged bangs and whumps.

I will not become like him, she told herself then. *I will never let that happen. I will die first.*

She waited until he was so close she could make out the

lines of his face in the gloom, and then she attacked him with her magic. She struck out with ferocious determination, using every bit of power she could summon. She met his gaze squarely, locked his eyes with hers, and went after him. He was not expecting it. The force of her assault jolted him back a step, shook him from head to foot. His mouth opened in surprise, and his eyes went wide. But he did not collapse as Danny Abbott and Robert Heppler had. He kept his feet. His face underwent a frightening transformation, and for a moment she could see clearly the depth of his evil.

"You foolish little girl!" he hissed in undisguised fury.

He came at her again, stronger this time, breaking past her defenses, brushing aside her attack. She retreated from him, trying to bring more power to bear, to slow him, to keep him at bay. The feeders were scrambling and leaping wildly, closing about, tightening their circle. She felt their anticipation, sensed their readiness. They would feed soon. They would feed on her.

Then she saw Wraith. He left the ground as if catapulted, his huge, rippling body uncoiling, his muscles stretching. He crossed the open space between them in a handful of heart-beats, paws tearing at the earth, jaws spread wide. A high-pitched snarl broke from his throat, so dark and terrible that for a second everything seemed to freeze with its sound.

In that second, Nest was certain he was coming for her and she was about to die. She brought her arms up quickly to shield herself and dropped to one knee.

But it was the demon Wraith had targeted, and he flew through the air in a blur of black and gray tiger stripes, crashing into his creator and bearing him to the earth in a bright flash of white teeth. The demon disappeared under the beast, body twisting, arms flailing in an effort to find purchase. Nest staggered back from them, nearly falling, not understanding what had happened. Why was Wraith attacking the demon? The demon screamed in rage and pain as the ghost wolf tore at him. It seemed as if the beast had gone insane, attacking with such ferocity that there was no stopping him. Feeders broke over them both, writhing and twisting jubilantly in response to the battle, frenzied in their eagerness to dine. They scattered momentarily as the demon threw off Wraith with a superhuman effort and struggled to his feet, torn and bloodied and battered. But Wraith was on top of him again in an instant, jaws snapping.

The demon screamed something then, just one time, a name that Nest heard clearly. *"Evelyn!"* There was recognition in the cry; there was rage and terror. *Evelyn!*

Then Wraith was all over him, dragging him down and ripping him apart. Blood and flesh flew in ragged gouts, and the demon's screams turned to muffled gasps. Arms and legs flopped wide in limp surrender, and the demon began to come apart, throat and chest gaping, insides spilling out. Feeders tore at him hungrily, swarming out of the night. The demon's savaged body lurched upward as if jolted by electricity, and something dark and winged and unspeakable tried to break free from the gore. But Wraith caught it as it emerged, and his jaws snapped down with an audible crunch. Nest heard a single, horrifying shriek, and then silence.

Wraith moved away from the demon's body then, head lowered, jaws dark and wet with blood. The demon lay crumpled and motionless before her, no longer recognizable as anything human, reduced to something foul and wretched. She stared at it a moment, watching it collapse on itself as the maentwrog had done, watching it sink into the earth and fade to an outline and then disappear.

The rain was falling in a steady downpour now, and thunder rumbled through the darkness, approaching from the west. The feeders faded back into the night, reduced to a scattering of lantern eyes that winked out one by one like searchlights being extinguished. Wraith shook himself, a gesture that seemed almost dismissive. His huge, tiger-striped face lifted into the darkness and his gleaming eyes fixed on Nest. For just an instant, and Nest was never certain afterward if she had actually seen it or just imagined it, she thought she saw Gran's sharp old eyes peering out of the ghost wolf's head.

Then Wraith turned and walked back into the trees, melting away into the darkness, becoming one with the air.

* * *

Nest went to Pick first, breaking off the pin that secured the cage door and gently lifting the sylvan into the open air. Pick sat dazed and shaking in her palm for a few moments, holding his head in his hands as he collected himself. Then he smoothed back the leaves that were clustered atop his head, brushed at his wooden arms and legs, and without looking at her, asked about Daniel. When she told him, fighting back her tears, he shook his head sadly and told her in a calm voice not to cry, but to remember that Daniel had been a good friend and never to forget him.

Then he looked directly at her, his narrow face composed, his button eyes steady. His voice was sandpaper rough. "Do you understand what's happened here, Nest? Do you know what your grandmother did for you?"

Nest shook her head slowly. "I'm not sure. I know I heard the demon call her name. And I think I saw her eyes in Wraith's, there at the end." She sank down on her knees in the darkness and rain. "I think she was there with him in some way."

The sylvan nodded. "She was there, all right. But not the way I had it figured. I had it wrong, I admit that. I thought that she had created Wraith to be your protector. But it was the demon who made Wraith. What your grandmother did was to stir up the magic a bit. She must have realized where Wraith came from when you first told her about seeing him. She must have understood right away that it meant the demon planned to return for you someday. And she knew when he did she might not be strong enough to stop him! Sharp as a tack, your grandmother. So she used her magic, all of it, to turn his own creation against him. On the outside, Wraith looked the same. But inside, he was something different. If the demon ever came back for you, Wraith was waiting to have at him. That was the secret ingredient your grandmother's magic added to the mix. The demon never figured it out, but that's why your grandmother didn't have any magic to protect herself when he came for her. She used it all to change Wraith."

"But why did Wraith protect me this time when he didn't

protect me before?" Nest demanded quickly. "Why didn't he attack the demon in the park or down in the caves or even in church?"

Pick lifted one forefinger in front of his grainy face and shook it slowly. "Use your brain. Your grandmother wanted to be certain that Wraith didn't intervene unless it was absolutely necessary. She didn't want any mistakes, any mix-ups. Wraith wasn't supposed to protect you unless you tried to protect yourself! Do I need to draw you a picture? It was your magic, Nest! Your grandmother reasoned that you would only use it if you were in the worst kind of danger. Remember how she cautioned you against using it foolishly? Reminded you over and over again, didn't she? That was because she wanted you to save it for when you really needed it. Think about it! That was the reason for your grandmother's note! She was admonishing you to stand and fight! If the demon came after you and you summoned up even the littlest part of your magic to save yourself, Wraith would have to help!"

He was animated now, infused with the passion of his certainty. "Oh, I know you would have done so anyway. Sure, I know that. But your grandmother wasn't taking any chances. It was a clever trap, Nest. Criminy, yes! When Wraith came to your defense, the demon was facing a combination of both his own magic and your grandmother's. It was too much for him." He took a deep breath and exhaled slowly. "That was the sacrifice your grandmother made for you."

Nest stayed silent, stunned. It was difficult for her to imagine her grandmother doing what Pick had described. But Gran had been her fearless champion, and Nest knew the sylvan was right. Gran had given up her magic and thereby her life for her granddaughter.

She set Pick upon the ground then and bent over John Ross. He was stirring at last, trying to right himself. His pale green eyes fixed on her, and for an instant she saw a mix of despair and resolve that frightened her. He asked what had happened, and she told him. When she was finished, he reached for his staff and levered himself slowly and gingerly to his feet.

"You saved us, Nest," he said. He brushed at his clothing, a muddied and rumpled scarecrow in the rain-drenched gloom.

"I was worried about you," she replied softly. "I thought the maentwrog might have . . ."

She trailed off, unable to finish, and he put his arm around her and held her against him. "I'm sorry this had to happen to you, Nest. I wish it could have been otherwise. But life chooses for us sometimes, and all we can do is accept what happens and try to get through it the best way we can."

She nodded into his shirt. "It never felt as if he was my father," she whispered. "It never felt as if he was any part of me."

"He was part of what's bad about the world, but a part that happened to be closer to you than most." Ross stroked her damp hair. "Put it behind you, Nest. It won't happen all at once, but if you give it a chance, it will go away."

"I know. I'll try." She hugged him gratefully. "I'm just glad you were here to help me."

There was an uneasy pause. His hand stopped moving in her hair.

"What's wrong?" she asked.

He seemed to be thinking it over. "What do you think would have happened, Nest, if your father had touched you?"

She was quiet for a moment. "I don't know."

She heard him sigh. "I'm going to tell you something I've kept secret until now. I'm going to tell you because you need to know. Because someday the knowledge might save your life."

His face lowered into her hair. "I dream about the future, Nest. I dream about it every night of my life. I dream about the way things will be if everything breaks down and the feeders consume us. I dream about the end of civilization, the end of the world. The dreams are real, not pretend. It is the price I pay for being a Knight of the Word. It is a reminder of what will happen if I fail. More importantly, it is a window into time that lets me discover exactly what it is I must try to prevent."

He stepped away from her, keeping his hands on her shoulders. Rain glistened on his lean face and in his mud-streaked hair. "I found out about you through my dreams. I found out that the demon was your father. But most important of all, I saw what you became because he touched you here tonight, in this place, in this park. I came to Hopewell to stop that from happening."

"What did I become?" she asked, her voice shaking.

He shook his head. "It doesn't matter. It can't happen now. The window of opportunity is past. The demon is gone. The events can't re-create themselves. You won't become what I saw in my dream. You will become what you make of yourself, but it won't be a bad thing. Not after what you did tonight. Not after you've heard what I have to say."

His smile was tight and bitter. "Some of what I do as a Knight of the Word is difficult for me to live with. I can't always change the future with words and knowledge. The demons I hunt are elusive and clever, and I don't always find them. Sometimes they accomplish what they intend, and I am left to deal with the results. Because I know from my dreams what those results signify, I must change them any way I can."

His brow furrowed with hidden pain. "It was necessary for you to face your father and reject him. I came to Hopewell to see if you could do that. I would have destroyed him beforehand if I could, but I knew from the beginning that my chances were poor. I knew it would probably be left up to you. I gave you what help I could, but in my heart, Nest, in my soul, I knew it would come down to you."

He stood tall in front of her, suddenly unapproachable, become as impenetrable as the darkness that shrouded them both.

"Do you understand?" he asked softly. "If you had failed in what was required of you, if the demon had touched you and you had become what he intended, if you had been unable to withstand him and your magic had darkened to his use . . ."

He took his hands from her shoulders, his voice trailing off. Their eyes locked. "My purpose in coming here, Nest, was to stop you from becoming the creature I saw in my dreams." He paused, letting the full import of his words sink in. "I would have done whatever was needed to accomplish that."

Recognition of his meaning ran through her like shards of ice, and she stared at him in horror and disbelief. *Whatever was needed.* She tried to say something in response, to let him know what she was feeling, but she could not find the words. The chasm he had opened between them was so vast that she could not find a way to bridge it.

"Good-bye, Nest," he said finally, stepping back from her, his mouth crooked in a tight, sad smile. "I wish I could have been your father."

He stood there a moment longer, a lean, hunched figure in the rain-drenched night. Her savior. Her executioner. She felt her heart break with the realization.

Then he turned away, his black staff gleaming, and disappeared into the night.

TUESDAY, JULY 5

CHAPTER 32

By morning, news services from as far away as Chicago were reporting the story. Variations in word usage and presentation aside, it read pretty much the same everywhere. A disgruntled union worker at MidCon Steel in Hopewell, Illinois, had attempted to sabotage a fireworks display sponsored by the company. Derry Howe, age thirty-eight, of Hopewell, was killed when the bomb he was attempting to plant within the staging area exploded prematurely. Also injured were Robert Freemark, aged sixty-five, of Hopewell, a retired member of the same union; two members of the staging crew; and several spectators. In a related incident, a second man, Junior Elway, aged thirty-seven, of Hopewell, was killed attempting to plant a bomb in the fourteen-inch mill at MidCon during a break in his work shift. It was thought that the dead men, longtime friends and union activists, were acting in concert, and that the bombs were intended to halt efforts by MidCon to reopen the company in defiance of a strike order and to initiate a new round of settlement talks. Police were continuing with their investigation.

In a second, much smaller news item, the weather service reported extensive damage to parts of Sinnissippi Park in the wake of a thunderstorm that passed through Hopewell sometime around midnight. High winds and lightning had toppled a white oak thought to be well over two hundred years old as well as several smaller trees within a heavily wooded section of the park. The storm had moved out of the area by early morning, but phone and electrical lines were still down in parts of the city.

Nest heard most of it from television reports as she wandered back and forth between the Community General Hospital lounge and the lunchroom waiting for her grandfather to wake up. It had been almost midnight when she walked home through the driving rain, the park deserted save for a cluster of patrol cars parked in front of the pavilion and toboggan slide, their red and blue lights flashing. Police officers in yellow slickers were stringing tape and examining the grounds, but she didn't attach any particular significance to the matter until she got home and found another cruiser parked in her driveway and more officers searching her home. She was told then that her grandfather had been taken to the hospital with a broken shoulder, cracked ribs, and possible internal injuries following a bombing attempt in the park, and that she had been reported missing and possibly kidnapped.

After determining that she was all right, they had driven her to the hospital to be with her grandfather. Old Bob had been treated and sedated, and she was told by the nurses on duty that he would probably sleep until morning. She had sufficient presence of mind to call Cass Minter to let her know she was all right and to tell her where she was. Even though it was almost one in the morning, Cass was still awake. Brianna was there with her, spending the night, and Robert was at home waiting to hear something as well. It was Robert who had called the police, telling them about the man poisoning trees in the park and insisting he might have gotten hold of Nest. He had even suggested, rather bizarrely, that the man might be using a stun gun.

Nest dozed on and off all night while her grandfather slept. Cass came up with her mother to check on her the following morning, and when Mrs. Minter discovered what state she was in, they took her home to shower and change, made her a hot meal, and then drove her back again.

When they left around midafternoon, she called the Lincoln Hotel and asked for John Ross, but was told he had checked out early that morning and taken a bus west to the Quad Cities. He had left no forwarding address.

Her grandfather was still sleeping, so she parked herself in a quiet corner of the lounge to wait. As she read magazines and stared into space, her thoughts constantly strayed to the events of the past few days. Faces and voices recalled themselves in random visits, like ghosts appearing from the shadows. The demon. John Ross. Wraith. Two Bears. Pick. She tried to listen to them, to understand what they were telling her, to fit together the pieces of jagged memory that lay scattered in her mind. She tried to make sense of what she had experienced. She thought often of Gran, and doing so left her sad and philosophical. It seemed, in the wake of last night's events, as if Gran had been gone a long time already. The news of her death, so fresh yesterday morning, was already stale and fading from the public consciousness. Today's news was all of Derry Howe and Junior Elway and the bombings. Tomorrow's news would be about something else. It diminished the importance of what had happened, she thought. It was the nature of things, of course. Life went on. The best you could do was to hold on to the memories that were important to you, so that even if everyone else forgot, you would remember. She could do that much for Gran.

She was dozing in the lounge, listening with half an ear to a television report that said authorities were dragging Rock River above Sinnissippi Park for a missing Hopewell man, when one of the nurses came to tell her that her grandfather was awake and asking for her. She rose and walked quickly to his room. He was sitting up in bed now, a cast on his arm and shoulder, bandages wrapped about his ribs, and tubes running out of his arm. His white hair was rumpled and spiky as he turned his head to look at her. She smiled back bravely.

"Hi, Grandpa," she said.

"Rough night, wasn't it?" he replied, seeing the concern in her eyes. "Are you all right, Nest?"

"I'm fine." She sat next to him on the bed. "How about you?"

"Stiff and sore, but I'll live. You heard what happened, I suppose?"

She nodded. "This guy was trying to blow up the fireworks

and you stopped him." She took his hand in hers. "My grandpa, the hero."

"Well, I didn't stop him, matter of fact. He stopped himself. All I did, come right down to it, was to make sure people knew the truth about what he was trying to do. Maybe it will help ease tensions a little." He paused. "They tell you how long I'm going to be here?"

She shook her head. "They haven't told me anything."

"Well, there's not much to tell. I'll be fine in a day or two, but they might keep me here a week. I guess they plan to let me out for your grandmother's funeral. Doctor says so, anyway." He paused. "Will you be all right without me? Do you want me to call someone? Maybe you could go stay with the Minters."

"Grandpa, don't worry, I'm fine," she said quickly. "I can take care of myself."

He studied her a moment. "I know that." He glanced at his nightstand. "Would you hand me a cup of water, please?"

She did, and he took a long drink, lifting his head only slightly from the pillows. The room was white and still, and she could hear the murmur of voices from the hall outside. Through cracks in the window blinds, she could see blue sky and sunlight.

When her grandfather was finished with the water, he looked at her again, his eyes uneasy. "Did you run into your father out there last night?"

Her throat tightened. She nodded.

"Did he hurt you?"

She shook her head. "He tried to persuade me to come with him, like John Ross said he would. He threatened me. But I told him I wasn't coming and he couldn't make me." Her brow furrowed. "So he gave up and went away."

Her grandfather studied her. "Just like that? Off he went, back to poisoning trees in the park?"

"Well, no." She realized how ridiculous it sounded. She looked out the window, thinking. "He didn't just go off. It's kind of hard to explain, actually." She hesitated, not sure where to go. "I had some help."

Her grandfather kept staring at her, but she had nothing left to say. Finally, he nodded. "Maybe you'll fill me in on the details sometime. When you think I'm up to it."

She looked back at him. "I forgot something. He told me about Gran. He said he tried to come after me, and she chased him off with the shotgun." She watched her grandfather's eyes. "So she wasn't just shooting at nothing."

He nodded again, solemn, introspective. "That's good to know, Nest. I appreciate you telling me. I thought it must be something like that. I was pretty sure."

He closed his eyes momentarily, and Nest exhaled slowly. No one spoke for a moment. Then Nest said, "Grandpa, I was wondering." She waited until he opened his eyes again. "You know about Jared Scott?" Her grandfather nodded. "They took his brothers and sisters away afterward. Mrs. Walker says they're going to be put in foster care. I was wondering if, maybe after you're home again, we could see if Bennett Scott could come stay with us."

She bit her lip against the sudden dampness in her eyes. "She's pretty little to be with strangers, Grandpa."

Her grandfather nodded, and his hand tightened about hers. "I think that would be fine, Nest," he said quietly. "We'll look into it."

She went home again when her grandfather fell back asleep, walking the entire way from the hospital, needing the time alone. The sun shone brightly out of a cloudless sky, and the temperature had fallen just enough that the air was warm without being humid. She wondered if it was anything like this where John Ross had gone.

The house was quiet and empty when she arrived home. The casseroles and tins were gone from the kitchen, picked up by Reverend Emery, who had left a nice note for her on the counter saying he would stop by the hospital to visit her grandfather that night. She drank a can of root beer, sitting on the back porch steps with Mr. Scratch, who lay sprawled out at her feet, oblivious of everything. She looked off into the park frequently, but made no move to go into it. Pick would be at work there, healing the scarred landscape of the deep woods. Maybe she would look for him tomorrow.

When it began to grow dark, she made herself a sandwich and sat eating alone at the kitchen table where she had sat so often with Gran. She was midway through her meal when she heard a kitten cry. She sat where she was a moment, then got up and went to the back door. There was Spook. Bennett Scott's kitten was ragged and scrawny, but all in one piece. Nest slipped outside and picked up the kitten, holding it against her breast. Where had he come from? There was no sign of Pick. But Spook couldn't have found his way here all alone.

She put milk in a bowl and set the bowl on the porch for Spook to drink. The kitten lapped hungrily, a loud purr building in its furry chest. Nest watched in silence, thinking.

After a while, she picked up the phone and called Robert.

"Hey," she said.

"Nest?"

"Want to go for a bike ride and visit Jared?"

There was a long pause. "What did you do to me last night?"

"Nothing. Want to go with me or not?"

"You can't visit Jared. He's off limits. They've got him in intensive care."

Nest looked at the shadows lengthening in the park. "Let's go see him anyway."

She hung up and when the phone rang, she left it alone. With Robert, it was best not to argue or explain.

Twenty minutes later he wheeled into her drive, dropped his bike in the grass, and walked up to her where she was back sitting out on the porch steps. He brushed at his unruly blond hair as he strode up, bouncing defiantly on the balls of his feet.

"Why'd you hang up on me?" he demanded.

"I'm a girl," she said, shrugging. "Girls do things like that. Want a root beer?"

"Geez. Bribery, yet." He followed her into the kitchen. "How's your grandpa?"

"Good. He won't be able to come home for a while, maybe a week. But he's okay."

"Good for him. Wish I could say the same."

She cocked one eyebrow speculatively. "What's the matter? Did I hurt you last night?"

"Ah-hah! You admit it!" Robert was ecstatic. "I knew you did something! I knew it! What was it? C'mon, tell me!"

She reached into the refrigerator, brought out a can of root beer, and handed it to him. "I used a stun gun."

He stared at her, openmouthed. Then he flushed. "No, you didn't! You're just saying that because that was what I told the cops! Where would you get a stun gun, anyway? Come on! What did you do?"

She cocked her head. "You mean you lied to the police?"

He continued to stare at her, frustration mirrored in his narrow, bunched features. Then he crooked his finger. "C'mere."

He led her back outside, down the steps and into the yard. Then he shook the can of root beer as hard as he could, pointed it at her, and popped the top. Cold fizz sprayed all over her. He waited until she was glaring openly at him, then took a long drink from the can and said, "Okay, now we're even."

She went inside to wash and change her T-shirt, then came back out to find him dangling a length of string in front of Spook, who was watching with a mix of curiosity and mistrust. "Are you ready?" she asked, picking the kitten up and depositing him inside the house.

He shrugged. "Why are we doing this, anyway?" He dropped the string and walked over to retrieve his bike.

She kicked at his tire as she walked past. "Because I'm afraid Jared might not come back from wherever he's gone if one of us doesn't go get him."

They wheeled their bikes to the top of the drive, climbed onto the seats, and began to pedal into the twilight. They rode down Sinnissippi Road and across Lincoln Highway to the back streets that led to the hospital. They rode in silence, watching the city darken around them, its people settling in behind lighted windows in front of lighted screens. Children played in yards, and lawn mowers roared. Starlings sang raucously, and elderly couples walked in slow motion down the concrete sidewalks that had become the measure of their lives.

When they reached the hospital, Nest and Robert chained

their bikes to the rack by the front entry and went inside. It was after nine o'clock, and the waiting room was quiet, most of the visitors gone home for the night. Side by side, they walked up to look in on Nest's grandfather, but he was sleeping again, so they didn't stay. Instead, they found a stairwell that connected the six floors of the hospital and stood just outside, glancing around surreptitiously.

"So, what's the plan, Stan?" Robert asked, lifting one eyebrow.

"He's in five fourteen," Nest answered. "Just off the stairway. You go up the elevator and talk to whoever's working the nursing station. Ask about Jared or something. I'll go up the stairs and slip into his room while they're busy with you."

Robert smirked. "That's your whole plan?"

"Assuming you intend to help."

He stared at her. "Tell you what. I'll help if you'll tell me what you did to me last night. The truth, this time."

She stared back at him without answering, thinking it over. Then she said, "I used magic on you."

He hesitated, and she could tell that for just half a second he believed her. Then he smirked dismissively. "You're weirder than I am, Nest. You know that? Okay, let's go."

She waited until she saw him stop in front of the elevator; then she entered the stairwell and began to climb. She reached the fifth floor, inched the door open, and peered out into the hall. It was virtually deserted. She could see room 514 almost directly across from her. When Robert stepped out of the elevator a moment later and walked over to the nursing station, she slipped from her hiding place.

A moment later, she was inside Jared's room.

Jared Scott lay motionless in a hospital bed, looking small and lost amid an array of equipment, eyes staring at nothing behind half-closed lids, arms and legs laid out straight beneath the covers, face pale and drawn. The room was dark except for the lights from the monitors and a small night-light near the door. The blinds to the street were closed, and the air conditioner hummed softly. Nest glanced around the room, then back at Jared. A bandage covered the top half of his head, and there were raw, savage marks on his face and arms from the beating he had received. She stared at him in despair, her eyes shifting from his face to the blinking green lights of the monitoring equipment and back again.

She had been thinking about coming to see him all afternoon, ever since leaving her grandfather. Spook had decided her. She would use her magic to help Jared. She didn't know for certain that she could, of course. She had never used the magic this way. But she understood its potential to affect the human body, and there was a chance she could do some good. She needed to try, perhaps as much for herself as for him. She needed to step out from her father's shadow, from the dark legacy of his life, something she would never be able to do until she embraced what he had given her and turned it to a use he would never have considered. She would start here.

She walked over to Jared's bed and lowered the railing so that she could sit next to him. "Hey, Jared," she said softly.

She touched his hand, held it in her own as she had held her grandfather's that afternoon, and reached up to stroke his face. His skin felt warm and soft. She waited to see if he would respond, but he didn't. He just lay there, staring. She fought to hold back her tears.

This would be dangerous, she knew. It would be risky. If the magic failed her, she might kill Jared. But she knew as well, somewhere deep inside, that if she failed to act, she would lose him anyway. He was not coming back alone from wherever he had gone. He was waiting there for her to come get him.

She leaned over him, still holding his hand, and stared down into his unseeing eyes. "Jared, it's me, Nest," she whispered.

She moved until she was directly in his line of sight, her face only inches from his own. The room was still except for the slight hiss and blip of the machines, cloaked in darkness and solitude.

"Look at me, Jared," she whispered.

She reached out to him with her magic, spidery tendrils of sound and movement that passed through his staring eyes and probed inward. "Where are you, Jared?" she asked softly. "We miss you. Me, Cass, Robert, Brianna. We miss you."

She nudged him gently, tried to reach deeper. She could feel something inside him resisting her, could feel it draw back, a curtain that tightened. She waited patiently for the curtain to loosen. If she pushed too hard, she could damage him. She experienced a sudden rush of uncertainty. She was taking an enormous chance, using the magic like this, experimenting. Perhaps she was making a mistake, thinking she could help, that the magic could do what she expected. Perhaps she should stop now and let nature take its intended course, unhindered by her interference.

She felt him relax then, and she probed anew, stroking him, brushing lightly against his fragile consciousness, the part he had locked deep inside where it was dark and safe.

Within her body, the magic hummed and vibrated, a living thing. She had never gotten this close to it for this long. She could feel its power building, working its way through her, heat and sound and motion. It was like trying to direct the movements of a cat; you felt it could spring away at any moment.

"Jared, look at me," she whispered.

Careful, careful. The magic prodded gently, insistently. Sweat beaded on Nest's forehead, and her chest and throat tightened with her efforts.

"I'm here, Jared. Can you hear me?"

Time slipped away. She lost track of how much, her concentration focused on making contact with him, on breaking through the shell into which he had retreated. Once, she heard someone approach, but the steps turned away before they reached Jared's room. Her concentration tightened. She forgot about Robert, about the nurses, about everything. She stayed where she was, not looking up, not shifting her gaze away from Jared, not even for a moment. She refused to give up. She kept talking to him, saying his name, using her magic to bump him gently, to open the door to his safehold just a crack.

"Jared," she said over and over. "It's me, Nest."

Until finally his eyes shifted to find hers, and he replied in a hoarse whisper, "Hey, Nest," and she knew he was going to be all right.

* * *

On a Greyhound traveling west between Denver and Salt Lake City, John Ross sat staring out into the night, watching the lights of ranches and towns hunkered down in the empty flats below the Rockies flash by in the darkness. He sat alone at the rear of the bus, his staff propped up against the seat beside him, the roar of the engine and the whine of the wheels drowning out the snoring of his fellow passengers. It was nearing midnight, and he was the only one awake.

He sighed wearily. Soon he would sleep, too. Because he would have to. Because the demands of his body would give him no choice.

Almost two days had passed since he had left Nest Freemark standing in the rain in Sinnissippi Park. He had gone back to the hotel, gathered up his things, and waited in the lobby for the early-morning bus. When it arrived, he had climbed aboard without a backward glance and ridden away. Already his memory of Hopewell and her people was beginning to fade, the larger picture shrinking to small, bright moments that he could tuck away and carry with him. Old Bob, greeting him that first day at Josie's, believing him Caitlin's friend. Gran, her sharp old eyes raking across him as she sought to see through the façade he had created. Josie Jackson, sleepy-eyed and warm, lying next to him on their last day. Pick, the sylvan, the keeper of Sinnissippi Park. Daniel. Wraith. The demon.

But mostly there was Nest Freemark, a fourteen-year-old girl who could work magic and by doing so come to terms with the truth about her family, when anything less would have destroyed her. He could see her face clearly, her freckles and quirky smile and curly dark hair. He would remember the long, smooth strides she took when she ran and the way she stood her ground when it mattered. In a world in which so much of what he encountered only served to reinforce his fears that the future of his dreams was an inevitability, Nest gave him hope. When so many others might have succumbed to their fear and despair, Nest had not. She represented a little victory when measured against the enormity of the battle being fought by the

Word and the Void, but sometimes little victories made the difference. Little victories, like the small events that tipped the scales in the balance of life, really could change the world.

I wish I could have been your father, he had said, and he had meant it.

He wondered if he would ever see her again.

He straightened in his seat, looking down the aisle past the slouched forms of the sleepers to where the driver hunched over the steering wheel, eyes on the road. In the bright glare of the headlights, the highway was an endless concrete ribbon unrolling out of the black. Morning was still far away; it was time to sleep. He had not slept since he had left Hopewell, and he could not put it off any longer. He shivered involuntarily at the prospect. It would be bad, he knew. It would be horrendous. He would be bereft of his magic, a night's payment for his expenditure in his battle with the maentwrog. He would be forced to run and to hide while his enemies hunted him; he would be alone and defenseless against them. Maybe they would find him this night. Maybe they would kill him. In the world of his dreams, all things were possible.

Weary and resigned, he eased his bad leg onto the padded bench and propped his body between the seat back and the bus wall. He was afraid, but he would not allow his fear to master him. He was a Knight of the Word, and he would find a way to survive.

John Ross closed his eyes, a warrior traveling through time, and drifted away to dream of a future he hoped would never be.

Available in hardcover
the dazzling sequel to
RUNNING WITH THE DEMON:

A KNIGHT OF THE WORD
by Terry Brooks

In accepting the black runestaff that channeled the magic
of the Word, John Ross accepted a solemn trust—and a
terrible burden. Each night he dreams of hellish futures
wrought upon the world by the Void. Each dream is of a
future that will come to pass unless Ross can prevent it in
the present. He drifts across America, a modern-day
knight errant in search of the agents of the Void.

But when an unspeakable act of violence shatters his
weary beliefs, John Ross turns his back on the Word. A
fallen Knight makes a tempting prize for the Void, so mer-
ciless demons soon stalk Ross and those close to him. His
only hope is Nest Freemark. She must restore Ross's
faith, or else his life—and her own—will be forfeit . . .

A KNIGHT OF THE WORD
The Sequel to
RUNNING WITH THE DEMON
by Terry Brooks

Please read on for an excerpt
from this chilling new novel . . .

He stands on a hillside south of the city looking back at the carnage. A long, gray ribbon of broken highway winds through the green expanse of woods and scrub to where the ruin begins. Fires burn among the steel and glass skeletons of the abandoned skyscrapers, flames bright and angry against the washed-out haze of the deeply clouded horizon. Smoke rises in long, greasy spirals that stain the air with ash and soot. He can hear the crackling of the fires and smell their acrid taste even here.

That buildings of concrete and iron will burn so fiercely puzzles him. It seems they should not burn at all, that nothing short of jackhammers and wrecking balls should be able to bring them down. It seems that in this postapocalyptic world of broken lives and fading hopes the buildings should be as enduring as mountains. And yet already he can see sections of walls beginning to collapse as the fires spread and consume.

Rain falls in a steady drizzle, streaking his face. He blinks against the dampness in order to see better what is happening. He remembers Seattle as being beautiful. But that was in another life, when there was still a chance to change the future and he was still a Knight of the Word.

John Ross closes his eyes momentarily as the screams of the wounded and dying reach out to him. The slaughter has been going on for more than six hours, ever since the collapse of the outer defenses just after dawn. The demons and the once-men have broken through and another of the dwindling bastions still left to free men has fallen. On the broad span of the high bridge linking the east and west sections of the city, the combatants surge up against one another in dark knots. Small figures tumble from the heights, pinwheeling madly against the glare of the flames as their lives are snuffed out. Automatic weapons fire ebbs and flows. The armies will fight on through the remainder of the day, but the outcome is already decided. By tomorrow the victors will be building slave pens. By the day after, the conquered will be discovering how life can sometimes be worse than death.

At the edges of the city, down where the highway snakes between the first of the buildings that flank the Duwamish

River, the feeders are beginning to appear. They mushroom as if by magic amid the carnage that consumes the city. Refugees flee and hunters pursue, and wherever the conflict spreads, the feeders are drawn. They are mankind's vultures, picking clean the bones of human emotion, of shattered lives. They are the Word's creation, an enigmatic part of the equation that defines the balance in all things and requires accountability for human behavior. No one is exempt; no one is spared. When madness prevails over reason, when what is darkest and most terrible surfaces, the feeders are there.

As they are now, he thinks, watching. Unseen and unknown, inexplicable in their single-mindedness, they are always there. He sees them tearing at the combatants closest to the city's edges, feeding on the strong emotions generated by the individual struggles of life and death taking place at every quarter, responding instinctively to the impulses that motivate their behavior. They are a force of nature and, as such, a part of nature's law. He hates them for what they are, but he understands the need for what they do.

Something explodes in the center of the burning city, and a building collapses in a low rumble of stone walls and iron girders. He could turn away and look south and see only the green of the hills and the silver glint of the lakes and the sound spread out beneath the snowy majesty of Mount Rainier, but he will not do that. He will watch until it is finished.

He notices suddenly the people who surround him. There are perhaps several dozen, ragged and hollow-eyed figures slumped down in the midday gloom, faces streaked with rain and ash. They stare at him as if expecting something. He does not know what it is. He is no longer a Knight of the Word. He is just an ordinary man. He leans on the rune-carved black staff that was once the symbol of his office and the source of his power. What do they expect of him?

An old man approaches, shambling out of the gloom, stick-thin and haggard. An arm as brittle as dry wood lifts and points accusingly.

I know you, he whispers hoarsely.

Ross shakes his head in denial, confused.

I know you, the old man repeats. *Bald and white-bearded, his face is lined with age and by weather and his eyes are a strange milky color, their focus blurred. I was there when you killed him, all those years ago.*

Killed who? Ross cannot make himself speak the words, only mouth them, aware of the eyes of the others who are gathered fixing on him as the old man's words are heard.

The old man cocks his head and lets his jaw drop, laughing softly, the sound high and eerie, and with this simple gesture he reveals himself. He is unbalanced—neither altogether mad nor completely sane, but something in between. He lives in a river that flows between two worlds, shifting from one to the other, a leaf caught by the current's inexorable tug, his destiny beyond his control.

The Wizard! The old man spits, his voice rising brokenly in the hissing sound of the rain. *The Wizard of Oz! You are the one who killed him! I saw you! There, in the palace he visited, in the shadow of the Tin Woodman, in the Emerald City! You killed the Wizard! You killed him! You!*

The worn face crumples and the light in the milky eyes dims. Tears flood the old man's eyes and trickle down his weathered cheeks. He whispers. Oh, God, it was the end of everything!

And Ross remembers then, a jagged-edged, poisonous memory he had thought forever buried, and he knows with a certainty that is chilling that what the old man tells him is true.

John Ross opened his eyes to the streetlit darkness and let his memory of the dream fade away. Where had the old man been standing, that he could have seen it all? He shook his head. The time for memories and the questions they invoked had come and gone.

He stood in the shadows of a building backed up on Occidental Park in the heart of Pioneer Square, his breath coming in quick, ragged gasps as he fought to draw the cool, autumn night air into his burning lungs. He had walked all the way from the Seattle Art Museum, all the way from the center of downtown Seattle some dozen blocks away. Limped, really, since he could not run as normal men could and relied upon a black walnut staff to keep upright when he moved. Anger and despair had driven him when muscles had failed. Crippled of mind and body and soul, reduced to an empty shell, he had come home to die because dying was all that was left.

The shade trees of the park loomed in dark formation before him, rising out of cobblestones and concrete, out of bricks and curbing, shadowing the sprawl of benches and trash receptacles and the scattering of homeless and disenfranchised that roamed the city night. Some few looked at him as he pushed off from the brick wall and came toward them. One or two even hesitated before moving away. His face was terrible to look upon, all bloodied and scraped, and the clothes that draped his lean body were in tatters. Blood leaked from deep rents in the skin of his shoulder and chest, and several of his ribs felt cracked or broken. He had the appearance of a man who had risen straight out of Hell, but in truth he was just on his way down.

Feeders gathered at the edges of his vision, hunchbacked and beacon-eyed, ready to show him the way.

It was Halloween night, All Hallows' Eve, and he was about to come face-to-face with the most personal of his demons.

His mind spun with the implications of this acknowledgment. He crossed the stone and concrete open space thinking of greener places and times, of the smell of grass and forest air, lost to him here, gone out of his life as surely as the hopes he had harbored once that he might become a normal man again. He had traded what was possible for lies and half truths and convinced himself that what he was doing was right. He had failed to listen to the voices that mattered. He had failed to heed the warnings that counted. He had been betrayed at every turn.

He stopped momentarily in a pool of streetlight and looked off into the darkened spires of the city. The faces and voices came back to him in a rush of sounds and images. Simon Lawrence. Andrew Wren. O'olish Amaneh. The Lady and Owain Glyndwr.

Nest Freemark.

Stefanie.

His hands tightened on the staff, and he could feel the power of the magic coursing through the wood beneath his palms. Power to preserve. Power to destroy. The distinction had always seemed a large one, but he thought now that it was impossibly small.

Was he still, in the ways that mattered, a Knight of the Word? Did he possess courage and strength of will in sufficient measure that they would sustain him in the battle that lay ahead? He could not tell, could not know without putting it to the test. By placing himself in harm's way he would discover how much remained to him of the power that was once his. He did not think that it would be enough to save his life, but he hoped that it might be enough to destroy the enemy who had undone him.

It did not seem too much to ask.

In truth, it did not seem half enough.

Somewhere in the distance a siren sounded, shrill and lingering amid the hard-edged noises that rang down the stone and glass corridors of the city's canyons.

He took a deep breath and gritted his teeth against the pain that racked his body. With slow, measured steps, he started forward once more.

Death followed in his shadow.

A KNIGHT OF THE WORD
The Sequel to
RUNNING WITH THE DEMON
by Terry Brooks
Available in bookstores everywhere

Join us online to find out about
RUNNING WITH THE DEMON
and its dazzling sequels,
A KNIGHT OF THE WORD
and
ANGEL FIRE EAST,
available in hardcover

RUNNING WITH THE DEMON
A KNIGHT OF THE WORD
ANGEL FIRE EAST
by Terry Brooks

Visit us at

www.randomhouse.com/brooks

to find out more about the author,
take our demonic quiz,
sign up for the Terry Brooks
E-Mail Reminder Service,
and much more!

Visit www.delreybooks.com—
the portal to all the
information and resources
available from Del Rey Online.

• Read sample chapters of every new book,
special features on selected authors and
books, news and announcements, readers'
reviews, browse Del Rey's complete
online catalog and more.

• Sign up for the Del Rey Internet Newsletter
(DRIN), a free monthly publication e-mailed to
subscribers, featuring descriptions of new
and upcoming books, essays and interviews
with authors and editors, announcements
and news, special promotional offers,
signing/convention calendar for our authors
and editors, and much more.

To subscribe to the DRIN: send a blank e-mail to
sub_Drin-dist@info.randomhouse.com or you can
sign up at www.delreybooks.com

The DRIN is also available at no charge for your PDA
devices—go to www.randomhouse.com/partners/avantgo
for more information, or visit www.avantgo.com and
search for the Books@Random channel.

Questions? E-mail us
at delrey@randomhouse.com

 www.delreybooks.com